Breeding

GEOFFRY FORDYCE

THE RURAL PUBLISHING COMPANY

First published by The Rural Publishing Company 2023.

Print (Paperback): 978-1-923008-22-9
eBook: 978-1-923008-23-6

Cover Design: The Rural Publishing Company
Layout and Typesetting: The Rural Publishing Company

The Rural Publishing Company
Email: hello@theruralpublishingcompany.com.au
Website: https://theruralpublishingcompany.com.au

This book is for our first grandchild, Abigail,
heralding our family's next generation of wonderful young people.

Chapter One

The brahminy kite soared and glided into land on a mangrove tree just five metres from the dinghy. It hardly made a sound as its talons wrapped around the bouncing branch. Twenty-two-year-old Bruce sat very still in his three and a half metre tinny close to the salt-water creek bank. The bird was magnificent. Its perfect ochre-coloured feathers against the white were brilliant. Its yellowish curved beak was beautifully honed to take its prey with ease. Its magnificent eyes with large black pupils were taking in every detail.

Bruce was quite a self-assured young man. He was happy with his own company and needed to be, as life on the family cattle station, three hours to the west, more often than not, required him to be working alone, or 'with all his friends', as his mates would tell him.

Bruce was fit and healthy. So far, his six-foot frame had not been broken by any unplanned parting from a horse or motorbike during mustering or other station work. He always prided himself on looking good. He kept his hair short and neat. He shaved each night, as he just liked the clean image it portrayed, rather than the lazy rich-kid image portrayed with a week or two of carefully-or not-so-carefully-manicured beard. Bruce had a fairly slim build, with not an ounce of 'white muscle', a consequence of daily hard yakka, which he relished. His jaw was square, and his mum told him he had a perfect nose. She wanted him to have a tassel of hair to better frame his handsome face. Again, that's what city boys did, he reckoned, as they had time to continually curl their hair behind their ears or shake their backwards-tilted heads to throw their hair back. In the bush, hair is not much of an asset, which cemented Bruce's preference for a clean short-hair look.

Bruce also liked to be neatly dressed, and unlike most young blokes, was happier in new jeans and an ironed shirt than an old comfy set of clothes that should have gone to an op shop long ago. His one concession was his old Akubra, which over the years had soaked up so much sweat it was now getting quite smelly. He could get away with it down the creek or down the paddock, but his mum would not have a bar of him wearing it near her house. Today, he had the Akubra on, a beige company shirt, and some long black shorts he only wore fishing.

This Saturday was magnificent. There had hardly been a cloud in the sky when Bruce launched his dinghy at daybreak. And there hadn't been a breath of wind, which meant there was not a ripple in the creek, except that created by fish darting after their prey and by the fleeing prey. It was now mid-morning and a few cumulus clouds had grown out of nothing. Against the distant hills on such a clear day, the vista was magic. Bruce knew his photography skills were close to rubbish, but he just had to try and capture the scene with his mobile. He knew it looked fantastic in real life, but for the life of him, he could not work out how to frame a photo to make it look like it did in real life. His mum Doris had the art, but he had inherited his dad's complete lack of skills on the art front. No matter, he assured himself, I'll make the lads jealous they're not here, even if the photo isn't a hot one.

With a few deft strokes and taps on his mobile, he loaded the photo onto Facebook. This was coastal country with plenty of people, which meant there was plenty of mobile coverage; the ether plucked up his photo and it was around the world in microseconds.

He snapped a few shots of the kite as well. It didn't move. It was used to people in the creek and had come to feast on whatever titbits it could get without having to hunt for live bait. Even though Bruce knew it was the wrong thing to do, he dived into his bait bucket for a small mullet, which he launched as high as he could toward the middle of the creek. The kite had been waiting. Like all wildlife, it was not slow to react like humans are. The bird was in the air as Bruce's arm swept its arc to release the hapless fish. That poor mullet never got to swim again, as the kite snatched it mid-air with easy precision. Without further ado, in full flight, the bird reached to its talons and took the fish in its beak. In a twinkle, the kite was gliding again, the mullet now fuelling its motor.

Bruce shook his head in wonderment as he always did. No matter how many times he'd done that, it was always pure majesty. Maybe he'd bring someone down the creek one day, someone who could take a photo and a video, and get them to capture what enraptured him. And maybe then his mates would stop telling him he was full of it when he tried to explain what he saw. His story-telling skills were ordinary too, he thought.

Even though he was no artist, Bruce knew he had some other skills. He never bragged about it, just did what he did well. In the creek, he rarely went home without a decent fish and at least one mud crab. He knew that a majority of people more often than not went home virtually empty-handed. Though others thought they'd been fishing, Bruce reckoned they more likely had been boating. Crabbing should be easy. But it wasn't. The pro crabbers virtually raped the creeks. They had pots everywhere. You could pull up your pot with as many as five and six mud crabs, but they always seemed to be one to five millimetres shy of a hundred and fifty across their shell, making them illegal to take if they were bucks.

In the maze of creeks through the mangrove swamp where he regularly went crabbing south of Townsville, Bruce had done some serious scouting to find the best places to drop his pots. These were mostly way up narrow mangrove-choked gullies that could only be reached at mid-tide in a small boat like his; it kept the pros at bay as they usually worked in much larger craft. At low tide there was often not enough water. At high tide the overarching network of mangroves made it impossible to get through. The tide was coming in and it was time to check the pots. Even though he had one good fish in the esky, a decent forty-eight-centimetre grunter, the fish were not very hungry today for some reason, so he reasoned he would not miss a good fish if he did not take too long.

The kite had gone, probably to salvage a feed from another fisherman. As he reeled in the lines he had out, there was constant popping of mud holes above the water line made by the swarms of tiny crabs. There were mobs of mudskippers, amphibious fish, sliding in the mud. He saw one that would have been a hundred and fifty millimetres long. Proper ugly buggers, Bruce thought, the toads of the fish world. Only something as ugly as a mudskipper or as crafty as a croc would thrive in the mud, which was bottomless if you were silly enough to try and step into it.

The mangroves also enthralled Bruce. Most were a very common mid-sized variety. But among these there was the occasional old short-statured tree with a thick trunk, usually on higher mud. These mangroves were truly majestic. Bruce had no idea how old they were, but the scars they carried suggested they were not young. The whole swamp is a war zone in a big flood, and these old trees would have had to withstand a major assault each time, the antithesis of the pristine day Bruce and the mangroves were currently enjoying.

Bruce fired up the trusty thirty horsepower Mercury outboard motor. He had the dinghy side-anchored, so all he had to do was lean forward to untie the knot and haul in the anchor. It had been jagged in mud, so he rinsed that off before bringing it onboard. As he rearranged the gear on the boat floor in front of him, Bruce nudged the boat into forward gear and slowly poked out into the main channel. The space he'd made would allow him room to pull in crab pots, sort out what was in each, remove the bait, and then stack them. Out in the channel, he opened to full throttle. The small craft lifted slightly on the nose and then settled back, high on the water, planing beautifully. Pure pleasure. He knew these creeks well, but even if he didn't, he'd always be on the outside of the bends where the deepest water is.

He let the throttle right off and the boat quickly sank down as Bruce wallowed at a crawl to enter 'his' creek that he'd christened Gater Gush for the high flow rate of water through the narrow entrance and his sighting of a two-metre saltwater crocodile there previously. The tide was just right. He angled the boat carefully through the tangle of mangroves, ducking under low branches, and pulling some branches aside to get through. He had to replace his favourite old, battered Akubra with a cap to do this because the branches would have taken the hat very quickly. And he wasn't getting in the water to retrieve it for any money, given the high chance of a large hungry nearby lizard waiting to have lunch. He had about two hundred metres to negotiate before he got to the first pot. Steady, steady.

He saw the float of the first pot high on the mangroves where he'd thrown it to reduce the chances of the ropes getting tangled and making it much easier to retrieve his pot. Bruce kept going. He was going to do the furthest pot first and work his way back, to make it easier to negotiate the creek with the stacked pots back in his boat. Bruce had three more pots spaced at about fifty metres up Gater Gush. He struggled his way to the last one, down beside a large mangrove that he could not get past. To enjoy it more, Bruce cut the motor, letting the boat drift to the pot, to stop and listen to nature. As they say, he wouldn't be dead for quids, he thought.

Bruce sidled up to the rope. The boat was going nowhere unless you pushed it through this mess, so he didn't have to worry about floating off while he concentrated on the pot. The water was fairly clean today and together with the broken sunlight invading the swamp on such a nice day, it gave the spot a magical perspective.

There was no evidence while the pot was submerged that it held anything, but that changed as he grabbed the rope and took the tension. The pot was only in about a metre and a half of water, but it was heavy. I might be lucky, he thought. The pot broke the surface. He was lucky alright. There was a big cod in the trap, a jenny and two buck crabs, one of which was rusty coloured and covered in barnacles and looked like it was legal. Bruce was salivating, just thinking about the crab sandwich he was planning for dinner. That big crab had to be full. The fish had not been attacked by the crabs, so either the crabs or the fish or both were fresh in the pot. Even luckier.

Bruce rinsed the mud off the bottom of the pot before getting it in the boat. First things first and he emptied out the fish onto the floor of the boat. To handle fish, Bruce had an old heavy work shirt that he placed around the animal to get a decent hold without being skewered by spines, gashed by gill blades or the sharp teeth, or losing his grip because of their protective slime. This worked well. Into the esky went the cod. Bruce then carefully tipped out the jenny and small buck from the pot back into the creek and then got the pot on the boat floor to check the size of the big buck. Bruce had a simple wooden arc he'd fashioned from a piece of ply with a one-fifty-millimetre space between the insides of the two wings. He could not fit it outside the tips of the shell spines. The crab was dinner. He would be juicy.

Though right now the crab was angry. Bruce tipped him out on the floor and the crab flared out both nippers as he slowly tried to crawl away. But Bruce had dealt with crabs before. He just went in behind him and pincered him with his thumb and middle finger, wedged behind the back wading legs. Once he had the crab under control, Bruce simply placed the unlucky crab in the esky on ice, along with the cod. The coolness of the esky slowed them right down, making them much more tractable when it was time to clean them. Bruce was not coming back on this trip, so he cut out the old bait and threw it in the water, a free feed for crabs lurking down there, making them bigger and better for the next trip. Man, this fishing is good fun, Bruce was thinking.

The next two pots yielded small crabs, nothing legal, and no fish. Just wasted bait. Bruce always consoled himself that the baits were helping the crabs grow for him and not the pros and be ready when he next came crabbing.

Bruce was hoping for another crab from the last pot as he worked his way towards it. The tide was coming in and there was at least a hundred millimetres more water than when he'd set off up the creek. He grabbed the rope, pulled in the float, and took the tension. This pot was full of something, he exclaimed to himself. It was heavy. As it broke the surface, Bruce could see why. There were another two large cod that were flapping vigorously and at least four crabs. He just could not see how many amid the fish and the bait. 'This is the life,' Bruce was thinking.

He hauled the pot onboard after giving it a bit of a rinse to clear most of the mud from its base, and quickly worked to get the cod out, which he then dumped into the esky to give himself a bit of room to work the crabs. There were five. Two were jennies. And two of the bucks looked legal. Bruce tipped the pot and started working out the jennies and the small buck. One of jennies had her nipper snagged in the pot mesh. As he was working on her, one of the potentially-legal bucks almost got free. Bruce had the pot on the edge of the boat and quickly pulled it inboard. The crab dropped to the floor and went for cover under the three pots already stacked. Bruce left the buck and went back to getting out all but the other large buck that he then grabbed, checked if it was legal, which it was, and plonked it in the esky. Salivating ...

He was cleaning out the pot's bait, when, 'Farrrrrk,' he screamed. He knew instantly what was happening. He'd forgotten about the first crab. Bruce had stepped near to where it was hiding. The crab had latched on to his left big toe with its powerful right claw. He didn't even have boots on to give some sort of protection. The pain was excruciating. Bruce dropped the pot. He'd always anticipated that one day someone in his boat might cop this, and always kept handy side cutters and pliers to deal with it. The only solution was to cut the nipper points off, because the crab will not let go, preferring to toss its nipper and regrow another. He grabbed the side cutters from the holster on the inside of the boat. It was a lot more difficult to do what he had to do than it looked. The pain was not helping, and he tried to put it aside as much as he could. And then the crab had a second claw that it had flared and was obviously prepared to use if Bruce put himself in the wrong spot. Even so, within twenty seconds, and it seemed like half an hour to Bruce, he'd got the side cutters around the nipper point and crunched. Immediate relief.

But he still had a rogue crab that needed a trip to the esky. No way was he going to lose this tasty piece of work. After the pain inflicted on him, the crab was to pay with its life. Bruce really had no hard feelings for the crab; if he was the crab, he probably would have attempted to do much worse. It was his own stupidity that caused the problem.

The toe did not look too good. The crab had broken the skin top and bottom and had jammed hard onto tendon insertions and bone. It was throbbing, oozing blood, and needed attention. Just like the crab. Bruce grabbed the crab and tossed him into the esky to let the cool send him to sleep. He knew enough about first aid to know that playing with his toe in this filthy situation was not going to help. Driving was going to be a hell of a challenge. He grabbed his phone, thankful for the availability of such amazing technology in this situation and dialled his sister in Townsville.

'Frances, I have a problem.' Bruce gave her a synopsis.

'Any chance you could pick up Mum or Dad and meet me at the ramp, please?' he asked. 'I can't drive and need someone to collect the Cruiser and boat and get me back to Townsville to get a band-aid on this stone kicker.'

'You're lucky, Bruce. I can leave right now and will get Dad. See you shortly,' Frances replied.

Even though the early afternoon was glorious, Bruce couldn't see it. His toe was killing him. All he could do was grimace, get the outboard going and get back to the ramp, painful as it was. Half an hour later he was there, and he did not expect Frances for at least another hour. It would not have been so bad if the light sea breeze that had sprung up had not created a bit of rippling in the creek, which created a constant vibration in the boat.

Normally he would consider the boat was at one with the water and would not have thought anything of the high-frequency buzz of the hull as it skimmed along in the creek, but today, his toe was acutely responsive to anything and everything. Fortunately, he still had his cap on, and Akubra stowed, so he would not have to change. The wind in his face would not have made it easy to keep on his favourite smelly old hat as he planed along in the creek.

An older bloke in a pair of faded blue shorts and a faded long-sleeved khaki shirt was at the ramp, loading his boat. 'Hey mate, any chance you could give us a hand, please?' Bruce asked as he gingerly brought his tinny alongside the concrete pontoon at the ramp. 'A bloody crab has given my toe a real workover. Hopefully I'll have my sister here shortly to help get me out of here.'

'I'm Lenny Pavarotti,' the bloke said. 'I'll just get this thing out the road first, if that's okay, and I'm all yours.' Lenny looked across at Bruce and could see he was looking a bit grey and very uncomfortable. He had been leisurely hooking his own tinny on to drag it out of the creek, but now Lenny quickly went about the task he'd done hundreds of times before.

'Thanks mate,' replied Bruce. 'I'm Bruce. Bruce Arnold.'

It was not his usual *modus operandi* to be asking for help, and it embarrassed him a bit. But he could see the bloke was one of those genuine older blokes who'd be just perfect for what he needed. As he sat there waiting, the toe was only getting sorer. While he had been moving and getting himself back to the ramp, the movement may have helped dampen the pain. Now he was sitting still, the throb was waxing.

Lenny came scooting down as soon as he had sorted his boat. He had a fold-up chair in his left hand. Lenny quickly scanned what was in front of him, and then he was all business.

'Just stay put till I sort this show out, Bruce,' he said. 'I'll park you up in this armchair while I get your tinny organised for you.'

'That's my ute, on the left there,' Bruce said. His clean, but obviously well-used white tray-back Land Cruiser, had a modified boat trailer hitched on behind. Bruce had pulled the trailer apart a year earlier to upgrade the suspension and replace the tyres with the same as what he had on his ute, which made it safer and easier to pull the boat from home, especially on the gravel sections. 'My outboard stabiliser is on the passenger seat floor with the tie down straps under the boat net,' he said as he handed over his car keys. 'And, ah, can you also grab my phone charger in the console too please, Lenny. And my wallet? I know I probably shouldn't leave it there, but I do. It's in the glove box. I have a funny feeling I'll need them before I see my ute again.'

'No worries, mate,' replied Lenny.

'And if you don't mind, there's a packet of Panadols in the glove box. I reckon they might help a bit,' Bruce asked his new-found mate.

Lenny grabbed the anchor rope and tied the boat, fore and aft, to the jetty.

'Now let's get you out of there,' he said. Bruce literally crawled out of his boat onto the pontoon, wincing in pain.

'That toe doesn't look too comfortable Bruce. Bloody crabs,' Lenny said as he helped Bruce to his feet and kept hold of his left arm as Bruce hobbled up to where Lenny had the chair set.

Once he was sitting, Lenny took off. In quick time he had the Panadol for Bruce and a water bottle to help get the drugs where they were needed. Ten minutes later, Lenny had Bruce's boat out of the water, tied down on the trailer and ready to go.

'Hey Lenny, do you want my catch, mate? By the time I get to clean it, it'll be buggered, so please take it,' Bruce said.

'Are you sure?' asked Lenny. 'I don't want to cut you short on anything.'

'Definitely, mate,' replied Bruce.

Lenny heaved Bruce's esky out of his boat and opened it. 'This has to be the guerrilla that got you,' he said, when he found the one-nipper crab parked up on top of the catch beside a nipper with the top point taken off. 'Three real nice cod, a ripper grunter and three crabs. Maria will reckon I've been to the fish shop on the way home because I don't usually do this well. Thanks Bruce. But I feel like a real mongrel taking it.'

Lenny was no novice. First thing he did was tie up the one-nipper crab. The cod were still moving as he shifted the lot into his own esky in the back of his ute. He took Bruce's esky down to the ramp and gave it a decent clean up, before taking it back to Bruce's boat.

'Thanks for that, Lenny,' Bruce said.

'No problem, mate. Least I can do,' replied Lenny who then finished packing up his own ute to leave.

'What's happening with your ute, Bruce?' Lenny asked as he came back to Bruce. Bruce told him the plan. Lenny said, 'Bruce, there's a few shifty buggers that come through here from time to time, so I'll stay till your sister gets here, just to be sure. No dramas for me. If you have a phone number, can I take that too, so I can check how you end up?'

'Thanks, Lenny,' Bruce responded. 'You're a bloody champion. And I'll take your number too please, mate. That okay?'

'Only too happy to help,' said Lenny as he messaged Bruce his number. Bruce called Frances who she said she'd hopefully be there in forty-five minutes after she had mustered his dad.

The chat had helped Bruce get his mind off the throb a bit, but now he felt it surge. He was thinking about all the fishing filth that would have found its way into the wound and what a nice little recovery he had in front of him. Not. Even a simple fish hook puncture can end up nasty. This one was going to stew up really well, thought Bruce. He winced at the thought of all he'd not be able to do for a bit till the toe was okay. Lenny was a bit like Bruce, not inclined to talk needlessly. So, they mostly just sat there waiting for Bruce's sister and

Dad. Bruce found out Lenny was a cane farmer from Brandon and Lenny learned Bruce was in the cattle game, but they did not share too much detail. Bruce's toe was too sore to get him conversational as he sat there unsuccessfully trying to will away the festering mess at the end of his back leg.

Lenny heard the vehicle coming first and then saw the dust. 'They're nearly here, Bruce.'

'You beauty,' Bruce replied in hushed tones, straining to avoid expressing himself in the same tone as his toe pain.

Frances must have been worried. The vehicle was coming at pace. The dirt track to the boat ramp was corrugated and they could hear the vibration of the suspension as the Honda SUV hurtled their way. 'Hope no wallabies are out for an early feed,' Bruce mused as he let a half smile get past his grimace. 'If they run into my sister, they might hurt themselves.'

'No chance on a day like today, Bruce,' Lenny said. 'It's such a magic day they'll be flat out under a bush, soaking it up.'

Frances and Bruce's dad, Merve, pulled up beside the two men. Lenny was out of his chair, but Bruce waited. 'You been teasing the seafood, Bruce?' Merve said.

'Well,' said Bruce, 'can't say I blame the poor buggers. I suspect they don't love me, Dad.'

Merve was sixty-three years old. He had a well-built six-foot frame, and all visual clues, including his even tan and his large work-beaten hands, suggested he was fit and strong. The cues were correct. His strides over to Bruce were purposeful and without wasted energy. As he placed a strong hand on his son's shoulder, he summed up the situation quickly. Everything was completely under control except Bruce's toe. 'You right to jump in with Frances, or do you need a shoulder, Bruce?' he asked.

Bruce was okay and let his dad know. He struggled up and turned to Lenny. 'You're a sensation, Lenny. Thanks, mate. Hope you can convince the bride you caught those fish!' With that, he hobbled to the car and eased himself in.

Lenny's eyes, planted below a brow deeply furrowed with concern, followed his new-found young mate. 'No problem at all. I'll hear from you when you get that claw sorted.'

'Merve,' Merve said as he introduced himself to Lenny who let him in on who he was. 'And that's Frances,' as they glanced towards Bruce's industrious sister who nodded briefly towards Lenny.

Frances was a clean freak, a bit like her brother. Bruce was currently filthy with a matching smell. Getting into her precious, sweet-smelling Honda grated her, but she was firmly between a rock and a hard place. When she'd pulled up, she'd gone straight to the boot to get a towel for the seat to at least try and reduce the mess her brother would make. She knew it was not his style to be untidy, but the rock was there, and they were wedged.

As Bruce and Frances headed off, Lenny and Merve had a brief yarn before they both followed the youngsters.

The car ride was a bit like the boat, Bruce thought. The Honda was quite smooth at the worst of times, but on the corrugated gravel road he felt every bump. His toe felt like it was on fire. He just tried to forget about it, about work waiting at home, and just concentrate on something constructive, like improving the genetics of the herd. Bruce had spent a bit of time trying to work out what he needed lately, but he was going in circles a bit and he could not get his head right around it.

But first he had to ring his head stockman on the property. 'Col, I'm going to be a couple of days down here. Not home tonight. Sorry. I busted me hoof and am just heading to the toe shop to get her fixed. Righto?' Col had enough experience not to be told what to do while Bruce was not there. Bruce listened to Col and replied, 'No, Col, nothing serious. I'll tell you the story when I get home. Useless bugger I am.' He could now concentrate on cattle genetics, with his main concerns under control or heading that way.

Frances took Bruce straight to the Townsville University Hospital emergency department. It was a quiet afternoon, so before he knew it, Bruce was sitting in the air-conditioned triage area answering a flood of questions from a young very-overweight nurse who looked like she had trouble walking, yet alone be able to bound into action in an emergency department, which is where she was. She seemed as interested in him as he was in being where he was. She wheeled a stainless-steel trolley with a computer on it and it was as though she could not break away from it. Every answer he gave, she tapped it into the computer with the zest of a dead fish. He knew he didn't know much about medicine, but he thought at least they should have taken a few vital signs, though she did attach a white wrist ID to Bruce she'd printed out from her trusty computer. She was way more interested in his medical history than in the acute problem he had. This was not looking promising, thought Bruce. Her interrogation was not even allowing him to escape to his cattle genetics virtual haven.

Somehow or other, whatever that nurse had done, resulted in his rescue. The grilling had finished a few minutes earlier and Bruce had been left right where he was, parked out in the open-plan area with only himself for comfort. There were all sorts of medical staff floating around, none in a sweat that he could see. Plenty of gossip. Coffee a favourite conversation topic. And it appeared that every nurse he had seen was hooked by an invisible umbilical cord to a computer on a trolley. He'd never seen that before, even on TV.

As he sat there, he saw a young nurse with a bit of purpose and no computer trolley come into the room. She had a case clipboard cradled in her left arm. It was hard for Bruce not to notice her. Crikey, her looks even seemed to melt his pain away. Her blonde hair was neatly held in a ponytail. She was trim and immaculately dressed. She was smiling, saying hello to staff she passed, with a beautiful dimple in her right cheek. It emphasised her flawless skin and perfect features. Bruce was watching for her to go scooting past when she zeroed in on him.

'Bruce Arnold?' she asked, as she checked his arm band to see that it matched the data on the clipboard.

'Yep,' he smiled back. It was the first time he'd been able to stop his grimace since Cancer had done his damage.

'I'm Therese,' she said. 'I get to take you through for treatment.' She glanced at the war zone on the end of his left foot. 'That does not look good. Who did that?'

'I was in the creek fishing and a crab got me. I'm such a Wally. Not only did the mongrel mince my toe, but you can't imagine what sort of fishing muck has carefully infected it. I'm more worried about the staphs than the physical damage just now,' he replied.

'Yes. I can smell you and you're obviously not dressed for a wedding. And if I know anything about blokes and fishing, that means you also haven't had a feed since before dawn this morning?' she remarked.

'No,' Bruce replied. 'I'm down there to fish, not to eat. I do that when I get home. When I'm down the creek I never seem to feel hungry. I just take a water bottle and chew on that.'

'That's pretty handy if the docs have to use anything strong on you,' nurse Therese said, as she neatly jotted down what she had gleaned. 'Righto, let's get you going,' she said, as she dropped the clipboard onto the back of Bruce's chair.

'Here comes the orderly,' Therese said, as a young bloke in staff dress, including a hair net, strode up. He was pushing a hospital bed. He asked Bruce if he would need help to hop on board. Bruce gingerly transferred himself without help, though he would not have minded if nurse Therese had taken a bit of weight in the process. The orderly unlocked the wheels and the pair of them wheeled Bruce away through swinging doors, down the corridor and into a procedures room. 'We'll leave you here, Bruce,' said Therese, and off her and orderly floated.

Bruce was met by a young Doctor Alan and a nurse Sammy who grabbed his file from the end of the bed and immediately started their visual examination of his horrible swollen and bloodied stone kicker. Bruce answered all their questions, and nurse Sammy entered a few more data into her adjacent four-wheeled computer.

'First things first,' Doctor Alan said. 'We'll get an x-ray, Bruce, if that's okay, and then we'll work out what to do. Then we'll get you cleaned up and smelling a bit better so we don't kill anyone with the pong. Sorry, Bruce. And then we'll get onto that toe. Fair chance we may have to get you to sleep for a bit so we can do what we do.'

The orderly reappeared and he and nurse Sammy took him off for an x-ray, which was quickly done. They then wheeled him to a wet room where he could strip down, bag his filthy clothes and shower.

Bruce did his best to keep his toe away from the water as it was on fire. When he was more presentable in a hospital gown, he was immediately brought back to the procedures' room.

In the meantime, Doctor Alan organised an anaesthetist. When Bruce returned, he was told he had no fracture, but they needed to give him some heavy sedation and local anaesthesia to work on his toe. The last thing Bruce remembered was the anaesthetist squirting something into the drip line he'd inserted into his left forearm.

Bruce reclaimed his senses in the recovery room. His toe throb was gone. What a relief. He could feel the toe was firmly and comfortably bandaged. And he still had a drip in that was powering away. He felt thirsty. There was a nurse right there who must have stirred him awake. But he just closed his eyes again, still feeling quite dopey.

'Bruce, wakey wakey,' the nurse was saying. 'We need you to wake up now Bruce.'

Bugger, he thought, and opened his eyes for the nurse. She was a hustler and was not going to let him lie there like a slug.

'Do you reckon you would feel well enough for a wheelchair ride?' the nurse asked.

'Probably,' said Bruce. Bruce had not heard the orderly who was waiting with a wheelchair. Making sure he didn't fall, the orderly and nurse watched Bruce as he slowly got out of bed and settled himself into the wheelchair. The orderly then wheeled him off to a waiting room where he was plied with sandwiches and a cup of tea. Bliss. Bruce needed that after no feed all day and nothing to drink since lunchtime.

'You have visitors,' a nurse told him. In came his mum and sister. 'The doctor will see you before you leave. He'll tell you about that toe of yours.'

'How's it going, love?' asked his mum. She was not looking that well, as usual.

Bruce was all good and ready to head out. Doctor Alan appeared. 'That toe should be fine as long as you keep it dry and keep it out of harm's way for a couple of weeks, Bruce. You're a lucky bloke. The crab gave the tendon attachments a fair bruising, but all is intact and we were able to get the wound clean, and almost sealed up too. Just make sure you finish those antibiotics we have ready for you as that monster would have left a nice concoction of bacteria we won't have been able to fully remove. Did you get the crab to have your revenge?'

'I did Doc. But I gave it to a bloke who helped me out down the creek. I know he'll enjoy the crab every bit as much as I would have.' Bruce had to swallow as he started to salivate just thinking about the crab sandwich he was going to miss.

Bruce changed into a fresh set of his father's clothes that Doris had brought with her. A nurse then signed him out with a course of antibiotics and some firm advice about looking after himself before they headed over to his parents' place. Merve and Doris had bought the house in West End, not far from the city centre many years ago as an investment that they had rented. When they had decided to move to Townsville, they waited till the tenants' contract ran out before a major renovation. It was a low-set block home on a thousand square metres. It had a beautiful open-plan living area with a magnificent kitchen. Merve's pride and joy was his shed, a feature in his manicured lawn and garden. Merve had built a high shed with one hundred square metres of lock-up area fronted with three large roller doors, and a further fifty square metre covered area, all concreted. It was ideal for get-togethers. Bruce loved his shed television where he could watch the rugby league and the cricket, allowing Doris to watch whatever she wanted on the lounge television.

Merve with the Cruiser and boat awaited them. Merve had even washed down the boat for him and the unit was ready to head back to the station.

'Will that toe handle the drive back, Bruce?' Merve asked, knowing his son well, 'or do you reckon you should camp here a day or two before heading back? Col will be fine without you for a couple of days I reckon.'

'What would I do here, Dad?' Bruce did not enjoy being inactive. He knew his parents would love him to stay, but if he got back to Bovale he'd be able to do something useful. His toe was comfortably bandaged and if he kept it off the clutch pedal, it should be fine. Bruce did not really want to leave so quickly, knowing his parents and sister would dearly have loved some time with him. And the truth was he loved spending time with them. But the boredom ... he just had to be doing something, toe or no toe. Given it was almost dinner time, he relented.

'I'll stay tonight.'

Immediately he could see all three of them lift and they set about making dinner and getting a bed ready for Bruce and his toe to settle for the night.

Chapter Two

Frances came around at piccaninny for breakfast. A real bush show with steak and eggs, toast and coffee. Then it was time for Bruce to head off. He could see the tear in his mum's eye and almost one in Frances's eye as well as he hugged them tightly in goodbye. Merve was not into hugging but the love for his son was obvious in his look as he firmly shook Bruce's hand, indicating they'd see each other soon.

Bruce was back on the road. He spent a lot of time in his Land Cruiser. Almost as much time as in bed at times. He had bought it with beautiful plush bucket seats obviously designed for urban cowboys, but he quickly got rid of them. A flat comfortable seat with a canvas cover was more functional when getting in and out all the time covered in work's grime. And in his business, grime was too often dust and cow dung. The air conditioning was well maintained, and he had installed an expensive sound system so he could listen to his favourite music when it suited. Today it didn't suit. He was looking for peace and quiet, and the unavoidable rumble of road noise was enough without more noise, even if it was Taylor Swift.

It was May. Pastures were haying off after the wet season. It was a beautiful time of the year with minimum and maximum temperatures reliably close to perfect for Bruce for weeks on end. Ideal for Bruce was about eighteen in the morning and up to twenty-eight degrees during the day. It was one of those days, and he did not need the air conditioning, just fresh air. Bruce was a veteran long-distance driver, so the short stint home of two hundred and fifty kilometres was almost a stress-free event. The highway was great, and Bruce set cruise control on one hundred and ten kilometres per hour, which was the local speed limit.

Initially, Bruce was thinking about a hundred different random things, mainly from the last two days. But by the time he got to Woodstock he decided dreaming was finished. Time to work out a few things. In the short term, he'd need to change what he'd planned, and give his toe a chance to heal without breaking out in a nasty infection.

Thinking cap on. Genetics. What was he really aiming for with his herd? The cattle breeding world was very confusing for Bruce. He had trouble reconciling all the descriptions of bulls he'd heard cattle owners waffle on about at sales, at shows, at the pub, wherever the subject came up. He'd heard recently of EBVs that were claimed to help, which apparently stood for estimated breeding values, produced by some mob in New South Wales. If they were estimates, they can't be up to speed for what he wanted. He wanted solid evidence, not estimates or best guesses or whatever they were, that his bulls would sire profitable progeny. He needed to download the head of someone who understood all this stuff, both the science stuff and practical stuff that most station owners had to work with. Maybe his mate in the agriculture department in Toowoomba could help? Back to random thoughts.

It seemed no time before Bruce was driving over the grid into Bovale. His senses immediately came to life; he was home. He liked to think he would not miss much as his eyes spent way more time on what he was passing through than the seven-kilometre road to his homestead, but that was okay because he kept the road in good order.

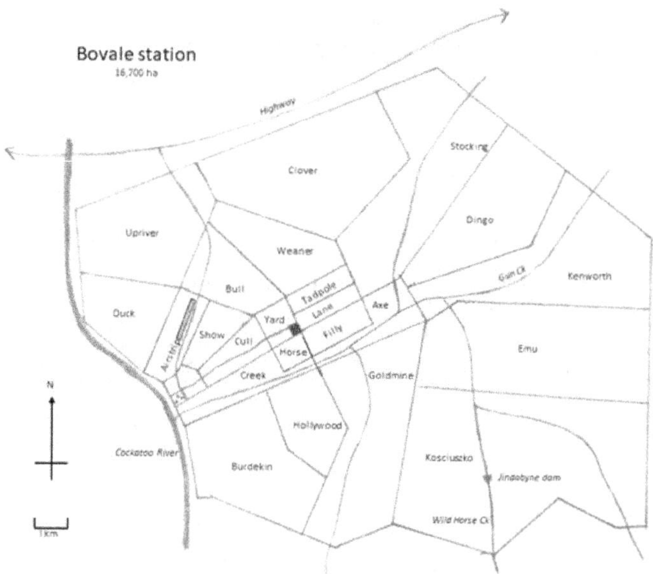

The country was in good order. The amount of bird life was part testament to that. Bruce was always amazed at the number and variety of birds. In the middle of the day, they were not so obvious, but at first light, the cacophony of calls from many birds of many species anywhere he went around the property was music. Bruce lightly touched the brakes as crested pigeons, as they do, left it to the last second before taking flight from the road to avoid being steamrolled. As he sped up again, he was momentarily distracted as a pair of pale headed rosella parrots flew from his left side. Thwack. One of them hit the windscreen. 'Damn,' Bruce cursed. He hated hitting anything, but these beautiful birds live a long time and pair for life. There was now one lonely poor parrot out there.

Over the grid about two kilometres into his place, Bruce noticed a small mob of bulls in his bull paddock on the trot as he drove along. Strange, he thought. Usually, they were either camped, ambling along or steadily grazing, depending on the time of day, and may look up to see for sure all's okay. They may even sometimes amble towards him, just in case he had some treats like lucerne hay. But not today. He could not see a dingo on their tail. They were just heading out away from him. It was that time of the day when they'd be ambling towards water in single file along well-worn tracks. But they were not even heading in that general direction. 'Why?' Bruce asked himself aloud.

As he passed the airstrip on his right, Bruce could see the homestead looming ahead to the south on a slight rise, perched with a brilliant view of the south-flowing Cockatoo River to the west on its way to join the mighty Burdekin River. He could also see the range his place ran up into on the southern boundary, and the beautiful gently undulating flats to the east across the station. I'm in love, he was thinking, with this joint. Pity I get to share it with myself, now Mum and Dad are in Townsville. The Cruiser rattled across the grid set about half a metre above ground level, standard practice to stop it filling and reducing the chances of cattle learning to jump it; Bruce was heading out of Airstrip paddock into the small Home paddock.

Bruce pulled up outside Col's house. The homestead ahead was fenced in a yard of about half a hectare, with well-watered lawns and gardens. There was a central area in the housing complex of about half a hectare to the east of the homestead. This lawn was kept green, greeting the team after a typical hot, dry, dusty day's work, always immediately lifting them. It was almost as good as heading up to the lush Atherton Tableland for an eyeful of green grass and rain, terrific therapy for those farming these areas. Merve had created the lawn about thirty years earlier when polythene pipe became readily available. He'd spent weeks establishing the sprinkler system that was replaced with a modern pop-up version only three years ago. His sweat might not have paid any bills directly, but he reasoned a happy head made good decisions. Central to the lawn was a magnificent Bowen mango tree that had thrived on Merve's attention since he planted it as a small seedling. The tree did shed a few leaves, and the mess underneath needed almost daily attention when the flying foxes steadily set about their noisy nocturnal raids on the crop just before Christmas each year. However, for the rest of the year, it was a large, brilliant, shade tree that Bruce and Frances had sprawled under many times with a book in their idle youth. The tree was a favourite of the common koel, birds that arrived before the wet season with their distinctive calls that every tropical bush dweller immediately associates with the build-up, a hot, humid few months late in the year punctuated with unpredictable violent tropical storms.

The head stockman's house was on the north side of the lawn beside a large machinery shed on the eastern side. It was Sunday morning and Col Wattle was home with his wife Simone of twelve years, and their two young children, Lachlan and Carina.

'G'day Carina,' Bruce chirped as he hobbled towards their front porch.

Carina had heard him arrive and charged out of the house to greet the favourite person in her small world. Bruce was a charmer. She looked up at him, 'Dad's home. I'll get him.' Before she turned, her beaming smile vanished, replaced with a worried frown as she saw the left leg lameness and the medical handiwork on his foot. 'What did you do to yourself, Bruce?' She hovered. At just six years of age, her caring maternal instincts poured out.

'Would you be shocked if I told you a croc bit my toe off?' he said, desperately holding a straight face.

'Were you frightened, Bruce?' she squeaked as she held her arms up awkwardly against her chest in a wince.

Bruce liked to lark, but he could see this was not heading in a good direction. 'Well, it was no croc and I still have my toe. I didn't say a croc did it, just that what would you say if it was a croc. Sorry if I scared you. A crab bit my toe. My own fault. No big drama. She'll be right in pretty quick time.'

Carina headed inside to get her dad. Bruce rested his arm on the bottom stair post, staring at nothing on the ground.

'G'day, Col.' Bruce greeted his head stockman who lunged forward with his massive right hand to shake his boss's hand.

He was the boss now Merve had moved to town. It was a worry. Doris had felt the station life was wearing her down, even though she was only fifty-one. Merve and Doris had reaped the rewards of some very astute investments when the seasons and prices had been good in nineteen eighty-eight to nineteen ninety-one, just before the seasonal and prices' situation had become quite difficult. They'd been gradually building their nest egg whenever they could, which had allowed them to leave Bovale in the capable hands of their son and live independently of station resources. Merve had not been keen on the move initially as he was still firing on all cylinders, but he respected his wife's wishes. He was not totally against the move as life running a large beef business was never an easy gig; he was not going to miss the troughs on the roller coaster ride that it was. Any reticence he had was resolved when his good mate Roger had asked him to manage a rural equipment supplies business he'd set up to serve the flocks of hobby farmers in and around the big village on the coast. 'Farmin Stuff' kept Merve well and truly out of mischief, and he was happy with the work it brought and the customers he dealt with. The key challenge Merve and Doris had yet to resolve was succession, as their daughter Frances was also part of the equation.

Almost all the calves had been branded this year, and weaning was starting in a week. Bruce knew he could not defer this without paying a massive business cost. Come hell or high water, she was on. He'd have to get someone in to do his job if he was to give his stone kicker a chance to heal.

'Crippled myself, mate,' Bruce sheepishly said. 'Nothing serious. It'll heal okay, as long as I give it a chance. Bloody crabs.'

'The weaning?' Col immediately countered. 'What's the plan to take that on?'

'Well, you're right. The cows won't think it's too funny by the end of the dry season if we don't get those calves off next week. And the chopper's booked. So, she's all systems go, with a cripple in tow. Do you like that bit of rhyming, Col?'

'Bruce, you are so talented,' Col said as he grinned at the silliness. He liked this young man. Pity Carina was not ten years older, he mused.

'We can't have Simone on the muster because she has to look after Carina,' Bruce said. 'Who should we get to do my job so I can practise my princess routine over the muster?'

Col replied, 'Do you want me to ring around the neighbours to see who might be up for it?'

'Yep. I'll see if any of my mates are free or if my cousins near Rockhampton have anyone spare. At least they might have some sympathy for me,' Bruce chuckled.

Simone came out behind a skipping Carina with eight-year-old Lachlan right with her. 'Hello Bruce,' she said. 'Carina tells me you've been battling crabs. Did you keep the devil for your revenge?'

'Simone, I would have liked nothing better than to eat the big fella, but I was not in the frame. I gave it to a real good bloke I met at the boat ramp. Lenny. Sorry, I know you would have killed for a nipper.'

'That's okay, Bruce. As long as that toe of yours gets back to normal, I'll forgive you.'

'Hey, Dad,' Lachlan said, earnestly, 'if Bruce can't go mustering, can I get off school and help?' Lachlan was thinking ahead, reasoning that if Bruce's toe was buggered, Bruce may not have a full roster on the muster, and he just might need someone as useful as Lachlan. It was typical bush kid maturity that belied their ages.

'Mate, I'd love you to, but you're doing school,' Col replied, smiling gently at his fast-maturing and increasingly-capable son. Col knew school was a tough grind in the bush for everyone. Lachlan and Carina spent about five hours a day in the school room, taking lessons over the internet from the teacher in Charters Towers, and doing tasks set by the teachers. Simone was the teacher's aide as they could not afford a governess. Since Lachlan had started school, her time available for the station had dropped off a lot, so it was a double whammy for them: less income and increasing costs associated with education and other needs of her growing children. But she was not begrudging it for an instant. Even though it was not easy, and Carina and Lachlan were not always easy to manage in the school room, she knew she was lucky in a way to be a constant witness to their primary school experience.

'How's your mum?' Simone asked Bruce.

'Same,' said Bruce. He didn't know what to make of them moving to town, though the upside was he had a brilliant and rare opportunity as a young man to take the reins of a large business, albeit with on-going regular advice from Merve who knew firsthand that Bruce would appreciate the help. The station was one hundred and sixty-seven square kilometres. As long as he kept the herd at about a thousand tonnes, he could sell about three hundred tonnes of live weight annually. Gross income of three quarters of a million last year sounded like a lot when he first worked it out. But then he had the costs. Staff. Vehicles. Diesel. Rates and rents. Maintenance of all the station equipment and infrastructure. Supplements. Weeds. Bull purchases. Insurance. And then there was that nice little annual challenge of paying the interest on the business loan, just shy of two point five million, trying to get some principle paid off, and investing in super for his future. The list went on and on. It would have been easy to spend a lot more than he had, but the reality was he had to run a very tight ship to sustain gradual station improvement and keep operations running smoothly. It was all not too bad except when the market troughs came along. Fortunately, they were not in that situation currently as sale yard prices had finally been increasing.

'I have some groceries in the ute that need to be in a fridge, so I'll leave you to it,' Bruce said. 'I'll talk to you if I can get a hand sorted Col and let me know if you hit gold. Oh, and by the way, Col, any chance you could do a quick run around Bull paddock, please? Something's up there. No idea what. The bulls were stirred up when I came through just now.'

'No problem, Bruce. Sounds a bit odd,' Col replied. He sauntered back inside the house to get his UHF harness, boots and hat to tackle the job.

Lachlan was hot on his heels. 'Can I come, Dad?'

'Yeah, mate,' Col replied. 'Get some jeans and a hat on and make sure your bike is fuelled up.' Lachlan did not need a second invitation. He was off like a rabbit in the headlights. Col knew he'd be safely saddled up on his Yamaha Grizzley 90 sooner than he could get to the shed himself. He mused about what a champion his son was turning out to be.

It would not have been twenty minutes and Col called on the UHF, which was always on in the homestead kitchen. 'You have a dead bull Bruce, along that fence line you cleaned up with the dozer two weeks ago. Just looks like he's just laid down and died. And not that long ago. He's still warm and not stiff yet.'

It was a shock. Bulls were a major investment. A dead bull was a major loss. 'Which bull, Col?' Bruce asked.

'It's that polled Cool Valley bull with the dark patch on his nearside blade you bought in Charters Towers recently,' Col said.

Bruce immediately cringed. They had paid seven thousand dollars for the bull a month ago and he was only twenty-three months old now. The family had high hopes of many mating seasons and many calves from him. 'Just check him for any signs of a stray bullet, just in case one of those town yobbos has been lurking.'

'Yeah, I had a good look over him, Bruce, and I can't find a damn thing that looks like it might have killed him. He's just lying there, dead as a maggot. He didn't even thrash around like most cattle do in their death throes.'

Bruce thought for a moment. 'I don't reckon it can be botulism, Col, because he's vaccinated. This is not good. I'll get onto the vet straight away and see if she can come out and work it out.'

'OK Bruce. I'll have a bit more of a look but so far, nothing else looks out of place,' Col offered.

Bruce sat there, looking into space. I don't need this, he thought. Damn. Wonder what happened to the poor bugger? Nothing came to mind. He hoped it was not catching, whatever it was. He knew he had to act even though the news was a gut punch. Bruce slowly got up and found his phone and rang Eileen Cook, the cattle vet he knew in town. She was good value and with any amount of luck would be able to drop everything and head out. He was in luck, even if Eileen wasn't. Being a vet meant the weekend on call was anything but planned, often darting from one emergency to another while her private life was parked up. Eileen was just finishing up one job and would head out within fifteen minutes and be there before lunch.

Like Eileen, Bruce was also quite used to dealing with the unexpected. He hobbled around the kitchen, putting away what he'd brought home and then set about getting some lunch for the pair of them before they did the bull. It was going to be much easier to tackle a bull post-mortem in the hot sun, topped up on glucose and fluids.

It was about eleven-thirty when Eileen arrived. She had been out to Bovale a few times and knew the drill. She knocked on the door yelling out, 'I'm here,' as she tugged off her elastic-sided boots and made her way into the kitchen without Bruce having to say a word.

Bruce looked up from the article he was reading in the Country Life newspaper. 'G'day Eileen.'

He was always a little taken aback with Eileen. She was stunningly beautiful, a really nice lady and smart and skilful on top of that. Eileen had only completed her degree a year earlier. Bruce had dreamed about her a few times but when reality checked in, he reasoned to himself there was no way he was in her class. He told himself, settle down and don't waste your time chasing her; you'll just get bruised and broken in the stampede to win her heart.

'You're not the Bruce I usually encounter today. What's up?' Eileen asked. As she said this, she glanced down and saw the bandaged toe. 'Uh oh, what got you?'

'Would you believe a dingo?' Bruce said.

Eileen looked sideways at him, trying to read him. She knew he was prone to take the piss if he could and she was trying to be one step ahead. 'Yeah, what were you doing, poking your foot in the jaws of a dingo?'

'Well, I didn't say it was a dingo, did I,' Bruce said with a broad smirk. 'Just wondered if you'd believe it was a dingo. It was a muddie,' he said. 'I wasn't concentrating. But the bugger was not skilful enough to do serious damage, so it should be okay, as long as I keep up my new diet of antibiotics on toast.'

'I'll be able to catch you now, Bruce,' Eileen commented with a bland face.

Bruce turned to her with arched eyebrows, 'Don't know why I'd be running, but it sounds interesting,' he said. More than that, he thought. Better leave it there.

'I've built a couple of corned beef and pickle sandwiches if you're hungry. And I'll turn the jug on for a cuppa.' He went to rise awkwardly, taking care of the wounded toe, but Eileen tapped him on the shoulder, suggesting he stay where he was while she did the jug.

When they'd finished lunch and cleaned up, Bruce said, 'I'll just call up Col and let him know we're heading out. Okay if I come with you?' Bruce knew it was way easier to just use Eileen's car, a four-wheel drive, as she'd have her kit on board.

'No problem,' Eileen replied.

The road into the homestead was through Bull paddock, so there was no need for Bruce to go through the agony of opening any gates. He guided Eileen to where Col had said the bull was. Col and Lachlan had beaten them there.

Bruce felt useless while he just watched as Col helped Eileen do the autopsy. No-one said much except Eileen who directed Col and described what she saw as she went along. Lachlan was enthralled and moved about trying to keep out of the way, watching every move and not asking annoying questions as his dad had told him earlier to keep out of this job, just watch, in case he picked up anything nasty.

The bull had gone down on his right side, so the first job was to roll it onto its left. They then positioned it where the carcass could be burned later if Eileen suggested that needed to be done. She went to work, looking over the bull in detail, finding nothing except some frothy discharge from the nose, then slicing him on his bottom line from his chin to his scrotum. After the skin and front and back left legs had been incised and folded back, Eileen opened the chest cavity by slicing between each of the ribs, cutting them off at the sternum and then breaking them off at the junction with the vertebral column. The lungs looked quite normal, but Eileen noted a jelly-like lump near the heart and there was a lot of fluid around the heart. Before going further, she dissected out the tongue, and holding it, dissected out the windpipe and oesophagus to the chest cavity, allowing her to then cut out the lungs and heart in one piece that she placed on a section of skin that she had prepared after peeling it back earlier. The lungs contained some froth, but it was the heart where the real problem became apparent.

As Eileen cut into the heart cavity, fluid poured out and exposed the heart surface which looked like it had suffered severe bruising. 'Crikey, this is spectacular. Haemorrhagic rhabdomyonecrosis,' she said. Little doubt this is why he died.' Eileen had the heart in her left hand, knife in her right, as she turned to Bruce and Col, 'Have you guys done any dozer work in this paddock recently?'

Bruce replied, 'Yeah, we cleaned up around the water just up from the yards a couple of weeks ago. Sounds like I shouldn't have,' Bruce said as he almost recoiled at the suggestion he'd created the problem himself.

'This is almost certainly blackleg,' said Eileen. 'We don't fully understand how this happens, but we know that young cattle get the spores from worked up ground which then end up in the muscle in cells called macrophages, just waiting till something happens to trigger them to produce toxin. Unfortunately, it's a very powerful toxin and kills extremely rapidly, especially if it hits the heart which it does in seventy percent of cases.'

'What causes that trigger, Eileen?' Col asked.

'Not sure Col. The good book says injury, but a university colleague of mine reckons a dose of exercise might be enough, say, if he'd had a lap round the paddock for some reason.'

'Bugger me,' said Bruce. 'On the way home this morning I saw the bulls lapping for some reason. Any clues why Col?'

'No, Bruce,' replied Col.

Eileen chipped in, 'For this to happen, he must never have been injected with five-in-one vaccine, or for some reason it has not worked if he was done.'

'No idea Eileen,' Bruce said. 'We certainly didn't give him a shot, and I don't know what the protocol is where he comes from. Eileen, what's the deal with the rest of the bulls? Are we going to have a calamity here or what?' Bruce was panicking inside, trying to control his worry.

'Well, the good news, Bruce, is it rarely affects an animal over two years of age, and from the bulls I saw here on the way in and just now, you're pretty safe. But I'd get any of them dudes up to three years of age at least in a yard and vaccinated as soon as you can.'

'Bad as this is, that's some good news Eileen. I was getting a bit worried,' Bruce said.

Eileen did not find anything of interest in the rest of the autopsy, but she took lots of samples, all tidily packed ready for shipping to Brisbane. 'I'll try and get these samples away today fellas, and it will probably only take them a couple of days to confirm the bug in the heart. Are you giving all your calves five-in-one in the cradle?' she asked.

'Yeah, that and the three-year botulism vaccine,' replied Bruce.

'My advice is to give them a five-in-one booster at weaning and then you'll be safe. And make sure you hit any young bulls that come onto the place again. Now you know you have the spores here, they can hit you any time you're not prepared, but only for the next hundred years or so.' Eileen smiled at her own silly joke and Bruce smirked, loving her cheek.

The job was done, everyone was clean, and Eileen had packed up, ready to head back to town. 'What did you think of that?' she asked Lachlan who was obviously over-awed by what he'd just seen and heard.

'Can we get it, Miss?' Lachlan blurted out. He was more concerned with his own questions than what he'd been asked.

'No, Lachlan,' Eileen replied. 'Just lucky, as it's very deadly. Drops them in their tracks in no time flat.'

'I've never seen a post-mortem,' Lachlan said, 'and if that's what vets have to do, I don't really think I want to be a vet.'

'Yes, it's not for everyone, Lachlan. This is one part that can back off a grown man if he's not prepared for it, but as much as I love animals and spend all my time trying to make them healthy and happy, I find this part of the job really interesting.' Lachlan had no answer. He just looked at the aftermath and at Eileen, stunned that anyone could find such a gruesome task interesting.

When the job was finished, Lachlan stayed with Col to burn the carcass. Eileen dropped Bruce back to the homestead. She turned to him as he carefully extricated himself from the car, 'Do you need a hand with anything Bruce before I head back? I hope that toe's okay under that impressive bandage.'

'I think I'm okay, Eileen. Thanks. If it gets tricky, I've got Col and Simone on hand. They're terrific. And their young fella, Lachlan, he's really good value, even if he isn't going to be a vet.' Bruce smiled.

'Bruce, I'm off call next weekend and a few of us are going to have dinner at the pub on Friday night, and then head back to our place for a game of cards. If your toe will stand it, we'd love you to join us. We've already conned your crazy mates Craig and Mick to join us,' Eileen asked hopefully.

'I'd love to Eileen. I reckon I might stand a chance as long as the toe doesn't end up a bucket of pus. What games do you play?'

'Five Hundred is one of our favourites, but we play other games too. Boring mob of women we are, but we reckon we could spice cards up if we flog the socks of you blokes. What do you reckon? Do you stand a chance?' she teased.

'I reckon as long as the company's good and we can have a couple of painkillers, maybe some light beers so I can get home afterwards, it'll be fun to play easy and give you a chance,' Bruce replied.

Eileen daintily flicked a bunch of wayward locks behind her left ear, raised her eyebrows, and rolled her eyes up to take in Bruce, almost through her lashes, as she smiled broadly, 'Well, we'll see. Don't underestimate how many tricks I learnt in my mis-spent hours at uni over five years.'

'Sounds like my kind of night. Looking forward to it Eileen,' Bruce said. 'I'll meet you guys at the pub by seven hopefully.' Bruce realised he was hardly registering what was going on with his toe. This lady is asking me out? Wow. Steady on, she might be luring me in for one of her mates; I know what those sheilas get up to.

'Good, Bruce. I'm holding you to it. See you then. Bye now.' Eileen rolled up the windows and headed back to town, and probably another call-out.

Vaccinating the bulls was on Bruce's mind. He had to rely on Col who was already under the pump. But that's what happens in the beef business; always a ton of challenges and always a solution to all of them, well almost. Bruce called up Col an hour later when he knew he'd be back from burning the bull carcass. They agreed Col and Lachlan could poke the bulls into the yards first thing in the morning. Bruce would take down the vaccine. Lachlan would be as happy as a pig in mud, especially if it delayed him getting back to school, and even if his mum, Simone, would hit the roof.

***

Bruce spent the rest of the week doing what he could. It was not much fun trying to keep his toe in cotton wool. Each night when he went to bed it was throbbing, a result of his almost continual motion, more so than any bumps. The doctor had prescribed him a very good pain killer, Meloxicam. He made sure he never missed a tablet because after showering each night when he changed the bandage, he needed to grit his teeth as it more than just tickled. The toe looked mucky as the doctor had suggested it would. But it was not oozing pus and it did not feel too bad when he woke each morning, so he reasoned good things were happening with it. The first night he had a shower, he wondered how he'd keep the toe and bandages out of the water. He rang his mum who asked Merve who had the solution.

'Put a preg testing glove on your foot and a rubber band round your ankle. It works perfectly for an arm or hand and should do the trick,' he said.

And it did. Merve was very disappointed he could not go out for the muster but now he was committed to Farmin Stuff, leaving him little option other than to let Bruce sort out the problems, busted toe or not.

Though all Bruce's mates and relations were mustering at the same time and could not get away to help him, at least they had an extra now. Col had rung their southern neighbour, Scott Olden. Scott was quite sympathetic to Bruce's plight. He'd be right to help muster and with some yard work. Bruce was okay with the plan. Scott was a good bloke, a good neighbour, a good beef business operator, and he needed a man who knew how to handle himself around livestock. Simone was breaking her neck, probably more so than Lachlan, to get back into cattle work. Col and Bruce planned their logistics to get as much done as possible outside school hours. Lachlan was on cloud nine. Carina was not overly impressed as it meant she had to be in the yards whenever Simone was there. At least Mum let her play with her dolls in the stock-free area of the yards, and only occasionally asked her to do something that was safe enough for a small girl. In a couple of years, she would be doing what Lachlan was, almost a man's job, as the development in pre-adolescent station children is extraordinarily rapid as they take on vast responsibilities that city children rarely have the chance to experience.

Water runs and fence checking were a constant in station life. Bruce had over one hundred and eighty kilometres of fencing by his calculations, with fifty-three of that as the boundary alone. Most of the time they remained intact, but as the muster neared and cattle were drafted into new paddocks, fences needed to be in good order to keep cattle where they were put. In addition, Bruce ensured all cattle had a phosphorus supplement till after weaning each year, fed as ten-kilogram blocks adjacent to waters, with cattle licking up whatever their appetite suggested. This meant water runs doubled as lick runs. Col had done a big water and lick run covering the east of the property where the breeding cows were, plus all the country south of Gun Creek flowing west-south-west in a fairly-straight line that split the property roughly equally north and south; the homestead was on the northern side of where Gun Creek joined Cockatoo River. So, after giving his toe a few days respite, Bruce reckoned he was able enough to check potential weak spots in fences and check some waters in the close-in smaller paddocks where the bulls and fresh weaner steers would be going. The paddocks had been spelled, so there was no lick feeding needed.

On Wednesday morning, Bruce packed a sandwich and some tea bags, filled his thermos with hot water, strapped on his radio harness with the fully-charged UHF, hobbled over to the machinery shed, and saddled up in the Kubota side by side vehicle they had recently purchased. It was not yet full daylight at a quarter past six. The cacophony of early-morning bird calls really was music, even if they sang the same song over and over. The ever-increasing population of feral cats had not yet taken enough birds to silence the bush.

It was fortunate the crab had mangled Bruce's left toe as he needed his right foot to drive the Kubota. He pressed the brake and turned it on, shattering the bush silence. At this early hour before the sun rose and stirred the lower atmosphere with its heat impacts, every animal within kilometres would recognise the farmer was on the move. Unlike you could on a horse, there was no chance of coming on to cattle without alerting them well beforehand.

Bruce headed east through the cull paddock towards the main cattle yards that were about four and half kilometres to the east, far enough from the house to avoid the dust and noise that emanated from there, especially at this time of the year when most prevailing breezes were between south-westerly to south-easterly. This was a long way compared to most other stations where the yards were adjacent to the big house, a legacy of days of yore when motorised vehicles did not exist. Many years earlier, Merve relocated the yards to be the epicentre of the station, with only a small set near the homestead. Bruce and Col had kept the yards track in good order as they used it many times daily. The Kubota made the drive a lot easier for Bruce than it would have been on a motorbike, though the track was not smooth and the toe, carefully wrapped as it was, was feeling every bump.

The motor may have prevented Bruce from listening for whatever he could, but that never dulled his vision or his smell, both senses being primed at all times. The tracks he covered were mostly across gently-undulating country covered in open forest with a well-managed grass and legume pasture. The ridges with stonier low-fertility soils supported ironbark trees. The flats were home to box trees. In areas of higher fertility soils, tall Moreton Bay ash trees predominated. In between, there were many shrubs, interspersed with hardy narrow-leaved acacia and eucalypt species. Across the station, Merve had established buffel grass wherever he could. This hardy species had evolved under the hooves of massive African grazing herds. Its substantial roots supported a plant that grew well and that stock loved, as did the graziers. Merve had also colonised seca stylo across the station. This hardy legume had come from dryland tropical areas of southern America. It provided protein for cattle early in the dry season and fixed nitrogen that enhanced the growth of buffel grass. Together, these species had increased live weight production of Bovale's cattle by over twenty kilograms annually.

It was almost a relief to have to get out to open a gate, check a water or fix a problem; hobbling seemed to get the blood flowing a bit better in Bruce's throbbing big toe. The herd drank up to one hundred thousand litres of water daily. Fortunately, the almost automatic station water reticulation system seemed to be humming along just nicely with only one trough found leaking. It was near the main station access road on the north side of Weaner paddock to the north of the yards, separating yearling heifers to the east from the bulls with seemingly no morals whatsoever, to the west. It looked like a wild pig had been in the trough, bending the float valve arm, which Bruce straightened as he struggled to keep his dodgy foot dry and out of the muddy mess made by the leak.

Four hours after he'd left the homestead, Bruce was just about back when his mobile phone rang. He let the vehicle come to a halt and he switched it off. He was near enough to the signal booster system they'd installed to have reception. It was Merve.

'G'day Bruce. How's everything out there?'

'Good, Dad. I've just ventured out on a water run, and everything looks okay. I reckon I should be able to do something useful next week,' he replied.

'Bruce, it's not so good here I'm sorry to say. I took your mum to the specialist today. He confirmed your mother has non-Hodgkin lymphoma.' The tremor in Merve's voice was evident, and he was a long way from his usual ebullient self.

'What's that exactly, Dad?'

'A type of leukaemia, Bruce.'

Bruce was stunned. He just stared at the steering wheel, but really at nothing. His mind was muddled and in shock. His mum! Cancer! No wonder she'd been crook for a while. She should have gone to the doctor sooner. Damn.

'What's going to happen, Dad?'

Merve paused. 'We don't really know yet, mate. We had an idea this might have been the case for a few weeks now. The GP thought it was likely, and once we got to the specialist and he did the tests, well, it confirmed it. Basic plan first up is chemo. Unfortunately, the chances of a cure are not high. But apparently the doctors can keep it under control and keep you alive for years in most cases. I'm devastated Bruce. But I can't imagine how your mum feels.'

Bruce was stunned to realise his eyes were watering. He just had nothing to say, but knew he needed to, for his dad. 'Should I come down straight away, Dad?'

'Look Bruce, it would be heaven to see you every day, but this is no emergency for you. Unless it'll help you, I reckon a regular chat to your mum on the blower would be best and come down after the weaning's under control.'

'Yeah, you're probably right, Dad. I'd come down there and hang around bored senseless, looking for an excuse to come home, even though I know Mum loves having me around. I just want to see her before this goes much further.'

Merve replied, 'I'll hand the phone over to Mum. See you when I'm looking at you, Bruce.'

Doris held the phone to her right ear, cradling the mouthpiece in her left hand, and with a bowed head she whispered, 'Bruce, sorry to give you the news.'

It was too much for Bruce who lapsed into uncontrollable sobbing, leaving Doris hanging. But she understood and just waited with glistening eyes for her little boy to come to terms with what he'd just learned. Eventually Bruce restored his composure, 'Sorry, Mum. Such a shock.'

'Thank you, Bruce,' she replied.

Bruce said, 'I'd love to come down straight away, but that may disrupt plans here and I can see you soon anyway. Just know I'm thinking of you and love you.'

It was Doris's turn to sob. It was breaking both their hearts. When his mum was composed, Bruce said, 'Mum, it's probably fair to say treatment won't be all roses for you, but in a modern world I am sure we are a long, long way from losing you. Medicine is amazing these days. I reckon if we strap in for the ride and let the pros control the show, you'll be right.'

'I hope so, Bruce,' Doris said. 'My dream is to enjoy grandchildren and that means I need to be sticking around for quite a few years before you and Frances achieve that. And you will.'

'Nothing like a bit of pressure, Mum. I probably shouldn't lob that on any girls that are silly enough to spend time with me, but I'll keep it in mind.'

Doris's revelation had unnerved Bruce a bit. Serious dating was unchartered waters, yet alone the prospect of breeding. It wasn't like the cattle, where you simply put the males and females together in the same paddock and waited three weeks while the level of hanky panky went off the scale, day and night.

'Just be you, Bruce, and you'll be amazed what girls notice. If I was twenty again and found you single and lonely, you'd be in trouble. I might be biased but I reckon your time is closer than you think.'

Whoa back, Mum, Bruce was thinking. Sounded good, but it did not sound like reality to him. The main thing he could do was make Mum happy.

'Righto Mum. I'll just be me, within striking distance of the fairer sex and see how I go,' he chuckled to her. He was thinking of the coming Friday night, and Eileen.

They chatted for a few more minutes about life at the station before hanging up. Bruce immediately felt like he'd landed in an alien world. Sure, this was home, always had been. But that chat had taken him to another planet, nothing like home. It was nice to talk to Mum and Dad, but not about signing off with cancer. Bruce just sat there, staring into the unfocussed distance, absorbing what they had just discussed. Slowly he thawed and eased himself, and his bandaged stone kicker, back into Bovale. The short drive to the shed was slow.

Bruce realised he hadn't noticed his toe for the past ten minutes. But crikey, the pain was arcing up again. He had thought the easy water run would be okay, but he had not considered just how seriously upset his immune system would be, raging at him via high-speed pain receptors from the end of his left foot. He hobbled to the homestead.

Chapter Three

Friday came. The muster plan and preparations were done. They would start tomorrow, maximising the opportunity to involve Simone and Lachlan, who was pumped. The chopper would arrive soon after first light, and move straight into Kosciuszko paddock, almost three thousand hectares on the south-east of the station. Ian, the pilot, was well-acquainted with their operation, having mustered Bovale multiple times. Prior to getting his licence, Ian had also done some contract mustering for the Arnold family. All he needed to know was a paddock, a time, expected stock numbers and class, and where the on-ground team would be, and he was ready to go.

But it was not yet Saturday, it was still Friday. Bruce could have done the trek to Townsville and back to see his mum, but he had a better offer just now. Charters Towers beckoned. Hormones helped make great decisions he reasoned to himself. The toe was much better. Though he could still not pull on a boot, Bruce was certainly up to chilling out with his mates in town, especially if it was with Eileen and her house mates. The boys liked to drink and lark a fair bit, but Bruce told himself, tonight was one night where he'd try the snaffle bit on the lads, and just enjoy some good clean fun with only a couple of drinks. Good luck with that, he thought as he shook his head a bit, thinking how Craig and Mick might react to playing cards with the ladies instead of drinking in the loud music and all the add-ons the local pubs had to offer young people off the leash.

The winter solstice was only a month away and the days were short. By six o'clock when Bruce crawled into his Land Cruiser, it was getting dark. Sundown was a difficult time of the day to drive as the eyes had to constantly adjust between the shadowed earth surface and the still-light sky. No amount of concentration could pick out all the road-side nocturnal wildlife, the wallabies, kangaroos, rabbits, kangaroo rats and occasional wild pigs and chital deer that were stirring into feeding action after a long day of rest. All, and especially wallabies, adopted what appeared to be, near-random escape routes when vehicles approached at night, which meant collisions were not uncommon. The wildlife always came off second best, and the vehicle almost unscathed if it had a steel bull bar like Bruce's. Tonight was no exception. He'd only just left the house, still in Bull paddock, when a wallaroo, a particularly solid buck, flew out of the grass just metres in front of him. It left Bruce no chance to react to the high-speed kamikaze trajectory, straight at the bull bar, mid-way between the spotlights, probably thinking it was heading to safety between the lights. Instant death. Bruce stopped and pulled the still-flinching carcass off the track and washed his hands using water from the tank mounted under his Cruiser tray. It was essential to move the body to prevent anyone hitting the rotting carcass, though the pigs out of the river may have demolished it before dawn anyway.

When Bruce got to the pub, Eileen, her buddies Jane and Brenda, along with Mick and Craig were already on their first shout. They were on a large open-air deck with a few potted palms as décor. It was a family area, well away from the public bar. They liked the outdoor setting as it enabled them to talk without having to shout. Friday night and the pub was full of revellers, all eager to share the week's happenings. The racket emanating from possibly fifty different conversations bounced off the hard walls and ceilings throughout the pub, a nightmare for anyone with industrial deafness.

Only Eileen had seen Bruce with a lame back leg as Craig called it. Mick met Bruce and told him to get seated; he'd shout him a beer. Bruce was up for pale ale. He immediately realised the sheilas were up to no good, well, probably it really was okay, when Jane and Eileen found a seat between them that Bruce could take. I wonder if pigs enjoy getting trapped as much as this, he thought.

The girls were dolled up in dresses, which Bruce loved. Jeans were okay when working, but he loved seeing the femininity of dresses. Eileen's dress was quite sensible for the coolish evening it was. It was a simple, elegant, pastel green dress with a gathered waist. It matched the lustre of her pearl earrings and the pearl pendant she was wearing. I could get out of control here, thought Bruce as he surreptitiously checked out each of the girls with a special check on Eileen. Stunning.

'No more crook ones or dead cattle, Bruce?' Eileen asked over the din in the pub, genuinely concerned.

'No, and thanks to you we probably are safe on that front,' Bruce replied.

'Here, have a sip on my lemon, lime and bitters while you wait for your beer. You look like you could drink a trough dry, Bruce,' Eileen said as she offered her drink.

'Thanks. Hope I don't give you any boy germs,' Bruce laughed, thinking just how good it would be to catch some girl germs.

'Not possible. I'm immune, Bruce. I've had all my shots against football and cricket,' she offered, giving Bruce a wickedly beautiful sideways smile.

'I meant to get back to you with an interim result on that post-mortem, Bruce. The heart muscle was positive for blackleg, so we got the diagnosis and advice spot-on. Probably won't make you feel any better about losing that bull, but I'm sure you won't let it happen again,' Eileen added.

'You can bet on that, Eileen,' Bruce replied. 'Thanks.'

Dinner was full of non-stop banter, interspersed with more serious talk about work and families. Looking after himself at home was always a tough chore for Bruce since his parents had moved to Townsville, so having a seriously-large, medium-cooked, rump steak served up with chips and salad, without having to either prepare it or clean up afterwards was the stuff dreams were made of. The regular mild flirts between Bruce and Eileen kept a smile on his face. Jane and Brenda were doing their best to ensure this continued. Craig and Mick were blind as bats to what was going on. But their blindness was no inhibition to good fun, and all had plenty.

The night was young when they headed back to Lizard Street where the girls lived in a typical old miner's cottage. It was an old, but serviceable fibro house. It had a tonne of character, partly because of the girls' embellishments of what they called 'The Villa'. The lounge room had a large coffee table made from mango tree slabs. Surrounded by comfy chairs, none of which matched, the slab, as the girls called it, oozed charm with its rough edges and undulating, polished, pock-marked surface. The slab was the scene of countless TV dinners and if it could have learned anything, would have been an expert card player as the girls were always playing with one eye on the television.

It was Bruce's first visit to The Villa. Nice. He noticed a few empty vases around as he ambled through the lounge into the small kitchen at the back. A hint? An opportunity, he was thinking. Maybe. Let's see how it goes.

'Coffee everyone?' Jane asked.

Mick had brought an esky with half a carton of a light beer, nestled under the ice.

'I think we'll start off with an analgesic,' Mick said as Bruce, Craig and he dived into the ice and then headed for the lounge, each with a stubbie in hand. Jane shrugged her shoulders and headed for the fridge. She came back with three glasses and some Chateau Cardboard, which is what the girls called their regular favourite, a cask of Chardonnay.

On his way to the pub earlier in the night, Craig had loaded up with several packets of chips and two blocks of rum and raisin chocolate, which he had brought into the kitchen for the girls to dish out with whatever they thought was best for nibblies. What more could a man want, Bruce thought. Well, other than for everyone to accidentally take off back to town for a serious session of clubbing except him and Eileen of course. But that was not going to happen. Slow down boss, he told himself. Dream real.

Brenda had the cards. 'Oh Hell,' she said.

'Oh what?' responded Bruce.

'It's a card game for any number of players, Bruce. Great fun. We'll teach you,' she told him.

'Hopefully you'll just get it Bruce before we flog the pants off you,' Mick threw in. He was obviously familiar with this game and enjoying the opportunity to get one up on his good mate.

Oh Hell turned out to be a great game, a bit of luck, a bit of skill, and tonnes of fun. Bruce's luck was not going well but was consoled by Jane who wore an all-knowing smirk, 'Bruce, unlucky at cards, lucky in love, they say.'

'I'll have a harem before the night's out,' reckoned Bruce. He was coming stone motherless last, but it was not dampening his spirits nor anyone else's. It was simply fun playing, just maybe potentiated by all the flirting going on.

Bruce had carefully given Eileen a one-armed side hug for excelling in one hand and she had reciprocated in consolation when he'd gotten his call completely wrong, with the worst result for the night.

'Bruce,' she said with a sparkle in her eye and not looking directly at him, 'don't drop your lip whatever you do, or I'll have to kiss it better.' That certainly livened the party even further with both Craig and Mick hopping into the discussion suggesting Bruce's top lip was almost at his waist and his bottom lip was where she shouldn't be kissing. Eileen blushed. Bruce smiled and looked at her gently, which only enhanced the glow in her cheeks.

The neighbours' cats would have been disturbed by all the banter, but the neighbours never complained; they probably just turned the volumes up on their televisions to hear the rugby league commentary.

Before they knew it, it was eleven o'clock. Bruce knew he was being a proper Cinderella, but he said, 'I need to get home good people. I have an early start, and the hoof needs a rest before I abuse it all week. I think I'll cut for it.'

'Not before I have a coffee in you, Bruce,' said Eileen. In no time she had the jug boiled and the brew ready for Bruce, just the way he liked it. 'Thanks for coming in tonight, Bruce. I've had a great night. Let's do this again soon.'

'Bloody oath, but it'll have to be after the first-round muster,' agreed Bruce, together with the other four, as he hobbled out to his Cruiser.

By the time he got back to the Bovale homestead and eased himself into bed, it was closer to one o'clock than midnight. His alarm was set for four-thirty. At least he'd have some pretty good dreams tonight, he thought, even if they're not going to be long enough. Within five seconds the sleep genie had snared him, locking down his consciousness.

***

Overall, the muster went well, in no small way due to the meticulous planning by Bruce and Col. Little happened that they had not anticipated and planned for. In the yards, every draft had been organised and estimates of what was going to end up where. It reflected the tidy well-organised mind of Bruce. He had worked on other places occasionally where they thought about the draft as they loaded the race with cattle and every day had a different plan. This was all too random for Bruce. He liked to ensure that cattle were mustered or came through the yards a maximum of twice annually. Any more than that he reasoned indicated he was not sufficiently prepared for mustering, pasture utilisation, supplementation, mating, marketing or whatever was likely to occur. It relied on having a good understanding of all aspects of the business and constant monitoring and recording of pastures and the cattle, in addition to costs.

The muster was up and down for Bruce's toe. It was in a lot better shape than it had been since resting it after the water run. Bruce rued not being able to get a boot on because this left his foot very exposed; he almost felt half naked, but there was little he could do other than wait for healing to happen at its pace. In the paddock, he rode in the side-by-side, which Simone would usually have done. But he was the princess on this muster and had to be content on a throne rather than his usual practice of riding the Kawasaki two-wheel ag bike, sometimes a bit like Mad Max might have when the cattle were not behaving as they should. The Kawasaki was parked up in the shed as Scott from next door had brought over his own 'tin horse', as he called his motorbike. Scott was very handy to have on the musters, but he could not spare the time to help in the yards. In the yards, from mid-afternoon when school was done, Bruce just worked the rear slide gate of the vet chute, making decisions while Col did the drafting. Simone and Lachlan kept the cattle coming. Simone drafted out of the small forcing yard into the pound, where Lachlan worked the gates, sending weaners into a side yard and cows and bulls up the race. Though the job was physically steady, it wasn't such a huge challenge as these cattle were quite well-behaved. Occasionally, Col would have to fly back and assist yarding up, but mostly the yard work went smoothly, even if the constant bellowing of separated cows and calves was sometimes deafening.

At the end of each day that cattle were mustered, Col would settle and feed the weaners. Early next morning before school with his wife and son, they would put culls in Cull paddock, which headed back towards the homestead, bulls into Bull paddock, and freshly-weaned cows into either Lane or Tadpole paddocks, to let them settle down for a few days before driving them back to where they were drafted to go.

While this happened, Bruce looked after Carina, as he moseyed around doing minor jobs that an unshod painful toe could handle. Carina was in heaven being with her idol. In the yards she was under the watchful eye of her mum, Simone, while she played with her dolls. But when Mum was gone, she came to life, trying her best to do everything possible to please Bruce.

During the muster, Bruce had more time than usual to assess his cattle. They were Droughtmasters, a red composite breed originally derived from two main breeds, Brahman and Beef Shorthorn in the Burdekin River catchment in the decades after World War Two. This combination enabled the astute cattlemen who achieved this to combine desirable traits from both breeds at a time when neither parent breed was fully developed for beef production in tropical Queensland. Though Bruce considered his dad, Merve, had done a great job bringing the herd to what it currently was, he perceived there were too many cows with small mature size, which might be reflected in low growth of the steers they bred. There were also too many horned cattle when cattle without horns were needed as dehorning was preventable cruelty if done in the traditional way. Bruce was thinking their fertility was ordinary. He was only weaning about eight hundred calves from thirteen hundred cows each year and he was sure he could do better but did not know how.

Four weeks later, all calves were off their mothers that were back in their paddocks. Col, with assistance from Bruce, Simone and Lachlan when they could, had finished the weaner training, the daily after-school ritual at each muster when they were not drafting a new mob. Bruce, with toe back to normal almost and happily dealing with boots, had been regularly ringing his mum. He now had a chance to head down to Townsville for a day or two while Col kept the operation afloat. It was a Tuesday afternoon as Bruce headed off. He eagerly anticipated seeing his family, and especially his mum, after such a torridly-busy few weeks at Bovale. This was also a chance for a break.

***

As Bruce parked in the driveway of his parents' place, his mum emerged from the front door. She had been eagerly waiting to see her little boy. 'Bruce, it's so good to see you,' she said as she embraced him warmly. Bruce gave her his best smile; he was really happy to see her.

Merve appeared in the doorway. 'G'day, mate,' he added as he gave his son a firm handshake.

Bruce grabbed his bag from the Cruiser's passenger side and followed his mum inside, with Merve behind, closing the door. 'Frances will be here for dinner and I'm preparing a stuffed topside roast because I know it's a favourite for you both,' Doris said. Bruce hardly needed her to tell him. His nostrils and sinuses were being caressed with the glorious aroma of roasting beef and veggies.

'Did I ever tell you, you're an amazing mum?' he said to Doris.

'Just doing what mum's do,' replied Doris as she busied herself with some further preparations for dinner. 'One day you'll know exactly what I mean. You'll have your own children. If they end up anything like you and Frances, you will be blessed.'

Merve had grabbed two stubbies of beer from the fridge and a can of lemonade. With a little bit from each stubbie, he made his wife a shandy in a tall glass, which she always enjoyed before dinner, found some stubbie coolers to insulate the beers and offered one to Bruce. 'Cheers, mate,' he said. 'Cheers, Honey,' he toasted to his wife, 'Here's to a perfect dinner.'

Merve and Bruce perched themselves on stools around the kitchen island as Doris kept working on dinner and all three caught up with each other. Though Merve and Doris had almost daily had an update on the muster, there was nothing like hearing it from Bruce in person as the chat cues prompted questions that seem to get missed in a phone conversation. Merve was very impressed how his son had handled it, and especially how he had worked so well with Col and his young family. 'You're a born leader, Bruce,' he offered. 'You're doing a lot better than I would have done at your age.

'Bit of nuisance about that bull though, Bruce. They say, when you have livestock, you have dead stock, but it surely doesn't have to be the most valuable one you own,' Merve despaired. They had a good yarn about blackleg and how Bruce might prevent any future deaths. 'That vet seems pretty handy, Bruce. She did a good job when we got her out to preg test the heifers a few months ago.'

Handy is one way to describe her, thought Bruce, who was inwardly assigning a whole pile of more flattering descriptors to Eileen.

Bruce agreed. As much as discussion about Eileen brought an unstoppable smile to his face, he thought he should steer the discussion well out of that territory before he dropped his guard and admitted he'd more than had her out for veterinary work. 'That Kubota has been brilliant, Dad,' he offered. 'It was great when my foot was out. Now I understand why Simone likes it so much.' Merve was eager to discuss vehicles, and Bruce breathed easier.

Just before six o'clock, Frances arrived, prompting Merve to get her a beer as well. She too was very pleased to see her brother. 'Good to see your lameness has gone, Bruce. Is the toe good now?' she asked.

'It's only a few weeks, Frances, and it's as good as it could be. It's amazing how nude I felt, not being able to get my boot on. Maybe I should wear steel-capped boots next time I go crabbing?' he replied.

'Yeah. How long do you reckon you can stay? I'd love to take you out on the town, maybe tomorrow night?' Frances asked hopefully.

'I'll stay for that Frances. Sounds like an offer I can't refuse,' Bruce replied.

'Knowing you, you haven't been out the gate of Bovale for weeks, brother. You need socialising,' Frances added.

'I might have snuck into town just once, Frances,' Bruce said with just a hint of the pleasure look in his eye.

Frances was sharp. She did not miss it. 'And what was on in town, Bruce? Maybe not just Mick and Craig getting you anaesthetised?' she queried, certain she'd spotted guilt of some sort.

'Just for a change Frances, I was good. We went to the pub and had a steak and a beer,' Bruce said.

'You three don't just have a beer, Bruce,' Frances teased gently. 'I just hope it was clean fun and I suspect it might have even been that, given your back leg was lame, as Craig calls it.'

Doris had dinner ready, and they descended on the dining room table. Doris had set the table with a small vase of leafy gum tree twigs and flowers at each end. The tablecloth was one of her finest. The silver cutlery was set alongside placings from her beautiful dinner set. Doris was creating the best ambience she could for a special dinner with the most precious people in her life.

Bruce had to lick his lips a few times. He was salivating so much in anticipation of the feast, the aromas of which were driving his senses giddy in delight. 'Thanks, Mum, this is Christmas,' he said. Merve and Frances agreed as they all waited to be served and for Doris to sit before they hoed into the magnificent tucker.

They had all finished their beers. Merve had brought out a bottle of shiraz and added it to the table earlier. Not only did it give the setting even better ambience, he knew they would all enjoy it immensely. At some stage in the past, he had learned the simple art of how to attractively wrap a serviette around the neck of the bottle to avoid spillage, which would help keep stains off the tablecloth. With a bit of ceremony, Merve poured wine for himself, Frances and Bruce into the crystal glasses Doris had set. Doris was envious as she had to stick with a sparkling water; no sense in reducing the chances of chemotherapy doing its job.

'A toast to you, Bruce, and how you're handling Bovale,' Merve said. All raised their drinks.

Bruce said, 'Thanks everyone. It's a full-on gig, but I really enjoy the work and the challenge.'

After they'd cleaned their plates, Doris surprised them with Bruce's favourite dessert, rice pudding and canned peaches. Doris even playfully called it 'Bruce pudding' as she knew how much he craved it. Bruce had not had such a delectable feast since his mother last cooked for him. He was going to suggest it would have been great to still have her at the station so he could enjoy more such delights, but he thought better of it in case it upset her. Being stuck in a city and having to undergo chemotherapy for cancer was not good fun.

After dessert, Doris and Merve gave Frances and Bruce an update on the treatment. There was not a lot they could tell them, other than it made Doris quite ill during the two-week treatment cycles she had to endure, two weeks on and two weeks off, maybe for about six cycles. 'It's all for the better,' Doris said. 'This will get me back to how I want to be, looking after the three most important people in my life.' She was very pragmatic and was dealing with the situation very well as far as Bruce could see.

Merve had been quiet for a few minutes, just listening to the other three, before he sensed a conversation lull. 'Your mother and I have been thinking through a few things since all this health thing has blown up. We need to sort out where we're going in our lives a bit better and what this means for you two.' Bruce and Frances were silent, respectfully waiting for more as they could see it was not easy for Merve to say what he was saying. 'We mainly have to sort out succession, which will impact our wills. Horrible to work through that with Mum in her predicament, but we just have to do it, and do it now,' Merve said. 'We're no specialists on this and we'll need specialist advice, but before we go there, we'd like to talk it through with you two first. To get your thoughts, just so we give ourselves the best chance of getting it right for everyone.'

'Dad,' Bruce said, 'you know Frances and I will accept whatever you and Mum agree is best. You obviously have some ideas and you've caught us cold, so how about you tell us what you think would work as a start?'

'You won't be aware of some of this stuff, Frances, so please bear with me as I explain my ideas.' Merve took a breath and had a sip of shiraz. 'There's a couple of major options to start with. One is to sell Bovale or keep it. If we sell it, we will fairly much cut off our main ties with the land and the cattle industry. We also potentially cut you out of the industry, Bruce. Unless you pair want that, we don't want to go that way. Which led us to our second-tier options that were based on which one of you two should take responsibility for Bovale. Let's assume this is you, Bruce. We think giving you joint ownership is not a good plan. Like a body with two heads. We want you to be friends, not competing. You get on great now, but one day you'll both be married with children and the equation may change if envy crops up, even thirty years down the track, so let's not plan for failure.

'I used the word responsibility. It's not so much about inheritance, but about taking on a large business including all assets and liabilities and continuing its success. Your mother and I want to invoke full succession; we want to be independent of Bovale. We need to have enough resources to enjoy the rest of our lives. And we don't need or want liabilities or even assets associated with Bovale.

'Frances, so you know, our current loan is almost two point five million dollars. We have been paying about one hundred and seventy-five thousand in interest alone each year. When possible, we work on knocking down the principle, but it's not that easy as Bruce will tell you.' Frances showed her concern, having known her parents had debt, but not being aware of its scale. She was starting to understand what her father meant by responsibility for the asset.

'But against that, we estimate the property is worth something like twelve point five million dollars and the herd is worth another three million, which means the business net worth is a fair bit. The reality is the real estate aspect of rural business is becoming increasingly dislocated from the agricultural business. Return on investment is shockingly low in beef if only the agricultural side is available for income, but unfortunately, unless you're playing the real estate game, we have to wear that. That's why we're loath to sell. If we sell out, we have no chance of ever getting either of you back into it again.'

'I really had no idea about all this, Dad,' Frances said. 'But as Bruce said, I'm going to happily accept what you decide, which must firstly suit you.'

'Thanks, Frances,' Doris said.

Merve continued. 'Fortunately, your mother and I started on the superannuation process many years ago. We own this house, and we have great investments. On top of that, I reckon I have at least another ten years in the workforce in me. The main concern for us is if we have to face major medical bills or one or both of us has to go into care. We need to budget for that without imposing on you two.

'What Mum and I believe too, is that you, Frances, should fairly share in some of the family wealth without jeopardising its security. If we do as I'm suggesting, Bruce will end up with considerably more wealth, but balance dictates some sort of cost for that privilege.' Merve paused to let that sink in. He sipped some more shiraz.

'Doris and I are proposing to transfer the station and the full business loan to Bruce and in the process extend the loan by a further seven hundred and fifty thousand dollars, if the bank will allow that. Five hundred thousand to Frances as a lump sum and half that to us. That money for you, Frances, could be invested now in housing, shares or super, depending on what you want, but it will be a great boost for you. Just like the boost you will get Bruce, including the boost in interest payments, probably to about two hundred and twenty thousand a year,' Merve added with a wry smile.

Bruce and Frances stared at their father, taking it all in, remaining silent. Doris was focussed on her two beautiful children and could see the extraordinary appreciation both of them had for what her husband was proposing.

'Does that sound reasonable to you both? Do you think I'm being fair, Frances?' Merve asked with obvious concern.

'Dad, I'm really chuffed you think I should get that much. But I really can't accept it if it means there's a risk to Bruce being able to keep the business afloat,' said Frances.

Merve replied, 'I reckon he'll be right. He's young. There'll be ups and downs. If the prices happen to spike for a year or two, and that happens occasionally, he'll be able to get the principle down a fair bit quickly and be sailing a lot easier. Add to that, land prices just seem to continually increase at a much greater rate than most other assets, so that will give him the buffer of increasing equity that he can borrow against if markets dive for a bit, or seasons are particularly bad. I wouldn't be suggesting this if I didn't think it's doable. What I don't know yet is whether the banks will take us on, though I reckon they will, and what the tax implications are. I just didn't want to do any negotiations until I knew we were all on the same page.'

'When do you plan to have our accountant assess the plan, Dad?' Bruce asked.

'Well, I made an appointment for tomorrow on the chance you'll be able to come with me. I'd love you to come too, Frances, if you can duck away from work. As you know, your mother goes in for more chemo tomorrow and I've organised for us to do this while she's having that. Doris would rather we do something productive than sit around in the hospital waiting for her cancer to get zapped,' Merve said.

'Looks like it's a full-on day. Are you okay with this, Mum?' asked Bruce.

'Yes, I am Bruce. I would much rather you be doing something useful. And I really don't need anyone waiting for me while I'm having the treatment. Tomorrow night I'll probably feel a bit tired, so my preference is for you to go out with Frances. That would be lovely. I'm enjoying tonight. It's so lovely to have both of my beautiful children here,' Doris said.

'You've made a beautiful dinner for us, Mum,' Frances said. 'Thank you. You are such a beautiful mum.'

Bruce stood up and went around to his mum, leaned down and gave her a hug and a kiss on the cheek, drawing a tear from her. 'Thanks Mum,' he said.

Merve was riveted, oozing pride in his children. In a moment of major change in their own lives, they had put the previous few minutes aside, their focus firmly on their mother who needed their love as much as at any time in her life. 'Wow,' he said. 'Doris, thanks for the lovely meal. And Frances and Bruce, I can't express just how proud of you I am.' He raised his glass to them and had a sip. Bowing his head slightly he shed a small tear, which did not go unnoticed.

***

The following day, while Doris received treatment at the hospital, Merve, Bruce and Frances met with their accountant. Merve outlined his proposal, which the accountant suggested would need a bit of tweaking, but would work satisfactorily, as long as the banks extended further credit. While still at the meeting, they booked an appointment for the following day with their bank manager.

Bruce was in the hospital waiting room while Merve went to sit with Doris as the staff finished off the chemotherapy, removed the drip and ensured she was in good shape to go home. It was much better being there than in the emergency department having his toe sorted out. He had no desire to go anywhere near that part of the hospital again. Bruce was standing, casually observing comings and goings, when he saw a familiar face coming in through the main entrance. The bloke immediately recognised him too. It was Lenny Pavarotti, the bloke who had helped him at the boat ramp a few weeks earlier. 'G'day Lenny,' Bruce said.

'Bruce, it's good to see you, mate,' Lenny replied. 'How's that toe of yours?'

'Pretty good, Lenny,' Bruce said. 'Pure luck I'd say, but that monster did not do any serious damage. It was mainly bruising and tearing of skin and soft tissues. Fortunately, I work with some excellent people, and I was able to give it the rest it needed and keep it clean enough.

I've still got a bandage on so I can keep it clean and wear a boot and it's healing really well.'

'Good to hear, Bruce. I was fairly worried when you left, as to how you'd go,' Lenny said.

'Lenny, you're just a champion bloke and I can't thank you enough for what you did. Somehow, we'll get even and I'm going to enjoy that,' Bruce said.

'You in for a check, Bruce?' Lenny asked.

'No, mate. Since we met, Mum's been diagnosed with some sort of leukaemia and she's in having chemo today. Dad's with her now. We'll be taking her home shortly when she's done here,' Bruce replied.

'Gee, that's not good news. Hope she's going to be okay,' Lenny said.

'Yeah. As far as I know we don't expect a complete cure. But it's just amazing what modern medicine can do, Lenny. The docs reckon they can keep a lid on it and slow progression to bugger-all and I'm sure hoping they're right.'

Bruce frowned. 'You're not here for any problems yourself, mate?'

'No, Bruce. I'm just dropping in to pick something up from my daughter. She works in this joint. Loves it. Me, I just get in and get out, quick as I can. I don't like being in either hospitals or schools. It must be that I subconsciously associate them with ordinary experiences or something like that. Catching me here is as likely as intercepting a stray bullet, I'm through the place so fast.' Lenny laughed at his own joke.

'Lenny, I was thinking the other day I might drop by and catch up when I get a chance to come down fishing again. I'm with you on hospitals and schools, so I'll let you scoot. But, looking forward to catching up soon,' Bruce said.

'Fantastic, Bruce. I'll hold you to it. Though I might have to go to the local fish shop and buy a crab so we can have a proper sandwich,' Lenny suggested, laughing again. He really liked this young bloke.

Bruce watched him disappear into the bowels of the hospital. It's amazing how providence hooks a man up with new mates, Bruce was thinking. That Lenny is a good bloke. Bruce decided Lenny just might need a good hunk of premium beef about the time he visited him. Ten minutes later his parents appeared, ready to go.

Doris felt surprisingly fine after her treatment, and instead of what Frances had proposed, the four of them went out for dinner at a quiet restaurant back from the Strand. The next day, while Doris had another chemotherapy session, Merve and Bruce met the bank manager who agreed with the proposal, mainly because the bank's mortgage on the property ensured there was close to zero risk for their institution. Merve and Bruce then spent the rest of the day initiating the required legal processes to implement the actions agreed over the past days.

Dinner that evening was a quiet affair. Doris was feeling the effects of the chemotherapy drugs. She just wanted to rest. So, Merve decided he'd do some steaks on the barbeque at the shed. The men also organised a bit of salad and some bread rolls and set about preparing the evening meal in the basic shed facilities, well away from Doris's kitchen that they wanted to leave as clean as possible. By the time Frances arrived, they were about to move inside with the meals to join Doris perched on her favourite lounge chair in the living room, watching the television, which they turned off. Beers in hand, except for Doris with her sparkling water, they quietly ate their dinners and chatted about the achievements of the past two days and where it might take them.

Chapter Four

The next day, Saturday, Bruce headed back to Bovale. He left his boat at his parents' place as he'd be sure to visit them on the way when he got a chance to go fishing. He was hoping that would be soon. As he drove along, he had plenty to think about. Foremost in his mind was what had transpired over recent days and how that would affect his life. It was increasingly dawning on him just how big it was. Sole responsibility for a multi-million-dollar business was no minor undertaking. His debt would be large, so he'd have to be very careful. No matter what happened, he could not afford to let Col go, as long as he and Simone wanted to stay. All the evidence suggested they would, so that was good.

Try as he might, Bruce could not keep Eileen out of his mind. She was a tantalising lady. And she had clearly shown interest in him. Just maybe? Bruce was passing Mingela when he thought, bugger it, no use thinking about it. Action. He rang his mate using the hands-free system in his Land Cruiser.

'Hey Mick, what are you up to next weekend?' Mick had nothing planned. 'I was thinking. If you and Craig come out to my place and we invite the girls, as long as everyone is clear to come, we could have a bit of fun, play some cards, have a barby, whatever, just have some fun and relax. Even a game of cards; I really liked that game the other night. Sound like a plan?'

Mick was keen. It had been a while since he'd been out to Bovale. 'I'll organise Craig and the sheilas, mate. No problem. What if next weekend won't work?'

'Simple, try the one after that. Biggest challenge might be cornering Eileen. She's on call half the time. Maybe try her first?' Bruce suggested.

'I'm on to it Bruce,' Mick said. 'And what are you up to between now and whichever weekend we're doing the Bovale thing, mate?'

'Plenty Mick. I've been laid up a bit with this mongrel toe, which means I have not been pulling my weight. I'm weeks behind on all the maintenance I usually do. We're also preparing and trucking culls to the meatworks shortly. Plus, there's never ending water runs and checking of cattle. After that blackleg episode, I'm spooked,' Bruce added.

'Gotcha mate. You sound like you need a wife or two to keep you alive and operating right. Buggered if I'm going to let that happen too quick, because Craig and I need our mate to keep us entertained,' Mick stressed.

'That makes three of us for having good times, Mick. But I also like the steady fun like that card night. Maybe I'm changing Mick, getting ancient.'

'I'm reliably informed that blokes can still breed when they're a hundred, Bruce. You're making me worried, starting to think like a sheila,' Mick responded.

'Yeah Mick. I know. Thing is, since Mum's diagnosis, lots of things have changed. I'm on my way back from Townsville just now after a few sobering, but very enjoyable days, with the folks. Mum and Dad are never coming back to Bovale to live, so my days of relying on Dad are gone. I'm the big bwana now. I just have to get used to doing that more and playing less.'

'I understand, Bruce. A bugger about your mum. How's she going?' Mick asked.

'Real good Mick, given the circumstances. She's a really good mum. Each dose of chemo knocks her back a bit, but she's doing fine. In a way it's better we know what she's got, and we can see a better future because of that. Thanks for your concern. You're a real good mate.'

The pair chatted on for a bit, catching up with interesting, but essentially useless information, all part of the spice of life, before they hung up. By the time Bruce got to Bovale, his head was back in the cattle business zone. He knew for sure his good friends were coming out in a week or two and he'd let them work out when. In the meantime, his focus was on keeping a business going.

No sooner had Bruce pulled up in the shed, Carina appeared. 'I missed you, Bruce,' she shyly said as she stood there with her left foot planted on top of her right, her left arm up the side of the Cruiser just behind the door and her right hand clutching her left elbow.'

'I missed you all too, Carina. It's great to be back in my favourite place,' Bruce said, looking down and smiling broadly at the sweet girl. 'My mum said to say hello to you. She misses you too.'

'Are you going back to Townsville, Bruce?' she asked.

'No, Carina. Your dad and I have a lot of work to do and I'm not planning on going anywhere.' Bruce was beaming.

Carina was visibly pleased too as she lowered her arms, still crossed, looked up at him, and asked, 'Do you need help with anything to the house?'

Bruce thought, this girl will make a mighty wife for some lucky man one day. She is just a darling. I couldn't refuse the offer. 'That would be great, Carina. Thanks. There are some groceries on the passenger side. If you get the wheelbarrow, it might be easier to get them to the house that way. Just don't take too much at once; make a couple of trips.'

Carina immediately uncoiled and skipped off to get the wheelbarrow, happy as a magpie with a worm. Bruce knew she would be careful, so let her take the responsibility. If she couldn't lift anything straight up, she'd find a solution. He knew she would not only take the groceries to the house, she'd also take them inside and put them neatly in the fridge and pantry as well. And then without asking, she'd get the broom and sweep the kitchen. What a girl. He'd concentrate on other stuff.

Col also came over to the shed. He'd been out on a water run that morning and was back for lunch. 'I hope Carina's not in the way Bruce. Sorry if she is.'

'No Col. Not at all. She's one mighty fine young lady. You should be immensely proud of her,' Bruce replied.

'Yeah. She's very good. Simone and I are very lucky. How's your mum?'

'Good, Col.' Bruce gave him a summary of the situation. Bruce was feeling he might have picked up some magnetic qualities in Townsville, because hot on the heels of Col, probably from an interrupted lunch, were both Lachlan and Simone. Lachlan welcomed him back home. Simone wanted to know about his mum. 'What are you doing for dinner tonight?' Bruce asked Simone and Col. 'I brought some premium rump steak from Townsville, and I was wondering if you'd like to have a barbeque over at the big house?'

Col looked at Simone waiting for her to respond. She said, 'That would be lovely, Bruce. What would you like me to do?'

'I reckon I'll get everything together okay, Simone. How about you just come over?' He glanced over at Carina who was toiling away, getting groceries to the house. 'Fair chance my favourite princess will give me a hand if you let her, because I'd bet my butt she'll ask you, as soon as she finds out what the plan is.'

'I'll let her come over about six, Bruce. We'll be half an hour later. Don't want to be too late on a winter's night, though your fire will keep us warm.' Bruce had a barbeque that was simply high-tensile steel screening mesh in a steel frame under which he lit a fire, usually of ironbark, creating red-hot coals about forty-five minutes later, perfect for steak. He had a margin of rocks around it, so it doubled as a campfire once the cooking was done. It was perfect for winter nights as rain was as rare as rocking horse manure in this part of the world in the cooler months. Winter nights were mostly cool, clear and dry, with an absolutely brilliant array of stars; though when the moon was up, it did reduce the visible star population.

About thirty seconds after six o'clock, Carina was at the front door of the homestead, knocking and asking to come in. Bruce was ready, as he knew she'd take no longer than half a minute to get from their house to his and would have been waiting for her mother to give the all clear to head off at six o'clock exactly, cued by Carina herself of course. 'Come in, Carina Wattle.'

Carina came in, eyes looking everywhere, trying to work out what she was going to be able to do. 'Mum said I could help you, Bruce.' Carina had already had a shower and was in her winter pyjamas. She was one sweet kid, thought Bruce.

'I'm cooking up a real rough apple crumble, Carina. I've got a base from the supermarket here, and I've got some crumble to put on top. What I need you to do is get all this canned apple into the base and cover it with crumble, and then we can get it in the oven and be ready for a warm dessert on a cold night. Do you reckon you could do that?' Bruce had already opened the cans of apple. Carina took a brief look and headed for the utensil drawer to get a dessert spoon. She was too short to do the job without elevation, so Carina then picked up a chair from the kitchen table and carried it to beside the bench where Bruce had put the workings of the apple crumble. As tiny and young as she is, no flies on this lady, Bruce thought. He left her to the task while he made a salad and prepared some bread rolls, fresh from his supermarket visit that morning.

The barbeque was in the middle of Bruce's front lawn. A one-metre-high mesh fence surrounded the yard, mainly to keep the wildlife out; nighttime grazers are excellent at destroying gardens. Until recently, the fence also kept a kelpie cross dog that had been the family pet for fifteen years separated from the wildlife. Polar had become very arthritic and was obviously struggling to enjoy life. Bruce took him for a drive down the paddock and shot him, to give old Polar a quick, painless and good death. Frances had called him Polar because she reckoned he was always on top of the world where the polar bears live. Bruce had not gotten round to replacing Polar, but it was on the agenda. A dog in the yard was a good deterrent, not only to wildlife, but also to visitors who might be unwelcomed. Polar had given Doris security and the comfort that goes with that for many years.

Inside the fence and up against it was a hedge that hid the fence. It created a great wind break on cool nights. The front yard had one large feature tree. Merve had planted an African Mahogany that had thrived. The tree had grown very quickly and provided splendid shade, welcomed on long hot days. However, what's above ground is often matched by what's below ground, and this tree had massive roots that regularly strangled the in-ground sprinkler system. Big trees can also make big messes, which is fine in the cattle paddocks, but not so fine in the house yard. It was a daily task to clean it up when the large seed pods with a pronounced internal spike were falling. Despite its shortcomings, the shade it provided, and its visual splendour saved its life, though Bruce often muttered to it that murder might be on the cards one day.

The lawn of buffalo couch was green and well-tended. It sloped gently down to the west, facing the river of which it provided an attractive panorama as the house was atop a rise. Bruce loved to keep the lawn in perfect condition. He also had a wide fringe of lawn around the house, a fire break, with a line of mango trees set ten metres apart around the whole yard perimeter. It was a simple, yet attractive setting.

Two hours after Carina had built the apple crumble, the five of them perched around the fire were licking their lips, savouring the dessert. 'Who made this, Bruce?' Col asked.

'Your daughter, Col. She's dynamite,' added Bruce as he smiled across the warm glow of the barbeque embers at Carina. She was curled up in a camp chair, obviously struggling to keep her eyelids apart just below the edge of her beanie as tiredness attacked her.

'You sure are, Princess,' Col said to his daughter. 'I reckon it's close to your bedtime, the both of you. We'll clean up. Off you go. Mum and I will be home soon.' Lachlan was also glad to be heading off to hit the hay. His non-stop days took their toll and by this hour he was almost if not comatose most nights. The two youngsters toddled off to bed after bidding everyone goodnight.

'They're brilliant children, Simone and Col,' Bruce told them. 'I know you're proud of them and so you should be.'

'Thanks, Bruce,' said Simone.

'It's a reflection of their parents. I'm so lucky to have you pair here. Thanks.' Bruce did not want to dwell there. He'd said what he wanted to.

'I must tell you what happened in Townsville. It was pretty big for Frances and I,' Bruce said. Simone upper eyelids lifted a little and she cuddled in against Col, her legs crossed and hands firmly wedged between her knees making sure no cold air sneaked in to make her uncomfortable. This is interesting, she thought.

Bruce continued, 'Mum and Dad are implementing succession. I'm going to be sole owner of this place. Well, me and the bank. I'll have a fairly hefty debt, but we reckon it's not an overwhelming risk. Dad's settling in well with Farmin Stuff and neither of them any longer want either the asset or liabilities associated with Bovale. Mum especially is keen for the change. She never liked the debt. With her current problems, lifting them completely out of debt is a huge boost to her well-being. She's over the moon.'

'So, you're now the big boss, Bruce,' Simone concluded as she slowly nodded her head with a gentle smile. 'Congratulations.' She untangled herself and stepped around the fire to give Bruce a hug.

'Congratulations,' Col added. He was comfortable in his chair and had his arms firmly crossed over his chest and his shoulders shrugged, keeping the warmth in.

Bruce said, 'For you good people, no change for mine. And I can't see any change on the horizon unless it comes from you. The big change for me is the full responsibility. I hope I can pull it off and make this place even better.'

'Speaking of which,' Col said, 'I see there's a field day of some sort on breeding cattle management over at Koolburra Station next Thursday, Bruce. If you're okay with it, I'd like to go.'

'That makes two of us,' Bruce said as he chirped up. 'That sounds like the sort of outing I could definitely handle. I know it's a school day, so your call completely, but I'd be real happy if you and the kids came too, Simone. It's not every day we get a chance to get together with the locals and I'd hate you to miss it if you can wrangle the day off.'

'Thanks, Bruce,' replied Simone. 'I like the idea. I can't imagine if we accidentally had a day off that anyone would lose an eye. And I'm sure the kids will be as pleased as I am to be able to go. Thanks.'

It was getting colder, and the embers were beginning to give up their heat; it was time to either build the fire or go to bed, and they chose their warm beds. Bruce refused their help with the clean-up. It was his pleasure to do that, especially as he'd already done most of it and what was left would only take ten minutes.

Mick rang on Sunday morning just as Bruce was heading out on a lick and water run in the Kubota. 'She's on, mate. We'll head out there Friday after work. Lock up your sheilas and tie up your dogs. We're on for a big one.'

'Mick, you're full of it,' Bruce said, loving his mate's expressions. 'Fantastic. I'll turn the hot water system off because you'll need cold showers all weekend by the sound of it.'

'Do that, Bruce. But I reckon you'll end up walking funny. The ladies are likely to drop your agates out if they have to shower on a cold night.' Mick was firing on all cylinders this morning. He was as excited as Bruce about a weekend party at Bovale.

'Should be good, Mick. Short-term pain, long-term gain. I'll end up a big fat cuddly eunuch and all the sheilas will love me. I've always wanted a harem.'

Mick had no come-back at hand. 'Look, mate, I'm on a job at the moment; have to go. We'll be in contact during the week. Lookout Bovale!' he exclaimed as they ended the call.

A smile never left Bruce's face as he did the water run. He headed out over Gun Creek. Even after just three days in Townsville, he missed this place. The beauty of the bush enraptured him. Healthy gums were an elixir for him, and these were in abundance on Bovale, especially along creek banks where majestic Moreton Bay Ash grew tens of metres tall with dark tessellated bark on the lower thick trunk, transitioning into a smooth creamy white for the rest of the trees' trunks and branches. The Moreton Bays attracted great flocks of sulphur-crested cockatoos when they were in flower, usually around Christmas. These large, majestic birds screeched all day as they chewed off flowers and twigs, creating unholy messes beneath each tree. Fruit tree growers loved this, because while they were chewing into trees out bush, they were not ghosting into their orchards like silent assassins, demolishing valuable trees and crops.

The country was in good condition, something Bruce had his father to thank for. He had healthy productive pastures and excellent ground cover across the station. In addition, there were very few weeds. It made management easy and ensured there was a solid base for live weight production, his income. He knew that many graziers in the district liked to utilise every blade of grass they could, which certainly created more live weight in the short term, but it also created huge problems. The biggest was that rainfall infiltration was drastically reduced, causing a negative feedback loop on pasture growth, creating either scalded country or a paradise for low-value or even useless unpalatable species and weeds. This underpinned massive risk and the costs that accompany those risks in low-rainfall years. Ultimately, average net business return was drastically slashed by this neanderthal practice and all fauna, flora, and humans in those landscapes were assigned to ugly; immediate human greed was sated, but all else was forsaken. Merve had instilled in Bruce the value of a long-term view when managing these dry tropical landscapes.

The only downside, if it could be called that, was Bovale was not contributing at all to the nation's and the cattle industry's progress towards lower net carbon emissions, which was currently riding on the back of the man-made tree thickening problem in northern Australia. Bruce was not about to change that. As he drove around, Bruce was assessing each paddock, especially the juvenile trees, commonly called suckers or regrowth. When Ludwig Leichhardt had first explored the region in the mid eighteen forties, he described it as lightly-wooded expansive grasslands. Since 1900, there had been gradual woodland thickening and in parts was now heavily forested. At Bovale, it certainly was no longer open grasslands; it was moderately forested with suckers appearing every year. The regrowth needed control. He'd heard the agriculture department blokes say the main reason for this was ever-reducing use of fire in landscape management. Fire killed young suckers, but anything bigger than a few metres was only temporarily set back. Though the solution to woodland thickening was obvious, the problem was that to get a good fire meant the paddock had to be locked up for a full wet season to create a good biomass for a fire and for subsequent recovery. After the burn, cattle had to be kept off the country for another full wet season as any grazing caused a permanent shift to non-native undesirable species. Because of this, they had to burn whole paddocks at once, with loss of that paddock for production for eighteen months. If they burnt ten percent of the place every year, they had about fifteen percent less production potential in the short term. However, in the long-term, prevention of woodland thickening would repay because woodland thickening could easily reduce pasture production by more than fifteen percent. Fire was an investment in the distant future of the business, and Bruce was planning to still be in the game then. It made good sense to burn, which is why he was assessing which paddock they would lock up before the break in the season this year.

It all sounded good on average, but nothing is average, one of the many challenges for Bruce. Though the objective was to burn one paddock annually, some paddocks like Kosciusczko paddock, made up about fifteen percent of the place. Burning that paddock was planned to coincide with *La Nina* years if they occurred as expected. That burn was linked with the burning of small paddocks on years either side. This needed a forecast two years ahead, but the Bureau of Meteorology was still lucky to forecast a few months ahead. So, they did their own guesses, as good as anything the BoM appeared capable of.

Burning could also damage fences, even the wire. As part of the station's fire plan, they had built fences along lines where it could be cleared of trees and kept clear, and it could be mown or disced annually to make fire breaks and protect the fences. One good secondary outcome was they always had good station access via any of the fence lines.

Bruce was as busy as ever till Wednesday. There was always plenty of maintenance, whether it be vehicles, buildings, fences, yards, pastures or fence lines. This week he mounted the tractor and slasher and manicured many kilometres of fence lines. Pasture growth had ceased for the year, and it was paramount to have breaks in place early, both for controlled burns and wildfires. While Bruce did this, Col maintained his routine of weaner feeding, water and lick runs, cattle checks, fence-line checks and other maintenance.

On Wednesday afternoon, just as the sun was dipping out of sight for the day, Bruce's phone rang. It was Eileen of The Villa. 'G'day, Bruce, Eileen here,' she greeted cheerily.

'G'day Eileen. How's everything in the veterinary world?' he asked.

'Good, Bruce,' Eileen replied. 'Nice and busy. I've been doing a lot more cattle work lately, which I like. The small animals are fine, but the owners aren't always a pleasure to deal with. They even get me quite upset occasionally, but I just put it behind me, and look forward to the majority of animals and people who are really nice.'

'Sounds like today might not have been a good one?' Bruce commented.

'No, not one my best. But I'm home now and Jane and Brenda have me back in a great mood. How's your week been?' Eileen asked.

'I've had a good one thanks, Eileen. Spent most of it on a tractor slashing fence lines. I'm pretty happy how they're turning out too. Tomorrow we're going to that Koolburra field day. Col and his wife and two kids are coming over as well. Should be great,' Bruce remarked.

'I'm jealous,' said Eileen. 'I saw on the flyer they've got a couple of people there who know their stuff. But I'm rostered on in the surgery here in town tomorrow. Bugger.'

'Ah well, I'll take some notes and give you all a lecture on Friday night,' suggested Bruce, rather cheekily.

'I'll be a keen student, Bruce,' Eileen chirped. 'Actually, can't talk all day. Just ringing to see what we need to bring this weekend. The girls and I are just heading off to the supermarket.'

'You've got me cold. I haven't really thought too much about it to be honest. I've got plenty of meat, so don't bring any of that. Maybe some fruit and veggies, bread and milk type stuff. Just enough for the weekend as we don't want waste. You can be sure Mick and Craig will load up on the important stuff like chips, chocolates and beer, so don't get any of that,' Bruce suggested.

'Righto. Got to go. See you Friday night, Bruce. And by the way, do we need a swag?'

'If any of you have one, bring it, Eileen. Looking forward to having you. See you then,' finished Bruce.

Seven o'clock Thursday morning, Bruce, Col, Simone and the children headed out for Koolburra. They used the Wattle's twin-cab ute so they could all fit in one car, arriving forty-five minutes later. There was a small crowd starting to build. Bruce was thinking they must have been shouting cold beers all day to lure this many out of the scrub. But more likely it was just good timing, a relative lull between mustering rounds, coupled with some potentially-good information being shared on the day.

Bruce was most interested in two segments. One was on bull power; the other was genomics, new and exciting stuff. Both offered some potential to improve the production and efficiency of the Bovale herd. He needed some fresh ideas as he was almost certain there was potential to improve.

Wayne Greenhough, an experienced veterinary scientist from Rockhampton in central Queensland, in a team presentation with a local grazier, talked about bulls. He first described why a bull needed to produce about twenty million sperm for a fertile ejaculate, making it sound like heaps. 'A mature bull produces fifty thousand sperm per,' he hesitated for effect, 'second.' He let it hang. 'Four billion per day.' He let that soak in too; the audience was attentive. 'So, every five minutes, yes, in just five minutes, he produces enough sperm for a fertile ejaculate. That's a lot of potential pregnancies per day. But go easy on him. He also has to eat, chew his cud, catch up with his mates, check the footy score, have a camp, all typical bloke stuff, every day. But we know from research that whatever else bulls do, ten matings a day is a piece of cake for a fertile bull. That's at least three hundred a month. So why do some people have four bulls per hundred females?' Wayne shrugged his shoulders and eyed the audience. 'Because someone else used that many. No other reason. The fact is that one fertile bull per hundred females is oodles, but we do like to add one extra for the paddock, just in case a bull breaks down during mating.

'What this means for many of you, is you can drastically cut your bull team down. This can at least halve the costs per calf from over one hundred dollars, which is what many of you currently pay. If you save fifty dollars per calf and you wean one thousand calves a year, that amounts for most of you to the value of a new twin-cab ute. You could build your wife a fabulous new kitchen, every year, not just one. Don't go home and not think about it,' Wayne concluded.

This information ignited Bruce's thinking. He asked Wayne, 'What if there's hilly country and thick timber, it's raining and, say, you have six bulls with five hundred cows in five thousand hectares; will that affect conception patterns?'

Wayne smiled. He had met this young man at smoko before the discussions started. 'Bruce, when we're your age, we all know where to go Friday night. Believe me, so do the cattle. They're cattle, not humans. No foreplay involved, just wham, bam, thank you mam. Better still for the bull, the females get into what's called sexually-active groups and seek the bulls that are territorial. We've tested this under some pretty tough conditions, and it is no problem. You just have to ensure bulls pass their cattle vets' soundness test, and that must include sperm morphology, and Bob's your uncle. No risk. Much lower costs. Big return.'

Bruce absorbed that. He had at least one gem to take home and apply. Though he knew Col would not think it was a good idea up front. Col was a very good man, but he was steeped in old ways and was a bit hard to change without witnessing the benefits. Just lucky

I'm the boss, thought Bruce. He was smiling again. His mum might be crook, but lots of other good things were happening.

Chantelle Menzies provided an insight into genomics for the crowd. 'When you take a tail hair root or an ear skin snip sample and send it to the lab, you get a genotype. That's a fifty thousand-long string of one of four letters. It's the DNA code and it's useless to you and I. But it's gold for a geneticist. They've worked out the DNA patterns for high fertility versus low fertility, good temperament versus bad temperament, *et cetera*. If you get your bulls wrong, you've penalised your herd genetics for up to fifteen years. It makes no sense at all in the modern world that you would not screen your bull herd to ensure you have none lurking there that have poor genetics for your most important traits. It's quite cheap, only about seventy dollars per bull.'

Bruce was impressed. He had thought from the bits he'd heard that these new breeding values offered great potential. He asked Chantelle, 'Can you use these tests to understand your current genetics, not just test your bulls?'

Chantelle was obviously impressed with the quick thinking that would have been behind that question. 'Yes, you can. Bruce, isn't it?' she asked. Bruce nodded. 'Bruce, if you take a DNA sample from fifty random heifers from an age group, say at branding, and have them genotyped and the genomics done, from their breeding values we can produce a clear and accurate picture of your herd's genetics in relation to all herds across northern Australia. That will help you define your breeding objectives, and in turn, dictate the relative emphasis on various traits when you're screening bulls.'

Bruce had not picked up such gems before at a field day. What he'd heard was not difficult to implement. It made good sense. And it had the potential to make him some serious dollars, just when he was fronting up to take on a business debt of nearly three and a quarter million dollars. As another speaker droned on about something he wasn't interested in, he mused to himself, these guys, especially that Greenhough dude, must have more pearls than just how many bulls to use. Over lunch, he approached Wayne and asked if he had a minute. 'Wayne, I understand you have experience with most aspects of breeding herd fertility,' Bruce indicated, 'Do you do consultancies, like come to my place and help sort out opportunities to improve the herd?'

'I do, Bruce,' replied Wayne.

'Well, you're a vet, so what if you came to my place, did a breeding soundness evaluation on all my bulls, and we spent a bit of time assessing what's happening to see if we can do better?' Bruce asked.

'I'll be up for that,' Wayne replied. They continued their discussion, working out a mutually suitable time for the visit. Bruce was pleased as punch. Fresh in the saddle as the big bwana, he was feeling he was already powering Bovale into the lead in the twenty-first century. Bruce wasn't driving home, so it was a good day to celebrate with a few beers. Simone and the kids were having a ball with the local ladies and children; they were in no hurry to head home. It was almost a disappointment when Col suggested they should head home. The crowd was pretty thin by this stage, and if they didn't go now, it may have been embarrassing to be the last to leave.

'That was one fantastic day,' Simone declared as they finally headed off. There was agreement all round, though Col was not overly impressed as he'd had to stick with sparkling water rather than beers because he was the driver. 'Thanks for driving, honey,' Simone said. 'I know it was tough on the water. But the kids and I had a blast. Thanks to you too, Bruce. You think you're a greenhorn, but we think you're a legend.'

***

Friday at Bovale went too quick for Bruce. A day off on Thursday and a full weekend ahead of frivolity meant he had a lot to do in just one day, which included ensuring the homestead was in a fit shape to receive his friends, especially if he wanted to impress the ladies. Somehow, he made it through his jobs list before dusk, and rushed in to clean his carcass before the cavalry descended on him. He'd only just walked into the kitchen when he heard the boys arrive in Craig's V8 Land Cruiser ute. There was no way to disguise the throaty note it made, even as they idled up to the homestead. Craig had fitted an exhaust system to enhance what he called the 'tune' from his beloved vehicle, earning him plenty of derision from his mates.

Early Friday morning, Bruce had put a large piece of corned brisket into each of two slow cookers. He'd taken them out after his late lunch, perfectly cooked. He knew he was going to run out of time this evening to do anything special. He lassoed the lads into peeling a few spuds that he diced into chips, covered with olive oil and some spices, before placing them on baking paper in the oven. He'd never win a prize for the best traditional dinner, but the elements were all solid tucker in their own right. Corned beef and pickles is an irresistible favourite in the bush. And who could resist chips with or without tomato sauce and or salt on a Friday night with a beer? Certainly not Bruce, and he was hoping, also his friends. Bruce also had another of his favourites ready to add, canned corn and peas.

'I hope those sheilas aren't too far away,' suggested Craig. 'I'm getting proper hungry and dinner's about ready to lay our fangs into.' He'd hardly gotten the words out when the lads heard the vehicle arrive. They wouldn't die of starvation after all. Craig headed outside to help them bring their bags and food inside while Bruce and Mick finished setting the table and worked on getting the meal ready to serve.

Jane bounced into the house, full of beans. 'Bruce, you'll make one hell of a good wife for a nice bloke one day. Dinner smells just fantastic and all we had to do was turn up with our tiaras on and eat it.' She lurched forward to Bruce and hugged him. Jane and Eileen followed suit, hugging Mick and Craig as well. All were pleased to see each other.

'You should have been here earlier, Jane, when we turned up,' Craig said. 'Bruce gave us both a big sloppy kiss. I reckon he definitely is going for a bloke. You ladies are safe as a house when he's around.' Craig was very impressed with his own joke and was laughing hard.

'I'm worried about you Craig,' said Brenda. 'A man who enjoys a kiss from his mate as much as you obviously have is also gay, which is fine. But the real problem is you only seem to have just realised that.' The whole six of them were in stitches with laughter. 'We ladies only have to be wary of Mick it seems,' she managed to get out between fits of giggles as she teased Mick with another hug, throwing her head back as she did so.

The hunger pangs of the lads, seriously potentiated by the great aromas, settled them quickly. 'Dinner's about ready everyone, so let's attack it,' Bruce announced. It was all action as the ladies stowed what they had brought where it needed to go, and the lads got dinner into plates on the table.

True to prediction, Mick and Craig extracted a chilled Sauvignon Blanc and a Cabernet Sauvignon. 'You got any plonk glasses in this joint, Bruce?' Mick asked.

'In that top cupboard on the left,' replied Bruce. 'And if you're more comfortable drinking out of Vegemite jars, there's a stack in the pantry.' Bruce smiled at his own joke.

'Vegemite or coffee jars are as good as any crystal, Bruce. Agreed. But I reckon we'll use these glasses tonight,' Mick declared as he set out six red wine glasses on the table. Everyone was in good form for cheek tonight it seemed.

'Here's to a great weekend,' Bruce toasted as all raised and chinked each other's wine glasses before taking a sip.

'Bruce, this is not quite restaurant-style tucker, but it tastes very good,' Eileen declared. 'Thank you. This corned beef is fantastic. I can't cook as good as this. You'll have to tell me later how you did this.'

The banter continued for two hours around the dinner table as they slowly munched, drank and talked each other's ears off, mostly about frivolous stuff, though occasionally giving a serious topic a glancing blow. 'Mick, can you get that pack of cards you brought, and we'll clean this table up for a serious game of Oh Hell,' Bruce said. As he set about cleaning, the girls launched into helping him and in no time the eating gear was stacked in the dishwasher. 'We'll wash those bigger pots later, I reckon,' Bruce said.

'No. Let's do it now,' said Eileen. She buried herself in the task with help from Brenda as Mick finished other tidying before the card game.

Oh Hell was as big a hit as it had been the previous time they played at The Villa. Bruce again found himself lagging the field in the two games they played, each taking over an hour. 'Are you sure you're not married to someone already?' Craig asked. 'When a man's as unlucky as you are at cards, no question he's in love.' It was the standard joke, but everyone still thought it was funny.

'So far, only in love with Bovale folks,' Bruce replied. His thoughts were firmly on Eileen but there was no way known he was going to get caught glancing her way as he declared this. So, he just poured himself another shiraz and focussed on the glass. 'When I work out how you're stacking the pack Craig, I won't say a thing. I'll just use the same against you.' He laughed as he gave his good mate a friendly shoulder pat.

It was nearing midnight and all six had hardly noticed how much time had lapsed. When Mick suggested he'd turn into a pumpkin if he didn't choke down some time, they all realised it really was time to get their pyjamas on. There had been no previous routine for such a get together, so it was almost bedlam as they organised their beds and swags, cleaned their teeth, and finally hit the hay.

Bruce lay awake for a short time before he drifted off. It had been a great evening. No flirting even. Everyone had respected everyone else. His parents would be pleased to see this. He was ecstatic. And Eileen was sleeping under the same roof as he was. So near. Yet, so far.

Bruce had decided that on Saturday, they would have a picnic at Jindabyne, which is what Merve had christened the beautiful dam he had constructed in Kosciuszko paddock about fifteen years earlier. The dam was fed primarily from Wild Horse Creek that rose in the hills on the southern boundary with a catchment of about five hundred hectares. It covered almost eight hectares, was about seven metres deep when it was full and held approximately eighty-five megalitres. After the recent good wet season, it was close to full. Even ten percent of average rainfall running off the catchment would yield more than double the dam's capacity. The permanence of this magnificent water supply made the dam an ideal wildlife habitat, especially as it was fenced off to cattle.

The previous year, Bruce had purchased three hundred barramundi fingerlings he had put in the dam. The plan today was to see if the barra were still there and eager to latch onto his line. It was not an ideal plan as fishing at either sunset or sunrise would have been more fruitful. Bruce put the hunter inside him aside in favour of having fun with his friends, even if they never caught anything edible.

Bruce had also seeded the dam with redclaw, a native crayfish, that he had caught in the river nearly eighteen months earlier. He had never tried to snare their descendants since, but tomorrow was hopefully going to be the first catch. That was, of course, if the local wildlife had not taken on redclaw as a delicacy and wiped them out. He was fairly sure barramundi were partial to redclaw, and he'd bet his liver most of the larger birds that frequented the dam would also gleefully consume all they could find.

Heading up to Jindabyne dam had the added advantage of providing the opportunity to check some waters, check the cattle and fix anything that needed attention. No opportunity was wasted by Bruce on Bovale. He had his usual paddock gear, some fishing tackle and a couple of yabby traps in the tray of the Kubota. He would jam two people in with him and the other three would go in a four-wheel drive.

Everyone was up before dawn on Saturday. All had been looking forward to this weekend and had all slept lightly. The first songs of the bush birds around piccaninny had easily roused them fully awake as most windows in the house were open. Breakfast was almost organised with everyone keen to pitch in to getting a mountain of fried bacon, eggs and tomato inside them and a picnic smoko and lunch of corned beef and pickles sandwiches built and packed. The aromas of coffee and fried bacon and the din of rowdy chatter would have jolted anyone out of bed if they had been trying to sleep in.

As they were about to head off, Jane grabbed Eileen and declared, 'Eileen and I are going with Bruce.' She said to Eileen, 'You get in the middle, and I'll stay on the outside and open the gates.' They all knew the unwritten law in the bush that whoever sits in the front passenger seat opens and shuts the gates. No variance from this ever occurs unless that passenger is incapacitated, someone else volunteers, or the passenger has the authority to ask someone else to do it; on family trips, parents quite often ask their back seat children to do the gate. I like this, Bruce said to himself as Eileen literally jammed herself in close to Bruce to enable Jane to get in.

Jane jumped in the vehicle, and they set off. 'Now, Bruce, don't grab Eileen's leg accidentally instead of the gear change. Righto?' She was smiling wickedly at them both as she delivered this delicious advice to Bruce, who raised his eyebrows, looked ahead, nodded slowly and grinned broadly.

'Wouldn't even dream of it, Jane,' Bruce managed to stumble out. 'Then again, maybe I would,' he declared on reflection. Eileen blushed furiously and threw a scowl at her extroverted good friend, without betraying a massive inward glow.

The Kubota led the way as it was open air. Craig, Mick and Brenda had the windows up and the air conditioning on in the ute, which meant they had no issue with the dust coming up behind the Kubota. At each gate, Jane let both vehicles through before shutting it, and the ute crew waited till the Kubota trio led off.

Bruce could have taken them straight across Gun Creek and then headed east in quite a direct route to the dam, but he took what he told them was the scenic route, up along the north side of Gun Creek past the yards so he could check more as they went. He'd come home the more direct route instead. His friends enjoyed getting to see Bruce's backyard and the many stops to check waters. Bruce took the chance to ask their opinion on many aspects of his infrastructure, pasture management and cattle management. His main focus drifted to the cattle and the chat was earnest and lengthier each time they pulled up.

All five of Bruce's friends were either partly or very acquainted with beef systems in this region and all were keen to contribute. Bruce was impressed with Eileen's knowledge, which was obviously reinforced by her veterinary training that had not only covered health management, but also the science behind interventions that could improve production. As they drove along, they discussed what he'd learned at the Koolburra field day and his intention of having Wayne Greenhough conduct a business assessment for him. Eileen agreed with Bruce's interpretations and gave him strong support. And as they drove along, they carefully gave each other some surreptitious snuggly pushes, all the while struggling to keep Jane in their conversation. But Jane didn't mind; she knew what was going on and was as pleased as punch for her friends.

It was only a twenty-kilometre drive to Jindabyne, but they'd taken almost two hours because of all the stops and engaging discussion each time. It was no surprise they were all hungry and thirsty as the dam came into view.

'This is beautiful, Bruce,' Jane exclaimed. 'Why have you kept this secret from us?' she added as an almost rhetorical statement while she leaned forward, enraptured. They were approaching the dam along a ridge from the north-west of the east-west wall, the water backed up to the south in full view. Trees had been cleared from below the water line when the dam was built, resulting in a lawn-like verge of short green couch grass about one to ten metres wide all around the dam that was about three hundred millimetres below maximum capacity. Tall trees and pasture grew right up to the edge of the couch grass verge, providing a stunning contrast. The vegetation and dam looked pristine as no cattle were able to enter the water and break down the verges, though some dug-up areas clearly indicated a few wild pigs were enjoying the dam as much as the native animals.

The water was clear and blue from their approach angle. The shallower waters were filled with flowering lotus lilies, presumably having been introduced by wading birds such as ducks and herons. On the southern side of the dam was an area of cumbungi that Bruce planned to get rid of. It looked great now, but he knew it would continue to grow right around the dam and choke it. It was easy to kill with an overspray of glyphosate, something Bruce avoided if he could, but weeds needed to be controlled.

As they approached, they disturbed several wallabies and a few kangaroos that had been camping on the ridge. A cloud of whistling ducks rose from the dam and circled wildly in unison before settling back on the dam at the southern end. A family of five black swans stayed on the dam but headed for deeper water; there was every chance they were breeding and had a large nest or two in or around the cumbungi. Two tall jabirus were standing in half a metre of water. As the vehicles approached, these shy birds daintily lifted one leg after another as they strode forward in the deep water away from the vehicles, flapping their broad wings as quickly as they could to lift them out of the water and gain height before reaching full majestic flight.

Eileen was stunned by what she saw. 'Those birds are beautiful,' she almost breathlessly exclaimed as Bruce brought down the Kubota's speed so they could all feast on a dust-free perfect view.

Just as they went through the gate near the wall's western end, a large flock of crimson-wing parrots whistled past, just above their heads. 'Wow. Those birds are beautiful,' Jane said as they tried to keep sight of the birds disappearing into the bush. 'They're my favourite. Even more beautiful than the pale headed rosellas that are so plentiful around here,' she added.

Bruce led them about one hundred metres along the western edge of the dam to where a gully entering from the west created a beautiful spot for the day's camp. 'There's fish here, ' declared Mick with complete assurance as they all got out of the vehicles and stood at the water's edge admiring the view. 'Pelicans aren't here for nothing.' Three of these awkward-looking birds were cruising along on the south-east side of the dam. They lifted their heads and their pace but did not fly off immediately. From the water's edge they could see petite and beautiful jacanas skittering across lily pads.

'Smoko time,' declared Brenda. She was hungry and led the charge to unload the feed and drinks onto a tarpaulin Bruce had brought and laid out on the couch grass.

'Hey, Craig,' Bruce said, 'there's a block buster on the back of the Kubota. If you grab that and head up the gully, you're sure to find some wood you can take apart to get a fire going here. Craig responded. Within fifteen minutes they had a small fire going on the water's edge with a four-litre billy-full of water in the centre. The Ironbark wood created a lot of heat, and it did not take long before the water was bubbling. Craig tossed in a handful of tea leaves and lifted the billy out of the fire with a stick by its arched wire handle and placed it nearby, tapping the edge of the billy with the stick to settle the leaves.

'This tea tastes out of this world,' declared Eileen as they all sipped on a mugful. 'It's amazing how all the wood flavours end up in the brew.'

'I wonder what all the poor people are doing today?' queried Mick. 'Bet they're not enjoying today as much as we are. This is sensational, Bruce. Thanks, mate,' he chirped, happy as a dog on a beach, as he munched into a corned beef and pickles sandwich and washed it down with billy tea.

Mick was impatient. He was experiencing a desperate urge to exercise his Neanderthal hunting gene. As soon as he had scoffed his smoko, he headed for the yabby traps in the Kubota and baited each with some dried dog food Bruce had brought for the purpose. He also stuffed a few green leafy twigs in each trap, hoping that would lure more redclaw. 'Bruce, does that canoe perched on the pump shed work?' he asked.

There was a small shed on the western end of the dam wall housing a pump driven by a diesel motor to lift water into a thirty-thousand-litre, stock-water tank on the ridge to the west. The pump was a reserve these days as a new solar powered system had replaced it, requiring less supervision and maintenance. There was an array of solar cells facing north along the dam wall, adjacent to the shed.

The canoe was a hit. It could seat two and there were two double paddle oars, which are usually used for propelling kayaks. Mick dropped the traps in deeper water than he would not have been able to without it. Bruce commandeered the canoe early in an attempt to lure a barramundi, patiently casting on the fringes of the lily beds. The fishing was not going well. Inevitably, the canoe was the focus of all the fun as it became a racing machine. The innovation for competition that emerged in the absence of a second canoe included rowing styles and direction stability. The frivolity culminated in distance competition with a mug of water perched on the rower's head. This created no end of cheating and so much laughter that none realised how time had flown, and that if they didn't have lunch, they might just die of hunger and thirst, despite playing in a lake full of drinkable water.

Mick's worms were the first to stir. Once he declared it was lunch time, the canoe was quickly parked up. There was a dramatic transformation as the industry in preparing lunch was intense. Craig was once again hailed as the best tea lady in the country when his perfectly-brewed billy-full of ironbark tea, as he christened it, was used to wash down the delectable corned beef and pickles sandwiches.

Rehydrated and re-energised, Mick checked his traps. The complete lack of success on the fishing front was countered by two traps burgeoning with crustaceans. Mick claimed it was his catch. Eileen was quick to respond with as much humour as she could muster. 'Mick, who built the dam, introduced the redclaw, brought the traps, provided the bait and lent you a canoe?'

'I did all that, Eileen,' Mick immediately claimed, laughing uncontrollably, which then had everyone once again back in a great mood.

'Redclaw for dinner, troops,' declared Brenda. 'What's your recommendation for cooking them, Bruce?' Without actually doing it, Mick showed how he'd tear off the head and thorax, then pinch off the rear flippers, drawing out the intestine from the body of the large tail. He would wash the tails and soak them in chilled salt water for an hour or so before grilling them over open coals.

'Sounds like a plan, Bruce,' Mick declared, reclaiming 'his catch'.

'I reckon if you reset those traps for another hour or so, Mick, we'll have enough to get a decent entrée for dinner,' Bruce suggested. 'I've got some steak ready as well. I'm starting to get weak at the knees just thinking about how good dinner's going to be.'

Bruce decided he, Jane and Eileen should head off first and check more waters. He asked Mick, Craig and Brenda to go home the way they came and re-check a tank that was not as full as it should have been when they looked at it earlier in the day. If it was still not filling, they'd check for a water leak on Sunday. Once again, Jane ensured Eileen was jammed in against Bruce all the way home and neither of them complained.

Bruce invited the Wattle family for the barbeque, which was a delectable feast. Mick's claims that his redclaw was better than the steak set off a major round of frivolity, spiked by Eileen's defence of Bruce as the real providore. 'I want to know what happened in the Kubota on the way home,' Mick said, beer in hand, his eyes bulging and grinning like a Cheshire cat as he stared at Eileen. 'Jane, what happened?'

Jane hesitated for a nanosecond. 'Well, about halfway home, we had to pull up because Eileen had to head off and get behind a tree. And while she was away, Bruce and I had a lovely cuddle.' Jane was desperately trying to keep a straight face, with her head slightly bowed, eyes rolled upwards, creased eyebrows and dark eyelashes setting off a visage of pleasant naughtiness. Even young Lachlan was cackling furiously. Carina, who was way too young to get the joke, was smiling with jealousy that she had not been the one getting cuddled by Bruce. Simone and Col did not miss the obvious connection between Eileen and Bruce. It was a good thing.

It was a cool night, so they headed back inside for the Oh Hell world championships, as Mick was proclaiming it would be. Simone and Col joined them for the first game, but then headed home as the children were dog tired. Cards did not last till midnight as the day had taken more out of them than they had realised.

'Early to bed, early to rise,' Bruce yawned as all six assembled to tackle breakfast at six o'clock on Sunday morning. The novelty was still alive, and sleeping was difficult when there was fun to be had. Breakfast was a repeat of the previous day, but with a little more order and a little less boisterousness; they were learning and accommodating each other's quirks, which is relatively easy for young adults.

Bruce's plan for the day was to muster the weaners for a booster with five-in-one vaccine. The booster was due, Bruce was desperate to prevent any blackleg deaths and he had a big crew who were all breaking their necks to join a muster. There were four two-wheel motorbikes in the shed and the Kubota side-by-side. Jane volunteered to be the one who missed out. She was the least experienced with cattle. Though she knew she would have enjoyed it immensely, she also knew that mustering weaners needed to be done with great care to avoid teaching any bad habits. Jane thought her lack of experience conferred on her the highest chance of making an error, leaving Bruce and Col with a headache they didn't need. Instead, she offered to cook some pikelets and scones for smoko; Simone and Carina would come over and help, though the chore was ninety percent socialising, which they both greatly enjoyed. It was a day off for Col if he had wanted, but he was keen to help by getting the yards and the vaccine ready. Lachlan was in luck. The adults were all too big for his motorbike, so he got to go on the muster.

Mustering and vaccination are serious business, a big contrast to the previous day. Once the weaners were yarded, the crew headed back to the homestead, interrupting a very pleasant and relaxing chat going on there. The fellowship and fun at smoko was on par with the previous day, thoroughly enjoyed by everyone. The pikelets and scones were first class. Bruce declared, 'Jane, you'll make some sheila a real good husband one day,' in his attempt to turn around Jane's declaration on Friday night.

Everyone went back to the yards after smoko where Eileen took on her professional role and taught the crew the finer details of exactly how to vaccinate, even to the extent of how to orientate the needle on the syringe for maximum efficacy. The job did not take long, and immediately afterwards, the weaners were walked back to their paddocks.

After lunch, Oh Hell was played in earnest before they pulled up to have smoko, pack up and leave. Jane almost had a tear in her eye. 'Bruce, this has been one fantastic weekend. Thanks, mate. She threw herself at him and hugged him tight. 'Thanks. It's going to be hard to top this.' All the boys hugged all the girls, sad to go and happy they'd been.

Bruce's heart arced up its pace as he anticipated the hug with Eileen. If he'd glanced at his hands, he would have noted a mild shake. But this was minor compared to what Eileen was experiencing. She was almost fainting but held her nerve for the moment. Eileen hugged Bruce, tightly and snuggled into him as much as she could in the brief moment, her head firmly on his shoulder. She lifted her head back and up at Bruce who still held her. 'Thanks Bruce,' she said lightly. Eileen then leaned up and gave him a quick kiss on the lips, their eyes locked on each other. It caught Bruce completely off guard, but not enough to let her go.

Bruce hugged Eileen's head back into his shoulder again and whispered, 'I have had one almighty good weekend. Thanks.' They then parted, but not before everyone had caught the 'event' as Mick proclaimed it to Craig on their way back to Charters Towers.

Chapter Five

Monday morning and Bruce was back to reality, sharing the homestead with his friends, as his mates had suggested to him. Try as he might, he could not get his mind off Eileen. That was okay as he headed out on the jobs he and Col had planned the previous week, as the day to day work could sometimes be done almost with the mind parked in neutral. However, Bruce's mind was in top gear. He had spoken with his parents the previous week and the arrangements to refigure the business, placing him in sole ownership of Bovale, were advancing rapidly. This meant Bruce had to take responsibility for a loan of three and a quarter million dollars. In turn, it entailed him having to ensure timely sales to service at least the interest, in addition to managing his business costs. It was time to do the first budget for which he would be fully responsible.

Bruce had helped his father prepare a budget before. He thought the best option he had for this budget was for Merve to help him. He knew Merve would be keen to help, but he'd be restricted to weekends as he could not leave Farmin Stuff during the week without forward planning. On Monday night he had a great chat with his parents. His mum was feeling reasonably well. His dad was firing on all cylinders. Both were as eager as a young child at the local show to hear about Bruce's weekend. Bruce regaled them with plenty, carefully omitting any evidence that sparks flew between him and Eileen. But Doris had a mum's sixth sense. 'Eileen sounds pretty special, Bruce,' she suggested.

'You're right, Mum,' Bruce agreed. 'I have some fabulous friends,' he added, trying to deflect the comment. Doris let it slide, as happy as any mother can be when their little boy is little no longer and attracting the attention of an excellent prospect of the fairer sex.

'We'll see you Saturday then, Bruce,' Merve said as they finished up their call.

During each day that week, Bruce and Col were busy across the station. Bruce was more relaxed now he had blackleg vaccinations up to date. He had been fretting the previous week that he would experience more deaths before the booster vaccine. Each night, he flicked off the television after the news and concentrated on building a budget for the up-coming twelve months. Bruce had limited experience with spreadsheets, but each night as he struggled, he became a little more literate. It was amazing how much help Doctor Google could be.

Bruce was grappling with creating a budget that would not leave him in trouble and unable to pay the interest. He could not see how he could cut costs without compromising income in either the short or long term. He could always sell more cattle, but that would reduce his potential to achieve payments in subsequent years. Increasing his debt was another option, though Bruce desperately wanted to avoid that for now. He could have banked on the cattle price rising as it was currently on the way up, having increased by fifty percent to three dollars a kilogram of live weight through the year already. But banking on good prices and a good wet season was a game for fools, as his father had drilled into him. Bruce grew increasingly worried about it as the week progressed, and only consoled himself by knowing his experienced father would most likely have the solutions that, so far, seemed out of reach.

Bruce also thought that Wayne Greenhough might also have some insights, on top of what he had already gleaned. He rang Wayne to organise a visit. Wayne's primary concern was whether the bulls were currently in reasonable condition and were not losing weight. Bruce assured him they were in good order.

'If bulls are in backward condition, Bruce, it is a worthless exercise assessing them because the loss of condition alone knocks down the percentage of normal sperm to below threshold levels for fertile matings,' Wayne assured Bruce. Wayne was able to come up and spend two days on Bovale in two weeks' time. It was quite an investment, but it would yield well if it led to costs being cut and or sales increased, even by relatively-small amounts. Bruce was confident this could be achieved.

On Wednesday night, Mick rang. Ostensibly he was checking in after the weekend to make sure they had not unintentionally left behind any problems for Bruce. However, his real agenda was to see how Bruce was going on the Eileen front. Mick didn't know whether his mate was being coy or telling the truth when Bruce told him they had not been in touch with each other since Sunday. 'Just let it slide, Mick,' Bruce pleaded, though inwardly he was chuffed that his friends were batting for him on a relationship. Bruce had also sensed Eileen's friends were doing the same for her. It seemed it was just a matter of one of them taking the step to close the gap. Bruce was not forward on the romance front at the best of times, but in this situation, he was going to do the waiting; you'll just have to hang in there, Mick, he thought.

'Mick, I need a beer with you blokes to let my hair down. How about Friday night? I'll camp at your place if that's okay, and head on to Townsville Saturday morning.'

'Mate, done deal,' Mick responded. 'I'll organise Craig and hopefully the girls.' Bruce had expected nothing less.

Bruce packed a bag plus a backpack with his computer and his scribblings on the budget and headed to town Friday night hoping to see the whole crew, especially Eileen. When he got to the pub, only four were there. 'Eileen's staying at Warrigal Station tonight,' Brenda told him. 'She's doing pregnancy diagnoses today and tomorrow out there. She would have loved to have been here. Sorry, Bruce.' Bruce was sorry too, but the end of the world had not come; neither of them were going anywhere fast. He'd enjoy tonight anyway, which he did, especially cards at The Villa, which, after just two nights, they agreed was a 'tradition' that must always occur.

Doris had a smoko for champions ready when Bruce arrived at their home on Saturday morning. Frances was there too, though Merve was stuck at Farmin Stuff till lunch time dealing with the smallholders who had city jobs during the week and were spending on Saturdays to keep their hobbies alive. Bruce's favourite smoko diet was what his mum called custard kisses, shortbread with an icing laced with custard powder. Doris had slaved away in the kitchen earlier in the week making enough to rectify Bruce's acute deficiency on the weekend, plus some to take home for Frances and for Bruce and Simone. She decided to keep none in the house as Merve also had an addiction that was hard to satisfy. Merve's addiction was fuelling the development of what was looking like early pregnancy. He was still adjusting to eating less in a job that was far less physical than cattle station life. Doris was not keeping sweets if they were going to blow out Merve's bulging gut any further.

The family had a late lunch when Merve arrived home. All four of them savoured the family at the table experience. It struck Bruce just how fantastic it would be one day to have a family of his own around the table at mealtime. Crikey, he thought, maturity is sneaking up on me, but it doesn't seem all that bad. 'Did you come from Bovale this morning, Bruce, or did you have a session in town last night?' Merve asked.

'I went in for a country at the pub, Dad,' Bruce replied. 'After a week by myself each night, I needed those mates of mine to lead me astray.'

'Where did they lead you?' Merve queried.

'Well, once we'd had a steak and a beer, we went around to a friends' place and had a game of cards. Five of us, Craig and Mick, Brenda and Jane. Better than getting drunk. Must be getting older,' he said, smiling broadly at his father.

'You are, Bruce,' Merve agreed. 'Can't say I see any negatives in that. It's good to see you able to get away from Bovale, even when it's now becoming a stone around your neck.'

'A good gibber though, Dad,' Bruce added. 'There could be worse outcomes for a man than having to live at Bovale forever.'

'What cards do young folk play these days?' Merve asked.

'Oh Hell when we have a crowd, Dad. It's a game needing a bit of skill and some luck and any number can play it. We love it,' Bruce replied.

'How about you teach us after dinner tonight? Just the four of us. I haven't had a game of cards for ages and would love to try something new if you reckon it's good,' Merve suggested.

'Sounds like a plan, Dad,' Bruce said.

It was two-thirty in the afternoon before they finally settled around Merve's computer. Bruce uploaded his budget spreadsheet, and they pulled it up on the big monitor in the office. 'I'll get you to go through what you've done, Bruce,' Merve suggested.

'No problem, Dad. Well, actually, about sixty thousand problems. I just don't have any solutions I like yet,' Bruce replied. 'I've cut out all the frills already, I reckon. It would all be solved if the price of cattle stays where it is or goes up, but we can't bank on that. What I'm really worried about is if the price goes right back down to where it's been for the past couple of years.'

'No, you sure can't bet on better prices, Bruce,' agreed Merve. 'Best starting advice I can give you is to use the Stockdale paradox. He was an American Admiral and naval fighter pilot who ended up a long-term prisoner of war in Vietnam. His main tenets were to be confident you will succeed and to confront the brutal facts. There's a solution. Always is, even though sometimes she takes a year or two to emerge – the joys of cattle business. Luckily we're bred tough.' Merve was wistful for a moment.

'I'm sure it'll be right, Dad. I suppose what I'm doing here is asking you to help me work out which line of expenditure is going to cop the brutal axe.'

'The first thing we should do is have a look at projected income,' Merve indicated. They poured over Bruce's calculations. Annual projected sales comprised about two hundred heifers, one hundred and sixty cows, four hundred feeder steers and fifteen bulls. 'What average market price did you use?' Merve asked.

'Two dollars seventy-five a kilogram, Dad,' Bruce replied. 'I'm not game to set it any higher as markets never seem to go up for long and just now, it's as high as it's been in five years. Bound to take a correction.'

'I can't disagree, mate,' Merve said. 'But how does it look when you use the current price? What is it? About three dollars?'

'Pretty close, Dad,' Bruce said. 'Yes, at three dollars it will square up as long as I keep the costs where they are. The extra interest is a challenge, but I have no problem with that. I know it's like paying superannuation and all will be good once I get a windfall year. I just hope that isn't too many years away.'

Merve had spent many years slowly building his wealth and had secured sufficient equity to enable him to employ a head stockman. It wasn't a luxury. It had enabled him and Doris to live a more normal life and not work themselves to the bone. He knew that letting Col go would be an easy way to solve the problem but having experienced the pain of no permanent staff himself for so long, he didn't want his young son to do the same struggle, especially as he was still single and struggling alone could be devastating.

Merve and Bruce spent the next two hours going through every detail in Bruce's calculations. As they got to the end, Merve said, 'This is a job well-done, Bruce. I can't say I could have done it as well at your age. I'm impressed. I reckon you've drawn the right conclusions on the balance.'

Both men stopped talking, looking at the screen. Neither heard the dramatic movie music from the television in the background as their whole concentration was on the budget. Bruce was in the computer's driving seat, using the mouse to slowly move over the spreadsheet as he reconsidered the budget. Merve, seated just to his right, with his right elbow on the desk, cupping his chin with his right hand and left hand resting on his right biceps, cogitated Bruce's dilemma. He had an opinion, but decided he was not going to spoon feed Bruce. He'd see if his son could reach the same conclusions he had, or an even better one. 'If I wasn't here, what would you do?' he asked Bruce.

Bruce looked down at the desk and then slowly came around to face his dad, his lips pursed and forehead creased in concentration, sitting on his hands as he looked up and to the left, not directly at Merve. Merve relaxed, giving his young son all the time he needed. It took Bruce almost a minute before he changed his gaze to Merve and responded. 'I reckon we just play it by ear, based on what I've done. If the price doesn't go down from where it is now, it's doable. If the prices keep rising, I'm on easy street. But if the prices head south, I'll find a solution then.'

'Totally agree, Bruce. To do otherwise would be jumping at shadows.' Merve stood and hugged Bruce 's shoulders with his left hand. 'Ten out of ten, mate.' Merve was oozing pride.

It was beer o'clock and Merve had a few cold ones in the shed fridge, which was where they headed. Frances and Doris abandoned the movie they had been watching when they realised what was going on and followed the men outside. All four were very quickly sipping on cold drinks. Doris was the only one not throwing down a lager as she was unfortunately restricted to sparkling water, which wasn't so bad, she thought; not being able to have a beer is totally unimportant compared with being able to sit here with the three most important people in my life.

'When are you taking the tinny out next, Bruce?' Frances asked.

'I suspect my sister has a crab deficiency,' Bruce teased, smiling gently at his sister who he loved dearly. Frances smiled with her mouth closed and sparkled her eyes, demonstrating that Bruce was indeed correct.

'I have been thinking of calling that bloke who helped me at the ramp that day to see if he wants to come with me one day fairly soon. I owe him big time.'

'What's his name again?' Merve asked, frowning and squinting as his brain ticked away.

'Lenny. Lenny Pavarotti,' Bruce replied. 'Remember I caught him briefly at the hospital when I was down last. Great bloke. A cane farmer down the Burdekin somewhere he told me.'

'Can he sing?' Merve asked, immediately bringing to mind the famous opera singer with the same surname.

'Wouldn't have a clue, Dad,' Bruce replied. 'If he can, I'll arc him up down the creek because I reckon it'd sound brilliant on a still morning there. Though, just from looks, I'd bet his singing's about as good as my knitting. He strikes me as a real practical bloke, tonne of common sense, salt of the earth, but with limited skills in the fine arts.'

'A mate of mine told me, 'You can tell a man by his men, Bruce,' Merve said. 'Yeah, if you know their friends, their long-term employees and especially if you know their dog, you'll know for sure what sort of person someone is. Very philosophical and I've found it spot on. I'm not at all surprised you've hit it off with Lenny,' Merve added, knowing his son was a young clone of the bloke he described as Lenny.

'In the meantime, though,' Bruce said, 'I have a vet coming up from Rockhampton. He was a speaker at a field day we went to at Koolburra the other day. He spoke a lot of common sense. I'm getting him up to test all the bulls so we can cut our bull costs back and make sure our genetics are on the right track. While he's at it, I'm going to bleed his brain for a few more pearls of wisdom on how I can get the place operating better.'

'Who is it, Bruce?' Doris asked.

'Wayne Greenhough, Mum,' Bruce replied.

'Are you thinking of cutting the mating percentage back, Bruce?' Merve asked.

'Too right I am, Dad,' Bruce asserted. 'When Wayne explained why we can and we should, it was obvious as a boil on your nose that we have too many bulls. They cost an arm and a leg at present, and it doesn't look like that's going to change any day soon. Any chance to get the bull numbers back will be a bonus,' he added.

That night, they had a sumptuous roast dinner that everyone enjoyed, though Doris was a bit cross with herself as she knew it would be an unfortunate bonus for her sweet husband's gut. After they were sated, washed down with shiraz, Bruce introduced his family to Oh Hell, which induced a riotously good night.

Bruce was staying in Townsville till Monday. The previous week his parents had informed him the documentation for transfer of Bovale to him was ready to sign. They would be visiting the bank in the company of their solicitor. Bruce had been quite relaxed about the situation while his attention had been focussed on budgeting. But now they had resolved his concerns about the budget, the full moment of what was about to occur started to seep into him. Frances and he had decided on Saturday night they would take their parents on a drive to Paluma dam. It was on the ranges to the north-west of Townsville and was a primary water supply for the city. Having a family excursion was good therapy for Bruce's nerves.

Paluma is nearly one thousand metres above sea level. It has cool beautiful weather in summer, so much so that many from Townsville opt to have a summer house in Paluma rather than a beach house, the latter being a sweaty hotbox on a typical north Queensland summer day, sea breeze or not. In the middle of winter, it was quite cool and overcast. Despite this, the dam was beautiful as it always is. They had packed a picnic lunch they shared in one of the shelters on the shore. In all the years they had lived in the area, Doris had never visited the dam. The only downside of the day trip was the long slow winding road up and down the mountain that Doris found very tiring, but not tiring enough to stop her vowing she would be back to enjoy the peace and beauty, topped by a Devonshire tea on the way home in the small village. Bruce promised to bring her back, but not before he took her to Wallaman Falls, a bit further north, west of Ingham on the same ranges, a stunningly beautiful spot.

Monday was everything Bruce had feared. He was shaking so much when it came to signing, he had to take a moment to compose himself. Frances was also a blithering mess, not made any better by seeing her usually so self-assured brother so obviously expressing his emotions. 'We should have brought some whisky and had a medicinal shot or two before we did this,' remarked Merve.

After he'd signed the last document, Bruce stated, deadpan, 'No turning back now.' He turned and smiled, firmly shaking the hand of his father, warmly embracing his mother, and giving his sister a brotherly cuddle. 'Life will never be the same,' he declared. 'Onwards and upwards.'

'Let's go and have that shot Bruce,' Merve declared.

'I'd enjoy that,' said Frances, with Doris and Bruce nodding in agreement.

They headed to a lounge in the city's Palmer Street precinct where they settled for a long chat and a couple of stiff drinks. Doris's licence was suspended for the duration of her treatment at least, so she could not be the designated driver. 'No problem,' said Bruce. 'If we're not legal when we're ready to go home, Townsville's full of taxis, that can resolve the problem.'

Two hours later, they decided to scout the street for the best-looking restaurant. They found one that met their needs and settled in for another couple of hours of companionship.

Before they got too settled, Bruce excused himself and walked outside and dialled up Col. Col was in the shower and Simone answered the phone. 'What's up Bruce? Everything okay?' she asked.

'All good Simone. I'm on a high and just wanted to let you and Col know the transfer of Bovale to me went seamlessly today. It's a bit daunting, but I'm sure I'll handle it fine.'

'Congratulations, Bruce,' Simone responded. 'Are you out celebrating?'

'Yes, we are, Simone,' Bruce replied. 'Also just wanted to let you know that Dad and I did our budgeting today. Everything is perfect for maintaining the status quo. In truth I was wondering how I was going to meet all of my commitments, but we reckon we've got that sorted. I'm really happy. I just had to tell you.'

'That's terrific, Bruce. When do you expect to get home?' Simone asked. Bruce indicated it would probably be the next day. Simone asked him to get some groceries if that was okay. She would text through a list later. Bruce would have taken the supermarket home for her this night, but some bread, milk and a few other items would be sufficient this time. However, he would definitely include some chocolates and flowers for her and Carina, two very special ladies in his camp.

Bruce's impulse to ring the Wattle's had even surprised him. It made him realise just how important they were to him, the next best thing to family. He knew he'd have to do everything in his power to keep them happy and wanting to stay at Bovale. He need not have worried because the feelings were definitely reciprocal.

***

Back at Bovale, Bruce finally felt like he owned the place. Well, the eighty percent the bank didn't own. It was a great feeling, but he was acutely aware of the responsibilities that came with it. For a man of just twenty-two years, he was quite mature. His good looks, perpetual trim and neat appearance of himself and everything around him, plus his quiet respectfulness made him a great catch for some lucky lady. Though no-one had him on the hook, he was heading that way for sure, he thought. Eileen, she kept charging into his thoughts.

Bruce and Col had plenty to do to keep the business operating smoothly. Both were eagerly looking forward to the visit by Wayne Greenhough. Bruce had made the decision to involve Col in the process so both would clearly understand any changes that might be implemented. They didn't have too much to prepare, though the veterinary chute at the yards needed some minor attention to ensure it was safe to restrain the bulls for examination and semen collection. Bulls, typically weighing six to eight hundred kilograms, are powerful creatures. There could be no opportunity for harm or injury to either the bulls or people during the process. Happy bulls made life a lot easier for the bulls, and therefore the herd and the people.

Bruce almost expected a call during the week from one of the gang. Jane rang on Wednesday night. 'Oh Hell at The Villa on Friday night Bruce, after we do dinner at the pub. Are you on?' He was on alright. He knew he could roll his swag out at Mick's place for sure, saving him a late-night trip home.

The pub was a hive of action by the time Bruce arrived on Friday night. Him and Col had worked till almost dark. After a quick shower, Bruce headed for town, arriving after seven thirty. By then the gang had already had two rounds of drinks and demolished their dinners. Bruce had rung ahead, and Mick had ordered him a steak which came out just after he sat down. 'Thanks, Mick,' Bruce said. 'How is everyone tonight? I'm feeling lucky, so get your money on me at cards tonight.'

'We've stacked the pack, Bruce,' Jane declared. 'You have no chance. You and Eileen will be stone motherless last, I can guarantee.' Without being specific, Jane had clearly suggested they were going to be terribly unlucky at cards, but quite lucky at love.

'We'll see,' Bruce said smugly as he slowly chewed his way through the massive rump steak he'd been served. Eileen never said anything and was trying her best not to highlight her obvious attraction to Bruce.

The ladies were well organised tonight. They had prepared some tasty snacks rather than use junk food to fill their bellies after a week of work. 'This is sensational,' Craig said. 'You girls are diamonds.' Craig was feeling particularly pissed off with himself because he'd essentially done nothing to add to the occasion other than turn up. No-one else minded, but he did. He'd fix that. Why waste time, he thought. Surreptitiously, he just left the house, and headed to the supermarket, still open to deal with the late-night shoppers. He scooped up some chocolate-coated berries and two boxes of mouth-watering ice-creams.

It had not taken Craig long and no-one had noticed him gone. But as he went to put the chocolates in the fridge and freezer, Brenda pulled him up, 'Craig, you brought dessert,' she exclaimed loudly enough that everyone heard. 'You're my man.'

Quick as flash, Bruce saw his opportunity, 'Eileen and I are safe from the wooden spoon tonight. Looks like it's Craig and Brenda.' That caused both Craig and Brenda to blush, while the other four laughed at their discomfort. That's interesting, Bruce thought. He had not previously noticed any real connection. It was interesting to him how all six of them were so similar. They were good friends, but all were innately shy, finding it hard to initiate more personal relationships. Maybe that's a good thing, he thought.

Bruce was very much enjoying the company of Eileen and every chance they had, they focussed on each other. When the card game was finished and everyone was preparing to split for the night, Mick pulled out a look of pure innocence and asked, 'Eileen, are you camping at our place tonight?'

'Mick, you're an unsubtle gorilla in The Villa,' Jane said, scolding him. Jane was the most forward of the group. She admired Mick's never-ending efforts to encourage Eileen and Bruce to get more personal with each other, but she was annoyed with Mick this time.

Bruce playfully grabbed Mick's arms, holding them behind his back. 'Now, Jane, I'll hold him while you flog him.'

Jane broke out in one huge smile, her anger evaporating. Thanks Bruce, she thought. She went up to Bruce, head thrust forward, hands on her hips and looked him fair in the eye from about ten centimetres for more than five seconds, an age it seemed. Mick was not moving an inch, giggling gently and doing his best to outdo her stare. And then she kissed him. None of the six had laughed so much in all their lives.

Wow, Bruce thought. If I interpreted what I've just seen correctly, here I am thinking their focus is all on Eileen and I when the whole time there's two other potential relationships, with everyone having been covertly focussed on one other person. We're a weird mob, he silently concluded, just what the Australian author, Frank Hardy, had written about. Bruce had really enjoyed the night, even though him and Eileen had not made any further advances towards each other. It'll happen when it should, he thought. It was almost certain that all six of them had concluded the same before they entered the land of Nod that night. Just as all six were thinking about the next get together.

Bruce was up and gone from Mick's place before daylight on Saturday. He had to clear his usual routine for early next week so they could accommodate Wayne for a couple of days. They wanted no distractions during that time. On Monday afternoon they mustered the forty Droughtmaster bulls. They would be ready to start fertility assessments straight after breakfast on Tuesday.

Chapter Six

Wayne arrived at five-thirty on Monday afternoon, a nine-hour drive from Rockhampton. After he'd had a stretch and moved his bags into a room Bruce had prepared for him, they settled into a discussion about the world and the weather over a cold beer. As they did this, Bruce worked on dinner. He had the Wattle's coming over for a barbeque. It was quite cool this afternoon, so Bruce decided they'd eat inside after cooking on the barbeque. At a quarter past six, Carina appeared, having been given the all clear by Simone to head over to the homestead.

'G'day Bruce,' she said as she shyly came into the house. 'Mum said I can come over and give you a hand.'

'Thanks Carina. Carina, this is Mister Wayne.'

'Hello, Mister Wayne,' she said as she glanced up at Wayne through eyebrows held down. She shyly placed her hand over her chin, and immediately returned her attention to Bruce.

Bruce said, 'Carina, I'll just go out and light the barbeque. Can you please keep Mister Wayne entertained? He might need a beer, and some crackers with cheese.'

Bruce disappeared. Carina immediately skipped to the pantry and found a packet of rice crisps that she brought back to the kitchen. She knew exactly where in the fridge Bruce had cheese. After she'd collected a chair and set it up beside the kitchen bench, she quickly had a plate full of cheese pieces and crispy rice biscuits ready.

'You are one amazing young lady,' Wayne remarked to her.

Carina was not sure how to respond. She asked, 'Do you want another beer, Mister Wayne?'

'I'd love one, please, Carina,' he replied. This sent her scurrying off to the cold room from where she retrieved two beers, one each for the men. She had noticed that Bruce's beer bottle was empty too. She gave one to Wayne and then replaced Bruce's in the stubby cooler. Carina then took both the empty bottles out to the rubbish bin.

It wasn't long before Col, Simone and Lachlan arrived. The conversation was mainly focussed on learning about each other's lives and families as they prepared for dinner. About a half an hour later, Bruce took the meat out to the barbeque. He was back in a bit more than ten minutes with perfectly cooked steaks, signalling the start to the evening's feasting.

Simone had brought dessert, simple but brilliant. It was ice-cream and mango she had frozen before the previous Christmas. 'I'll have to factor in the amazing hospitality when I eventually do the invoice for this job. This dinner was amazing, everyone. Thanks,' Wayne said.

'Do you want another beer, Mister Wayne?' Carina asked.

'No thanks, Carina. I'll have another glass of wine. If you go to the fridge, you'll see in the door that I've put some pig food there. Can you get it for me please?' Wayne asked her.

Carina was walking sideways, staring disbelievingly at Wayne, completely confused about having to get some pig food. She didn't say a word as she hurried to the fridge and opened the door. There, on the left was a box of flavoured chocolates she had not noticed earlier. Now she knew Mister Wayne was playing a joke. Having experienced such tricks many times from her father and Bruce, she decided to play her own. She held the door open and leaned around, looking at Wayne. 'There's a gap here in the door, Mister Wayne, and I can't see anything a pig would eat. I saw Lachlan in the fridge before dinner and he ran outside with something and never came back for ages. Maybe he ate it?'

'I did not eat any pig food,' replied an indignant Lachlan. He looked wildly at his mother, sure she'd be angry with him. 'Mum, I didn't do anything,' he pleaded. With that, he stood up and headed for the fridge to see if he could work out what was going on.

'Tricked you, Lachlan,' squealed Carina as she plucked the chocolates out of the fridge door and raced to the table. 'Here, Mister Wayne.' Lachlan smiled and headed back to the table, sitting up like a well-behaved Kelpie, hoping like hell he'd get a few of the chocolates.

Wayne handed the chocolates to Simone. 'You'd better take charge of these,' he said, which Simone did amid uproarious laughter as everyone played the game of eating pig food, pig-style.

Eventually the temporary silliness settled. 'If we're going to have a look at what's happening at Bovale and work out what we might do better, how are we going to do that, Wayne? Bruce asked.

'In a nutshell, the best way is for you to describe to me the performance and production of your pasture and herd, plus your business costs, and we'll judge if you're operating at an achievable level or not. Then we can look at everything you own and everything you do and don't do to see how they may affect your ability to meet achievable targets,' Wayne replied.

'That sounds fairly intense, Wayne,' suggested Col.

'Yes, it can take a bit of effort, Col, but unless we do that, we won't have the evidence for making change that will improve business performance,' Wayne explained.

'And once we reach conclusions, that's not the end of it. You'll have to work out how to change a system, not bits and pieces, because when you change one aspect, invariably that affects many other elements. It will take a bit of time, but it'll set you up for much more efficient regular assessment in the future. You should then be able to assess whether anything you come across is worth incorporating into what you do here,' Wayne added.

'The herd we have, Wayne, weighs about one thousand tonnes. And I aim to produce and sell about three hundred tonnes annually, which we do. Does that suggest we have room for improvement?' Bruce asked.

'That's brilliant you know, Bruce. Rarely do I come across producers who understand what their business product is. Without data on the pasture and on reference production measures, it's hard to judge,' Wayne replied. 'For a start, do you know the annual growth of heifers or steers?'

'Not off the top of my head. I could probably work that out,' replied Bruce.

Simone cut in. 'Wayne, Bruce, if you don't mind, I'll take the children home. I think they'll enjoy the blanket show better than this technical discussion. We'll see you tomorrow. See you later, Col,' she said as she, Carina and Lachlan headed off.

'Yes, it's been a long day. I'll need to nestle under a blanket before too long too, but before then, let's sort out what we're doing for the next two days.' Wayne suggested.

'We're ready to go first thing in the morning with the bulls, Wayne. There's forty of them,' Col said.

'Righto,' acknowledged Wayne. 'By the time we buggerise around *et cetera* and get into them, we'll hopefully get them done by lunch. I need to get a perspective on your pastures, cattle and infrastructure before we can get on the same page and discuss business management, so how about we get around a few paddocks to see breeding cattle, heifers, steers and weaners. And then on Wednesday we'll park up and build a strategy. Sound like a plan?'

'Sounds perfect, Wayne,' Bruce said.

***

It was six thirty when they arrived at the yards the next morning. Wayne walked in to where the veterinary chute was to assess the situation. He then set about preparations. Before they'd left the shed earlier, Bruce had them load a solid table into the back of the old station Land Cruiser. Col and Bruce got the table to exactly where Wayne wanted it. They then set up their generator in a safe location away from the work area to reduce noise pollution and ran a lead from it to the table.

Wayne set up his microscope and sampling gear on the table. He also rigged up his electroejaculator, ready to go.

'Gee, that thing doesn't look like it'd be too comfortable,' Bruce said, wincing uncomfortably, when he eyed the electroejaculator probe. It was about four hundred millimetres long and almost a hundred millimetres in diameter with two handles at the blunt end for connection to a power supply. Along the length of the base of the probe were three electrodes.

'Yes, it shocks most people when they first see it, but the truth is, it looks ordinary, but it's actually perfectly designed,' Wayne explained. It has to be that big to sit comfortably in a bull's rectum; they're big animals with big bums and they need a big probe to maintain a good connection with the rectal wall. The current we use is exactly the same as physios use on people every day and just like in physio, we use pulsing stimulation. The handles are curved out and up so the shit stick can sit comfortably in between, holding the electrodes exactly where they need to be, immediately above the organs holding the semen ingredients. The pulse we apply initially holds their bum hole closed, which is good as we don't want them crapping it out. Then we pulse it till the muscles contract and expel the semen. I've never had the experience, but my perception is they find it odd, and in some cases a bit frightening, giving their butt a tickle. Tropical bulls like these seem to tolerate it really well. But those black southern cattle sometimes squeal a bit. I don't know whether that's because it hurts or because those cattle like vocalising way more than tropical cattle; my perception is they get a fright more than experience pain.'

'I'll believe you, Wayne,' Col said, 'but no way you're going to be getting a sample out of me with that thing.' This gave both Bruce and Wayne a good laugh.

Wayne then explained the procedure and what their tasks were. One of Bruce's jobs was to record all the data. Initially Bruce would open the head bail, just enough so the bull could get his head in and out as they wished. Col would put a rump bar in behind the bull to hold it forward. Wayne would then examine the scrotal contents. After that, Col would put the probe in, Wayne would operate the pulse generator and Bruce would catch the semen in a test tube jammed onto a funnel on the end of a metre-long handle. Semen collection was done via a small door that opened out on the lower left side of the chute, commonly called a dicky door. Wayne would then take the sample and do measurements under the microscope while Col would remove and clean the probe and Bruce would use a pair of custom-made pliers to get a skin sample for DNA from the bull's ear.

It took the team just one bull to get into the swing of the process, despite neither Col nor Bruce having seen it done before. The electroejaculator caused the bull to get a very large erection, making collection with the small funnel a tricky exercise. Wayne was examining the semen and suggested, 'Have a look at this fellas.'

Bruce walked over and peered down the microscope, seeing what looked like hundreds of sperm swimming wildly around. 'That's really good sperm I've rated at eighty percent motile. I hope we keep seeing this all day,' Wayne commented.

The second bull reacted completely differently, not having an erection. He ejaculated into his sheath, which Wayne efficiently stripped directly into the funnel as he held both the funnel and the opening of the bull's sheath with his left hand. 'It's better they get an erection,' Wayne explained,' and then I can see if there's any problems with the penis.'

'That looks a bit dangerous the way you grabbed onto that sheath, Wayne,' Col suggested.

'Fortunately, I've done it thousands of times without dramas,' Wayne replied. 'I reckon I have two things in my favour. One is it puts the bull in a difficult situation; if he kicks me, he also kicks himself in the sheath. I suspect that's a good deterrent. The other thing is the way we've set this up. You see how he has his head comfortably resting in the head bail? What that effectively does is blind him to what I'm doing. I have all the advantage in my court. I'm giving him none. The worst thing I could do is create a situation where he would try to kick because the most likely outcome is he'd hurt himself. We don't want that, at all.'

Only a few bulls later, Wayne was again assessing sperm. 'Check this one, Bruce,' he said.

Bruce again squinted down the microscope. He could see about one hundred sperm, he guessed, but almost none were swimming. 'Problem?' he asked Wayne.

'I think so. We'll get another sample and see,' Wayne responded. A second good sample had the same problem. 'He's a dud, Bruce. Sorry, mate.'

After they had done a group of six bulls, Wayne would get in the yard with them and walk them around while he assessed each in detail to complete his veterinary examination. Wayne was looking intently at one bull as he walked. 'This one has stringhalt, Bruce. He's out.'

'What's that, Wayne?' Bruce asked.

'An inherited anatomical defect of the stifle joint. If you look carefully, you can see the click in that joint up in his flank. That's equivalent to our knee. The kneecap in this bull is partially dislocating. When he passes the genes on to his daughters, they end up completely locked up in the back legs when they get in poor condition, like when they're lactating.'

'I've seen that,' Col said. 'I wondered what it was.'

After Wayne assessed the semen of each bull, he put a few drops in a small tube that he labelled. 'We'll send that down to the lab for morphology assessment. We can't do that here because it takes high-precision microscopes we can't use in the yards and it needs assessment by people who are specially trained and accredited.'

Because everyone had prepared so well, all the bulls were done without any significant problems. Bruce was disappointed when Wayne failed four of the bulls, with more potentially to fail if they did not have at least seventy percent normal sperm. 'No problem, Bruce,' said Wayne. You only need half the bulls you have here, so we have to get rid of twenty. What we're doing here is two things. Firstly, we're knocking out anything that has suspect calf-getting ability. And of those that are fertile, we'll eliminate those that have poor genetics for key traits like growth, fertility and temperament.'

'When will we get the results, Wayne?' Col asked.

'The semen morphology will be within two weeks,' Wayne explained. 'But the genetic tests are slower, unfortunately. We send the ear samples you took today to a lab where they read about fifty thousand bits of DNA, which is proper gobbledygook to you and me. It's called genotyping. They give the genotype to a geneticist for genomic analysis, which means they can calculate for each trait the genetic merit of the bull. All up, that process can take up to two months at present. A bit slow, but you have time on your side, so all good. I'll show you an example tonight of what we can do.'

After lunch, Col walked the bulls back to their paddock, while Bruce took Wayne for a drive to Emu paddock, about fourteen hundred hectares to the north of Kosciuszko paddock. Emu was one of four paddocks usually reserved for mature cows. Wayne was full of questions, trying to understand the details of Bruce's system. For now, his 'head-top' analysis would suffice till he was able to access specific data for a desk-top analysis.

'I'm really impressed with your pasture management, Bruce,' Wayne commented. 'You understand it as well as you should, and your country is fairly much in A condition.'

'Thanks, Wayne,' Bruce replied. 'I had a great teacher. Dad. I know my feed base underpins every dollar I make this year and for many years to come. I'm very conscious I don't create a problem today that I don't feel the consequences of and can't fix easily in many years' time.'

'Do you do your own pasture budgeting?' Wayne asked.

'I do now, Wayne,' Bruce explained. 'Initially Dad had me do some training with the agriculture department people and they came out to help me early on. I also did a three-day course on grazing land management, which really helped me get a concepts' understanding. It also taught me a lot of the details. Once I understood all that, I've been doing it myself. I still have questions and there's always the local department people to answer them for me.'

Wayne asked many questions about how many cattle of each age and sex Bruce had, their weights, and his sales and purchases. All the while, Wayne made copious notes, mainly when they pulled up to see something, as writing while driving on a bush track was proving quite difficult. 'You obviously have some of the information I'm looking for, Bruce, because you're able to tell me the live weight of your herd and its live weight production. We'll do a bit of work on that tomorrow.'

'Are you getting any ideas on what I might do to make this place more profitable, Wayne?' Bruce asked.

'You're already aware we can do a lot with the bulls, reducing their costs and getting your genetics more focussed on your business objectives. But there's potentially a few other changes you could make that will improve your margins,' said Wayne. 'You can take that further by breeding some of your own bulls. I might be wrong at this stage, but my rough guess is your weaner production is only a bit over one hundred kilograms per cow and it really should be at least thirty to forty kilograms more than that. There have to be reasons other than genetics that has your weaner numbers down where they are. We need to look at pregnancy and losses through to weaning in both heifers and cows. That may require some changes to mating and weaning management, to supplements and or to vaccinations. There will be a web of interacting factors and we'll need to clearly identify what's driving any problems because it's the drivers we need to change.'

'I agree, Wayne,' replied Bruce. 'I have been thinking for a while we should be weaning more calves.'

'Do you do any pregnancy diagnoses and monitor the outcome, Bruce?' Wayne asked.

'Yes we do, but I must say I haven't exactly calculated the losses we may be experiencing. The pregnancy rates are pretty low in the lactating cows, and I thought that's maybe where the main problem is,' Bruce suggested.

'What about in your females calving for the first time; do you know if they have any major losses?' Wayne asked.

'Come to think of it, we only keep pregnant heifers, and there's usually a fair percentage, maybe twenty percent, that don't come in with a calf at branding,' Bruce replied. 'That's a real worry, now you mention it.'

They arrived back at the yards where Col was waiting. 'We'll head across to see the pregnant heifers and yearlings now, before we go back to the weaners, if that's what you want, Wayne,' Bruce suggested.

'Perfect, Bruce,' Wayne replied.

As they drove through each group, Wayne's main questions revolved around getting an understanding of annual growth of young cattle in this country. 'I reckon you are getting around a hundred and thirty-five kilograms a year in this country, Bruce. Are you happy with that?' Wayne asked.

'It seems fine, Wayne,' Bruce replied. 'But if I can get more, that would be sensational.'

'What sort of licks do you feed these young cattle?' Wayne asked.

Col answered as he did most of the lick feeding. 'We use a loose mix that has about thirty percent urea in it, Wayne. All the cattle get that through the dry season. And we like to start in early May if we can, to hold as much condition on the cattle as possible when the first frosts hit about the first week of June.'

'You don't feed phosphorus at all?' Wayne asked.

'Yes, but I'm not sure this country needs it as far as I know, Wayne. We haven't seen any bone chewing,' Bruce replied. Wayne knew Bruce was referring to the age-old bush diagnosis of phosphorus deficiency based on cattle chewing bones and even fresh carrion.

'How do you feed phosphorus?' Wayne asked.

Again, Col answered. 'We mostly use blocks because they're a lot easier to get out and we don't have to keep them out of the rain.'

'What vaccines do you use?' Wayne asked.

'Everything gets vaccinated against botulism, Wayne,' Bruce replied. 'We give the calves a shot of the three-year single-shot vaccine when we're branding. That means we don't have to vaccinate any steers again. We don't bother revaccinating female cattle till they wean their first calf. After that, them and the bulls get a booster every year. It's pretty easy to manage it that way. Also,' Bruce added, 'blackleg killed an eighteen-month-old bull here recently. So, we've now started giving all calves a five-in-one vaccine booster at weaning to follow up what we've been giving at branding.'

'That's interesting, Bruce. Tell me about the blackleg incident,' Wayne requested. Bruce and Col gave Wayne a detailed account of what had happened. 'That vet's pretty sharp. I would not have picked blackleg straight up, not just on heart muscle lesions. That's not typical blackleg in my experience. You live and learn,' he added.

'Do you use vibrio or pestivirus vaccines at all?' Wayne asked.

'We haven't so far, Wayne. Occasionally we'll buy a bull that's been vaccinated. But we don't do it as a rule. We've not seen any evidence of abortions,' Bruce offered. They were driving through Burdekin paddock at this stage, looking at the weaner heifers, just to the south and over Gun Creek from the homestead, on the river. It was very close to beer o'clock, so they headed home.

It was a very still afternoon. 'This is magic weather in a beautiful spot, fellas,' Wayne commented as they parked up in the shed and headed across the lawn between the shed and the homestead. 'I reckon

I could get used to living here.' The late afternoon had brought out the galahs and pale-headed rosella parrots that were feeding across the lawn. The rosellas had a particular liking for the sprinklers when they came on. Pairs of the birds fluffed up their feathers and bathed themselves for as much as five minutes at a time. All three men grabbed a beer and headed out to sit on the homestead's lawn as the sun was setting, getting close to the horizon across the river from where they were sitting. The red glow of the evening sky gradually emerged. It created a stunning contrast to the tall gum trees on the eastern high banks of the river. In the absence of any cloud, this was as beautiful a sunset as Wayne had seen in a while.

'What's the plan for tomorrow, Wayne?' Bruce asked.

'Well, after we have dinner, I'll spend an hour or two working over what I've seen today. First thing tomorrow, we might get what data you have together and build as accurate a picture as we can. I would like to see your business costs too, Bruce, if that's okay. That will give me further insight into exactly how the business is operating. Only then can we work out what will improve it,' Wayne replied.

Bruce had given Wayne extra information from his office, such as the makeup of the phosphorus lick blocks and how much was consumed, and the budgets and expenditure summaries for previous years that he didn't have on hand during their station inspection. At about eight o'clock that evening, the phone rang. Bruce was cleaning the dishes after dinner. Wayne was in the lounge with his computer and paper spread over the large coffee table, deep in thought. The phone call was from Mick. 'Are you heading into town this weekend, Bruce?' he asked.

'I'd love to Mick, but I probably should go down and see Mum. Since she's been on this chemo, she wants Frances and I there as often as we can.'

'How's it going out there with that Wayne bloke?' Mick asked.

'Good,' replied Bruce. 'Really good. It's a bit hard to judge what he's going to advise at this stage. We still have to finalise an interim description of the current situation in the morning. But I get the vibes some good stuff might come out of this.'

'That's great,' said Mick. 'From what you were saying, you had a feeling you could improve the situation, but just needed someone like that to help you work out what exactly to do.

'I saw Eileen down the street today. She looked great. She was asking about you, mate. You better look out. I think she's getting more set on you,' Mick said as he laughed a bit.

'Worse things could happen, Mick,' Bruce agreed. 'And how's Jane?'

'Good. She was with Eileen,' Mick replied. Bruce let that hang for a bit. Bruce could sense his good mate was in the discomfort zone. Mick obviously liked Jane, but just like himself, didn't quite know how to take the next step for fear of making a fool of himself.

'Just be yourself, Mick, and good things will happen. Sage advice from my best mum,' Bruce offered. Bruce was not totally sure about that, but Doris was no fool, and she was also a lady, so she would know things he didn't have a clue about.

Mick wanted to change the subject as he really didn't know how to discuss this sort of stuff, even with one of his best mates. 'How long will you be in Townsville, Bruce?' he asked.

'I'm thinking I might stay a couple of days, Mick. But not just in Townsville. I haven't been fishing since that mongrel crab got hold of me, and I'm keen to get down the creek again. Should be good this weekend. The tides are pretty good and there's not much wind forecast,' Bruce told him.

'Are you taking your old man fishing?' Mick asked.

'Probably not Mick. When he's not busy at Farmin Stuff he's at home keeping Mum company. He's not even in a position to come up here for a day, even though he's dying to get back for a visit. I've been keen to take that old bloke who helped me out when the crab minced my toe. I'll give him a ring and see if he's a goer,' Bruce said.

When Mick hung up, Bruce called Lenny. 'How's my old mate?' he asked.

Lenny was pleased as punch Bruce called. 'The cane harvest is in full swing, Bruce, but the contract harvester's not due at my place till late next week. I'm open to go fishing any time before then. Are you keen too, Bruce?' Lenny asked.

'You read my mind, Lenny,' Bruce replied. 'I am getting withdrawal symptoms from not having been, which is why I rang. Would Saturday suit?'

'Bruce, we can go in my boat if you like. How about you come to my place with a rod? I'll have some crab pots and bait, and we'll head down the creek from here,' Lenny suggested.

'I can do that,' Bruce agreed. 'Low tide is about eight o'clock, so if I get there by then, we can fish the rising tide and maybe pull out about mid-afternoon. Does that sound like a plan?' Lenny told him where to go and he'd see him then. Bruce loved fishing, and knowing he was going this weekend buoyed his spirits a lot.

Bruce and Wayne had breakfast at daybreak, which was about a quarter past six at this time of the year. Col came over shortly after and they gathered around the table with a cup of coffee each to help Wayne get an accurate representation of the herd. Like most beef producers, Bruce had not maintained a set of herd records that was designed to answer specific questions about performance and production. It was an unfortunate situation because the data was not that difficult to collect if there was a plan to collect it. But once the opportunity passed to collect it, it was lost. Despite this, Bruce and Col had enough records and memories to gradually put together a herd structure that closely resembled the true situation. This was made easier by Bruce keeping herd numbers and transactions fairly consistent as he did not over-stock, ever. This took about two hours.

Bruce was about to ask Col to make them all another cup of coffee when Simone and the children arrived. 'Smoko time, boys,' she declared. It was a bit earlier than they usually had smoko, but school of the air started in half an hour and Simone decided it was a good opportunity to let the children be with their father. Col was ecstatic, especially as Simone had baked a batch of scones that she had brought as well.

'Gee, I almost feel like I've died and gone to heaven,' Bruce suggested. He was salivating furiously at the thought of scones for smoko. While Simone boiled the kettle, he dived into his pantry for some syrup, his favourite scone topping. He liked it with butter, even though Simone had also brought cream and strawberry jam. All options were catered for today.

While they demolished the scones, Wayne kept working on the computer. Now he had a herd description, all transaction records and some reasonable estimates of live weights of each age and sex of cattle, he had calculations to do before they could progress any further together. 'If you blokes have something to do for an hour or so, that would give me a chance to pull this together,' Wayne suggested. Col and Bruce jumped at the chance to do a few odd jobs that were always waiting. They returned about eleven o'clock. Wayne was ready.

'I'm as nervous as hell just now, Wayne,' Bruce admitted. 'It's a bit intimidating, but also quite exciting to have a forensic examination of the business.'

'Like you, Bruce, I'm also excited. There are some good opportunities I reckon,' responded Wayne. 'But firstly, I'd like to have a yarn about future data collection. This job's been a bit tricky and I'm not absolutely sure we have the right answers because we've had to bodge up some data that didn't exist.'

'Yeah, sorry about that, Wayne,' Bruce replied. 'I'm kicking myself now. You are absolutely correct. Unless we ask the right questions, we don't know what data to collect, and unless we collect the right data, there's no chance of answering the questions. We're just lucky I had a bit of data.'

'To help you out, I have a set of questions here that I think you should be asking about your business as a routine,' Wayne told them. 'I've set these against the major management options you have available, so you can see how they link in. The key is to know the exact information you need to collect, and then plan to collect it. You already do a great job with your pastures. But my advice is you need to improve your cattle data. My main recommendation there is to get RFID tags on all your cattle. That way you can identify them using a transponder any time they come through the yards. When you put the tags in, put their age group and sex against the number in your data recorder. If an animal loses a tag, you'll lose that animal's data unless you have a second backup tag, but if you replace it and record the age and sex, at least you won't lose track of your numbers.

'The next recommendation is to get all your cattle through the yards at the mid-year muster when you do pregnancy diagnoses. It's a stock take. It's good business practice, no matter what your business is. When you do that, collect some data. The most important is the lactation status of female cattle. If you're doing pregnancy diagnoses, enter foetal age, not just whether they're pregnant or not. And get their weights if at all possible. Body condition is also useful, but it's not critical like lactation status is.'

'What about at other musters, Wayne?' Col asked.

'If nothing else, get lactation status. One way to do that simply is to draft off, say, dry or non-lactating cattle and run them past the reader that's been set up to record dry cattle on that day. Then do another session set up for wet or lactating cattle. The reason lactation status is so important is it describes if they reared a calf to weaning, and also if and when the calf was lost or weaned,' Wayne added. 'Basically, I'm suggesting you don't go to the yards without your data collection device and tag reader, and you at least record every animal that runs through the race every time. It's easy enough to do, just a discipline.'

'I'm keen Wayne. And I'll be keener if you can give us some pearls out of what we've been able to give you this time,' Bruce said.

'Thanks Bruce. As I indicated yesterday, there clearly is a problem with weaner numbers, which is knocking down your business live weight production by at least ten percent from what I can gather so far.

That's the bad news. The good news is I think I have a few solutions for you.

'The key to understand what I'll tell you is to understand live weight production. Live weight is your business product, as it is for any beef business, even feedlots. The definition of annual live weight production is annual weight change plus the weight of a calf weaned. So, if, for example, you have a cow that's four hundred and eighty kilograms last year and this year she's four hundred and sixty and weans a one and sixty kilogram calf, her live weight production is one hundred and forty kilograms. If she died and the calf didn't survive, her live weight production would be minus four hundred and eighty kilograms. A steer's live weight production is simply his annual weight gain as he weans no calf. If you add up individual live weight production of every animal in your business, that is exactly the same as sales over a period of time, hence the importance of the concept.'

'That's an interesting concept, Wayne. But what's wrong with using weaning rates, which is what we usually do to get an idea on how the females are going?' Bruce asked.

'Weaning rate is a performance measure, Bruce,' Wayne replied. 'Your product is live weight. You can alter production if it's not at an achievable level by changing performance. No-one pays you for good or bad weaning rates or mortality rates or growth rates. The most important numbers describe production, values and costs because they're what drive your margins.'

'How do you know how much a cow should be producing, Wayne?' Bruce asked.

'That brings us to your situation here. The main reference level is yearling growth because research has shown that in the same paddock in the same year, yearling growth is exactly the same as weaner weight per cow in the paddock. In other words, there is no such thing as magic. Damn.' Wayne laughed at his own joke. 'If it's one hundred and fifty kilogram country, that's what yearlings can grow in that year and it's what a cow herd, on average, can extract from the pasture for their calves.'

'You mentioned yesterday our weaner production was just over a hundred kilograms. What should it be?' Bruce asked.

'Yes, when I did the calculations, my suspicions were confirmed. On this place, I think it should average over one hundred and fifty kilograms at least,' Wayne suggested.

'Crikey,' Bruce exclaimed. 'That's massive. What are we doing wrong?'

'I don't have absolute proof, but my primary diagnosis is that you have a phosphorus deficiency. Yes, you're feeding phosphorus blocks, but at the rate the cattle are eating the blocks, they're getting insufficient available phosphorus to have any significant impact. I did some calculations after what I saw yesterday and from what I've seen in your purchases, the cattle are lucky to be getting one gram of available phosphorus a day from the blocks. They need at least five grams, and sometimes up to ten, daily.'

'But why wouldn't we have seen bone chewing if the cattle are phosphorus-deficient?' asked Bruce.

'Because bone chewing is a symptom of nutrient deficiency, and in most cases it's probably protein deficiency that causes it. It just happens that the most nutrient-deficient regions have both protein and phosphorus in low supply. If cattle get sufficiently deficient, they will eat fresh carcasses. I've seen them mobbing around roadkill up in the Gulf country before,' Wayne added. 'I'm drawing my conclusions mainly from your country types and that the cattle obviously have a primary nutrient deficiency. And it isn't protein.'

'You mean to say we've essentially wasted our money on those blocks, Wayne?' Bruce queried.

'Exactly. I'm sorry. Some people in my game call those specific blocks, tombstones. The manufacturers make it look like magic, but it's nothing of the sort. The phosphorus in those particular blocks is not readily available, and that's not clear in their statements. And secondly, the cattle are simply not consuming enough, and probably heaps of them are consuming very little. The fundamental error you've made is you've made a decision on nutritional needs without understanding it, if I read the situation right. Hope that's not too insensitive a statement,' Wayne added.

'No, give it to me straight, Wayne. Nothing we can do about the past. But we sure can control the future. What should we do?' Bruce asked.

'The main strategy with supplements is to work with a company that has a qualified nutritionist. If that person tells you it's good, then it's good. There's one such place in Charters Towers, I know. Almost certainly they will recommend you donate all the blocks to the poor people,' Wayne said, laughingly. 'Just put them out. They can't hurt the cattle, just like they can't help them, but they're better off not taking up room in your shed,' Wayne recommended.

He went on, 'They'll almost certainly recommend a loose mix. Yes, it's better if you have wet season shelters. But one method a few people use is to buy one tonne bags of it and leave the top open during the wet. You will lose a bit, but it gets around the cost of shelters. Up to you.

Cost out the alternatives to see what will work best. We could do some diagnostics, but we won't unless you haven't seen a lot of difference in the cattle already because the main diagnostic test has to be done at the end of the wet season and we've missed the window for this year.'

'How will we know if a different supplement is working?' asked Col.

'You should notice a few things. Firstly, young cattle will grow better during the wet season. It's critical they get this too. One of the things I've noticed is the pregnancy rates in your two-year-old heifers is barely making seventy percent. That's not good. They're simply not big enough. You should see them busting out of their skins in this country during their first mating and getting ninety percent pregnant or better,' Wayne advised.

He added, 'You should also notice calves growing faster, lactating cows in better condition, and then at weaning, you should get much higher pregnancy rates. All good outcomes that ultimately should increase annual live weight production, I guess, by at least twenty-five kilograms per animal. Across your business, that's a huge boost.

'But there is one aspect you need to account for. When you feed supplements like phosphorus to deficient cattle, the main effect is to cause them to eat a lot more pasture every day. That's the main benefit, much more than the specific nutrients in the lick. Therefore, you need to pull back your cattle numbers, probably by ten percent or so. Irrespective, if I'm correct, when you repeat the calculations next year, I'm expecting you to see station and individual animal live weight production much higher than where it is now.'

'I'm loving it, Wayne. But any other bad news?' Bruce asked.

'I think so, Bruce,' Wayne replied. 'I reckon you're losing too many calves between pregnancy and weaning. If you had been monitoring what's happening at an individual animal level, I think you would have seen levels close to twenty percent. And that chews into overall live weight production. On average, based on the detailed research that's been done, I'd expect each calf loss to be costing you about one hundred and twenty kilograms.'

'What level of loss should we be getting if everything was going well, Wayne?' Col asked.

'In this situation, I'd reckon eight percent or less. That means you should be able to pull it back by about ten percent, which would have a huge benefit for your business,' Bruce said.

'What do you think is causing the problem, Wayne?' Bruce asked.

'I'm not sure at this stage, but I have my money on two main options. The first and most obvious is phosphorus deficiency. One of the main reasons calves die is their mothers fail to start producing milk on the day of calving, the same problem as in many women. There's good research now that shows the main reason this occurs is poor feed quality immediately prior to calving, which causes the shift in the hormone support systems to not be ready on the day of calving. The cow's system essentially panics, taking about three days to properly arc up full milk production. But for some calves, that's too late, and they perish. The solution is to position your cows with the best quality feed possible within the situation around calving. I recommend starting wet season phosphorus supplementation for cows a few weeks before calving starts, even if the wet hasn't arrived.'

'Would we keep up the dry season lick at the same time?' Bruce asked.

'You could, but it would probably work best if you get your feed company to formulate a transition supplement, essentially lifting the phosphorus in the dry season lick,' Wayne suggested.

'The other issue I'm concerned may be affecting you is vibrio,' Wayne offered. 'There could also be pestivirus in the herd without you knowing, but vibrio is more likely to be consistently keeping pregnancies down and calf losses up. Has your vet commented on the empty uteri being bigger than expected at pregnancy diagnosis?' Wayne asked.

'Not that I can recall,' Bruce replied. 'She could have, and I might not have thought anything of it, and then carefully forgotten. Sorry.'

'Well, it doesn't matter in a way whether it's here or not, as my advice will be the same. First thing will be to start annual vaccination of all bulls against vibrio. In the first year, you'll have to give them a booster as well. It's a mongrel vaccine and they hate it, but it is an excellent vaccine that stops the spread of the disease and can even clear it from bulls. The second recommendation will be to cull all non-pregnant females because if the disease has been resident in the herd, there will be plenty of carriers that need a trip to America, chilled and in a box,' Bruce recommended.

'Do you think we can do that, Wayne? We haven't been able to previously cull non-pregnant cows because we don't get enough pregnancies,' Bruce queried.

Wayne replied, 'If you don't do it, you're going to perpetuate the likely problem. It really should be fine because if a suitable phosphorus supplementation strategy is put in place, you will get sufficient pregnancies. And to top all that, you have to get your numbers back a bit to prevent effective phosphorus supplementation causing pasture damage. All up, I don't believe there will be any dramas achieving it.'

'We'll need to make more room for cull cows as there will be quite a few non-pregnant cows that are in low condition and we'll have to fatten them to get reasonable returns,' Col suggested.

'Spot on, Col,' Wayne said. 'Like I said earlier, I'm making some recommendations that will have multiple ramifications. It's never easy to change. In this case, you are looking at quite significant change which will mean you'll have to think through all the consequences and how they will be dealt with.'

'Back to disease,' Wayne said. 'I would also like you to sample some cattle for pestivirus, to guide any action on that front as well. When the cattle are next through, I'd like you to get about a dozen bloods from your yearling heifers and a dozen bloods from some of your oldest cows that were born on the station. If the disease is here, it will show up as an antibody in the cows. And what we see in the heifers will guide your action plan. Maybe the best plan there is to work with your usual cattle vet to get those bloods *et cetera*. Will that work for you?'

'Too easy, Wayne,' replied Bruce. 'Should we sample for vibrio at the same time?'

'You could, but it probably won't help much because, as I mentioned earlier, no matter what you find, your action will be the same. The whole disease management issue, especially for vibrio, will also be helped a lot by reducing your bull percentages as you're planning,' Wayne added.

'There is another recommendation I have for you too, Bruce, that I mentioned yesterday,' said Wayne. 'It will help your rate of genetic improvement and it will cut your costs back quite a bit if you start breeding some of your own bulls.'

'I didn't think we could do that,' Col said. 'Don't you need to be a stud?'

'That's exactly what I'm suggesting. Set up a stud using your cattle, breeding bulls for you. You've been buying reasonable bulls for years, so the genes you need are in your herd. It's just a matter of doing it correctly and you'll reap some quite big benefits,' Wayne said.

'How would we start? Do we select bulls from the calves before we brand?' asked Bruce.

Wayne responded with, 'That's exactly what you don't do Bruce. That strategy is an industry favourite for sure, but it has a long history as a plan for failure, unfortunately. You have to start with females that you consider have the right traits. An example would be, select pregnant heifers that are polled, well-grown and with good temperament and conformation. Then use breeding values to select a bull that meets your breeding objectives and mate him to those heifers during their first lactation. Anything that is pregnant will have a potential star bull in the oven with the right genes for fertility, growth and whatever else you are aiming at. If these females have good udders, they are the foundation of your bull-breeding herd that you add to each year with pregnant heifers and take out anything that demonstrates problems. You still purchase a few top-shelf bulls if you can find them. On top of pulling down the cost per calf of owning bulls, a key outcome is you have full control of the genetics of your herd.'

'Does that mean if we muster Stocking paddock where we have the pregnant heifers, we can select our foundation that we could segregate for mating with a bull once we identify him?' asked Bruce.

'That's correct, Bruce. That's a good approach,' agreed Wayne.

'I really like the concept of breeding some of our own bulls,' Col added.

Wayne said, 'My experience is that after four to five years, you will really struggle to find bulls at any sale that meet the standards of the bulls you breed here. If you do it correctly, I'd virtually guarantee that will be what will happen.'

This development almost brought the conversation to a stop. Both Bruce and Col were contemplating bull breeding with a fair amount of pleasure. So, it was excellent timing that Simone appeared. 'How's it going here, boys?' she asked.

'We're brimming with great ideas,' Col replied, smiling. 'You know me. Old stick in the mud, not wanting change. But we've had a great discussion just now and for once, I'm seeing that we can make some really good changes here at Bovale. What do you reckon, Bruce?'

'Agreed, Col,' Bruce replied. 'Just at the moment though, my gut worms are screaming for a feed, so how about we give them what they want?'

'Hope you don't mind Bruce, but I've taken the liberty of preparing a lunch for all of us over at our house. It's ready now and the children are on a school break, so if you head over straight away, everyone's problems will dissolve at once,' indicated Simone, laughing freely at her own bonhomie.

'You are an A grade sheila, Simone,' Bruce said. 'No wonder Col married you.'

Col came back with, 'Bruce, we're waiting for you to match my achievements. It can't be too far off, and some lucky lady will pluck you clean off the shelf.'

'You've been talking to my mum,' Bruce responded, smiling broadly and offering no hints on how his woeful love life was progressing.

'Let's go,' Col said. 'Thanks, Simone.'

During lunch, the discussion was mainly around Col and Simone's family. Bruce was quiet and contemplative about their morning's discussion. When the conversation lulled a bit he asked, 'Wayne, you have given us a lot of recommendations just now. As you said, that's the first step. What do we do after lunch and beyond?'

Wayne suggested they spend the afternoon revisiting everything they had discussed. To create the change, they firstly needed to work through the details of implementing it. This included defining associated costs and savings. Once they had worked this through, by late in the afternoon, they might be positioned to redo the budget and look at overall potential business impact. Once they realised the scale of the afternoon's tasks, the men quickly finished their lunches and headed back to the homestead to knuckle down.

By sundown, they had broken the back of the job. It was once they had recalculated potential income and costs after the changes were implemented that Bruce realised how dramatic the process he'd started was going to be. His business margins might be lifted by as much as two hundred thousand dollars. And it would be better if prices escalated further.

'Yesterday and today have been fantastic, Wayne,' Bruce concluded. 'You've helped me no end. I can guarantee I needed help, but I didn't realise how much till we went through this. My only regret about today was that Dad was not here. But he really wanted to finish all his commitments with Bovale, so maybe he would have preferred to go fishing than talk filthy dirty about cows for two days?'

'That's great to hear, Bruce,' Wayne said. But the truth is, there's still a lot more you can learn and implement. I can see where your focus on the pastures has got you. If you now get some more detailed training in reproductive management, genetics, cattle nutrition and business management, I think you'll be amazed at the benefits. From a big jump now, further knowledge and skills will give you resilience, and you need that as much as anything to buffer against the changing climate and markets, both of which can give you a hiding any time you're not prepared for the tough times.'

'I'm hearing you, Wayne,' Bruce replied. 'It's sobering. As much as anything over the past couple of days, and actually since that Koolburra field day, I've learnt how little I knew. The worst part is, now that I know more, it has suddenly dawned on me how true that old adage is, you know the one, 'The more you know, the more you know you don't know'. I'm absolutely sure it's beer o'clock,' he declared to finish, shifting the whole conversation quickly.

Chapter Seven

The visit by Wayne had fired both Bruce and Col into a new orbit. Bruce was particularly pleased he had involved Col in the details of how the business operated and how they might change it to improve their profitability because Col was now fully compliant and a strong advocate for the changes. The challenge was working through all aspects of what they did throughout the year, taking account of infrastructure and available labour, to work out how to most efficiently transition. Bruce realised they could waste a lot of time trying to work it out in their heads alone; a sound written plan was required. He suggested to Col that both of them take some time to consider what they had learned and in the coming weeks they would plan half days where they would get together around a table and sort it out.

Independently of this, Bruce knew Col and his family were a valuable asset for Bovale. They would not be easily replaced if they left. The anticipated extra income that Bovale would generate had buoyed him because it was crucial in being able to provide suitable remuneration to keep the Wattle family at Bovale. As opportunity may arise, Bruce now felt confident he could formally employ Simone on a much more regular casual basis when she was available. He could not pay the children when they worked, especially Lachlan who was keen as mustard, but he could create opportunities for Lachlan and Carina that fairly represented their value to Bovale. At this stage, he was unsure what he would do, just sure he could do it.

Meanwhile, Bruce was gearing up for a weekend that he was very much looking forward to. He was so keen, he had left the station by three o'clock on Friday afternoon, heading to his parents' place in Townsville. When he arrived, he was met with the beautiful aromas of the dinner his mum was preparing. Merve was yet to get home, but Frances would not be far from arriving.

'What's that you're preparing, Mum?' Bruce asked.

'Fish and chips, Bruce,' Doris replied. 'Your father had a client the other day who gave him some barramundi fillets they were happy to share after a Gulf trip.'

'Wow. I love the way you do chips too, Mum. They come out really nice,' Bruce offered. 'I don't know how they cook chips in takeaway shops, but they give me a gut ache. The heat-treated vegetable oils they use is the main problem I know, but I'm sure they add some other rubbish as so-called flavouring.'

'G'day Frances,' Bruce said as his sister arrived. 'How's everything at your place?'

'Good, Bruce. Though I haven't yet finalised what I'm doing with all that money. It's not what I had ever been expecting,' Frances said. 'And I still feel really guilty about you increasing your business loan to enable it to happen.'

'Don't feel guilty, Frances,' Bruce advised. 'Yes, the truth is I was initially struggling a bit, just as Dad suggested, trying to work out how I was going to deal with it, but this past week I had a veterinary scientist come up from Rockhampton who has really helped. Col and I are furiously working out how to implement all the changes we reckon we should make. It should be well and truly worth it.'

'That's excellent. How's Bovale looking?' Frances asked.

'Really good. The season has been okay, so we have good feed for the cattle. Col and Simone and the children are terrific, and together we keep it pretty tidy and operating like a well-oiled machine,' Bruce said.

'Mum said you'd tried to catch a barramundi up at Jindabyne dam the other day. How'd you go?' Frances asked.

'Pretty ordinary, Frances. Didn't even get a bite,' Bruce replied. 'We went at the wrong time of the day to start with. And then we spent most of our time up there playing silly buggers in the canoe, which was a lot of fun. We caught a good feed of red claw, which really surprised me. Mick reckoned he was the world champion red claw catcher, which was pretty funny.'

'You have some really good friends. Mum said there's a vet called Eileen who sounds pretty special,' Frances said. Her smile gave away that she was probing into whether Bruce's love life was improving or not.

'You're correct there, Frances,' Bruce meekly replied, 'but she's a good friend, not a girlfriend. All six of our gang get on really well. When I had them out to Bovale for the weekend, it was as good a couple of days as we've all had in a while. We'll probably do it again as soon as we are all free to do it.' Bruce looked up at his sister, 'Would you like to join the show when we next do it? I reckon you'd enjoy it. It'd spice up a visit out there for you.'

'I'd love to, Bruce,' Frances agreed.

'I should ring Lenny before dinner,' Bruce declared, changing the subject, 'just to make sure everything's right for tomorrow.' He went and found his phone and dialled his mate. 'G'day Lenny. Everything ready for tomorrow?' Bruce asked.

'I haven't slept for three days in anticipation,' replied Lenny, laughing heartily. 'Mate, the wife's on my case. She's trying to get me to take sandwiches and that sort of stuff with us. She's more excited than me and she hasn't even met you. Do you eat down the creek, Bruce?'

'Never, Lenny,' Bruce replied. He knew exactly how Lenny felt. Water was all they needed. They'd eat when they got home.

'Beaudy, Bruce,' Lenny said. 'The bride won't like it much, but if she gets it directly from you in the morning, she'll live with it. We'll have smoko when we get home. After we clean all the fish and cook all the crabs that is.'

'You're sounding optimistic, Lenny,' Bruce said. 'Are we going past that fish shop on the way home you were telling me about last time?'

'No, mate. I'm taking you. You're my good luck charm. I can feel it in my bones. We'll get some good catches tomorrow, I'm sure,' Lenny declared.

'Whatever you do, don't feel it in your bones, Lenny,' Bruce told him, laughing. 'None of that feelings stuff. We're going down there to take control and not rely on any luck. Any word around about whether the professional fishers have been in the creek wiping it out lately?'

'Those bastards are always there with their nets and pots, Bruce,' Lenny replied, 'but they can't get them all. There're a few rippers down there with our names on them.'

'Righto, mate, we'll see you at about seven in the morning, after you've had a sleep,' Bruce told him. Lenny laughed heartily and bid his friend good night.

The Arnold family had a very pleasant dinner of fish and chips after Merve eventually arrived home. Bruce slept soundly that night and was up at five o'clock to have breakfast before heading down to Lenny's place.

Bruce always found it a refreshing jolt to his senses, encountering the lush green cane paddocks, coming from the dry tropical environment of Bovale. It was always pleasant; green is a good colour in agriculture. The harvest was in full swing at present. Many cane paddocks had already had their crop removed, leaving them bare other than for residues of the trash burning and stumps of the cane that would ratoon to produce next year's crop. This contrasted with the laser-straight drills of green young cane that had been planted a couple of months earlier and the yet-to-be-cut cane, most of which was metres tall and a tangled mess in its mostly-lodged state. The sugar mill at Giru could be spotted for miles across the coastal plain. It was an amazing factory where, on average every hour, over one thousand tonnes of cane billets are fed into the mill to produce one hundred and fifty tonnes of raw sugar, loaded onto rail wagons for shipping to the Townsville port. Bagasse, the fibre from the crushed cane stalks was used to generate power by the mill. The consequent smoke plus the steam rising from the evaporation pans rose from the mill, twenty-four hours a day at this time of the year.

Twenty minutes after passing Giru, Bruce drove into Lenny's place, only two kilometres out of the small village of Brandon. Off the single-lane bitumen road that serviced the area, Lenny had a manicured crushed-rock driveway of about one hundred metres into his home. The avenue was lined with mango trees that were currently smothered in flowers and smelling beautiful, as always. As he drove up to the impressive low-set red brick home, he could see there was a large machinery shed behind the house where the road led. Parked at the shed was Lenny's four-wheel drive that he recognised from 'the day of the crab', with the boat trailer hitched and ready to go. Bruce realised Lenny was probably in the shed because he could see the glare of blue welding flame and the smoke curling out of the work scene.

Bruce drove to the shed and parked beside Lenny's vehicle. As he got out of the car, a large athletic dog of no particular breed raced out of the shed to see him. The dog looked as happy as any dog Bruce had ever seen, not much of a guard dog, thought Bruce. It never even made a sound, leaving Lenny completely unaware of Bruce's arrival. I'm impressed, Bruce thought; if dogs are like their owners, this must be a great family, not just Lenny. The dog came straight up to him, stopping at Bruce's feet and looking up. It cocked its head at Bruce, as it clearly did not recognise him. Bruce looked down at the big fellow, admiring the shiny black and white coat. The dog clearly wanted a pat and Bruce delivered to expectations.

Bruce could see Lenny, leaning forward in concentration, holding on to some steel that another person was welding. He waited till the weld had finished and the slag was being chipped off before he walked up and called out, 'G'day Lenny. Hey, mate, your dog's attacking me ferociously,' he laughed as the hound pressed in against him, almost demanding to have his ears rubbed.

'Get away, Brutus,' Lenny yelled at the dog. Brutus wasn't too scared of Lenny. He just relaxed his demands of Bruce and stood about a metre away, obviously hoping Bruce would reverse Lenny's command.

'Come here and meet my daughter Therese, Bruce,' Lenny said. It was only then, as she flipped open her welding helmet, that Bruce noticed the welder was a young woman. She removed the helmet and smiled broadly at Bruce as he stepped forward and they shook hands. This woman was stunningly beautiful. He remembered her. She was the nurse who had introduced herself to him at the hospital where he had the mud crab injury dealt with. He was as impressed then as he was now with how Therese presented herself. This lady is special, Bruce thought. But the occasion left him dumb.

'Dad's been raving on about you, Bruce,' Therese said. 'Anyone would think you walk on water the way he talks about you. You must have been telling each other some dreadful lies down the creek that day. I remember you when you came to the hospital. Do you remember me?'

How could I possibly forget, Bruce was thinking. 'Yeah, I remember alright, Therese. Until you got control and took me in to get my toe welded up, I was thinking I'd gone to the wrong shop. Thanks.'

'How's the toe now?' Therese asked.

'Good. Look at that,' Bruce said. Bruce only had on his crocs. He slipped off the left one to show there was hardly a mark. 'Great nursing, Therese,' he declared.

'I didn't do much, Bruce, but I'm glad it's all good now. Just make sure you both stay out of trouble down the creek today,' she added. 'I don't need to see either of you in Emergency again.'

'We'll be saints,' Lenny assured her. As he said this, a lady who was obviously Lenny's wife and Therese's mum came over from the house. 'Bruce, meet my wife, Maria.' They shook hands. Bruce immediately realised why Therese was such a beautiful lady. Maria was also beautiful.

'Nice to meet you, Bruce,' Maria said. 'After all Lenny's said about you, I'm really pleased you're going fishing together.'

'Nice to meet you too, Maria. Lenny told me we'd be back here with a boat full of fish and crabs later this afternoon, so I hope you're hungry,' Bruce suggested.

'That fish and crab you gave to Lenny down the creek that day was superb. Just do that again today and we'll be really good friends. I like fresh fish as long as someone else catches it,' Maria said, smiling broadly.

'Are you blokes having a feed before you go or when you get back?' Therese asked both Lenny and Bruce.

'When we get back, thanks, Therese,' Lenny said.

'Yes, we'll be right till then,' Bruce added. He knew he had to add that, or they would have ended up with an esky full of sandwiches, which is exactly what they didn't want.

'I'll be here, Bruce,' Therese said as she looked up at him. Bruce had no inkling she was as instantly smitten with him as he was with her. Maria, however, certainly didn't miss it.

As Bruce got his gear from his Land Cruiser and loaded it into Lenny's ute, he was trying to reconcile his feelings for Eileen, because this Therese lady had just blown his socks off. Play it cool, he told himself; Therese could be as interested in me as she obviously is in fishing.

Lenny took Bruce to a place he had never fished before to the north-west of Brandon. There was a boat ramp there, which made it easy to get Lenny's boat in the creek. Loaded up, they headed up the creek at full throttle. It was the weekend, so they were not the only people in the creek. Dotted along the creek were the floats of many crab pots. Bruce had slipped off his old Akubra and replaced it with a cap while they were speeding along as the last outcome he wanted was to lose his favourite old hat. Their first task was to bait and set the crab pots. Lenny had eight collapsible pots in the boat. As they sped along, Bruce set about preparing each pot. The bait was mullet that had their fillets taken. Bruce bound each in a strong plastic mesh pocket and tied it to the inside base of the pot. Lenny suggested they simply put the pots out along the creek. If they never caught any crabs this way, they'd find some more inaccessible gullies. As each pot was ready, Lenny would slow down and Bruce tossed it in the water, taking care it would not sink base up and that the float was not entangled. Each float had Lenny's name and phone number on it, which was a legal requirement, and it also enabled them to verify it was their pot when they came to check them. As Bruce tossed each pot, Lenny registered the position on his GPS tracking system so they could easily track directly back to the pot.

Once they set all the pots, Lenny turned the boat around and they headed back down the creek to what Lenny thought might be a good place to fish. The noise of the motor made it difficult to talk over, so Bruce just enjoyed the experience as they planed along. He liked this creek, especially as it widened out with obvious snags that may harbour some decent fish.

Lenny slowed the boat down. 'This should be a good place to wet a line, Bruce,' he said. Lenny had all the latest toys. This included a GPS anchor, obviating the need for a metal anchor as Bruce was accustomed to. The GPS anchor, which resembled a small outboard motor, was locked horizontally on the bow of the boat. As they stopped, Lenny unlocked it into a vertical orientation, sliding the base into the water. The small plastic propellor on the base was controlled by a GPS, keeping the boat in the same spot no matter which way the wind or tide wanted to push it. This could be overridden by a remote control to reposition the boat in any direction.

As soon as Lenny set the GPS anchor, he immediately referred to the display on his sonar fish finder. 'I can see a few good fish, Bruce, but I'm worried I just saw what I suspect is a bull shark pass. If that's the case, he may spook the other fish.'

'The fish don't stand a chance with you around, Lenny,' Bruce remarked.

'I need all the help I can get, Bruce,' Lenny replied with a wicked grin, obviously happy that Bruce was impressed by his range of electronic gadgetry.

'We'll work along this bank here for a bit if that's okay with you, Bruce. I'll control the GPS anchor unless you want to have a go,' Lenny said.

Bruce had a light carbon fibre rod fitted with braid line. He was using an imitation prawn lure made of plastic and infused with a fish attractant that obviously fish liked, even if Bruce didn't think it smelled too fabulous. Bruce cast the lure adjacent to a submerged log, a branch of which came out of the water only two metres from the muddy mangrove-lined bank of the creek. When he cast the lure, he let it sink, then jerked it a bit, before reeling it in a little. This was repetitive to give a fish the illusion the bait was a wounded animal and an easy succulent meal. Repeated casts failed to have any impact on the local fish population that were either absent or not interested in Bruce's antics. Lenny was having the same impact, so after about ten minutes, he decided to shift the boat about twenty metres downstream where there appeared to be another snag, which was another large, submerged log. On his first cast beside the log, Bruce snagged a fish, 'I'm on,' he quietly said to Lenny. This was code to Lenny to get his line out of the water, quickly, to avoid them getting entangled with each other. Lenny was an old hand; he hadn't needed Bruce's cue and he was reeling in his line, eyeing off the landing net stashed against the starboard wall of the boat.

Bruce's line had major arc in it. Lenny noted that Bruce was completely calm, a sign of a great hunter which good fishermen need to be. The fish leapt out of the water, violently tossing its head in a bid to free itself of the hook. It was clearly a good-sized barramundi. 'You've got him, Bruce,' Lenny said, encouraging Bruce. Lenny grabbed the net, ready to scoop it under the fish when Bruce eventually pulled it alongside the boat. The fish bolted, taking at least twenty metres of line with it. Bruce calmly held on, then slowly worked the big fella back towards the boat. This happened several times, before Bruce got the barra to where Lenny could scoop him up with the net.

'Thanks, mate,' Bruce said, admiring the fish. Lenny was as happy as a little boy in a toy shop. He had an old shirt stashed beside him that he pulled out and put over the fish to achieve a stable grip as he removed the hook from its mouth. Lenny then took a grip on the lower lip of the fish as he put his hand under its body, lifting it clear of the net so Bruce could admire it.

Lenny then put the fish against the ruler he had along the side of the boat. 'Seventy-four centimetres, Bruce.' It was terrific to be fishing with someone who knew exactly what to do. It was so much easier than fishing by himself when Bruce often felt like he needed four hands. Today he had that. 'Grab it, Bruce,' Lenny said, which Bruce readily did. Lenny then reached for his mobile phone to get a good photo that he immediately sent to Bruce, Maria and Therese. 'The bride's going to be impressed with you, young fella,' Lenny said.

'Let's see what you can snag, Lenny,' Bruce suggested as they reorganised themselves to cast again. As it so often happens, and despite all the electronic fish-finding gear Lenny had, the only thing they successfully snagged for the rest of the day on their lines was logs. However, every two hours they stopped luring and took off up the creek to check the crab pots. They rarely lifted a pot without a crab in it, but most were jennies or under-sized bucks. They did finish with four legal crabs, which was plenty really. They only needed two each for themselves and their families, as long as the crabs were full of meat, and these crabs showed every sign they were.

They decided to finish the day after doing a run on the crab pots at about two-thirty. As they collected each pot, Bruce cleaned it out and collapsed and stacked it in the centre of the boat. After getting back to the boat ramp, they secured the boat and its contents on the trailer. In the back seat of his dual-cab ute, Lenny had left another esky. The fish and crabs were still in the large esky in the boat. This second esky held ice and cold beers. Just as they were getting in the vehicle to leave,

Lenny pulled one out for himself and Bruce. 'Get this into you, Bruce,' he said. Bruce was pleased. A cold beer as they pulled away from the ramp, heading back to Lenny's place, would help ease the frustrations of casting a lure for four hours without landing anything, after he'd caught the barra.

'I'm keen to do this again, Lenny, if you're up to it at some stage.' Bruce suggested. He had enjoyed fishing with someone who obviously shared the same passion. They would make a good team in the boat any time they went together.

'Me too, Bruce,' Lenny said as he savoured a few sips of his beer, driving slowly away from the boat ramp.

When they arrived at Lenny's place, Brutus bounded out to meet them. He detected the noise of the ute, probably as far away as Brandon as they approached, and was already well down the driveway by the time they turned in. Bruce could see he was very happy to see them as he raced alongside the ute, bouncing up and down trying to see who was in the vehicle.

Lenny pulled the boat and trailer onto a concrete slab beside the shed. This was clearly a wash-down area that Lenny used for farm machinery, very handy for cleaning the boat, which could be a messy task if parked up on dirt. As soon as Bruce opened his door, Brutus was rubbing up against him. 'Get out of there, Brutus,' Lenny yelled, sending Brutus slinking away.

As Brutus backed off, his mood changed as Therese and Maria came out of the house. Brutus ran towards them but knew not to touch them as the ladies held their hands high and told him to back off. 'How'd you go?' Therese asked Bruce.

'I think you've already seen everything we caught,' Bruce replied.

'It was an impressive fish, Bruce,' Therese exclaimed.

'Still is, Therese,' Lenny reminded her. 'Bruce, I want you to take it home with you. Please.'

'Lenny, I'll feel like a criminal if I take the whole fish, seeing we went in your boat. How about we fillet the big dude and we'll share it. You'll have a fish frame for crab bait, too,' Bruce added.

'Bruce, please take the fish,' Maria pleaded. 'You caught it.'

'How long since you've had fresh-caught barra for dinner, Maria?' Bruce asked.

'Ages,' she replied. 'But that's okay.'

'Today, you're taking the whole fish, Maria. I go fishing mainly for crabs. I do like fish, but I like crab better. Besides, we had barra fillets last night, so I have no problem leaving it all with you,' Bruce told Maria.

'Are you sure?' Maria asked, hands crossed on her chest and obviously very happy that Bruce was leaving the fish.

'I'm sure, Maria,' Bruce said.

'Thanks, Bruce,' she said. 'Every time I want a feed of fish, I now know what to do. I'll dial you and tell Lenny to get the boat ready.'

'You're a cruel lady,' Lenny said. 'I clearly remember catching some fish once.' Lenny was portraying absolute innocence.

'You're okay, Dad. You might not have the same knack as Bruce, but I've had plenty of lovely feeds,' Therese offered. 'Enough of this rot because we've made smoko and I'm starving. Let's go get it. The fish and the crabs can wait.'

Therse and Maria went to the house. Bruce waited for Lenny to go in with him. Smoko in the afternoon is solidly entrenched in the local farming communities. Farmers must have needed a break from what appeared to be the monotony of driving up and down in tractors, Bruce thought. He was not going to knock back a smoko. He was starving. And he'd been invited to share a feed with a very impressive lady.

Bruce was impressed with the beautiful décor of the house inside. 'I'm feeling like I need to have a bath before coming in here, Maria,' Bruce admitted.

'Don't be silly, Bruce. It's a home, so just be you,' Maria replied. The house was not new, but certainly had been renovated. Maria had all the toys a modern woman could want, just like her husband had in the boat, Bruce thought. I don't know what they'd make of the Bovale homestead, he wondered; it was clean and sound but quite dated. Maria and Lenny's open plan living area opened out to an impressive rear patio on the house. This is where they were ushered for smoko. Maria and Therese had a feast ready for the pair. Bruce looked at it. I don't have an appetite that'll go close to putting a dent in this, he thought. He retained his counsel, so he accidentally would not offend these ladies who were obviously dead set on impressing him.

After three perfect peach blossoms and several Italian sweets, the names of which eluded Bruce, he was full. The home-brewed coffee made the experience surreal, much better than any restaurant, especially in such terrific company.

'Therese, if we want this man back, we'll set the pots with peach blossoms,' Maria declared. These delightful sweets were two small sponge-cakes set together with a layer of cream icing. The whole thing was then dipped in raspberry jelly to provide pink colour, and then dusted with crushed coconut.

'You'll catch me every time, Maria. I'll be curled up in the pot, gnawing away happily,' Bruce agreed.

Maria and Lenny started to have trouble getting into the conversation as Therese and Bruce focussed on each other, asking each other about their lives. When Bruce described his business, and interesting aspects of how he operated it, they were all impressed by the scale of it. Lenny and Maria were very impressed with the maturity of this young man with responsibility for such a large asset.

Therese was simply impressed, rating Bruce as good a potential friend as she'd encountered. 'I'd love to come up to Bovale if that was possible,' she said.

'I'd love to have you, Therese,' Bruce agreed. Wow, he thought. 'I have this group of friends and we're planning to get together at Bovale some time in the next month or so, Therese. My sister's coming up too. I'll let you know when it's on.'

'I hope it doesn't clash with my shifts, Bruce,' Therese replied. Bruce asked about her roster at the hospital, and he quickly established what weekends would be suitable. He'd make it his business to enable Therese to come.

Before they realised, it was getting late. Lenny had not cleaned his boat. The fish had not been filleted. The crabs were also unattended. Bruce knew he'd better get going back to Townsville soon as he'd promised his family he'd be home for dinner. The four of them went out to the boat where Bruce grabbed his fishing gear and two crabs that he put in an esky he had waiting in his own ute. He thanked Lenny profusely for such a great day. Lenny was happy, really happy and they shook hands firmly. Maria gave him a big hug. 'Thanks again for the barra, Bruce,' she said. 'You come back here soon. We'd love to have you.' Bruce was absolutely sure that offer was completely sincere.

Therese had been standing back, but after her mother had hugged Bruce, there was no holding her back. She hugged him firmly, snuggling her head in his shoulder as surreptitiously as she could. 'Thanks, Bruce. I'll hear from you,' she said as she stepped back, hanging on to his hand that she gradually let slip.

Bruce finally accepted that Therese might think he was okay as a potential friend. He certainly enjoyed that hug, smelling her hair deeply for the brief moment he could, without hopefully either Lenny or Maria realising what he was doing. Maria understood everything that was happening in front of her and was not disappointed. Lenny was thinking about filleting the fish and when he'd next go fishing with his new-found mate.

'I'll be in touch with all of you soon,' promised Bruce. He drove up the driveway towards Brandon, tempted to break into song. But he first must let the family know when he'd be back. About a kilometre down the road, he pulled up and quickly sent a text.

***

Doris had once again cooked a beautiful meal. It was a blade roast, cooked to perfection with stuffing, and laced with vegetables. 'This is so good, Mum,' Bruce said. 'Thank you.'

'Anything for my little boy,' Doris said, looking up at Bruce who was anything but small. 'I think you like it so much because you don't have someone at Bovale to cook for you,' Doris commented.

'When I do, Mum, I'm sure it won't be any better than this,' Bruce replied, genuinely believing what he said.

The evening was terrific, as always. Since Bruce had taught them Oh Hell, it was now almost obligatory for them to have a game. It was way more fun than what the television had to offer. Before they started, Bruce killed both the crabs he had brought; it was an instant death as he skewered each into their body with a screwdriver at the point of the abdominal flap. Bruce cleaned them green and steamed them for fifteen minutes. The card game had to halt as he ducked off to complete each task. Once the crabs were cooked, he sealed one for the family and one for himself to take back to Bovale. Dinner tomorrow night was going to be exceptional, up there with the roast he'd just had.

The next morning, Doris was able to keep Bruce around till after smoko by cooking some sweets that he could take home. Doris really enjoyed doing this for Bruce. Once she had the biscuits packed and Bruce had had smoko, there was no holding him back. He bolted for his haven, Bovale.

Chapter Eight

Bruce arrived back at Bovale in the early afternoon. It was Sunday, so he expected the Wattle family to be relaxing for the day. He did not need Col's help at the moment, so had no plans to annoy them. Just as Bruce walked into the homestead, Simone was on the UHF calling him, 'Bruce, are you on channel?'

Simone sounded worried, with urgency in her voice. 'G'day, Simone. Just back. Everything okay?' he said into the handpiece.

'No, Bruce. We're looking for Lachlan,' she replied.

Bruce experienced a terrible cold shiver through his body. 'Are you home, Simone?' Bruce asked.

'No, Bruce. We've left Carina there by herself, hoping she'll be okay. Can you please check her and then come to the cattle yards as quick as you can?' Simone asked.

'Will do, Simone? Anything else you need?' Bruce asked.

'I don't think so, Bruce,' Simone said. Bruce detected a tone of desperation in her voice.

'Hang in there, Simone. I'll be there soon,' Bruce called back. He put the handpiece down and thought for a moment. He then picked up the phone and dialled his neighbour, Scott Olden. Scott's wife, Wendy, answered the phone. 'Wendy, Bruce here from next door. No time to chat. Sorry. There's a problem here. I've just got home from Townsville. Col and Simone are out desperately looking for Lachlan. Can you please call in a few people around here and help? Most importantly, can you please find a chopper pilot who's available. They will be our best chance I suspect. I know nothing more, other than they're at the cattle yards at this stage. Just tell anyone able to come over we're on channel twenty-three. Thanks. I'll fly. Ah, before I go, maybe best you stay where you are and coordinate if that's okay, please, Wendy? Thanks.' He knew Wendy was a good lady, totally reliable. 'I'll give you a cooee when I know more about what's happening. Thanks.' With that, Bruce hung up and dashed over to check on Carina.

Carina knew Bruce was home and had heard him on the UHF. She was waiting at the front gate when Bruce arrived. She was crying. Bruce crouched down and took her in his arms. 'Carina, tell me what's happened?' he asked.

'Lachlan's missing, Bruce,' she wailed. 'He went for a ride on his bike this morning and hasn't come back.'

'You don't know where he went?' Bruce asked. Carina looked at Bruce, holding her wails and shook her head, tears streaming down her face. It was breaking Bruce's heart. He could not imagine the anguish Col and Simone were experiencing. 'Did he have his UHF on?' Bruce asked. Carina numbly nodded.

'Carina, you can help by being a big girl now. For me, please?' Bruce softly said to her. 'I want you to help everyone who is looking for Lachlan.' Carina looked at Bruce, not understanding, but Bruce could see a slight glimmer of positivity sneaking through the face of misery. 'Some neighbours are coming. We need someone here at the homestead to tell them what to do. Can you do that?' Carina nodded vigorously, her eyes brightening. You know how to work the UHF, so keep listening to that. When someone comes, tell them we are on channel twenty-three. Okay?' Carina nodded. 'Do you have a mobile phone here?'

'Yes, Bruce. Mummy left hers here in case I needed it,' Carina replied.

'Well, one of us may call you on the UHF to make a call using the phone. I know you can do that. Are you still okay here if I leave now?' Bruce asked her.

'I'm okay Bruce,' Carina said, sobbing again.

'We'll find him, Carina. And then you'll be happy and laughing. You wait and see,' Bruce told her. That glimmer of optimism stopped her sobbing. It was time for Bruce to get to the yards.

Bruce charged over to the shed to his motorbike. He'd already donned a harness and fully-charged UHF before he left the house. The bike needed fuelling, which Bruce did as quickly as he could. 'Simone, Bruce here,' he called into the UHF as he was about to get going. 'I'm just leaving the house now. Carina is all good. See you soon.'

'Thanks, Bruce,' Simone called back. Bruce was not hearing an optimistic voice.

It did not take Bruce long to get to the yards. Simone was there, waiting for him, but he could not see Col. He pulled up next to Simone. She'd obviously been riding her bike, looking for Lachlan.

Bruce hugged her. 'Tell me what you know, Simone,' Bruce said, gently.

She looked up to Bruce, tears in her eyes. 'He went out after smoko this morning. He was desperate to do some work. You know Lachlan.'

'Yes, he's a fantastic boy, Simone,' Bruce agreed, nodding.

'Col relented. He told him to put on his UHF and water bottle and to check the trough in the middle of Dingo paddock, the one on the south side, you know, she said. 'Col had found the float arm broken yesterday and fixed it. It looked like pigs in the trough had done it. He knew it needed checking daily for a bit to make sure the pigs didn't cause more problems. That's all he had to do. Col told him, if he saw a problem, not to fix it, but to come home and Col would go back with him to fix it. But he just hasn't come back.' Dingo paddock was about one thousand hectares and one where they usually kept mature cows. It was to the north of Gun Creek on the eastern side of Bovale.

'Where's Col now?' Bruce asked.

'He's still searching, Bruce. He asked me to come back and coordinate some help. As I was coming home, you answered the UHF, so I decided to meet you halfway, here at the yards.'

'I have some people coming, and a chopper with any amount of luck, Simone,' Bruce explained. 'I've asked Wendy from next door to coordinate the help. It may be best we stick with that plan. It would be good if you could stay at the house and help, but I think it'll be better if you get the flying doctor gear together, please, and bring it to the water where Lachlan went. That way we'll also have some transport if we need it. The most likely outcome is he won't be too far from there, so best we have the help as close as possible when we need it. Bring it out in your dual-cab ute too, please.' Simone nodded. Bruce went on, 'Before you come out, can you please work out the coordinates for that water point? Leave a copy with Carina and she can pass them on if needed. Bring out some snacks for Col too; he'll need them. And chuck a jerry can of petrol in too please in case we need it. I'll get going and hook up with Col.'

With that, Bruce accelerated away from the yards on his motorbike. He had an in-built speaker and microphone, blue-toothed to his UHF, that he normally used when mustering. This would be very useful today. As Bruce approached the southern Dingo paddock water, Bruce held the speaker switch, 'Col, can you hear me, mate. Bruce here.'

Col immediately responded, 'I'm here, Bruce. I'm about halfway across to the water on the boundary with Stocking paddock.' Bruce immediately orientated Col as around two kilometres north-west of the water Lachlan had gone to check.

'Where have you checked and what do you think I should do, Col?' Bruce radioed back.

'I was a bit random to start with, Bruce, but now I'm trying to do some sort of grid pattern, south-east to north-west across the paddock, moving about fifty metres to the north-east at each crossing.' This matched the geography of the paddock, which was long and narrow, widening as it extended to the north-east boundary of Bovale. I found Lachlan's tyre tracks at the water, so he'd definitely been there. But I just couldn't pick up where he'd gone as the cattle have since come in for water and wiped out most of the clues.'

'That sounds spot-on, Col. Keep tracking exactly like that. If you like, I'll do something similar and work back the other way,' Bruce suggested.

'Perfect, Bruce,' Col radioed back.

'I have a few others coming to help too, Col. So, have a think about a plan for them too. And with any amount of luck, we'll get a chopper here soon as well,' Bruce added.

'You are a champion, Bruce,' Col called. 'Thanks, mate.'

'How's your fuel, Col?' Bruce asked.

'It's good thanks, Bruce,' Col replied.

'Simone is bringing out a snack for you and the flying doctor pack if we need it when we pick Lachlan up. When you're back on the southern fence line, rip down and top up if Simone's back too,' Bruce said.

'Thanks, Bruce. I'll keep going till then,' Col said.

The two men then methodically continued their searching, slowly moving across the paddock, standing on their bike pegs to see as well as they could, hoping they would not miss any signs of Lachlan. It was a slow, heart-breaking task. Their concentration was enormous, and both would need a good feed when it finished. The tall dry grass at this time of the year ensured it would not be easy for a ground searcher to pick up Lachlan, but they had to keep trying until a chopper arrived.

About forty-five minutes later, Bruce picked up the radio call of a chopper pilot, 'Bovale, Bovale, Ian Spencer here, approaching from the west in an R22.' The R22 was a small two-seat helicopter favoured by mustering pilots. Bruce could hear the rotor blades of the chopper as Ian spoke. He knew Ian was a good operator. Ian could still be a fair distance away as the elevation of helicopters enabled much greater transmission.

'Ian, Bovale here. Bruce Arnold speaking,' Bruce radioed back.

'Got you loud and clear, Bruce,' Ian responded, which indicated to Bruce he was closer than he thought and approaching fast.

'Righto, Ian. Simone, are you on channel?' Bruce called.

'I can hear you, Bruce,' Simone radioed.

'Simone, can you please read those coordinates of the water point to Ian?' Bruce called. Simone immediately read them to Ian who repeated them back to be sure he had them. Bruce then cut back into the conversation. 'Ian, Bruce here. As Simone said, that water point is where Lachlan has disappeared from. Can you please go to that point and start working a circular search pattern?'

'Will do, Bruce,' Ian called back.

'On the way, can you please fly past the homestead and check along the road to that water. It's fairly much in a line, probably about fifty degrees?'

'Will do, Bruce,' Ian responded.

Bruce felt a lot more confident now Ian was on the scene. Visibility from the air was immeasurably superior to what they could achieve on the ground. In addition, the speed of checking was far greater. Bruce didn't think Ian would need a second person on board to help spot, but he'd ask him if he did not have quick success in finding Lachlan.

'Col, Bruce here,' he called.

'Yes, I got all of that, thanks Bruce.' Col had correctly guessed why Bruce was checking in on him.

'How far away are you, Simone?' Bruce called.

'I'm in the paddock now, Bruce, heading up to the water,' Simone called back.

'Col, might be smart if you take that quick break now, mate. You may need some energy once we find Lachlan,' Bruce radioed.

'Roger, Bruce,' Col called back. Col was getting very tired, and the suggestion was exactly what he needed. He took stock of exactly where he was as a set-off point later, and then went directly back to the water to meet up with Simone. Simone had the feed ready for Col by the time he arrived. Both of them were silent in their grief. They knew there was nothing more they could be doing other than what was being done. The chopper had arrived at the water and hovered briefly, radioing in that he was starting his search pattern.

Ian had only been searching for less than ten minutes. 'Found him,' he radioed. This stopped everyone in their tracks. Bruce and Col switched off the bikes so they could hear more clearly. They could hear the chopper directly to the south of the water where Lachlan had been, towards Gun Creek, and in Kenworth paddock, not where they were. 'He's on the ground and moving; he knows I'm here. What's your instructions please, Bruce?' Ian called.

'Thanks, Ian. Can you please stay about two hundred metres to the north of him till we get there? And while you wait, see if you can raise anyone else who might be coming that we've already picked him up,' Bruce called.

'Roger,' Ian called.

There was a gate between the paddocks at the water. It was the best access point. Col and Bruce came directly in. Simone had the gate open for them, Col first, only minutes after the call, and closely behind him, Bruce. Neither waited for the other. They gunned their bikes directly for Lachlan. Simone shut the gate and followed at a more sedate pace. It was only about one kilometre to Lachlan. As Simone approached, she heard Bruce radio, 'We've got him, Ian. Thank God, he looks okay.' The words welled up tears Simone never knew she had left. She had to stop the ute for fear of having an accident herself. 'Ian, can you please call the RFDS?' Bruce called, words that made Simone freeze with fear.

'Tell them he'll need fixed-wing evacuation. It looks like he has a leg fracture and maybe an arm,' Bruce called.

'Roger, Bruce,' Ian called back.

Col had arrived at the scene first. He found Lachlan lying beside his motorbike. He still had his helmet on, but with the visor down he would have been perspiring freely. He'd be thirsty. 'Lachlan, Dad here,' Col said as he knelt beside Lachlan.

'Sorry, Dad,' Lachlan feebly replied.

'It's all okay, mate. Please don't be sorry. You relax and we'll get you sorted,' Col told him gently. This was easier said than done for Col. He was tearing up himself and felt a bit of vertigo. He stopped himself. Breathe easy, he told himself. Col's first action was to open the visor of the helmet.

Bruce arrived on Col's tail. The two men assessed the situation as best they could. It appeared as if he'd simply fallen off his bike. The reason was not obvious, nor why he was where he was. Lachlan was belly-down. His left leg was at an awful angle below the knee, obviously being broken. Lachlan's left arm was under his body. Lachlan had his head partly twisted to his right so at least he wasn't face-down. 'Where does it hurt, Lachlan?' Col asked.

'My leg and my arm under me, Dad,' Lachlan squeezed out.

'Does your head, your neck or your back feel sore at all, Lachlan,' Col asked.

'I think they're okay, Dad. It's just the leg and the arm. It hurts too much to move, which is why I couldn't radio,' Lachlan apologised. Bruce was immediately relieved that Lachlan could feel the pain in his leg. No pain would have indicated potential spinal damage, a disaster.

It didn't mean that was not the case, but they had to be very careful not to create a problem.

While Col was asking these questions, Bruce had his water bottle out. He radioed the situation and instructions to Ian in his chopper. He then added, 'Ian, can you go back to the homestead, please? I have a UHF in the kitchen. You'll get mobile reception there too. I think we'll need you there.' Bruce then tried to get some moisture to Lachlan's lips. They trickled it out and Lachlan lapped it like a puppy.

Simone arrived. She quickly came in and knelt beside Col over their son, giving him shade. 'Mummy's here, Lachlan,' she said, hoping that would help him relax.

'Before we move him, I'll try and get instructions,' Bruce said. He stood up and radioed Ian. 'Can you hear me, Ian,' called Bruce.

'Loud and clear, Bruce,' Ian called back.

'Ian, can you please get a doctor on the radio and act as a relay for us?' Bruce asked.

'Will do Bruce, I'll radio that in now, and then use the mobile phone once I've got the chopper parked,' Ian responded.

Bruce, Col and Simone had to wait almost another ten minutes before Ian landed the R44, shut it down, and then got to the homestead and called back, which seemed like an eternity. In that time, Simone talked gently to Lachlan, who was remarkably composed. He was lucid but obviously in considerable pain. Bruce and Col set about working out the best way to get Lachlan back to the homestead. They realised a stretcher would be useful. Bruce quickly cut two saplings of about two metres with a small axe he always carried in the Land Cruiser. They thought the best strategy was to use both of their shirts as the bed, with the saplings fed through either side and through the sleeves. But until they had instructions, they kept their shirts on.

'Bruce, are you on channel?' Ian radioed.

'Here, Ian,' Bruce called back.

'Tell us what you have, Bruce. I have a doctor on speaker phone so with luck you can talk directly if I do the handpiece of the UHF,' Ian said. Simone teared up, elated at this development. Col held his hand at her back as she gently stroked Lachlan where he wasn't sore.

'Hello, Bruce,' the doctor said. The transmission was not perfect, but it was good enough to do the job.

Bruce described the situation as best he could to the doctor. He then said, 'My assessment doc would be he's okay to move, but it'll help a lot if we can use some pain management. We're ready to get him to the homestead if you just give us the instructions.'

From Bruce's description, the doctor agreed. 'In the RFDS kit, you'll find some OxyContin five milligram tablets. Can you get half a tablet, crush it, and add a tiny bit of sugar, if you have it, and water to make a paste for Lachlan?'

'Will do,' replied Bruce. Col immediately set to the task, with Simone ready to help get the medication into Lachlan.

'That will give him some pain relief, but it may take ten to fifteen minutes before it works. After that, please use your best judgement on how to get him to the plane. We are leaving Townsville soon. If you need me on the way, just call.' The doctor was used to the station people being so incredibly resourceful and sensible. He had confidence these people would get it right.

Lachlan willingly ate the paste that had no sugar, but he didn't like it much. 'Sorry, mate,' Col said. Simone was crying. She couldn't bear to look at the twisted leg and she knew it was not going to be any better once they saw what had happened to his arm. She composed herself as best she could and trickled some water to Lachlan to help him dilute the paste taste in his mouth. Once Col was satisfied Lachlan had the tablet down the hatch, he and Bruce took off their shirts and rigged up the stretcher on Lachlan's left side as he lay, so they could roll him in. It took over ten minutes before Lachlan admitted the pain was starting to abate a bit. 'We'll wait another couple of minutes, Lachlan, till we're sure, and then we'll shift you.

'I'm sorry, mate,' Col went on, 'but even though you've had that muck, it's still going to hurt like hell. We'll do our best. We just have to get you to the plane.' Lachlan said nothing. He was terrified, though he didn't realise that his parents were equally terrified.

'Let's do this,' Bruce said quietly. 'Hang in there, Lachlan.' The first thing they did was remove the helmet. Lachlan was clearly sweating profusely and dehydrated. Simone helped him drink some more water before they went any further. She knelt at Lachlan's head and support-ed it, turning it slowly as the men did their part. Bruce had volunteered to take what he considered the worst role, which was turning the twisted leg. Col knelt over the stretcher and Lachlan, and slowly lifted the right side of his body with grips under Lachlan's shoulder and pelvis.

Once they began, they could not stop. This is the worst day of my life, thought Bruce as he held back nausea, watching the leg he was nursing move unnaturally as they turned Lachlan; I can't imagine just how much worse it is for Col and Simone. As they rolled Lachlan slowly, he screamed out, 'My leg, my leg.' The sound was dreadful, but they all held their nerve and kept going. Then Lachlan started screaming about the pain in his arm. As he rolled, they could see his left arm was also at an awful angle halfway between the elbow and wrist, clearly broken as well. The only good fortune was, there was no obvious compound fracture. The skin was not broken. Lachlan was now weeping loudly. 'Please stop,' he wailed again and again. But they knew they couldn't.

Finally, they had Lachlan on his back, with his left arm resting across his body. Simone decided not to unclip the UHF harness as it could not be pulled out from under Lachlan without causing more pain for him. His broken left leg was resting alongside his intact leg. All four of them were panting from the exertion and fear. But once Lachlan was on the stretcher, they could all breathe more easily. 'That's the worst of it, Lachlan,' Bruce told him. Lachlan's face was a distressing sight. It was streaked with the moisture of his tears, mixed with dirt. His eyes were red. He was still weeping, but more quietly.

Col and Bruce then gently lifted the stretcher. The weight of Lachlan pulled the two sides towards each other, which the men attempted to counter as best they could. Bruce walked backwards to the open door of the rear seats of the dual-cab ute. He then crawled in backwards and across the seat and out the other side, all the while holding Lachlan as steadily as he could. Col had the other end, at Lachlan's head. Simone held Lachlan's good hand on his right side. Lachlan never experienced anywhere near the pain during this that he'd just been through, judging by his subdued reaction. However, Simone was concerned as the grip his small hand had on hers became very firm and was slightly stronger each time there was any wobble in the stretcher. Once they had Lachlan on the back seat, they carefully slid out the support saplings. The plan was to replace them when it came time to get him out again, which was the reason the saplings were put in the back of the ute.

'Col, I'll drive,' Bruce said. 'You get ahead quickly and pack an overnight bag for Simone and meet us at the airstrip. With any amount of luck, Simone can go on the plane.'

'Good plan, Bruce,' Col replied, as he got on his bike and took off quickly, back to the homestead.

Lachlan was too tall to enable Simone to sit in the back. They had positioned Lachlan so his head was behind the driver's seat. Simone had to sit in the front. She pushed back her chair as far as it would go, giving her as much access as was comfortably possible for them both, before they set off, slowly. They were not driving on a well-maintained sealed road. Rather, they were going cross country, which caused many small bumps, no matter how carefully Bruce drove. He just kept going as carefully and as quickly as he dared. Bruce looked across at Simone regularly. Her face was fixed on Lachlan. It was contorted in fear, grief and pain. Tears streamed down her face as she consoled her boy while they drove along.

The trip was about thirteen kilometres, taking them forty minutes. They were just passing the yards, with about six kilometres to go, when they heard the RFDS pilot radio Ian, ensuring it was okay to land. Bruce always kept the one point three kilometre-long airstrip stock-free and in excellent condition. He had thought he might never use it, and the cost of doing this might be wasted. As he drove along, he thanked his stars he had been so diligent.

Once they arrived at the airstrip, the magnificent King Air B350, a twin-engine aircraft, was already parked, ready to take them. The doctor and nurses were ready, standing beside a collapsible stretcher fitted with medical accessories. Bruce drove up presenting them with Lachlan, feet first. It was a blur for all of them then. The medical team was brilliant. They summed up the situation very quickly. Before moving Lachlan, a drip was inserted in his right arm and he was heavily sedated. Simone was still finding tears, a mix of sad and happy ones, but she, Col and Bruce could do little more than watch. Bruce knew Col had on his bravest face, as he was sure he'd cry soon, but it just didn't happen. Col had been so focussed on the practicalities of saving his son, he was able to push aside his emotions so far.

The doctor's assessment matched Bruce's; the major injuries were a broken arm and a broken leg. They would get him to the Townsville University Hospital emergency department as quickly as possible, x-ray him, and then treat him once they were sure they knew what was required. After Lachlan had been transferred to the plane, Bruce retrieved his shirt from the back seat of the ute and donned it. He would have copped a bit of sunburn from not wearing it, but that was absolutely nothing against what Lachlan was dealing with. The pilot seated Simone safely where she could observe proceedings *en route*. With little fanfare, the plane and its precious cargo took off for Townsville.

Col stood watching. His heart was broken. He was empty. His beautiful boy was broken. His wife was away. There were several people there to witness this, apart from Bruce who stood silently as well. Scott from next door had arrived as had another two neighbours. Ian, the chopper pilot, had brought Carina down to the strip so she could see her brother safely head off to Townsville. Carina tugged on Col's hand, 'Daddy, is Lachlan okay?' she asked.

Col looked down at his stunning little six-year-old daughter with the first of a few tears appearing at the corner of his eyes. 'Yes, honey,' he replied. 'He's a bit broken just now, but they'll weld him back together and he'll be as good as ever,' Col said, forcing a smile.

'Smoko time,' Bruce said, glad he'd recently experienced the afternoon version of it, even if that had only been the previous day under extraordinarily different circumstances. Bruce thanked everyone sincerely and invited them back to the homestead for a cup of tea. Smoko didn't last long as Bruce remembered he needed to recover his motorbike and make sure all the gates were shut, something he ignored as they brought Lachlan across the station. As only first-class people and neighbours would, Wendy and Scott had brought dinner for everyone with them. They decided the least they could do was get everyone fed properly. Bruce was overcome with emotion when Wendy told him this. He thanked her tearfully. 'Scott, would you be able to drop me back to the bikes please, mate?' Bruce asked. 'That'll save Col coming out, and he needs to be here with Carina.' Scott was only too happy to do this while Wendy took brief control of the homestead.

As Bruce and Scott drove out to collect the motorbikes, both were silent for a while. Scott could clearly see Bruce was still in shock from the day's events. They had just passed the yards. Bruce shut a gate and climbed back into Scott's ute. 'I wonder why Lachlan was where he was and what he was doing?' Bruce said, half to himself, but also to Scott.

Scott could not answer. He still had not been to the scene and had insufficient context to formulate any hypotheses. 'I think the answer is pretty easy to find, Bruce,' he replied. 'Lachlan will be able to tell you himself, once he's back in one piece again.'

'Yeah,' agreed Bruce. 'No point in producing conjecture. Lachlan is not a reckless young boy, so there must have been a compelling reason for it. No matter, as you say, we'll find out in a day or two.' The men let the topic lay till they arrived where Lachlan's and Bruce's bikes were parked. Both of them silently surveyed the scene, slowly scanning for any clues for the cause of the accident. Bruce had his mobile phone and took a photo of the spot where Lachlan had fallen, looking back towards the water where he had come from. Scott and Bruce walked slowly together back across the approach to the fall. One dislodged small stick was their only lead, but it told them almost nothing. They loaded Lachlan's undamaged bike onto the back of Scott ute and headed back to the homestead.

Dinner was sombre. Wendy had ensured Col and Carina came over to the homestead to join them. It was a simple but delicious stew Wendy had cooked. 'Thanks Wendy,' Bruce said as he finished. 'What you and Scott have done for all of us here today is brilliant. You are wonderful people. Thanks.' Bruce's sincerity was no surprise to Wendy. She knew this young man was special. It was just disappointing to have to see him shine under such dire circumstances.

'Col, I rang Mum earlier and told her,' Bruce said. 'She was upset as you can imagine. But more importantly, she wants you and Simone and Carina to stay with them while you're in Townsville. It will save you the difficulty of finding a place and paying for it. And Mum and Dad will be very happy to have you.'

'Daddy, can we stay with Mrs Arnold please?' Carina pleaded with Col, obviously quite excited at the prospect.

'I expect we can,' Col said to her. 'Thanks, Bruce. That would be terrific. Who knows what we're in for with Lachlan. If it's okay with you, now I'm feeling a bit better, would it be fine if Carina and I took off for Townsville now? If Simone knows we're coming and we have a bed, she will have two major issues less to worry about.'

'I'm sure that'll be fine, Col. I'll ring Mum and let her know you'll be late. Give her a call when you get to the hospital, and you can organise the details then. I'll let her know what's happening,' Bruce replied.

After making sure everyone was right, Bruce eventually had a bath and got himself into bed. He was exhausted and it didn't take long for the sleep genie to take him away. It was one o'clock in the morning when Bruce woke, hearing his phone ringing. He felt awful dread as he raced to find his mobile, easy to spot, brightly buzzing in the kitchen darkness. 'Bruce here,' he answered groggily.

'Bruce, I'm so sorry to ring, but I couldn't stop thinking about you and just had to check you're okay and to let you know everything is okay here. It's Therese here.'

'Therese?' Bruce stammered, his forehead creasing with worry. 'What's wrong?'

'Nothing, Bruce,' she replied. 'You would not have known but I was at the hospital and in the team that met Lachlan when he came in. I had no idea who he was or where he was from until I went to see his mum as I went off my shift. We had a good chat and it was Simone who filled me in.'

'How are they, Therese?' Bruce asked, coming fully awake now.

'They're both well, Bruce,' she replied. 'This really shouldn't be coming from me, but it's only what Simone and Col can tell you anyway. The doctors assessed Lachlan and he should be fine. But they're holding him under heavy sedation till his body settles a bit more before they plate both his leg and his arm. Simone is really upset but happy Lachlan will be okay. I waited with her by Lachlan's side till Col and Carina came. They've all gone over to your parents' place now for a sleep. They'll be back after the surgery tomorrow, which will hopefully finish about lunch time.'

'Thanks, Therese, for letting me know. I can sleep a whole lot better now. Sorry that my worries have made your job a bit harder, but what you have done for Simone would have been really appreciated by her. Thanks. Col and Simone are gold to me,' Bruce added.

'Bruce, I am really happy to help. I was wondering after you were at our place how long it would be before we could get together again and then this happens. I should let you get back to sleep, which is also where I need to be too,' Therese said.

'Righto, thanks, Therese. I'll talk to you soon,' Bruce said as he hung up. He stood there, a bit dazed, but really happy his new friend had rung with some good news.

Chapter Nine

Change at Bovale was on hold. Bruce was going nowhere. Most of his energies were focussed on ensuring his cattle had on-going supplies of water and supplement and they remained under control. When he could, he was back at the homestead, at the kitchen table, writing down his thoughts on what was needed to get the changes underway. Bruce's ideas evolved somewhat randomly, and to avoid them being lost and to help retrieve them from their disparate development, Bruce started a section for each new strategy on separate pages within the same notebook. He planned to wait till Col could get back to the station and back in the groove of the station's work, before advancing the ideas into reality.

On Monday afternoon, Col rang to tell him the surgery had gone well, and Lachlan was back together with an excellent prognosis. The breaks were bad, but had not involved any joints or growth plates, which made full recovery a much more likely outcome. Col suggested he probably should come home as he was not achieving much in

Townsville. Bruce told him to stay there while Simone and Lachlan were there as they would need him, even if Col did not think so.

Col rang again the next day while they were visiting Lachlan in the hospital. 'He's back, Bruce. He's back.' Col was clearly elated that his son was in recovery and doing well.

'Has Lachlan told you what happened?' Bruce asked.

'Yes, Bruce,' Col replied. 'Yeah, when he got to the water, there were two dingoes there, chewing into what looked like a calf carcass. He wouldn't have known it, but it could only have been an abortion as no calves are due to be born for a couple of months. Anyhow, his reaction was to think the dingoes had killed it and he got angry and raced at them on his bike, but they just took off into Kenworth paddock. So, he went through the gate and got after them. He said they just kept trotting and galloping out of range, making it impossible to get close. He just wanted to run one over and kill it for what he thought they'd done. He said he was going fast, and he tried to change direction too quickly as he went over a stick, which threw the back wheel sideways, sending him head over turkey.'

'Scott and I saw the stick. Now I understand what happened. Mystery solved,' Bruce offered.

'I don't think he'll be out chasing dingoes any day soon again, Bruce,' Col said. 'Hang on. Simone wants to chew your ear.' Col handed the phone to his wife.

'Bruce, I haven't said thanks for everything on Sunday. You were wonderful. Col and I are in awe of what you did for us. Thanks. I'll give you a bear hug when we get home,' Simone said.

'I just did what had to be done Simone. I am just incredibly pleased Lachlan is going to be fine again. That was my main concern. How's he doing?' Bruce asked.

'He's good, Bruce,' she replied. 'The surgery sites look pretty awful, but at least his arm and his leg don't have those awful bends they had in them when we found him. I'm still having nightmares every time I think about it,' Simone admitted.

'What sort of progress timeline have they suggested, Simone?' Bruce asked.

'Overall, they think he'll be walking okay within a month, which is amazing,' Simone replied. 'His problem though is having both a broken leg and broken arm on the same side. We're here till he can be fitted with a wheelchair to enable us to look after him at home. By the time we get that organised and Lachlan is well enough to not need constant medical attention, it'll probably be Friday. We are really keen to get home.'

'I bet you are, Simone. Hospital is never a good place,' Bruce suggested.

This statement immediately lit up a huge grin on Simone's face, but Bruce couldn't see that as she said, 'And Bruce.' She paused.

Bruce was worried. He had an awful premonition that something bad was coming. 'What?' he replied, tentatively, not wanting to hear any more bad news.

'Hospitals can be okay,' Simone said, rather jauntily. 'I met Therese.' Bruce didn't say anything for a moment as Simone paused. 'She's wonderful, Bruce. You never told us.'

'Hang on, Simone,' Bruce protested. 'What has Therese been telling you?'

'Bruce, I know you're not boyfriend and girlfriend, but oh my, is she smitten with you,' beamed Simone.

This cracked the biggest smile on Bruce's face that he'd experienced in a while, but he wasn't going to be admitting too much or get ahead of any situation. 'We're just friends and we've only just met, Simone,' he suggested. Bruce knew immediately that his whole family would now be aware of Therese, as Simone would definitely have shared these pearls with his mother, which meant Frances would also be full bottle on her. At least he knew his dad would retain his counsel, even if Simone did something completely outrageous and invite Therese around to his parents' place. He could only hope Therese would baulk at the invitation; knowing the little he did about her, he was confident she would.

'Hang on, Bruce. Carina wants to say hello,' Simone said, as her daughter stood in front of her with hands out to her mother indicating she wanted the phone.

'Hello, Bruce. I met your girlfriend. She's lovely,' Carina declared proudly and innocently down the phone.

Bruce had to play this one carefully. 'Yes, Carina. Therese is a really lovely lady. But she's not my girlfriend, you know.'

'Well, I think she should be, Bruce,' Carina declared.

'We'll see,' Bruce replied. 'How's Lachlan?'

'He's good, Bruce. Dad reckoned if he was a cow, we'd have to shoot him. I think that's awful, but Lachlan thinks it's funny,' Carina responded.

'Fair enough, Carina. Can I have Mum back please?' Bruce asked.

Bruce wanted to get back on topic. 'When you get Lachlan home, Simone, will you need anything to help him?'

'Col and I think we'll cope okay, thanks Bruce,' Simone replied.

'Let's just see how it goes,' Bruce agreed. 'If we need to do more, we'll find a solution.'

Simone hesitated for just a second. 'Don't ever wonder why we think you are amazing, Bruce. It's not just Therese who has you on the top shelf,' she added, just to be sure Bruce never missed her opinion.

'Thanks, Simone,' Bruce said, mightily humbled. 'I guess I'll be seeing you on the weekend some time?' Simone agreed and they finished the call.

Mick rang that night. 'Bruce, gee, when I heard the news about Lachlan, I was shocked. Is he okay?'

'Amazingly good after what he's been through, Mick,' Bruce told him.

'Everything okay at Bovale?' Mick asked.

'Yes, thanks, Mick. I'm here with my friends at present but I have everything under control. The Wattle's will be back on the weekend and life will be back to normal pretty quickly. I'm looking forward to that after Sunday's effort,' Bruce added.

'I bet you are,' Mick said. 'Do you reckon another Bovale weekend would be in order one day soon?' Mick asked. 'I'm keen to see if those barra are really there or not.'

'How about we leave it a few weeks, Mick,' Bruce suggested. 'I'm actually pretty keen, but Col and I have to rejig a fair bit around here and we'll be short on time. Also, I'm keen to go easy on Col so he can look after Lachlan as much as possible.'

'I'm okay with that, Bruce,' Mick agreed. If I see any of the gang, I'll let them know.' Mick had tried to sound innocent, but Bruce sensed they were already planning to head out whenever Bruce gave the green light. He was pleased. It would be terrific to have another weekend together like they'd had. Not everyone had such good friends as he had.

'Mick, let me know when you mob in town have a suitable weekend coming up and I'll see if it matches my situation. When I was in Townsville the other day, I took the liberty of inviting my sister, Frances, to join us when we do it. Hope that's okay with you?' Bruce suggested.

'Sounds fantastic, mate,' Mick said. He indicated he'd be in touch before they finished the phone call.

On Thursday night, Wayne Greenhough rang. 'Just got your sperm morphology results back, Bruce,' he said. 'I've put that together with the other assessments we did on the day and am about to email it to you. If you can get on the computer, I can talk you through what it means, right now if that suits you.'

'It would,' replied Bruce. 'Just hang on while I relocate myself and turn it on. I've just finished dinner. How about I ring you back in about ten minutes? Will that work?' Wayne agreed it would, giving Bruce a bit of time to sort himself out and be ready to discuss the bull results with Wayne.

When he was ready, Bruce rang Wayne. 'Let me have it. Hopefully good news.'

'Well, fairly good, Bruce,' Wayne replied. 'As you'll remember, we knocked out four early last week.' Early last week, Bruce exclaimed to himself. That seemed like a month ago, so much had been happening at Bovale. Wayne went on, 'There's another four that have failed morphology. Disappointing, but the sort of outcome we'd expect in bulls that have not previously been put under the microscope, so to speak.' Bruce had Wayne's spreadsheet open on the computer. Wayne had highlighted the failures in red.

'Can you explain what's happened in each of those bulls, please Wayne?' Bruce asked.

'Sure, Bruce,' Wayne responded. He went on to show that each had in excess of fifty percent abnormal sperm, with one having only thirteen percent normal sperm.

'That's good, but if a bull has, say, thirty percent normal sperm, and he has a sperm-rich ejaculate, doesn't that mean he has way more than enough normal sperm to achieve a threshold fertilisation rate?' Bruce asked.

'The problem these bulls have, Bruce, is not how many apparently-normal sperm they have,' replied Wayne. 'Having more than fifty percent abnormal sperm is a direct indicator of dysfunction. So, for example, a bull with a low percent normal sperm might still achieve fertilisation, but then the probability of embryo survival is low. It's not so much that a bull needs a lot of normal-looking sperm, but that he needs to be producing sperm that are functionally-adequate. That's just one reason why sperm morphology is such a vital test. There is no value in having a bull with good genes if he cannot deliver them for fertilisation, especially in competition with other bulls.

'Another issue with lowered conception rates when percentage normal sperm is low, is the potential for delayed conception patterns, which then delays calving, which then reduces weaner size and may also contribute to lowered ability of cows to re-conceive during lactation. Those are direct financial penalties, though the truth is this outcome is unlikely if there are other bulls present that can cover for the dud. Again, the dud cannot adequately contribute to the gene pool.

'A third problem with low percent normal sperm is that this trait has a strong genetic correlation with ability to re-conceive during lactation. That means that, even when he does sire female progeny, when they come to breeding, even when mated to fertile bulls, they have delayed conceptions. Again, this is a direct cost to the business.'

'I'm getting the picture, Wayne,' Bruce agreed. 'I'm really pleased we've now identified eight dud bulls, though I'm quite stirred up about the business having unknowingly invested in dud bulls. No way is this going to happen again.'

'You'll be pleased to know, Bruce, that within that group of thirty-two apparently-useful bulls you have left, there are going to be some more serious duds,' Wayne reminded him. 'They'll be fertile alright. And they'll look okay, even grand. But the DNA testing we're doing will clearly show they'll be carefully delivering dud genetics. The genomics we're waiting for should deliver some really useful outcomes for you. I predict you'll want to cull more than twelve of what you have left, but you'll have to compromise and keep some bulls that are average.'

'I'm glad you're softening me up now, Wayne,' Bruce responded. 'Now I'm getting even keener on breeding some of our own bulls, maybe even a lot of them. But that also has its limitations, I can see, if we don't get the right foundation sire.'

'You are absolutely correct, Bruce,' Wayne replied.

'You may not have realised that you've just led me into embarking on finding a seriously-good bull, Wayne,' Bruce stated. 'This could be tricky but it sure will be a lot of fun.'

'Glad to hear it, Bruce,' Wayne commented. 'How are you and Col going with all the other strategies we started working on last week?'

'I hate to tell you, Wayne, but we've stalled,' Bruce replied. 'You probably didn't realise the world nearly came to an end here on Sunday.' Bruce went on to give a synopsis of what had occurred.

'So sorry to hear all that, Bruce,' Wayne said. 'When you're ready, get back to me. In the meantime, I'll be back to you as soon as those breeding values get calculated.' The men finished up their discussion soon after.

***

The Wattle family arrived home at lunch time on Saturday, six days after the accident. Doris had rung Bruce with their expected arrival time, which enabled him to have a plate full of fresh corned beef and pickles sandwiches, just as he knew they liked them, sitting on the table on the front porch of their home when they arrived. He had also added some individually-wrapped peppermint chocolates, an absolute favourite of Simone's, in a bowl beside the sandwiches. He was servicing his motorbike in the machinery shed when they arrived.

Carina was first out of the car. He saw her reach back in and extracted a plastic ten-litre bucket that had been on the floor where she had been sitting. She raced over to Bruce with the bucket. 'I've got a present for you, Bruce,' she announced, breathless and rosy with excitement. Bruce waited, wondering what on earth he was in for. As she pulled up in front of him, he peered into the bucket, at the bottom of which was a large mud crab, tied up.

'Wow,' Bruce said. 'Where did you catch that?'

'I didn't catch it Bruce,' she declared. 'Therese gave it to us when we left the hospital. She said her dad caught it for you.'

The situation was indeed looking rosy, Bruce thought. Not only is Therese one hell of a lady, she knows the sort of presents I like. 'Thanks, Carina,' Bruce said. 'How is it to be home again?' he asked as he took the bucket from her and placed it on the shed bench. He'd deal with the crab later. First priority was to help the family.

'It's good, Bruce. I liked staying with Mrs Arnold. She's nice.'

'Did you see Frances?' Bruce asked.

'Yes, she came up to the hospital when Therese was there,' Carina innocently replied. Uh oh, thought Bruce, before I know it my family will be better acquainted with Therese than I am.

Bruce ambled over to the ute adjacent to the right rear passenger door where Lachlan was sitting. Lachlan had opened the door, patiently waiting for assistance. Bruce reached forward and took Lachlan's right palm and gently shook it, looking him squarely in the eye, 'Welcome home, mate. Crikey it's good to see you back here and looking as well as you do. How do you feel?'

'Thanks, Bruce,' Lachlan said. 'I'd be a lot better if I didn't feel like a scrub bull tied up in the bush. Give it a few weeks and they'll take the ropes off. Hopefully they'll feed me and bring me a drink while I'm down.' Lachlan had obviously been thinking how he was going to greet Bruce. He liked to put a bright and slightly-comical perspective on whatever was happening. Bruce shook Col's hand and gave Simone a hug before picking up bags from the back of the ute and carrying them over to their house.

Col lifted Lachlan's wheelchair out and set it up. He then gently lifted Lachlan out of the car and onto the chair. 'How's that?' he asked Lachlan.

'Perfect, Dad,' Lachlan replied as Col took the chair and wheeled him over to the house where he backed up to the stairs. Bruce needed no instructions. He was reading the moves. He came in and grabbed the base of the chair at Lachlan's feet as Col lifted the back and together, they carried it onto the porch. 'Thanks, Dad and Bruce,' Lachlan said.

Simone had already been into the house and dropped a load. She had spotted Bruce's welcome gifts. 'Thanks, Bruce,' she said. 'That's very thoughtful of you. One less job I have to deal with just now.' She then set about making sure everyone, including Lachlan, had something to eat.

'You don't need me just now, so I'll keep working,' Bruce said, as he skipped down the stairs and headed back to the shed. He'd had lunch already. The crab awaited cooking, which he duly attended to.

Bruce built himself a thick crab sandwich for dinner that evening, but before he demolished it, he took a selfie of him and the sandwich, which he then sent to both Lenny and Therese. 'Thanks for dinner. Beautiful. Much appreciated. Wished I'd been with you to catch and share it,' he messaged.

On Sunday morning early, Col came over to the homestead to get an update on how the station survived in his absence. Bruce pulled out his notebook and they earnestly put their ideas together to finalise the changes. It was a beautiful day, like most recently. It had started out a bit cool at ten degrees, but quickly warmed to about twenty-five degrees and was forecast to hit a maximum of thirty degrees. There was not a cloud in the clear blue sky. There was no wind, just gentle breezes created by the daily heating by the sun. So, it was testament to the dedication and enthusiasm of Col and Bruce to be tolerating an inside job when then could be outside enjoying mother nature in her prime.

Working out the logistics of supplementation of cattle was the big task. After they had finalised how they would reset the herd groups across the station, they then calculated how much of each supplement would be required in each paddock every month. This was done to get orders correct for the dry season urea-based lick, a wet season phosphorus-based lick, a dry to wet season transition supplement for pregnant and lactating cows, hay for weaners and for other cattle when yarded and dry season supplements for small and big weaners. In ad-dition to this, they took Wayne's advice and planned for a short-term energy-dense supplement for heifers in late pregnancy, aiming to in-crease new-born calf survival rates and improve the chances of these animals re-conceiving within four months of calving. Supplements required storage space, infrastructure and labour for feeding out, and infrastructure to enable ideal access for cattle, all of which needed to be considered. It took all day to get their ideas sufficiently well formulated for Bruce to be able to take them to town and negotiate orders with a stockfeed company.

'I reckon you should get quotes from a company other than that mob in Charters Towers, Bruce,' Col said. 'If the overall cost is going to be in the order of a hundred thousand dollars, even if you get five percent off that, that's five thousand for something else.'

'I agree, Col,' Bruce replied. 'A luxury weekend on the Great Barrier Reef immediately comes to mind as a perfect investment,' he laughingly suggested. 'Yes, it's just as easy for a Townsville or a Home Hill company to ship us product as the guys in Charters Towers.'

Col left it at that. He was immensely pleased his employer involved him so intimately with planning the business. It was a lot more enjoyable than just doing what he was asked. Bruce was different to most employers. He wanted Col to take responsibility and he trusted him with it; this emanated from, and further enhanced, their mutual respect. It was a good feeling for Col, and so far, he and his family had been very happy in this situation because of it. Bruce was not going to be wasting any time. On Monday morning he made phone calls to several feed companies.

On Monday afternoon, Bruce and Col did a kill. It was a fat non-pregnant cow, one of several they had running in Cull paddock. Col mustered the small group in the mid-afternoon, leaving them to stand in the shade with access to water in the yards. At five o'clock they took the tractor with a loader hitched on the front down to the yards. Bruce had a rifle that he used to shoot the cow that was standing peacefully. After it fell, he used a knife to cut into the front opening of the chest and sever the major blood vessels feeding and coming from the heart, enabling clearance of a majority of the blood from the carcass. Col positioned the loader to lift the cow by the legs and place it, legs up and steady, on a low frame set on a concrete block just outside the yards. Bruce washed down the cow and the block before the men skinned her. The last stage involved re-lifting the cow by the back legs so the hide could be stripped from the back. Bruce removed the feet and head with the hide before he opened up the belly and chest of the cow to drop out all the organs with the skin. Some people like to preserve the kidneys, liver and heart when doing this, but neither Col nor Bruce liked offal, so in with the rest of the gut it went. The final task was to cut the cow in half, down the back line. Bruce had a clean tarp on the back of his ute. Col lifted the carcass high over the tray of the ute, lowering it so the front half of each body side rested on the tarp. Bruce then cut off each forequarter at the last rib. Col then lowered the hind quarters onto the ute. The tractor's loader arms could be simply replaced with a bucket. Col did that, and loaded the waste and took it away to bury in a hole he'd already dug. Bruce washed down the block while he did this. Both men then headed back to the homestead where they hung the quarters to allow rigor mortis to pass in the cool overnight air in a screened butchering room beside the cold room at the homestead.

On Tuesday, Bruce left home at five o'clock, after Col had come over to help get the carcass quarters hung in the cold room, heading for Home Hill, a bit over an hour to the south-east of Townsville. He had organised another appointment for mid-afternoon in Townsville. He was on the road for about an hour when he pulled up and dialled Lenny, before pulling back onto the road as he could speak hands-free, but not dial. 'G'day, mate,' Bruce greeted him when Lenny answered. 'What's for breakfast?'

'Are you in Brandon, Bruce?' Lenny replied.

'No mate, but I'm on my way to Home Hill this morning. On my way back to Townsville, I thought I'd drop in and say hello if you're lying around doing nothing.'

'I am, Bruce. I'm just starting a new novel this morning. I wish,' Lenny said. 'I've got the harvest contractor just about here, so I'm getting ready for that. But the good news is I'll be here. Are you coming for lunch?'

'If I pick up a couple of pies in Ayr on the way through, we can have them with a cup of tea if that suits,' Bruce suggested.

'Like hell,' Lenny said. 'Maria would cut both our throats. That would be too messy for everyone. You just come to lunch, just yourself. We'd love to have you.'

'Thanks Lenny, I'll do that. I'll give you a time when I know it,' Bruce added.

What Lenny didn't know was Bruce had his portable fridge in the Land Cruiser stacked with ten kilograms of high-quality steak, all neatly cryovac-packed in serves for two people. Lenny would love it, but Bruce knew him and Maria would offer a barrage of pretence about why they didn't need it. Bruce was looking forward to it. The pleasure of an imminent gift-giving had him on a high.

At the Home Hill stockfeed business, Bruce was warmly welcomed by the factory nutritionist. Lucia had a cup of tea ready for him, and he was ready for it, which meant it didn't last long in the cup. 'Now you've finished that, Bruce, do you want a look at the plant before we talk business?' Lucia asked.

'I'd love to,' Bruce replied. The business mixed dry rations, dry lick supplements and fortified molasses products for beef businesses, as well as providing ingredients for beef producers to mix their own sup-plements. Col and Bruce had considered molasses, an excellent cattle feed when fortified, though it required a lot of infrastructure they still didn't have, such as storage tanks, a feed-out mixer and feeding troughs. Back in the office, Bruce outlined his needs and what Lucia could offer to meet those needs. There were several options for Bruce to make decisions on as they progressed negotiations, and ultimately, they prepared the basis of what Lucia would quote on. After they had done this, Bruce asked a lot of questions about fortified molasses. The option sounded good, but Bruce decided it would be best to progress towards using molasses slowly as finances allowed.

Just before Bruce left Home Hill, he messaged Lenny. 'I'm leaving Home Hill. Collecting the pies in Ayr.' That should get a laugh out of him, Bruce thought. Immediately Bruce had a reply, an emoji thumbs up.

Brutus did not know the sound of Bruce's ute yet, so was slow off the mark as Bruce turned on to Lenny and Maria's driveway. Only ten metres down the track, Brutus appeared, racing towards him. Bruce thought he looked like he was grinning, just like his owner. Lenny was in the shed, as expected, and was by the car door, opening it, by the time Bruce turned off his ute. 'G'day, Bruce. What a great surprise to have you for lunch. The bride is over the moon,' Lenny said.

'I had to drop in and say thanks for the crab, Lenny,' Bruce responded. He jumped out of the Land Cruiser, shook Lenny's hand firmly, then walked around to his fridge. 'Got some crab bait and dog food here for you, mate,' Bruce said as he hefted out the two five-kilogram bags of meat. Lenny was beside him and closed the lid for Bruce.

'Looks too good for the hound,' Lenny observed. Bruce smiled broadly as they walked across to Maria who emerged from the house with open arms.

Maria hugged him like he was her own son and then looked down at the bags. 'What have you got there, Bruce?'

'Dessert, Maria. Hope you haven't made any,' Bruce said, laughing.

'Come in you bad man and show me,' she said. When Bruce opened the bags for her and Lenny inside, Maria said, 'Are you sure this is all for us, Bruce?'

'All yours, Maria. Get it all in the freezer for now. It's cryovac-packed in two-serve lots. If it's just you and Lenny for dinner, get one pack out. If you've got ten people for dinner, get five out,' Bruce said. 'Easy. It'll be tender and tasty. You'll love it.'

'Thanks, Bruce,' Lenny said. 'That looks real good meat. We might even demolish one for dinner if Maria doesn't have anything else ready. Let's have lunch,' he declared. Maria, of course, had prepared a huge, delectable feast for the three of them. Bruce would have loved to have stayed all afternoon in Brandon, but he had his appointment in Townsville at the stockfeed company. He left Lenny and Maria's place just in time to avoid being late. It might not have mattered much to the people in Townsville, but Bruce was not a person to ever be late or unreliable, and he wasn't starting today.

In Townsville, Bruce had a similar experience to what he'd had in Home Hill that morning. He encountered good staff working for a good business. Tom Smythe, the young nutritionist, was very impressive. He obviously had a sound, practical understanding of beef production systems, coupled with considerable technical knowledge. 'If you get a chance, would love to have you out at Bovale, Tom. We'll be in touch when you get a quote together for me,' Bruce said as he left.

After he was finished, he dropped by to have afternoon smoko with his mother. She was very pleased to see him. 'I'm so happy young Lachlan is good now. It was absolutely terrific having the Wattle family stay, but they were very sad about Lachlan, especially on the Sunday night when they got here,' Doris told Bruce.

'Thanks for having them, Mum. They appreciated it. They are overjoyed to be home again with Lachlan on the mend. He's a good lad,' Bruce commented.

'I hope you don't mind me mentioning it, Bruce, but the girls were all very excited about Therese,' Doris said. Bruce looked at her with a smile. 'I didn't go up to the hospital, so I never met her, but that'll happen at some stage, I'm sure,' Doris added.

'Thanks, Mum,' Bruce said. 'Yes, we're only friends. I get the impression the girls have been putting one and one together and getting eleven. The answer is two. She's a friend and like all my friends, you'll meet them at some stage.' Doris smiled broadly at Bruce with raised eyebrows, saying nothing more on the subject. There's some secret women's business going on here, Bruce thought to himself, and left it at that. Bruce was desperately tempted to call Therese and see if he could see her on the way home, but he thought that could wait. He'd waited all his life so far; what's another couple of weeks?

Bruce drove into the shed at Bovale just after dark. It had been a long day. Fortunately, he had stopped by a fast-food outlet on the way out of Townsville and collected a cooked chook. An excellent supplement for an easy-to-prepare dinner when he got home. It was chilling in his portable fridge. The next day, he went to Charters Towers to visit the stockfeed merchants there. He decided not to catch up with any of his friends as he may have been lured into dinner in town. He really wanted to be back at Bovale, so he snuck in and out of town, hoping he'd left the gang unaware of his trespass.

On Thursday night, Jane rang. 'I heard you were in town, Bruce.' The gossip trail in town never missed a thing.

'Yes, Jane. Sorry I didn't take time out for you guys, but life's been a bit busy and I only had time for a hit and run on town,' Bruce admitted.

'That's okay,' Jane said. 'We all heard about Lachlan's dreadful accident. That would not be helping you. Is he okay?'

'Thanks Jane. Yes, he's well and truly on the mend. It wasn't much fun when it happened, but somehow it all worked out well,' Bruce added. 'Lachlan's home now. He has to use a wheelchair for a bit, but I don't think it'll be too long, and he'll be bouncing around, back like a bought one.'

'That's great news, Bruce,' Jane responded. 'Mick told me you were keen to have another Bovale weekend, and he asked if I could let you know what suits us.' Bruce pricked his ears. Maybe that kiss she had given Mick had taken their friendship further, he wondered, though there was no way known he was going to ask.

'That's right, Jane,' Bruce agreed. 'I really loved that weekend here and I know you guys did too. Mick would have told you that Frances is keen to come the next time we do it, too, and I'm keen to have her. Hope that's okay with you.'

'We'd love her to join us, Bruce,' Jane replied. 'So, would either the end of next week or two weeks after that suit you?'

The end of next week would suit Frances and Therese, so Bruce agreed they'd do it then. Bruce had barely finished the call when he found himself sending a joint message to his sister and Therese. Whoa, he said to himself. Then he realised it was the smartest trick because they were already as thick as thieves with each other, and Therese could come with Frances. He'd say nothing and let them work it out, because as sure as his butt pointed towards the ground, that's exactly what would happen, whether he thought he'd help or not.

Over the next week, Bruce almost put the up-coming weekend out of his mind. He was so busy, not only doing routine physical work, but also straining his brain in implementing the system changes. Col and Bruce agreed they needed to draft out about fifty pregnant heifers from the two hundred they currently had in Stocking paddock. They mustered on Tuesday to do the job. They selected only polled, well-behaved heifers that were well-grown and looked well-muscled. These were sent to Airstrip paddock, which they had decided was going to be the stud's temporary home at least. The unselected heifers went back to Stocking paddock. Though there were bulls in Bull paddock, adjacent to Airstrip, they were not going to be anything more than a nuisance as the selected heifers were already pregnant. By the time the heifers wanted to engage in mating, they had planned to have removed half the bulls and have built a second fence to create a laneway to replace the short intervening fence.

Now the heifers were in place, the pressure was on to find the right bull. Wayne had advised them they may even already have that bull in their current bull herd, but they would not know until the breeding values had been calculated. Those results were still six weeks away. In the meantime, bull sales were happening across the state. They started scouring through sales where bulls were sold with both breeding values and certified as fertile, including sperm morphology assessment. They had anticipated having to assess a lot of vendor groups, but what they found was very few vendors offered any information with the bulls other than a photograph, a pedigree and some interesting comments that primarily reflected how well the bull had been fed in preparation for the sale. This was grossly inadequate for their purposes, which meant they then had to find a suitable bull from a small group of sales, but fortunately, sales with large bull numbers.

Screening bulls also required Bruce to establish breeding objectives for Bovale. Even though Wayne had given good instruction for this, Bruce initially tried to avoid the breeding objectives process. However, he quickly realised he was making excessively variable decisions about potential bulls. Wayne had copied them a spreadsheet that enabled Bruce to methodically work out his breeding objectives. It took him about four hours, but in the end, he was very happy he'd done it. The result he obtained had no obvious flaws and it provided the bonus of giving him the exact relative emphasis on each aspect of bulls. Once he recommenced reviewing bulls available in the market, he found the process was now relatively quick and clear-cut.

Before any of this began, Bruce realised that he would almost certainly be selecting elite bulls. There would be strong competition for such bulls. He had to be prepared to pay much more than they usually did for bulls. But this was tolerable as they were only aiming to source one new bull this year.

On Thursday morning before he bolted off on a water and lick feeding run, Bruce rang his mother. 'Happy forty-ninth birthday, Mum,' he sang.

'Thank you, Bruce,' Doris replied. 'It's happy so far. I'm feeling good.'

'That's great to hear, Mum,' Bruce responded. They chatted for a bit about what he had been doing at Bovale.

'Bruce, now I know how I feel after chemo, I know I am okay to come up for a visit between cycles,' Doris said. 'Would that be okay?'

'Mum, it'd be better than a visit by the Queen. Then again, you are the queen of Bovale. When are you thinking would be a good time?' Bruce asked.

'It'd have to be a weekend, Bruce. Your father and I could drive up on a Saturday afternoon and come home on Sunday afternoon. My next two weeks of chemo are the middle two weeks of August. So, maybe the last weekend of the month?' she suggested.

'I'll have the red carpet out, Mum. You'll know Frances is coming tomorrow and all my good friends this weekend. I'm really looking forward to it,' Bruce added.

'I'm really happy for you, Bruce. I know you'll have a great weekend,' Doris said before they wrapped up their call.

While Bruce was working on sourcing a new bull, the needs of the station still had to be met. Both Col and Bruce stopped everything on Friday to cut up the cow carcass that had been ageing in the cold room since being slaughtered the previous week. It was a big job. Before school started, Simone helped, as did Carina. Col wheeled Lachlan over so he could watch. Each quarter was methodically broken down into cuts. The meat was sliced if it was for steak. Off-cuts and some parts of the carcass were minced. As they went, all cuts were packaged, labelled and stacked in plastic bins for later transfer to freezers. Bruce had a passion for sausages. Some fatty mince was reserved for this, into which Bruce mixed sausage meal, iced water and flavouring, before it was fed into a casing through the sausage machine. It was a big task to complete the butchering, filling ten stacked bins, each with about twenty kilograms of packed beef, but they finished and even had the butchering room clean by four o'clock that afternoon. The snags remained hanging, along with two briskets. Five bins of bone and other waste waited, stacked in the cold room, ready for disposal, but that was not a job for today.

Chapter Ten

It was almost Friday night, and Bruce had visitors coming. He had
been so busy, Bruce had almost regretted agreeing to having the
gang for the weekend, but as it neared his excitement increased. He
definitely wanted to see his visitors this weekend. He had about two
hours to get the house ready, nowhere near sufficient, but he wasn't
that concerned. If they didn't like the situation as it was, well, their
problem not his, he reasoned to himself in his euphoria. Bruce had
just finished cleaning himself and dressing when he heard the note
of Craig's ute. Five minutes later, Mick and Craig were loading their
stores into the cold room. 'You blokes have stolen all the junk food out
of a fuel station, I'm sure,' Bruce declared when he saw what they'd
brought. 'Next time you go shopping, please take one of the ladies.
There's no hope for you blokes.' They were all laughing.

'What's for dinner, Bruce?' Mick asked.

'Snags, ' Bruce said. 'Special Bruce snags. You'll love them.'

'What else?' Craig asked.

'Nothing, mate,' Bruce replied, presenting the most serious look he could muster. 'Maybe you'll let us eat some of that muck you blokes brought?'

'Righto, sounds like you and the sheilas have it under control,' Mick concluded. 'I'll make sure everyone has a drink.'

It was half an hour before The Villa ladies turned up. Eileen, Jane and Brenda did their grand entrance with the boys' assistance, bags in hand and hugs all round. 'Righto, Bruce,' Jane asked. 'What's for dinner?'

'Didn't you bring it, Jane?' asked Craig. 'We're going to starve. Back to town,' he declared, pointing directly to Charters Towers, laughing his head off.

'Remember, my sister's coming. I've got the meat. She's got the onions, I hope. Let's light the barbeque,' Bruce declared.

Fifteen minutes later, Bruce spotted the approaching headlights of the final car while the gang was noisily having beers around the raging fire in the barbeque pit. Bruce casually let them be and met the last two visitors. Both Frances and Therese immediately warmly hugged Bruce. 'We'll unload first and then I'll introduce you to everyone,' Bruce suggested. Frances was like a little girl with a new doll, she was so happy to be home again, excitedly explaining every detail of everything they encountered to Therese. Therese was almost mute. It was a big occasion. When they had the bags and food inside, Bruce put one arm around each and led them outside and introduced everyone. None of his Charters Towers friends had any idea that Therese would arrive. Bruce could see they were all trying to work out whether she was Frances's friend or Bruce's friend. The only thing that was obvious was she was the friend of both. Bruce was sure the sheilas would have it all worked out before the night was finished so he left it hanging. 'Let's see if we can get a feed together,' he announced.

With so many willing hands, and a full larder to select from, in no time a feast had been assembled. What remained was for the snags to be cooked. Bruce went to the cold room where he had several strings hanging. Out of the sausage machine, a string is one long sausage which is then folded into sections of three sausages, typically producing at least twenty sausages that are hung till they're ready for storage or cooking. Bruce retrieved one string which was sufficient for the evening's meal. Beside the barbeque, he neatly cut the string into individual snags before dropping them on to the barbeque plate.

'I've never seen that before,' Therese remarked to him. 'Where did you get that bunch of sausages from?'

'I made them today,' Bruce replied, matter-of-factly.

'Wow,' Therese responded. 'You are one talented boy. I'm sure I'll see plenty of things this weekend I've never seen before.'

'So, you've not been on a cattle station before, Therese?' Bruce asked.

'No, Bruce, but I'm a farm girl inside and out,' Therese replied.

'That's not a bad thing, you know,' Bruce commented. 'You'll be amazed how adaptable your skills are to this situation. The only tricky part where you may need to start at ground zero is stock handling, but I'm sure you'll take that in your stride.'

'Surely we're not going mustering or something tomorrow?' Therese queried.

'Do you want to?' Bruce asked.

'Not the first day, please, Bruce,' Therese said, smiling broadly.

Dinner was sumptuous. Bruce's snags were lauded. 'Nearly as good as the redclaw I caught last time,' Mick claimed. 'Wait till tomorrow night before we judge this feast the best.'

'Mick, you're too modest,' exclaimed Jane.

'Always have been, Jane,' Mick responded, assuming as humble an air as he could muster.

Frances and Therese had brought desserts, which really topped off the feed. 'There is no way known any restaurant in the world could have matched what we had tonight,' declared Craig. 'Thanks Bruce. Thanks ladies. A toast to you all,' he declared as they all agreed, raised their beers and toasted.

'Enough eating,' Jane immediately added. 'Let's get this mess cleaned up and get the cards out. Oh Hell World Cup tonight,' she exclaimed. This invigorated the gang and it wasn't long before Bruce's kitchen had resumed a semblance of cleanliness and order. The game had to be played at the family dinner table inside the house, bringing them all close together. Everyone, except Therese, was an old hand at Oh Hell. With the simple instructions explained, it wasn't long before she understood it, and started to enjoy the game and the associated comradery as much as everyone else. Bruce was also very happy to see Frances in high spirits, totally enjoying being with him and his friends.

Craig came last in both games, which inevitably reduced the conclusion from Mick that he was currently very lucky in love. This hilarious conclusion was another revelation to Therese. Bruce could see Mick thinking for a bit before Mick announced in his most serious tones, 'Ladies and gentlemen, I think we need to sell this bloke. He's still single and the cards have spoken. He's ready to be snapped up.' This evoked uproarious laughter in the group.

'Hang on,' Bruce said, 'let's grab another drink first and we'll go outside around the fire and stoke it up. That should make this more interesting.'

Outside with the fire roaring again, Mick resumed the 'sale'. He was standing while everyone else was on garden chairs around the fire. 'Sale Oh, Sale Oh,' he called. This was the chant of the regional livestock auctioneers to denote the beginning of a cattle sale, used to call the bidding crowd together. Therese couldn't believe what she was seeing and hearing. This is hilarious, she was thinking. She then had an inspiration. She pulled out her phone and started videoing the mock sale.

Mick took a swig from his beer and adopted the chanting monotone of an auctioneer. 'Righto ladies and gentlemen, welcome to the sale here this evening. We have a special sale here tonight on account of Bruce Arnold Pastoral. There will be just one lot, an exceptional sire. The minimum bid here tonight ladies and gentlemen, will be two thousand dollars and all further bids will be in two-thousand dollar increments.' Mick's words and his serious presentation, as good as any auctioneer, had his seven friends in stitches.

Mick held up his hands to settle the frivolity. 'Ms Arnold, can you please lead the sire?' Mick asked, directing Frances to grab Craig by the arm and parade him across the lawn. As this happened, Mick continued. 'Righto ladies and gentlemen, you can see the quality in that sire. He's by a Melbourne sire out of a beautiful Townsville dam and has all the qualities that will improve any herd or family. Now, ladies and gentlemen, notice the excellent rump and the beautiful disposition of this sire.' Craig was in the spirit of proceedings. As Mick made this declaration, Craig suddenly kicked up his heels and let out a snort he thought a bull would be proud of. This spurred Mick on. 'What you've just seen, ladies and gentlemen, is just how strong his libido is as well. Just note how strong his legs are and the good spacing between the eyes.' Mick lowered his tone a touch for the next statement. 'Ladies, and gentlemen, we understand the sire has not been submitted for fertility assessment, but based on his pedigree, this should not be an issue.' This statement had everyone in fits of laughter. Craig stopped parading beside Frances and turned with a lop-sided look at his mate, grinning. Mick looked back, straight-faced. Craig shrugged his shoulders and kicked his heels up again, before continuing the parade with Frances. Mick continued. 'This sire is the number one lot we have on offer this year, so please take your opportunity to bid tonight.'

'Ladies and gentlemen, I know there is strong competition for this sire here this evening, but please don't let that deter you. We have Arnold Pastoral here. I know they're keen for a foundation sire with excellent quality.' Mick took another swig of his beer before continuing. 'There's some good families here also, and a sire like this would definitely set them up for life,' Mick declared as straight-faced as he could muster.

'Without further ado, ladies and gentlemen, let's commence this sale,' Mick declared before going on. 'Can I get a bid on this sire? Remember, this sire won't be equalled in any sale this year, so please take your opportunity. Any bid now, ladies and gentlemen, any bids now?' Mick had put down his beer. He had picked up a piece of firewood in his raised right hand that he was obviously using as his gavel. His left hand was outstretched towards his friends with palms open. This hand was searching for bidders he would point to as any were made. Mick was scanning all faces, except Craig's of course. He dared not look at Craig directly or he might just fall apart in fits of laughter.

'Any bid now, any bid now? Can I get eight thousand for this sire, now? Eight thousand dollars? Eight thousand dollars? Anyone got eight thousand dollars?' Mick chanted, punching out the values, searching the teared-up eyes of his friends. Mick changed into normal speaking tone slowly ramping back into a pleading, lilting chant. 'Can I get six thousand? Six thousand? A six thousand bid now? Four? Can I get four? Four thousand, anyone? Four thousand, now?' Mick reverted to normal speech. 'Ladies and gentlemen, just look at this quality sire. It's not clear why I can't get a good starting bid. Any bids, any bids, now?'

'Hup there,' Mick suddenly yelled, his hand pointing directly at Bruce who'd surreptitiously snuck his forefinger in the air, not missed by Mick's eagle eyes. 'We have a bid now,' Mick chanted. 'What's your bid, sir?' Mick asked of Bruce, serious as he could be.

Bruce stopped laughing for a moment, and through a broad smile, called out with a typical sale ring note, 'Two thousand.'

This set Mick off in a droning frenzy. 'Two thousand, ladies and gentlemen. We have a bid here, now.' Mick had his left hand firmly pointing at Bruce, the right hand with firewood cum gavel raised, his eyes desperately seeking any notion of a competing bid. 'Two thousand bid, two thousand bid, two thousand dollar bidder, now.' The last word was squeezed out slightly slower and at a higher pitch with a twang to emphasise the bid. To almost celebrate the bid, Craig again kicked up his heels, causing Frances to giggle uncontrollably to the point of almost having to stop parading Craig.

Jane saw her chance. She carefully positioned herself beside Brenda. Jane gently took Brenda's hand and lifted it just enough to set Mick off. 'Hup there,' yelled Mick. Mick's left hand violently changed its point of direction as he lifted it from Bruce and thrust it directly towards Brenda. 'Four thousand dollars. I have four thousand, now.' Brenda was bemused. She looked at Jane who just shrugged her shoulders feigning complete innocence. Jane still held Brenda's hand, and Jane noted she wasn't pulling it away, suggesting she might have more bids where that came from.

Mick droned on, his right hand still holding the piece of firewood aloft. 'Four thousand bid, four thousand bid, four thousand dollar bidder, now. Can I get six? Six thousand? Can I get six thousand, now? Six thousand? Six thousand? Anyone with six thousand, now?'

Mick paused slightly, which cued Bruce whose bidding finger quietly punctured northwards, re-energising Mick. 'Hup there,' Mick called in a crescendo as his left hand was simultaneously brought back to point directly at Bruce. 'I have six thousand. Six thousand. Six thousand, now. Six thousand dollars, six thousand dollars, six thousand dollar bidder now. Can I hear eight? Is there eight? Eight thousand? Eight thousand, now?' Jane lifted her friend's hand. Mick never missed it. 'I have eight,' he crooned. Without hesitation, Bruce poked his finger skywards again, looking Mick square in the eye; fortunately, Mick was looking at hands and fingers, not eyes. 'Ten, I have ten. Ten thousand dollar bidder, now,' Mick declared.

Brenda lifted her hand away from Jane's and bid again. Fantastic, thought Jane, smiling broadly. 'Twelve,' Mick shouted, his left hand having quickly gone from pointing at Brenda, to Bruce and back to Brenda. Craig was starting to laugh as he walked slowly, escorted by

Frances. Suddenly he feigned a limp. Mick never missed a beat in his drone. 'Ladies and gentlemen, a small issue. If there's any problem found with this sire, the vendors have promised to replace him if a reconditioning doesn't work. Now ladies and gentlemen, is there fourteen? Fourteen thousand? Fourteen thousand? Fourteen thousand, now? Can I get fourteen? Fourteen? Fourteen thousand now?' Mick paused and took another swig of beer. 'Ladies and gentlemen, if I can't get another bid, I'll have to knock him down at twelve. Any more bids? Any more bids, now? The bid's with the lady on the left here. Sir, do you have fourteen,' Mick enquired as he looked directly at Bruce. Bruce shook his head in laughter.

'Righto, ladies and gentlemen, we have twelve thousand. Twelve thousand, now. Any final bids? Any bids? I'm going to have to knock him down,' Mick declared. He lowered the lump of wood and was holding it above his left palm. 'Twelve thousand dollars. Going once. Twelve thousand dollars. Going Twice. Any more bids?' Mick paused, eyebrows raised in question. Mick gently slapped the firewood into his left palm. 'All done, out she goes,' yelled Mick. 'Sold to Brenda Holdings. The sire goes to a good home.' Mick breathed deeply and drained his beer as everyone clapped his performance. Mick walked over to Craig and draped his left arm around his shoulders. 'Sorry, mate,' he said to Craig. 'Couldn't help myself.'

'It's fine,' responded Craig. 'My parents would be impressed you got that much for me.'

'I think you should thank the winning bidder,' suggested Mick.

Craig walked over to Brenda, and they hugged. 'Thanks, Brenda, glad I've now got a real good owner,' Craig said.

'You're a very good buy, Craig,' she said, looking at Craig squarely. They both smiled broadly at each other, neither saying nor doing more.

'Did you get the whole auction?' Frances excitedly asked Therese.

'I'm pretty sure I did,' replied Therese. 'That was hilarious.'

Bruce had overheard them. 'Can I have a look?' he asked. The next half hour was spent reviewing Therese's video, telling Mick what a champion he was, and congratulating Craig on his new owner and Brenda on her new sire. The discussion was very silly, but because it was all done with such good nature, they all enjoyed it immensely.

It wasn't too long after that, the whole crew ended up asleep. They were a long way shy of an eight-hour quota of sleep, spurred on by the excitement building for the day ahead, before they were all in the kitchen again, enjoying breakfast and building a picnic lunch. Bruce, as well-organised as ever, had put two huge chunks of fresh corned brisket into two slow cookers just after they finished cutting up the meat the previous afternoon. It was cooked just after the auction, and Frances had transferred it back to the cold room, ready for sandwich making in the morning. The organised chaos abated by seven-thirty as they prepared to head off to Jindabyne dam.

Because Bruce needed to take the Kubota side-by-side, they needed two other vehicles. Once again, Jane assumed responsibility for who'd travel with whom. 'Therese and Eileen, can you go with Bruce, please?' she asked. 'Brenda can go with Craig, now she owns him, and Mick and Frances can come with me.' Brenda was shaking her head, highly amused, and not at all displeased.

'Therese, you get in the middle if you like,' Eileen suggested to Therese when they went to get into the Kubota. 'I'll open the gates.'

The previous night, unbeknown to any of the men or Therese, The Villa ladies had indeed done their due diligence on Therese. Frances had been discretely grilled. Eileen had been upset, but she vowed not to display it. She respected Bruce a lot. It made more sense to her now why Bruce had not previously been more forward. I can't make him like me more than he likes someone else, she had reasoned.

Bruce had told everyone they could go out anyway they wished as every vehicle had someone who knew how to find their way out and back. Bruce was going the long way, with a detour to where Lachlan had taken his fall. Therese had said she would like to see it, no matter how plain. As they drove along, Bruce engaged Eileen in an update on Wayne's visit and what they were doing as a result. Therese found it difficult to contribute as it was mostly foreign to her. She just asked the occasional question so she could get a basic grasp on what they were discussing. Eileen was very impressed by Wayne's achievements and the responses of Bruce and Col.

'This might sound pretty silly,' Therese said when there was a break in the conversation, 'but what is the specific objective of doing everything you do with the cattle? What benefits are there?'

Bruce thought for a moment and then said, 'Good managers ensure cattle always have good access to high-quality feed and good water and they don't suffer from infectious diseases. This removes many of the stresses and risks from the lives of rangeland cattle. The outcome is they live quite idyllic lives, except potentially for their last minute or so when they must face slaughter. But in a civilised society like ours, this is now a humane process. The benefit for us is high productivity of high-value product at reasonable cost. This is a complete contrast to those who harvest feral livestock. That results in low yields of low-value product at high cost. Also, the lives of feral livestock are frequently highly stressful as feed and water supplies and quality were never guaranteed, calves are never weaned causing many cows to die in lactation, and out-of-control bulls smash each other mercilessly, doing the same to cows that make the mistake of getting in the way. If we don't do what we do, they rarely ever enjoy a good life, yet alone a good death. The same applies to all livestock, whether they be horses, sheep, whatever, even wildlife.'

'Exactly,' added Eileen. 'I could not have put it better myself.'

As they travelled, Bruce was acutely aware of Therese snuggling firmly against him. He was not sure what to do, stuck in the vehicle with the lady who almost lit his flame and the lady who had put him completely on fire. The best strategy is to let things happen the way they should, he reasoned, building on what his mum had said. He was really surprised how happy Eileen was when it should have been patently obvious to her that Therese was in the driver's seat, so to speak. It's that secret women's business again, he thought. Little did he realise, he was absolutely correct.

They drove north-east up the Dingo-Kenworth paddocks fence line to the trough. 'This is where Lachlan found the dingoes eating the aborted foetus,' he told the ladies. 'He came through the gate, and then chased them straight towards Gun Creek. It's about a kilometre from here to where the stick caused his back wheel to slide out and the bike to fall. 'They all got out when they reached the site and Bruce explained what he knew and what had happened on that day.

'Bruce, it is amazing how you found him and then organised his recovery to us as quickly and as well as you did. Lachlan has a huge amount to thank you for and I know he knows that,' Therese said as she summed up the enormity of what had happened.

'You have an amazing man there,' Eileen said, which caused both of them to look at her expressionless, hiding their full feelings, and both absolutely, inwardly and pleasantly stunned by what they'd just heard. No-one made further comment.

They turned for Jindabyne dam. 'It'll be smoko when we get there,' Bruce suggested. 'I reckon Craig will have a perfect billy of tea boiled again.'

As they caught their first glimpse of the dam, Therese was as spellbound as the rest of Bruce's friends had been at their first visit. 'Those saltwater creeks where you go fishing with Dad are nothing compared with this, Bruce,' she declared breathlessly.

'That's interesting, Therese,' Bruce responded. 'I find the creeks remarkably beautiful. I agree this is also stunning. I just like them both I suppose.' Therese had out her mobile phone and asked Bruce to stop a couple of times to get a photo. She even had him turn the vehicle around so they could get a selfie with the three of them in it and the dam in the background.

They could see their friends ahead organising the picnic smoko. All except Mick, of course, who was out in the canoe planting the red claw traps where he thought he'd have most success. There was nothing else to do other than enjoy smoko when they arrived.

Frances was agog with pleasure. It wasn't often she had the chance to come out to Jindabyne. 'Thanks for asking me to come out with your friends,' she said to Bruce as she gave him a big hug. 'You are one fantastic brother, and you have the very best friends.'

After smoko, Jane took charge of what she was calling the Bovale Olympics. All the 'sports' involved the canoe. Mick was frustrated because he wanted the canoe to pursue the redclaw. 'They can wait, Mick. The longer you leave the traps, the more we'll get,' Jane declared. She was more interested in Mick capsizing the canoe and having an unplanned swim while attempting an outrageously-difficult manoeuvre. Bruce was keen to cast his line for a barra, no matter how slim the chances of catching one were. Maybe after lunch, he thought.

After the Olympics had been won, and lost, it was lunch time. Eileen was quietly standing near the verge of the long grass. Bruce came up and stood beside her. 'Thanks,' he said, giving her his most sincere look. 'You are also one amazing lady.' Eileen nodded slightly to him and smiled with difficulty. After a minute they both made their way to the middle of the lunchtime feast.

The corned beef and pickles sandwiches washed down with Craig's billy tea tasted almost as good as dinner the previous night. The Villa ladies had brought some home-made cupcakes for dessert. 'I know what I'm having every day for lunch when I get to heaven, if I'm not already there,' declared Mick. 'Every time I think you ladies have done something that can't be topped, you turn around and top it. Thanks. My body probably hates me, but my heart loves it.'

The exertion of the 'Olympics' had everyone resting for a bit. It was quiet. Bruce walked over to the water's edge adjacent to, and about ten metres from, where they were camped. He stood there, admiring the view, noting all the wildlife and what they were doing, and trying to imagine where the barramundi were lurking, and what would be required to get one on his line. Therese looked across at him in deep contemplation and walked over. As she walked up beside him, she slipped her right hand into his left, standing right up against him, resting her head on his shoulder. 'Thanks, Bruce. This is beautiful,' she murmured.

'Only matched by the lady standing next to me,' he responded so only she would hear, looking straight ahead. The scene had captured everyone. They all had their mobile phones out, quietly snapping what was a magnificent photograph. 'If we didn't have an audience, you'd be in deep trouble, Therese,' Bruce quietly added.

'So might you,' Therese said softly. They stood there for another ten minutes, just enjoying being able to lean into each other, before Therese said, 'I think enough photos have probably been taken by now.' They both laughed and turned to join their friends on the picnic tarp.

Bruce had invited the Wattle family to dinner. When they got home at about four o'clock, he took Frances and Therese over to see them. None of the family had expected to see either Frances or Therese and both Simone and Carina squealed with delight, with hugs all round, when they arrived.

'You look really good, Lachlan,' Therese told him. 'Bruce showed me where it happened today. I don't usually get to see where the accident victims come from, and it was special to see this one. You are a very lucky young man.'

'I know, Therese. Thanks for looking after me, too,' Lachlan replied. He was in awe of Therese and Bruce.

'What got sold last night?' Simone asked. 'We could hear the racket.'

'Sorry about that. We should have toned down a bit. Mick sold Craig,' Frances answered. 'It was hilarious. Brenda bid twelve thousand dollars for him. Therese got it all on video.' This prompted

Therese to show them her footage, which also had the Wattle family in stitches of laughter.

It was when Therese pulled out her phone to show the video, she noticed she had a message from Frances. When she was walking back to the homestead later, she checked the message. It was a photo, her and Bruce lakeside. She knew she'd treasure that photo.

The barbeque that night and the Oh Hell was as much fun as the one the previous night. The big difference was, Mick didn't sell anyone. Every now and then through the night, Frances would grab Craig by the arm and walk him around the room, stimulating calls for Mick to sell him again. Mick would have none of it. He was resting on his laurels. He knew that one auction too many was definitely too many.

While they were all enjoying dinner, Carina piped up, in glorious innocence, with the question of the evening, 'Craig, how is Brenda going to get all the money to pay for you?'

Amid the raucous laughter, Jane added, 'I want to know who she's going to pay.' This totally bewildered Carina.

Therese saved her. 'It wasn't real, Carina. We were just playing.'

'That's what you think,' Mick said. 'It was real alright. Brenda's going to the bank tomorrow to get a loan.'

Craig was smiling like a Cheshire cat. 'If it had been real, it would have been closer to twelve million. But the bank would still be able to loan that amount for a product worth at least four times that,' he modestly claimed.

'Now we're talking Monopoly money,' Mick assured him. Mick was still a celebrity. His haul of redclaw from Jindabyne dam was substantial. Mick refused all offers of assistance that afternoon when he cleaned his catch, soaked them in brine, and then roasted them over the coals. When Therese claimed, 'Mick, this is better than mud crab,' Mick puffed out his chest.

His great mood and self-assurance were further elevated when Eileen declared, 'Mick, your redclaw are amazing.' Bruce smiled to himself, very happy to see how well Eileen had adjusted to just being a friend. She was no longer unconditionally defending what she had perceived as Bruce's territory.

The next day, Bruce suggested they spend the morning in the river down from the house. Bruce maintained a mown track down to the junction of Gun Creek with the river. There was a gentle slope down from the rise the homestead was on. The riverbed edge was lined with massive and majestic weeping paperbark trees, indicative of substantial water availability. Adjacent to the homestead, the riverbed was one hundred metres wide. At this time of the year, it was an expanse of white-brown sand. Up against the eastern bank, the homestead side, was a waterhole with crystal-clear water that extended for over two kilometres, terminating at the junction with Gun Creek. This was the homestead water supply. At the river edge, shaded under the huge paperbarks, the water was one to two metres deep. The width of the waterhole varied and was near to twenty metres just below the house.

After the breakfast bedlam during which a picnic smoko had been prepared, when everything had been cleaned up and everyone had packed their gear, Bruce and Frances led them down to the river. They were heading to their favourite childhood haunt. The track was not particularly appealing, but once they reached their destination, all were in awe. 'Guys, we've been here for days, and right under our noses you've been hiding a gem,' exclaimed Jane. 'How nice is this place.'

'Any fish or redclaw in here?' asked Mick.

'Mobs,' replied Bruce. 'This is where I got the redclaw for Jindabyne dam,' he added nonchalantly.

'You're too cool, Bruce,' Eileen declared.

They could hear the Kubota slowly heading down. Col and Simone had loaded Lachlan in his wheelchair in the back and tied it down. The Wattle family were joining them. When they got down to the riverbed, the men unloaded Lachlan and carted him to a beautiful, shaded spot. He had to sit in the shade in his wheelchair. It was frustrating for Lachlan, but he knew he was lucky to be alive, so he complained little and was thankful Bruce and his friends invited them.

The morning was relaxed. Without a canoe, the river frivolity was far less vigorous than the 'Olympics' on Jindabyne dam had been the previous day. Smoko was an extended affair. Bruce had brought some firewood as the creek wood was not sufficiently dense to easily boil the billy. Before they all fell asleep from excessive Sunday morning relaxation, everyone headed back to the homestead for lunch. Despite the option of left-over meat from the barbeque, most opted for yet more corned beef; it was good.

When everyone decided to head home, it was clear they were all tired and needed a weekend to recover. Last to leave were Frances and Therese. They helped Bruce select some meat to take back to Townsville in a large esky for themselves and Merve and Doris. Before leaving, Frances strategically made herself scarce by going over to say goodbye to the Wattle's. When the two ladies finally drove away from the homestead, Bruce was bereft, a depth of feeling he hadn't previously experienced.

Chapter Eleven

With everyone gone, Bruce finished cleaning up after the butchering. He then spent a few hours stacking the freezers with meat. Him and Col were very methodical and organised, enabling them to find what they wanted when they needed it in the future. The meat supply was freely available to the Wattle's. Simone came over to the butchering room a couple of times a week to extract what she planned for them to eat. The choice now was good, with the freezers quite full again.

Col had done a lick and water run in the morning. After lunch, Bruce decided they'd have a closer assessment of the bulls he'd identified from sale catalogues the previous week. As he prepared for this, it suddenly struck Bruce that he'd become quite passionate about breeding on two fronts. One was obvious, the cattle. But in snaring the heart of Therese, he was doing exactly the same in his own life; it was all part of the process of ultimately sustaining his own genetics and having children. Wouldn't that be good, he thought. He didn't dwell on it because he quickly realised he had plenty of time to sort out his own breeding.

It was quite a different proposition with the cattle. They usually reached sexual maturity as yearlings. The cows were culled by ten years of age with some of them having weaned as many as eight calves by then. None of this happened without good management. Well-managed cattle herds were not left to decide what they mated to and when. Their human masters made those decisions for them, as well as when it was time for calves to be weaned.

Bruce wanted just one ideal Droughtmaster bull. He knew of potential bulls at four studs across Queensland. Their data, especially their breeding values, looked good on paper and the bulls looked great in photographs. But there was no way known he was paying big money for a bull without seeing him live. He also wanted to see the dam and sire of each bull of interest and get an overall perspective of the source herds to minimise the chances of getting it wrong. On Monday night Bruce rang the owner of the bulls most likely to meet his needs. Dennis Seccombe owned Red Leather Droughtmaster Stud in central Queensland. 'G'day, Dennis. Bruce Arnold from Charters Towers here. Are you free to discuss bulls you have in your catalogue for your upcoming sale?' Bruce asked. After the men had exchanged pleasantries and Bruce had explained who he was and what he was seeking, Bruce asked, 'You have six bulls in your catalogue I'm interested in. Is it possible I could visit and inspect the bulls and their sires and dams?'

'No problem, Bruce. We would love you to visit and do an inspection,' Dennis replied. Bruce and Dennis discussed suitable timing and they agreed the following Tuesday would be fine. Bruce contacted each of the other three studs and was invited the following week for inspections. Bruce had a big week in front of him, visiting one stud daily and driving between studs each day. He calculated the round trip was going to be over three thousand kilometres. With daily motel and meal expenses, this was adding over three thousand dollars to the cost of the bull. The upside was he would not have to attend sales in person, which would have been more expensive, as all vendors now offered online bidding.

Bruce had just finished his last phone call when he received one. It was Therese. 'Hello, Bruce. Hope I'm not interrupting anything important.'

'Any time you ring, it's my number one priority, Therese,' he replied. 'I've been on the phone a bit tonight but have just finished my calls.'

'Thanks for having me on the weekend. I really enjoyed it,' Therese said.

They chatted away for about ten minutes, or so Bruce thought. When they finished, he glanced at the clock. Forty-five minutes, he exclaimed to himself. It was nice. Better than that he said to himself; it was fantastic. Amid the challenges of the Bovale business, Bruce now found he had the pleasure of his blossoming romance. It was all new territory. He had to learn to accept that someone wanted to catch up with him daily, not necessarily to talk each other's ears off, but simply to hear each other and share their lives. It was the start of a much-anticipated daily ritual. It depended what shift Therese was on when the call would happen. Usually, Therese rang Bruce because she was more constrained by her formal work environment and city life, while Bruce was his own boss in a flexible work environment. Though she did have to ring when Bruce was likely to be in the homestead compound where they had mobile phone reception.

The tyranny of distance was in action. Two hundred and fifty kilometres to Townsville did not allow any quick visits. However, Therese was keen to come out to Bovale on her days off, and the next opportunity was Sunday and Monday. Bruce was heading south on the inland highway on Monday, so that would be good. He'd see Therese on his way home the following weekend when he came back north up the coast on the Bruce Highway.

During the week, quotes came in for supplements. Bruce decided on sourcing from each of the three companies, as not all provided the best deal on each product type. Overall, he concluded he had saved himself over three thousand dollars. That will help the bull acquisition cause, he thought; an island holiday will just have to wait.

Therese arrived at Bovale late morning on Sunday. Bruce had tidied the homestead as best he could and had neatly mown the lawns. It was the first time for just the two of them with no distraction. Wow. He couldn't just sit down and yap all day. They'd have to do something useful. Bruce decided a water and lick run during the afternoon would be good. It didn't sound much like a first date, but just being together was the main game. The Wattle's knew Therese was coming and were nearly as excited as Bruce. Simone christened her the princess of Bovale just in case Bruce was at all confused about how they viewed the situation. Bruce had invited them to dinner, which Simone initially refused, telling Bruce it just needed to be them. But Bruce pointed out they'd only be at dinner for a couple of hours, and both him and Therese would love their company. Simone was happy, very happy.

Carina was super-happy. Lachlan was still in awe. Col was saying nothing, but his thoughts were all good.

Bruce marvelled at the magical touch of a woman. Therese had arrived with some flowers, which initially had Bruce very confused. He thought, isn't it that the bloke is supposed to be giving flowers? Therese's plans soon became evident. She picked a few leaves from plants in the garden and made some simple floral arrangements to adorn the kitchen and living areas of the homestead. Somehow, she shifted a few items around, creating a cottage look that Bruce never even realised existed in the homestead. Therese had brought the ingredients of a lunch with her. 'This is beautiful, Therese,' Bruce commented. 'I could get used to having you here.'

After lunch, they headed off in the Kubota, loaded with lick. Therese was quite pleased to be doing the lick run. It would give her a chance to see and learn more about this fascinating and beautiful cattle station. And the bloke who owned it, well, about eighty percent of it. The vehicle was feeling the weight, so it was slow going till they reached the first feeding point in Burdekin paddock, south of the homestead. As they were driving north along the fence line between Goldmine paddock to the east and Hollywood paddock to the west, they encountered a smashed set in a dogleg. This set was three steel posts braced with cross bars welded in place. The structure normally took the strain of the taut sections of fence wires. The welds holding the bracing bars were broken. The wires attached to the set had also been broken. 'What would have caused this to happen, Bruce?' Therese asked.

'It looks like a mob rush, maybe dingoes herding the steers in this paddock?' Bruce supposed. 'We've got more than a fence to fix. We now have cattle in Hollywood paddock, which is what we're burning in a few weeks. We need the fence fixed and the cattle out. Ever been mustering?' Bruce asked Therese with a smile suggesting there was fun involved.

'Sounds like I'm going this afternoon,' countered Therese.

'We'll fix the fence first,' Bruce suggested. They needed a welder, which meant they had to go back to the homestead and return in the old station Land Cruiser with a generator and welder. At the shed, Bruce noticed that, as if by magic, Therese transformed into a worker. A shed was familiar territory for her. Bruce also packed a small fire-fighting unit, a knapsack that sat on your back and sprayed water from a hand-held nozzle when mechanically pumped. They would need this as grinding and welding sparks could easily start a bushfire.

Back at the wounded fence, Bruce said, 'Therese, I'll untangle this mess while you set up the gear and then I'll work the spray while you weld.'

'Sounds like a plan to me, Bruce,' she replied. Therese started the generator. After she'd donned a full-face mask, earmuffs and gloves, she set to work with the angle grinder, cutting and preparing surfaces. By the time she was ready to weld, Bruce had already extinguished four fires. In the welding helmet, Therese focussed on the job and hardly noticed that Bruce was continually spraying to swat the fires started by the sparks. As soon as she finished, she switched off the generator. Bruce was cooling the welds.

'Excellent job, Therese. I had my work cut out putting out the fires,' Bruce commented. He had noted what excellent welds she had done. 'If I didn't know better, I'd say your dad was a tradesman, teaching you as well as that,' he added. He was having increasing respect, not only for Therese, but also for her dad, his mate, Lenny.

'Yes, he's a boilermaker, Bruce. I'm a lucky girl,' Therese replied.

'And I am one lucky bloke,' replied Bruce with a huge smile. 'Righto, let's get this fence up and then we can sort the cattle.' While Therese packed up the gear she'd been using, Bruce set to work on re-straining the fence. In no time, it was as good as new. As they worked, Bruce was thinking how incredulously lucky he was. Therese has to be the most attractive lady in Queensland. She's great company. She says she's a farm girl, but she's obviously a farmer. She's obviously an amazing nurse. And she likes me. Me, he exclaimed to himself. I'm spooked, but this lady could be my wife one day. As he considered this, he stopped and looked at Therese, who stopped and looked back. 'Ten,' he said. Therese blushed and smiled coyly, knowing he was rating her as highly as one could. Bruce then got back to work, and Therese followed suit.

Back at the homestead, Bruce fitted himself and Therese with a UHF radio and then gave her a quick lesson on using it. Their brief radio checks alerted Col who cut in, 'Are you guys right, Bruce? Do you need a hand?'

'We should be fine Bruce. We've just fixed the fence between Hollywood and Goldmine. We're just heading out to push any steers in Goldmine back to where they should be. If we need help, I'll cooee,' Bruce radioed.

'No problem, mate. We'll watch the footy while you're working,' Col replied. Bruce was pleased as he knew he'd be with Lachlan, passionately cheering on whatever team they were supporting.

They started the muster at the south-west corner of Goldmine paddock. Bruce instructed Therese to drive slowly in the Kubota, keeping the fence to the west in sight. Bruce would sweep the paddock on the two-wheel bike, pushing steers to the west and in front of Therese. The creek that flowed north-south through the middle of the paddock was a slight hindrance, but in the end, the muster went smoothly. All the steers were in the northern third of the paddock. It was the widest section and he had to hold Therese back to give himself time to traverse the paddock without cattle ducking back behind them. Fortunately, the well-trained steers were happy to amble in front of Therese into the water square at the north-west corner of the paddock. Bruce counted them through the gate back into Hollywood paddock. 'Thirty-two,' he told Therese. 'They all look okay too. I was worried a few might have injuries after what they did to the fence, but it looks like we dodged a bullet.'

'That was fun, Bruce,' Therese commented.

'Thanks for the help, Therese. I was not feeling happy about our first date being a muster, but them's the breaks,' Bruce said as he half grimaced and shrugged his shoulders. They were standing in the water square, shutting the gate behind the steers. 'I feel like I need to have you on the payroll for that effort.'

'A hug would do fine, Bruce,' Therese said, smiling radiantly. They were both happy.

It was just on dark when they parked in the shed. They walked quickly over to the homestead as the Wattle's would be over soon. Somehow in the interim, they needed to get clean and dressed and prepare a meal. As they pushed through the front gate, Simone came on the UHF, 'Bruce, are you there?'

'I'm here, Simone. Sorry, we're running late.'

'It's okay, Bruce,' she replied. 'We could hear how you were going. Carina and I took the liberty of going over to the homestead and setting up a stew when we realised you'd be late. Hope you don't mind.'

'You're an angel, Simone. Thanks. Just give us some time to get presentable and come over again,' Bruce responded.

***

When Therese headed off on Monday morning, Bruce almost cried. Why do I feel like this, he asked himself. He had already packed his bags and not long afterwards, he headed off, aiming for his overnight accommodation in Blackwater, west of Rockhampton.

Bruce arrived at the Red Leather stud at nine o'clock the next morning. Dennis greeted him, 'Just in time for smoko, Bruce. Come in and meet the wife, Greta, and we'll get fed up before we see the cattle.' Bruce immediately liked the Seccombe family. Smoko was full of enquiry about each other's families.

Dennis had all fifty-four of his sale bulls in a yard where he was hand feeding them with a proprietary fattening mix. 'I suggest you just walk through the bulls in the yard, Bruce. Their numbers are branded on them. They're all dog quiet so you shouldn't have any dramas,' he suggested to Bruce. As Dennis stood in the shade of a large tree in the corner of the yard, Bruce slowly walked through the bulls. One by one, he found the six he was looking for. One was very upright in the front pasterns and when he observed very closely, he could detect the bull experiencing slight discomfort as he walked. A second bull had small growths between the claws of his rear feet. Bruce had previously heard these were called interdigital fibromas; they caused lameness and were heritable. The other four bulls looked terrific to Bruce.

'The bulls look great Dennis. You should be proud of yourself. I've marked several I'm keen to bid on at this stage,' Bruce told him.

'Thanks, Bruce,' Dennis replied. 'Let's go and have a look at the cows.' They drove several kilometres to a paddock where Dennis had about one hundred and fifty cows around a water point. The men walked together through the mob, that nonchalantly hardly moved as they stood or laid down, chewing their cuds. Bruce was impressed with what he saw. They were not overly-big cows. All were polled with no evidence of poor temperament. It took him fifteen minutes, with a bit of help from Dennis who knew each of the cows like one of his children, but eventually Bruce found the dams of all four bulls still in contention. One cow had over-sized teats and appeared to have previously experienced mastitis. This ruled out her son.

Again, Bruce made no specific comment on the individual cows. 'Your herd looks exactly like what I'm aiming for, Dennis,' Bruce commented. 'Thanks for letting me see these cows because they've totally cemented my conviction to bid at your sale. I'm sure I'll like the sires, if there is any chance we can see them too, please?' Bruce asked.

'Too easy,' Dennis replied. He drove them to the bull paddock where he pointed out the three sires Bruce had asked to see. Each looked terrific, backing up the information he had downloaded on these bulls. The sheath housing the penis of one bull was too large for Bruce's liking, as this rendered it more susceptible to prolapse, a condition cattlemen called a broken pizzle. A foundation sire for his own bull-breeding herd should not have this problem in its direct lineage. Fortunately, it was the sire of one of the three bulls he'd already discounted.

'I'm over the moon at being able to come and see these cattle,' Bruce said to Dennis as they drove back to the homestead. 'Thanks for giving me the opportunity and your time.'

'It's been a pleasure to meet you, Bruce, and help you,' Dennis replied. 'I hope you can pick up a bull that meets your needs at our sale,' Bruce concurred. He knew there would be good competition for these bulls. At least he had three to bid on, meaning if he was not able to bid high enough on the first one offered, he still had two more available to bid on, and still one more if the price of the first two exceeded his capacity to pay. And if he missed all three, a bull from another stud sale might be attainable, he hoped.

After a very pleasant lunch with the Seccombe family, Bruce headed further south-west for his overnight stay in Augathella. The country was unfamiliar to Bruce, but he enjoyed what he saw immensely. After living all his life in dry tropical, spear grass country, the beauty of the country between Springsure and Tambo was exemplified by the obesity of the cattle he saw grazing as he drove along.

The Augathella-based stud Bruce visited offered the same hospitality he had experienced at Blackwater. That afternoon, he had a long but interesting drive via Roma, Taroom, Theodore and Eidsvold through to Monto, west of Bundaberg. He admitted to Therese that night when he rang her that he was starting to feel like he was on holiday rather than doing a job. It had felt so good to have Therese at Bovale on Sunday night, and now he wanted her to be with him every night, especially when he was on holiday. Whoa back, he had to keep telling himself, every time he had that thought. Give it time.

By the time Bruce had inspected his target bulls at Monto, and then at Nebo, west of Mackay, he had confirmed a total of eleven bulls met his breeding objectives. This was not as many as he had hoped, but it was better than fewer target bulls. With the punishing schedule of close to three thousand kilometres in five days under his belt, Bruce was tired by the time he arrived in Townsville, where he went straight to his parents' place. Therese had a late shift that day, so he was unable to see her till Saturday.

Doris had had her last chemo treatment for this cycle that afternoon. She was resting when Bruce arrived at about six o'clock. His sister, Frances, and his father greeted him. Bruce crept in to give his mum a quick hug before he enjoyed a hot shower. Merve and Frances were over in the shed where he joined them for a beer. Merve was keen to get a debrief on Bruce's southern foray and Bruce was keen to update him. Merve was impressed with his son's endeavour. He could see his son was taking the Bovale business well beyond what he had achieved, which made him very proud. They needed a second beer to get through all they needed to talk about before Frances ushered them back to the house where they enjoyed a very quiet family dinner she had cooked.

Doris was well enough to join him and Merve for breakfast on Saturday morning. Merve was heading off to work shortly. 'When are we going to meet Therese, Bruce?' Doris asked. She was obviously abreast of the gossip.

'Not sure, Mum,' Bruce replied. I'm heading around to see her shortly on my way home to Bovale. She's on a late shift again today, so today probably won't work well. I've asked her to come out to Bovale next weekend, so you'll meet her then for sure,' Bruce replied.

'I've heard such nice things about her, Bruce, we just can't wait to meet her. She's friends already with Frances, which is really nice,' Doris said.

'Yes, she's a special lady, Mum. Her family is also great. I only met Lenny when he helped me down the creek that day, but he's now one of my good friends. And Therese's mum, Maria, is an older version of Therese. She is a great lady,' Bruce offered.

'What's their dog like?' Merve asked, laughing. Bruce knew the background on this question as him and his father had often noted just how extraordinarily similar dogs were to their owners.

'Brutus is the nicest hound I've ever met, I think,' Bruce replied, pleased as punch. Merve grinned broadly, very happy for his son.

Back at Bovale, Bruce was consumed by work. On Wednesday, they planned to burn Goldmine paddock, which was a high priority, but still routine jobs had to be done. The weather forecast was good. Bruce had already obtained a permit from the local fire warden. But they had to ensure they were well-prepared. Most important was good fire breaks. In the past week, Col had finished slashing the entire boundary of the paddock. Bruce had to run discs on the inside of the vehicle tracks the whole way round to give them further security. They had two main firefighting units that were basically a one-thousand-litre water tank that could be mounted on the tray back of a ute, a pump driven by a petrol motor and a hand-held spray nozzle that could be controlled by the person driving the vehicle. These had to be serviced and ready to use. One would go on the old station Land Cruiser. The other would be mounted on a neighbour's vehicle when they arrived for the burn. They also had the knapsack spray unit. Bruce would take this in the Kubota that he was going to control the burn from.

The most difficult part of the burn was going to be around the creek crossings at the southern boundary and the northern boundary just before it joined Gun Creek. It was difficult to create a secure fire break through the creek. Tall trees that grew there could throw embers beyond the fire break if the wind blew the wrong way when the fire was in the canopy. Bruce and Col spent most of Monday working on these creek crossings and deliberating on how they would manage the fire.

Burning was a communal affair. Each station helped their neighbours. This was in everyone's interest as no-one wanted a rogue fire. If a fire got out of control, any neighbour whose place may be threatened was exactly where they needed to be to make decisions on how to contain it and cause least damage. On Wednesday afternoon, eight neighbours and workers, Scott and Wendy Olden included, arrived to assist with the fire. The southern boundary of Goldmine paddock adjoined their station. Several had arrived, as planned, with fire-fighting units mounted on the back of their four-wheel drive vehicles.

Wendy came, armed with sandwiches and soft drinks. She knew the men would be hungry and thirsty doing this job, well before they got back to the homestead. Bruce had recruited Simone to prepare a barbeque. It would be a very simple affair, snags and steak on bread with tomato sauce, washed down with cold beer, exactly what the men enjoyed, despite their womenfolk insisting more needed to be added. Bruce had control and the men were going to get a man's feed. However, he knew for sure Simone would not be able to restrain herself and other special needs would appear like tomato and beetroot and onion and … the list would hopefully have an end.

Bruce took charge when everyone had arrived and assembled in the shed. Him and Col explained the anatomy of the paddock, how they planned to burn, and how they expected the fire to behave. There was a light south-easterly blowing, which was ideal. Bruce told the men, 'We'll start the fire in the north-west corner. One fire lighter will head along the north-east boundary, the other will head south-east along that fence line. We'll go steady and make sure it's back-burning slowly and under complete control as we go. After we have sufficient back burn, I will give the go-ahead to both fire lighters to progress slowly to meet at the south-east corner, with one firefighting unit working the break behind each. Three of us will remain and work along the western boundary and three along the northern boundary making sure we get quickly onto any spot fires when the main inferno rips across.'

Everyone had a fully-charged UHF set on the station frequency. Everyone had water. As they went, they agreed on tasks for each person. It was all done using a military-like approach. Everyone expected this as fires were dangerous for anyone involved. When everyone was satisfied with their tasks and Bruce was satisfied that everyone was as well prepared as they could be, they set off to do the burn.

Bruce was very pleased that ten people were on the job. It would make it so much easier and safer than if fewer had volunteered. Yes, the neighbours had their own interests at heart when they decided to come. But they also enjoyed the rare opportunity to socialise with their neighbours, which meant the evening barbeque was not going to be skipped by anyone if they could help it. They all liked to have a look at what their neighbour was doing as well and discuss anything novel they encountered that attracted their interest. This burn was particularly attractive as Bovale had a new owner and everyone was keen to see how the young pup was going and how well he'd manage the burn. They were not disappointed.

At three o'clock, Bruce lit the match and dropped it. 'She's on, fellas. No turning back now,' he said, turning and smiling to the assembled crew as he pocketed the box of matches. Scott had one of the drip burners. He lit the burner in the developing flame and started to work along the northern fence line. Everyone else waited till he'd gone about one hundred metres to see how the fire was behaving before Bruce gave the nod for lighting to start towards the south. A firefighting unit followed each fire lighter, ensuring there were no residual fires on the fire breaks.

Scott had three kilometres to light initially; the western fence line was a five-kilometre stretch. At five o'clock, Scott radioed, 'I'm at the corner, Bruce.'

'Roger,' Bruce replied. 'How fast is it back burning where you are?'

'Fairly quickly, Bruce,' Scott replied. 'I'd say it's taking about five minutes to get about ten metres.'

'Righto, Scott. When the other guys are through to their end, you'll be right to head south,' Bruce responded. It was another half an hour before the western fence line was completely lit.

'Off you go, Scott,' Bruce called.

'We're moving,' Scott called. Bruce gave it twenty minutes before giving the nod to the other crew. By this stage, the light was poor. The breeze was starting to drop. Both fire lighting pairs moved quickly. As they lit, the fire pushed by the breeze built very rapidly and moved very quickly. As the fire front approached the back burn on the other side of the paddock, the updraught caused by the fire from the east reversed the breeze on the western side, bringing both fire fronts, as planned, roaring straight towards each other.

In the fading daylight, Bruce was on the northern boundary at the creek crossing, witnessing the spectacular upsurge in the fire as the two fronts met and extinguished each other. But this was the most dangerous time as the swirling updraughts in the fire centre could lift embers and carry them a considerable distance. He was scanning towards Gun Creek when he saw a small fire start. 'I have a spot fire on the mid-northern boundary,' he quickly relayed through his VHF. Fortunately, he was already on the north side of the fence in his Kubota with the knapsack of water. He charged towards the fire, leaping out of the vehicle as it stopped. He grabbed the knapsack, threw it on his back and began pumping, spraying the base of the flames. He was lucky. The fire had not advanced anywhere in the light breeze and cooling evening, and he quickly had the fire out. Once he was satisfied it was out, he radioed, 'Spot fire under control, boys.'

Throughout all the action, Wendy drove non-stop between the groups, handing out sandwiches and cold soft drinks from her eskies. As Bruce came back onto the fence line, she arrived and pulled up. 'Some medication for you, boss,' she said as she handed him a peanut paste sandwich and a lemonade.

'Thanks, Wendy,' Bruce said. 'You are a megastar.'

'Anything else before I move on?' she asked.

'No, I'm right here thanks, Wendy,' Bruce replied. She scooted off to the next person scouting along the paddock boundary.

By eight o'clock, everyone agreed the fire was spent and it was safe to leave. Bruce radioed, 'Simone, we're finished here. Dinner in half an hour, please, if that's okay with you?' Simone had been monitoring the situation. Lachlan had discarded his wheelchair a week earlier. He and Carina were helping their mum, eagerly anticipating eavesdropping on the conversation where they would learn plenty about the fire, in addition to what else was happening in the neighbourhood.

Col took off on his motorbike before sunrise the next morning to check the fire. He was keen to spot any residual fire that may flare up and have the potential to start another fire once the day warmed and the breezes started up. The added threat was a fresh burn was fertile ground for whirly winds to start. These could lift embers and take them anywhere. Col's first dash around Goldmine paddock that morning was only the first of many as he kept constant vigilance all day.

Just before ten o'clock, Bruce logged in to register as a bidder in his first online auction sale experience. The auction was being streamed live from Monto. There were two bulls he had recently identified as potential sires being sold today. The first was Lot nine, early in the sale and the second was Lot thirty-one. Bruce was on tenterhooks. He had reviewed the relative potential value of each bull based on recent markets. He had decided he would not exceed twelve thousand dollars for either bull. That had helped his nerves as not having a definite ceiling was too much like gambling for Bruce and he did not like gambling.

The sale bulls, typically weighing six to seven hundred kilograms, were all approximately two years of age. They were fat and red, with sleek shiny coats and none had horns. They were physically and sexually mature and each struck an imposing presence. They looked at the crowd with virtually no expression, though for sure their hearts would have been racing in such a threatening situation for them. Each had a large highly-visible yellow paint brand denoting lot number on its back. They were drafted in pairs into a small arena where a handler moved them around continually so buyers could see them from all angles and could see how they moved. Pairing of bulls helped them settle, each presumably drawing comfort and security from the presence of the other.

When the bulls walked, it was with a rolling amble as their muscle and fat moved fluidly under their gleaming coats. The folds in the large dewlap below their neck flopped around heavily. They usually moved slowly in the selling arena, till the bidding for them was completed, which is when the exit gate was opened. The bulls immediately became alert. Their bulk became firm as they walked deliberately through the gate without coaxing. Some bulls trotted out; they were obviously the most pleased to escape the circus. Having the handler in with the bulls demonstrated how quiet they were. The more difficulty the handler had moving the bulls, the better. Such bulls usually had excellent temperaments, the most valuable trait cattlemen looked for in a bull. Bruce could see that all the bulls being paraded were very docile, matching his experience when he had inspected them.

At ten twenty-two, Lot nine was introduced by the auctioneer who rattled off a barrage of diatribe used to gee up the crowd and potential bidders. The previous eight lots had all sold well, ranging from eight thousand to seventeen thousand dollars. Bruce was a bit edgy about the ceiling he had given himself, but he chastised himself. He relaxed as he thought fondly about Mick's sale of Craig and how similar the scenario was. The auctioneer struggled to get a start-up bid. This is promising, thought Bruce. Then one of the three eagle-eyed spotters on the selling dais with the auctioneer yelled, 'Yes,' as he dramatically pointed to an on-site bidder who offered four thousand dollars. Very quickly the bull went to ten thousand dollars. Bruce had not yet bid.

As the auctioneer spewed out the usual gibberish trying to bait bidders, Bruce waited, and then he hit the bid icon. Immediately, the auctioneer declared, 'We have eleven thousand online.' This immediately evoked two more bids of twelve and then thirteen thousand dollars. Bruce realised he was competing against two others who were as keen as him and looked like they were keen to drive up the price a lot more as well. He withdrew his hand from the mouse and sat on it, watching the situation play out. Within a minute, the bull had been sold for twenty-one thousand dollars. Ten more options left, Bruce thought.

At eleven thirty, Lot thirty-one was introduced. This bull was even more popular. Bidding started at six thousand dollars and rose very quickly to sell for twenty-nine thousand dollars. Bruce didn't even get to bid on the bull. He wasn't feeling good about the situation, especially if every one of the bulls he had targeted over four studs was going to attract prices as high as what he had to compete against today. Maybe he needed to reconsider his ceiling, he thought. He'd discuss this with his dad when they came for the weekend.

Even if Bruce didn't have a good day, Col did. He drove back into the shed where Bruce was working at five o'clock. 'Turns out all my riding today was in vain, Bruce,' Col reported. 'It's a good day when you're checking fires and it turns out it's as exciting as watching paint dry.'

'Thanks Col. Sorry about no action, but I sure am pleased,' Bruce replied. He and Col both wanted a rogue bush fire as much as they wanted a poke in the eye with a burnt stick.

Friday was upon them. There was a great feeling around Bovale. The burn had gone well. But more importantly, Therese was arriving tonight after finishing a morning shift and Bruce's parents were arriving the next day. Simone met Bruce in the shed that morning. 'A royal visit, Bruce. The princess tonight. The king and queen tomorrow. I hope you have everything ready for them,' she said.

'No pressure when you put it like that, Simone,' Bruce responded. 'It's actually pretty good being part of the royal family,' he laughingly suggested.

'I haven't seen you with a tiara yet, Bruce,' Simone threw back at him, grinning broadly.

'You know, we could fix that, Simone,' Bruce said. 'I see on the local Facebook page there's a ball on in Charters Towers in mid-October. Just maybe I can get myself a partner and a tiara, maybe even a cloak, and head into town?' He was alive with smiles, thinking just how good it would be if he could take Therese.

'That might be possible if you could find a girl interested in you,' Simone suggested as she gave Bruce a sideways look, her face covered with a knowing smile.

'Simone, if it looks a goer, I'll buy you and Col a ticket too. I would love for you to be there,' Bruce suggested.

Simone was hesitant. 'Thanks. But who'd look after Carina and Lachlan?' she asked, her forehead creased at the dilemma.

'Easy fixed, Simone. I'll ask The Villa ladies to fix that for you. I'd bet my liver they'd rustle up a solution,' Bruce responded.

'That sounds like a good deal, Bruce,' Simone said, again smiling radiantly in anticipation.

Therese arrived tired but safe at seven o'clock, having driven directly from work. Bruce had just finished a phone call to Jane. His request to help Simone resulted in them agreeing that they should all go to the ball. Jane would organise the gang. They agreed Frances would almost certainly love to come, and Bruce would confirm. 'We'll do a group booking for twelve, Bruce. All of us with partners,' Jane said. Bruce agreed. Jane told Bruce she would also find a babysitter who could use The Villa if that suited. Jane was fired with excitement when he hung up.

'Fancy a night at the Charters Towers Cattlemen's Ball?' Bruce asked Therese.

'I'd love that. When is it?' she asked.

'Saturday the seventeenth of October. Do you reckon you can get the date off?' Bruce asked.

'Do wild bears live in the forest?' Therese said. They jumped into each other's arms and practised a clumsy waltz. 'I think we need practice, Bruce.'

'How about we just keep trying for about a week?' Bruce responded, with a very pleased look about him.

'How about you ring Frances,' Therese suggested when Bruce told her what he and Jane had been planning. Frances was agog with excitement. She was going to be there, come hell or high water.

Bruce had a few small jobs on Saturday morning, but otherwise he and Therese were focussed on getting the homestead ready for the patriarch and matriarch. Bruce mowed the lawns and Therese busied herself enhancing the home look that would make Doris happy. She had not yet met Bruce's parents and was like a cat on a hot tin roof.

'It'll be just like when I met your parents, Therese,' Bruce assured her. 'You shouldn't be surprised they are not a lot different, except they're graziers and not farmers. Minor detail,' he added.

'I don't know whether I have her house just as nice as she would like it, Bruce,' Therese responded.

'It's my house, Therese,' Bruce said, smiling. 'Her house is in Townsville. Mum will be expecting the 'Bruce look' and she will get to see this place as good as it has ever looked. Thanks. You'll find out as soon as you meet her that you fretted about nothing.'

Merve and Doris arrived at ten o'clock. 'Therese, I am so pleased to meet you at last,' Doris said as the two ladies warmly embraced.

Merve was not quite sure how to greet Therese, but she solved it by giving him a bear hug too. 'Great to finally meet you, Merve,' Therese said.

It was a late smoko, but it was still smoko. Doris produced some scones she had cooked before they had left. With the pikelets that Therese had freshly cooked, no-one was going to be short of a superb feed. They'd have to defer lunch to fit it in.

Doris's quick scan over her home of thirty years did not disappoint her. 'Bruce, you are looking after Bovale so well,' she exclaimed.

'I do my best, Mum,' Bruce replied. 'It's Therese's touch that makes all the difference. I don't know where she gets it from, but magic just flows out of her hands.'

'I can tell, Bruce,' Doris responded. They were sitting at the dining room table, the two ladies beside each other. Doris then took Therese's arm and with a broad and sincere smile said to Bruce, 'This lady's a keeper, Bruce. I've only just met her, and I know.' Bruce and Therese just looked at each other and smiled. Merve was laughing, supremely happy, but retained his counsel.

Merve was keen for a look around. Bruce took him for a short drive to see the weaners, steers and bulls while the ladies got to know each other and prepared lunch. After lunch, Bruce suggested they all go for a drive in his parents' dual cab to Jindabyne dam. His mother was just as keen to have a look as Merve was; they were both still referring to Bovale as 'home'. They travelled out through Burdekin and Goldmine paddocks, where Merve could see what a good burn they had achieved.

At Jindabyne dam, they all got out to survey the beautiful scenery. 'This only gets better as it matures,' Doris commented.

Bruce had brought the yabby traps and a bit of bait. He grabbed the canoe and dropped the traps against the lily bed. Merve boiled the billy. Bruce had brought fold-out chairs for a very comfortable picnic. After an hour, Bruce recovered the traps. He had already caught two dozen redclaw, which would make a nice entrée for the evening's barbeque; he was wishing Mick was with them to clean, soak and cook them for him. They went back to the homestead via the yards to see different parts of the station.

The Wattle's came over for dinner. Carina appeared by herself at about a quarter past six. She had obviously pestered Simone senseless about heading over, and Simone had relented. Carina desperately wanted to see the visitors. 'Hello Therese. Hello Mrs Arnold,' she said very quietly and respectfully as she came into the kitchen where the two ladies were chatting as they prepared a few items for the barbeque.

'Hello, Carina,' both ladies replied.

'How nice to see you Carina,' Therese said. 'Have you come over to help?'

Carina nodded shyly. She came alive when Therese asked her to peel two carrots and cut them up. Carina grabbed a chair and put it beside the kitchen bench. After grabbing two carrots from the fridge, she retrieved a potato peeler and a small knife from the drawer beside the sink and a small cutting board. She clambered up on the chair and set to work. The ladies were incredibly impressed with how at home she was in this kitchen.

Bruce was trying to resolve his bid ceiling dilemma with his father. 'I like your strategy, Bruce,' Merve said. 'But I think you might have to reconsider how you calculate your ceilings. Remember you are buying just one bull for the year. You would not have hesitated to buy four or five at a total that is more than your proposed combined expenses for one bull plus Wayne Greenhough's efforts.'

'I agree, Dad. The market's a bit silly at present with no sign of coming back. If what I need costs a few thousand more, then that's what he's worth,' Bruce responded. 'I'll put some more thought into it before the next sale. And that's on Tuesday.'

Chapter Twelve

Doris and Merve decided to leave after yet another afternoon smoko on Sunday. 'We're going home before we blow up from eating too much,' Merve declared.

Doris was tearful. 'It's been absolutely lovely to come out to Bovale and very special you were here, Therese,' she said. 'Next time we'll try and get out for a bit longer so Merve can get his hands dirty, and I can enjoy being back a bit longer. I miss this place.'

As Merve and Doris's dual-cab disappeared along the road out of the station, Bruce and Therese stood hand in hand watching. Bruce shed a tear. Therese saw it. 'A lady gets a good deal when she dates you, Bruce,' she said. 'You have a wonderful family.'

Monday dawned a stunning day. The air was cool and crystal clear. Around sunrise, there was a cacophony as birds of many species went about their daily business. The view from the front of the homestead out over the river was picture-perfect. 'And you have to live here,

Bruce?' Therese asked rhetorically, thinking just how brilliant it would be to also live at Bovale.

Therese did not want to leave that morning, but the afternoon shift in Townsville beckoned. Bruce watched her disappear and wanted to get in his Land Cruiser and follow. *I suspect I know why I feel like this,* he thought. *They say it's not good to rush these things, but I'm tempted to buck that trend.* They had agreed Bruce would head down to Townsville in two weeks in the middle of his mum's next cycle of chemotherapy, when he'd also go fishing and crabbing, hopefully with Lenny.

Tuesday found Bruce again tentative, not his usual self. The Augathella stud was having its auction. Bruce had four bulls in his sights. After the discussion with his father, he had decided to elevate his ceilings by four thousand dollars, but he was firm in his opinion that he must adhere to the settings he'd made for each bull. They varied from fourteen to twenty thousand dollars. The thought of forking out the latter amount for just one bull had him in a cold sweat. *What if I land that bull and he turns out a dud,* he wondered. However, he consoled himself that he had done due diligence as best he could, and he had an agreement with the owner for a replacement if the bull did not measure up.

As for his first online auction, it began at ten o'clock. One hundred and three bulls were being offered. Lots three, sixteen, seventeen and fifty-nine were the bulls Bruce was targeting. He logged in before the auction commenced and confirmed his registration as a bidder. He could see and hear there was a large crowd in attendance at the on-property sale, possibly more than one hundred people. This suggested competition would be as fierce as it was last week. *Ah well, Bruce* thought, it is what it is. When cattle prices were on the rise, market confidence grew, and good products sold well.

The auction was initiated after the vendor welcomed the bidders. As usual, the vendor offered bulls early in the auction that were likely to attract high bids, thus setting a high benchmark for prices. Lots one and two were expected to sell well. The handlers brought them into the selling arena together and slowly moved them around as the auctioneer did his work, his spotters on an adjacent elevated platform. In what seemed like a blink of an eye, the first bull sold for twenty-seven thousand dollars. Lot two sold for twenty-three thousand dollars. Bruce's highest upper limit was on Lot three at twenty thousand dollars. He braced for the action. The auctioneer was in full flight, 'Can I get eight thousand for this bull? Eight thousand? Eight thousand?' He paused. 'Ladies and gentlemen, this bull is worth much more than this. We all know that. Can anyone give me six, just to start it off. Six thousand? Six thousand dollars?'

Bruce considered the situation. He knew this bull was going to attract high bids. He had nothing to lose and a huge amount to gain if he was the opening bidder, especially if bidding was slow and he was able to get the bull well below his threshold. Bruce hit the bid icon. The auctioneer responded. 'I have six thousand online. Six thousand dollars.'

Just as the droning lilt of the auctioneer's voice started to power up, the power went off at Bruce's house. The computer was still on, but the internet receiver dish was not working. 'Damn,' Bruce exclaimed. After the hustle and bustle of the online auction, it was suddenly eerily quiet. The only sound was the faint whisper of the cooling fan in the computer. He could not hear anything else in the house, not even any of the fridges or freezers. His immediate reaction was it was a general power outage, but he needed to check. If it was the transmission line to the station, he could either wait for the power to come back on or fire up a generator to get temporary supply. If something on the station had earthed the power and tripped it, maybe he could identify the culprit and flick the earth leakage circuit breaker back on. That could be difficult, and he hoped that if this was the case, nothing serious had occurred, especially something that could cause damage to the station's power supply.

Bruce jumped up and ran to check the secondary power box at the back of the homestead. Nothing looked unusual. He then trotted across to the shed where he found the same thing in the main power box. As he was checking the power box, Simone came down the front steps of their house. 'Have you lost power too, Bruce?' she yelled out.

'Yes, Simone,' Bruce yelled back. 'Just when I didn't need to. Looks like a general power failure. I'm going to get the generator going.'

Bruce had a fifteen kVA generator that sat in a frame for easy loading and unloading from the back of the old station Land Cruiser. It was mostly used for power tools such as welding around the station. It was stored in the shed adjacent to the power box that was configured to take the generator power when the main transmission line failed. Bruce plugged it in and was about to start the generator when he heard Lachlan yell from inside their house, 'Mum, the power's back on.'

Bruce quickly unplugged the generator from the power box and put the leads back in their usual storage place. He raced back to the home-stead and dashed into his office. It took him three minutes to reconnect to the auction as an online bidder. As the auction reappeared live, the auctioneer announced, 'Righto ladies and gentlemen, Lot twenty-one is as good a bull as we've seen today.' As the drone continued, Bruce immediately realised he had missed the opportunity on three of the four bulls he was aiming to bid for. Most frustrating was he didn't know the price any of the three had attracted, which meant he didn't know whether the outage had thwarted him or not. Whatever the case, there was nought he could do. He just had to wear it.

As the sale progressed, Bruce could see the prices were generally high for the better bulls. Bruce's target of Lot fifty-nine was one such bull, well, in his opinion. He was hoping its price would not exceed the sixteen-thousand-dollar threshold he'd set for his bidding on the bull. The auctioneer suspended the sale after two hours when fifty bulls had been sold. It was lunch time. The selling team needed to re-energise for another two-hour stint. Bruce logged out and had a quick lunch himself before logging back in, in time to catch the sale re-start.

Lots fifty-nine and sixty were drafted into the selling arena half an hour later. The prices had not abated, which was good for the vendor, but had Bruce worried he was not going to get the bull. The auction-eer was waxing lyrically, issuing volleys of typically almost-completely useless information designed purely to switch buyers into hand rais-ing mode. 'Look at the style of this bull, ladies and gentlemen. His length, his eye muscle area at one hundred and twenty-seven square centimetres. One of the sale's gems. This bull is by Rockefeller out of a Red Leather dam, impeccable pedigree. His outlook is outstanding with a beautiful spring of rib. Righto, ladies and gentlemen, what is the opening bid on this bull?' Bruce was cringing hearing this in-formation. It was laughable, but somehow the big operators with deep pockets seemed to love it and it opened their wallets. Bruce was despairing that yet another bull would escape him, denying him a purchase opportunity.

A spotter found a man with a finger discretely held skywards. 'Yes,' he yelled as he pointed at the man, enabling the auctioneer to quickly pick him out and focus on him.

So much for the discrete finger raising, thought Bruce, as in almost the same fluid moment, the ring-side bidder called out, 'Seven.'

'I have seven thousand ladies and gentlemen. Seven thousand. Seven thousand dollars, Seven thousand dollar bidder, now.' The auctioneer was alight with passion as he and his spotters worked the sale arena, trying to create a bidding frenzy. It did not seem like anyone else was going to join the competition. Bruce didn't know whether this was the negative psychology trick, bidders used against the auctioneer's strategy. The idea was to delay bidding so that other bidders would be potentially lulled into thinking the Lot was not what the auctioneer had cracked it up to be, which may pull the ultimate price down. Bruce knew this, but he also knew he wanted, even needed, the bull. He hit the bid icon, which was spotted instantaneously, eight hundred kilometres south on a ring-side computer monitor. The auctioneer shouted, 'I have eight online. Eight thousand dollars.'

Bruce's bid immediately triggered a bidding battle. Bruce quickly realised there must have been many people with the same idea as him. The price rocketed straight past sixteen thousand dollars. The spotters had bulging eyes as they eagerly sought bids, with theatrical pointing towards bidders and calls of 'Yes' firing like shots from a semi-automatic 308 rifle. The bull didn't care a jot. He was waiting for someone to open the gate. Bruce cared. His opportunity was gone. He adopted a similar attitude to the bull. He just waited till the bidding was done and then he would exit the auction.

The bidding pulled up when the auctioneer declared, 'I have fifty thousand dollars, ladies and gentlemen. Fifty thousand dollars.' His emphasis on the first syllable of 'thousand' was dramatic. The selling team persisted but couldn't extract a higher bid. The bull was knocked down to another stud master with a flourishing smack of the gavel into the auctioneer's lectern as he called, 'All done. Out she goes. To the Red Leather Droughtmaster Stud. Congratulations Dennis and Greta,' the auctioneer finished with.

That evening, Bruce logged on to see the results of the auction. The list of bulls was displayed alongside their sale prices. Lot fifty-nine was the sale topper. Lot three went for twenty-seven thousand, two thousand more than Lot sixteen. But Lot seventeen went for just fifteen thousand dollars. Bruce had put a bid ceiling of sixteen thousand dollars on the bull. 'Damn,' he said out loud. 'Damn. Damn.' But then he reconsidered. The person who got the bull for fifteen may have simply out-bid him if Bruce had bid at sixteen thousand dollars. We'll never know, thought Bruce, but, damn. All but one bull had been sold at an average price of eleven thousand, three hundred dollars. This made Bruce's selection look excellent. Bruce could have bought many bulls at an affordable price, but he simply didn't want them as they did not meet his strict breeding objectives. Well, at least I can pick a good bull, thought Bruce.

He'd invested a lot of time into getting a bull and so far, and he had nothing to show for his endeavours. Despite the outcome, Bruce was happy for the stud owner. He sent him a congratulatory email. There were bull sales happening all over the countryside. Each stud selected their preferred date mostly somewhere in the August to October window when their sale bulls were approaching two years of age and were being purchased for mating immediately after the sales were completed. As the second-most popular breed in Queensland where approximately fifteen million beef cattle lived, Droughtmaster sales were a regular occurrence. The Red Leather stud sale was on in just three days.

It was back to more mundane station work for Bruce. He and Col spent much of Wednesday digging holes and building and cementing in strainer sets for a one-kilometre fence across the northern end of Airstrip paddock. It was parallel to, and fifty metres from, the existing fence. The objective was to create a laneway that would hopefully keep the bull paddock occupants far enough away from the fifty potential girlfriends in Airstrip. On Thursday, they strung four heavy barbed wires that they tied to galvanised steel pickets knocked in every eight metres along the fence line. This fence was strong, and needed to be.

On Friday, Bruce saddled up for another auction. This one would be shorter as only fifty-four bulls would be sold. The Seccombe family kept a beautiful lawn beside the yard where they had erected a large tent for the day. This setting was visible on the live feed. This sale was not a traditional auction. Rather, Dennis and Greta had opted for a Helmsman auction in which all bulls are sold simultaneously. Bidding opened at ten o'clock, giving everyone ample time to do their final inspections of the bulls on offer. The bulls were in groups of four to six in pens through the yard complex. The auctioneers had all bulls listed on a board. When a bid was made on a bull, the price was written on the board at the same time as being listed online. There was a cut-off time, twelve o'clock, when final bids had to be received.

The highest bidder on each bull at that time, secured that bull. This type of auction tended to start slowly and build to rapid bidding as the deadline loomed.

It was a good format for Bruce as he logged in online. He could casually bid at any time, and even have smoko or lunch as it proceeded. At the sale site, bidders continually inspected bulls and discretely discussed tactics with their bidding partners. The crowd zeroed in on the bid registration board during the high-concentration time, the last fifteen minutes before time was called. Bruce had three bulls in his sights. The challenge was how to not land all three, so his bidding had to be strategic. He had set his ceilings at fourteen, sixteen and eighteen thousand dollars. He decided to only bid initially on the bull he'd given the highest ceiling. He would stick with that bull unless the bidding exceeded his ceiling. If that happened, he'd switch his bids to the bull with the next-highest ceiling, leaving one last bull if the bidding again got away on him on the second bull. However, this would only be successful if bids escalated in a *pro rata* manner. He could easily find himself with nothing to bid for if both the other bulls were already past his threshold when the first bull exceeded his. At an auction, not much is predictable, so any further planning was difficult. Bruce wished himself good luck.

By eleven o'clock, bids had been placed on all three of Bruce's target bulls. Eight thousand dollars had been bid for his number one selection. Bids on the other two remained well short of Bruce's thresholds. At eleven-thirty, Bruce's number one target was already at sixteen thousand dollars. It did not look good, Bruce thought. Surprisingly, his number three selection was also at the same bidding level; goodbye bull, Bruce thought. With seven minutes to go, Bruce made his move.

He bid eighteen thousand dollars for number one. Only two minutes had elapsed before a bid of twenty thousand was made for the bull. Gone. Damn, Bruce thought, this is frustrating.

His only option left was number two. Fortunately, the bull remained within reach. He currently sat on fourteen thousand dollars. Bruce let another thirty seconds go by and then he bid fifteen thousand dollars. He almost held his breath, waiting for a counter bid. But it didn't come. The auctioneer counted down the time and at exactly twelve o'clock, he called, 'Time.' Bruce had a bull. He was elated.

Bruce immediately got on the UHF. 'We've got a bull,' he excitedly announced. There could have been no-one listening as he hadn't bothered to check first.

He felt a bit of a dolt, but not for long as Col came on. 'Good on you, Bruce,' he said with a similar level of excitement to Bruce's evident in his voice.

Straight behind him came Simone. 'Congratulations,' she radioed. 'Tell me more,' she excitedly requested.

'He's red,' said Bruce with a bit of a giggle. Crikey, I sound like a child, he thought. He was feeling in a particularly silly mood. He'd obviously had an endogenous release of some sort of brain stimulant that had him buoyantly care-free.

'That's an incredible surprise given all Droughtmasters are red,' radioed Simone.

Bruce quickly settled to his usual self. 'Sorry, Simone,' Bruce radioed back. 'He's just the sort of bull I was looking for. Somehow, no-one else saw what I saw, and they left him for me. Though I do have to part with fifteen thousand dollars for the privilege of bringing him home.'

Bruce climbed off cloud nine after lunch. He had rung his father and Therese, both of whom were at work. He apologised profusely for interrupting their days, but both were very happy for him. At two o'clock he had a phone call from the selling agent, 'Congratulations on the bull, Bruce.'

'Thanks, mate,' Bruce replied. He'd forgotten the bloke's name within seconds of him having introduced himself. They agreed on invoicing details.

The agent then asked, 'How would you like the bull to be consigned?'

'I hadn't seriously considered that yet. Do you have any suggestions?' Bruce asked.

'Yes, Bruce. There were twenty bulls bought by businesses in your region and the owner has booked a truck to take that lot to the Charters Towers sale yards. Would that work for you?' the agent replied.

'That would be perfect,' Bruce said. 'When can we expect the bull to arrive?'

'It should be early Wednesday morning, Bruce,' the agent advised.

After the call finished, Bruce rang his good mate, Mick, who worked for a business that owned a truck. 'Mick, how would you be?' Bruce asked. They went through the usual social update chat before Bruce introduced his reason for calling. 'Mick, I've got myself a bull. I picked him up at the Red Leather sale this morning. Pretty pleased with myself.'

Mick immediately worked out why Bruce had rung. They had done business like this before. 'Do you want me to go down and get him, Bruce?' Mick asked.

'No, Mick. Even better. They're bringing him to the saleyards in town. The plan is to have him here early Wednesday. Would it suit for you to bring him out once he's ready?' Bruce asked.

'That should not be a problem, Bruce,' Mick replied.

Mick arrived at Bovale before lunch on Wednesday. It was almost a royal welcome. Simone suspended school lessons and Col stopped what he was doing. They all gathered around the loading ramp at the cattle yard as Mick drove the truck up. Bruce and Col had the gates set for the bull to exit the truck before Mick had even managed to clamber out of the cab. 'You blokes are a bit keen,' Mick remarked, laughing. 'Anyone would think you've just taken delivery of a million-dollar bull.'

'He is, Mick,' Bruce replied. 'Fifteen grand is a fair bit of dough. Let's hope he's worth it.'

The bull walked calmly out of the truck into an empty cattle yard. The small crowd stood against the fence in the small yard where the bull stood and admired him. Mobile phones were busy as multiple photos were taken, including one with Bruce standing near his head. 'I like him, Bruce,' Col commented. 'He has everything I like to see in a bull. And if you say he has the right genes, you've done exceptionally well to get him for just fifteen thousand in the current market'

'Thanks, Col,' Bruce responded.

'He's a beauty,' Lachlan declared.

'Does he have a name?' Carina asked.

'He has a number, Carina. Do you have a name we could give him?' Bruce asked.

Carina creased her small forehead in thought for a moment. 'Can we call him Jasper?' she asked as she held her hands out and high, jumping on the spot, in anticipation of Bruce agreeing. Carina liked collecting pretty rocks. Her favourites were some beautiful red rocks she had found in the river that a visitor had confirmed for her were jasper.

'I like it,' Bruce said. 'Jasper it is. Thanks Carina. Do you like that name, Lachlan?' Bruce asked.

'Yes, Bruce,' Lachlan said. 'He's beautiful, just like Carina's rocks. But I hope he's a bit more useful than a rock sitting on the table,' he added, being the very practical lad he was.

After lunch, Bruce mounted his two-wheel motorbike and walked Jasper out. Bruce let him take his time. He was obviously hungry and was catching a mouth-full of feed at every opportunity as he strolled along. Jasper was too valuable to put with the other bulls in Bull paddock immediately. Jasper had to become accustomed to the feed, water and environmental conditions of Bovale, which were very different to the cosy situation he'd been reared in. He also had no social position within the herd; they were all strangers to him. Dominant mature bulls would have immediately given him a flogging just so he would know where he was in the pecking order. Bulls are powerful animals, and such encounters can cause broken legs, which results in the bull having to be shot. Bruce and Col had agreed the best place for him in the short term was in with the pregnant heifers he'd be mating after Christmas. The heifers would not hurt him. He would not hurt them, and he sure couldn't get any pregnant when they were already in advanced pregnancy. They'd relocate him after calving started in a month, before the cows started to cycle again, and after he'd have had time to adapt to Bovale.

The heifers had left the water to graze out in Airstrip paddock before Bruce arrived with Jasper. Bruce reasoned he'd be okay if he left him here in a very low-risk situation. Jasper now knew where the water was. He'd be like all other cattle that get introduced to a new paddock; he'd walk the paddock boundary to orientate himself, and he'd find other cattle and establish a social position. Being a bull, he'd naturally establish a territory. But Bruce had already done this for him, as well as selecting a high-class harem for him. He had the whole of Airstrip paddock, and no other bull could come waltzing in to challenge him. Perfect.

That night Bruce rang Dennis Seccombe. 'Thanks Dennis. The bull is perfect.'

'I'm glad you like him, Bruce. I reckon you were really lucky to get him at the price you paid, but that's the market for you,' Dennis replied.

'I agree, Dennis. You wouldn't have known, but I was one of the under-bidders on that bull you picked up at Augathella last Tuesday. Congratulations. That bull is superb, and I hope he works out well for you,' Bruce said. They had a great chin wag for another half an hour, mostly about cattle but also making sure they updated each other on the social front. Bruce felt he had found a good friend in Dennis. He hoped it would hold him in good stead in the future.

Bruce was on a high as he headed out on Friday afternoon. He was going fishing. He was seeing his family. Most importantly, he was seeing Therese. Therese was having her days off in Brandon, which was perfect for both of them. But first, Townsville. The family were all present to greet him when he arrived. 'Tell us all about this bull, Bruce,' Merve asked. Bruce had photos and videos to show them which he downloaded onto the family computer so they could all see it at once and enlarged on the monitor. Dinner would wait till they dissected all the information Bruce had.

'Explain to me these breeding values you keep talking about, Bruce. They're obviously important, but I really have no idea how they work,' Merve requested.

'How about we have dinner, because Frances has it prepared, and we can talk about that as we eat?' Bruce suggested. Merve disappeared to the shed and returned in no time with beers for himself, Bruce and Frances. Doris was in the middle of a chemotherapy cycle and was neither on the hops nor voluble for anything. She barely ate as they dug into the delicious fish and chips Frances had cooked.

'Dad, when we buy a bull, we buy him for two attributes,' Bruce explained. 'One is his DNA. The other is his ability to put that DNA where and when it's needed. The last bit is why we do a breeding soundness evaluation which involves a standardised assessment of his physical capacity, his scrotal contents, and his sperm motility and morphology. All those elements are critical. It doesn't matter how good his DNA is if he can't deliver.

'The real challenge though, is knowing whether the bull has the right DNA. The unfortunate situation is that you can't judge much of a bull's DNA simply by looking at him. Yes, you can with weight and temperament, for example, but critical traits like female fertility remain a mystery unless we use some way to work it out. An example of how successful this can be is selection for milk production in dairy cattle. For aeons, farmers and geneticists have been conducting progeny tests to find out which bulls sire daughters with the best milking capacity. It's slow, but it works.'

'So, why can't you just select the cows directly like we've always done?' Merve asked.

'There are a few reasons, Dad,' Bruce continued. 'The first is we have to keep most of the females we breed, so there's very low selection pressure. The second, and most important, is that bulls have about fifty times as much influence on the next generation as females do. A cow can have an average of say, zero point seven five calves a year, that is three calves every four years. But a bull can easily sire forty calves a year. Therefore, if we know whether the bull has the right DNA for fertility or not, we can achieve a vastly higher rate of improvement compared to just selecting females. A third reason is the corollary of the second reason; if we use bulls with the wrong DNA, we can be going backwards without knowing it and if we've planted the wrong genes in our herd, it can take ten to fifteen years to breed them out again. One of the big problems with only using selection on cow performance is that even though you can make some minor progress that way, every time you buy a bull of unknown genetic merit, you are randomly pushing the direction of change backwards or forwards much more rapidly, effectively completely over-riding every step forward you make with the females. Does that make sense?'

'It sure does, Bruce. Thanks. Now I know why you're running Bovale these days and I'm selling shovels,' Merve said. 'It's amazing what your generation is doing now that can solve problems we didn't even know we had.'

'It's not just my generation, Dad,' Bruce responded. 'Some of the smartest people using these methods are fossils. It depends on what presses your buttons. Breeding does it for me and that's why I've made it my business to learn about it and use it.'

Bruce continued with his explanation. 'The science on how to find bulls with the right genes for all the important attributes has been evolving quite rapidly over the past forty years or so. All the top studs enrol in a program where they get pedigrees and measure growth, fertility, adaptation, behaviour and carcass and meat quality in females, steers and bulls. The data is then crunched for each breed to calculate breeding values. So, for example, there is a widely-used breeding value for female fertility called days to calving, which is a measure of the time between when mating starts and when the cow has a calf; more fertile females have shorter days to calving. If we select bulls with a negative days to calving, that means his female progeny will on average be more fertile than at least half the cattle within the breed.

'Jasper has a breeding value of minus ten for days to calving. That is huge,' Bruce emphasised. He was fired up in his passion and Merve could see how important it was to his son, and to his business.

'What's really exciting is the scientists have now worked out how to read the DNA directly. We give them a bit of DNA, like tail hair roots or a snip of skin out of the ear. They read the DNA in the lab to get what they call a genotype. And then mathematicians use the genotype to calculate genomic breeding values. So now we can have a bull of any breed with no data available on him at all, and we take DNA from him and get breeding values for all sorts of traits. The most important for us is what they call P4M, which is pregnant within four months of calving while the cow is lactating. That's what we've just done for the Bovale bull herd, and we should get the results any day now. I'm just crapping myself that we'll have to get rid of too many bulls because they'll have dud DNA. But no point jumping at shadows.'

'Bruce, that is amazing stuff,' Frances said. 'I had no idea how much science goes into what you are doing. No wonder you're running Bovale and I'm doing someone else's dirty work in the big city.'

Frances, Bruce and Merve spent another two hours talking about Bruce's plans for breeding at Bovale before the sleep genie beckoned them. Bruce was up early, as usual, and headed for Brandon. He and Lenny were going to catch half the fish in the Burdekin River delta today, or so Lenny had assured him. They were using Bruce's tinny today as it needed a run after having been parked up in Merve's shed since the mud crab attack.

Brutus was a quick learner. He must have already tuned his ear to the sound of Bruce's Land Cruiser because as Bruce turned into the driveway, the big pan licker was waiting there with what looked like the biggest smile in the lower Burdekin plastered across his dog head. He raced up and down beside Bruce as he slowly went towards the shed. Bruce must have let out a woof at some stage to alert the clan because Therese was waiting for him as he pulled up.

Therese and Maria made sure their men did not go down the creek hungry. There was no way the ladies could understand why the blokes didn't want to take a picnic lunch with them, but they just had to accept that men are weird creatures who liked doing weird things in creeks and they'd fix their hunger when they got home.

Bruce took Lenny to his favourite fishing haunt. Bruce was very keen to see what Gater Gush would yield. The men had picked a good day for it. The tides were right, a bit over average height so there wasn't too much run. There was very little wind, which was a bonus at this time of the year when usually the south-easterlies hammered you. Most importantly, the fish and the crabs were hungry. They had set the crab pots and Bruce had anchored them in a stretch of the creek littered with snags. Lenny was the first to cast his lure. It landed only thirty centimetres from the bank, adjacent to a semi-submerged log. Instantly, his rod bent over as a fish hit the lure and took off, diving and veering away from the boat. It then shot upwards, breaching the surface, violently shaking its whole body in its efforts to dislodge the hook. It was a good-sized barramundi. 'I think you might have a fish there, Lenny,' Bruce said, as calmly as possible, grossly understating his inner excitement.

Bruce was reaching for the landing net. Lenny, in his ecstasy, was supreme in his irony. 'I think I have, mate. Probably just bloody crab pot bait though.' He held his emotions and concentrated on playing the fish. Fairly quickly, Lenny brought the fish in beside the boat and Bruce calmly scooped him out of the water.

'Well done, mate,' Bruce exclaimed. 'I haven't even had my line in the water and you're already way ahead of me.' They fished the incoming tide for two and a half hours and then the outgoing tide for another two and a half hours. They moved quite a few times to pick up the pace. They were having a good day. Lenny had landed a second barra, two good grunters and a pearler of a mangrove jack. Bruce had landed three barramundi, two finger-mark bream, and one mangrove jack. These fish were between quite a few under-sized fish they had released back into the creek.

'Lenny, you're my good luck charm,' Bruce declared. 'I reckon we have enough for today,' he said as they reeled in so they could slip up Gater Gush and retrieve the crab pots.

'It's the other way round, Bruce. I generally have difficulty catching a cold. But today, it's been magic. Thanks,' Lenny responded.

Out in the main channel of the creek, Bruce opened the throttle and the tinny planed beautifully. It felt like it performed better with the balancing weight of Lenny up front than it usually did when Bruce was in the boat by himself. As they reached the entrance to Gater Gush, Bruce throttled way back and had the boat in a slow cruise as they entered crab paradise. Lenny turned around to Bruce, 'Maybe we should have our steel-capped boots on today?' he joked.

'Don't tempt fate, Lenny,' Bruce suggested, laughing. 'The buggers don't need an invitation to take a piece out of you, and they'll probably bite your ankle and not your toe.'

They eased their way through the mangrove thicket, passing seven of the pots they had laid. When they got to the top-most pot, downstream from a large log blocking further access up the gully, Bruce cut the engine and they manhandled themselves into position to pull out the pot. Lenny grabbed the rope and tugged the float out of the mangrove tree they had thrown it into. He then took the weight of the pot and lifted it to the surface of the water. 'She's heavy, Bruce. Looks promising,' Lenny said. The dappled sunlight on such a pristine day gave them both a good look as the pot breached the surface. As it came clear of the water, a large cod in the pot thrashed wildly amid five crabs. 'Whoopee. We done good, Bruce,' Lenny yelled out, excited as a three-year-old with a new toy. Bruce watched as Lenny dipped the pot a few times to clear the mud from the base before he hefted it into the boat. Lenny deftly removed the cod. Bruce held open his large esky to take the fish in quick time.

'Looks like you've got two legals there, Lenny,' Bruce observed. 'Two jennies and a small buck it looks to me.' Lenny worked on the catch and just as deftly as he had with the cod, he had both large bucks confirmed as legal size and into Bruce's esky. While Bruce slowly manoeuvred the tinny downstream to the next pot, Lenny removed the old bait, collapsed the pot and stacked it in the floor of the boat. By the time they repeated the process eight times, they had nine good crabs and three cod.

'What a brilliant day, Lenny. Thanks. I'll remember this one for a while.'

'Better than that, Bruce, I'll remember it as what happens every time I go fishing. No wonder we like doing this,' Lenny replied.

As they drove up to the shed back in Brandon, Brutus, Therese and Maria were all excitedly waiting to see what had been achieved. Lenny casually got out of the car and declared, 'Well, no-one got bitten today. And the boat went really well.' He was packing on the irony as thick as he could.

However, Maria knew Lenny better than he did. She ignored the comment and went straight to the boat trailer. She climbed up and opened the esky. Her face lit up. 'Wow,' she said as she closed the lid and faced Therese with a huge smile. This prompted Therese to follow suit; she was also suitably impressed.

After the obligatory smoko, the men set to work cleaning their catch and the boat. The fish fillets were all packaged. Bruce was dropping some off in Townsville before he went back to Bovale. The crabs had to be dealt with fresh. Bruce would take three back to Bovale, two for the Wattle's and drop two off for his dad. That left four crabs for dinner. All four of them had fresh crab as a menu-topper. Bruce killed each crab, spiking it into the abdomen at the point of its flap. He then took off the carapace and cleaned the crabs, leaving the bodies, nippers and legs, ready for a fifteen-minute steaming.

Dinner was divine. The food was first class. The company was first class. Bruce was pinching himself. He kept thinking how amazing it was to have Therese as his girlfriend and that she came from such a fantastic family. As dinner wound up, Therese asked, 'Everyone ready for Oh Hell?'

'I'm in,' replied Bruce.

'We've never played it,' Maria added. 'Can we learn?'

Within minutes, Therese and Bruce had Lenny and Maria schooled in Oh Hell. The next hour was spent pitting their wits against each other. 'That was fun,' declared Maria.

'Nowhere near as much fun as a port,' Lenny responded. He had headed over to his liquor stash in a lounge-room cupboard. He set down four small glasses and a bottle of expensive South Australian port on the table and poured a glass-full for each of them. 'A toast to a great day,' he said as he raised his glass and sipped, joined in unison by the others.

'I'd like to toast Bruce and Therese,' Maria said, suddenly inspired. 'You are such a beautiful couple and Bruce, Lenny and I are absolutely thrilled that you are Therese's best friend.' She raised her glass and sipped.

'Hear, hear,' Lenny prompted in agreement. He raised his glass and gulped the whole lot. 'That's how impressed I am,' he said. 'Very.'

'Thanks Mum and Dad,' Therese said. She was tearing up.

'Thanks Lenny and Maria,' Bruce said. 'If you're impressed with Therese, you can't imagine how much more impressed I am,' he added. He paused. 'I think I need a drink.' Bruce was trying to hide his embarrassment of having suddenly blurted that out. He need not have been concerned.

'Do you have your suit for the ball next month yet, Bruce?' Maria asked.

'No, not yet. I should get onto that. I'm hoping to get into town late next week and can organise it then,' Bruce replied.

'Has Therese given you any suggestions?' Maria asked.

'Not yet, but I'm all ears,' Bruce responded. They spent the next quarter of an hour working out what Bruce should do. Bruce learned that Therese, with plenty of assistance from Maria, was well-advanced in her preparations for the ball. It was a huge event. The discussion fired excitement in Bruce. He'd never experienced going to a ball with a girlfriend before. The ball would be almost an official public debut of their relationship. When Bruce had that realisation, he knew why the ladies were so serious about their preparations. It also dawned on him that The Villa would probably be in pandemonium, working through all that had to be done to turn up looking like a million dollars with a partner to match. He thought he probably should stay a night in Charters Towers with the gang to make sure all was going well.

After breakfast on Sunday, Lenny jammed Bruce and Therese in his ute and they had an inspection of the farm. Bruce had little understanding of the process of sugar farming, but by lunch time he was much wiser. Half the tour involved checking out all Lenny's toys, as he called them. He had an impressive array of machinery and implements with one three-hundred-horsepower tractor that looked to Bruce like it would have experienced no engine strain at all dragging the family home to Townsville and back. Therese was in her element. She was clearly a competent grease monkey, able to service much of the machinery and do all sorts of maintenance on the implements. 'I can see now that when we fixed that Hollywood fence, why it was such a simple task for you, Therese,' Bruce said.

After yet another sumptuous lunch of Maria's special hand-made ravioli, Therese left for Townsville as she had an afternoon shift. She took the fish and crabs to Merve and Doris's place as that would allow Bruce to take the short-cut, taking about forty minutes off the drive to Bovale. The Wattle's were ecstatic to see him back. 'Crab for dinner,' Lachlan cheered.

On Monday, Bruce and Col had finished for the day when Bruce's mobile rang. It was Wayne Greenhough. 'Bruce, I've just received the breeding values back for your bulls from the University of Queensland team. I'm about to email them to you.'

'Is it good news or bad, Wayne?' Bruce asked.

'Bit of a mixture, Bruce,' Wayne replied. 'There's some serious rubbish I'd advise consigning to the meatworks. But I reckon you'll have enough bulls that you'll be happy with, but it may take you a bit to accept some of them. I'll email the data now and we can talk about the details later. Would tomorrow suit?'

'That would be perfect, Wayne. Any time after sunrise will work for me, before I head out to do some jobs,' Bruce replied.

'Where have you got to with the recommendations we worked out a while back, Bruce?' Wayne asked.

'I reckon we've advanced as much as possible at this stage, Wayne. It's been a hoot,' Bruce indicated. 'The best outcome is I nailed a foundation sire for breeding our own bulls. We got him home just the other day. I'm very happy with him.' Bruce gave Wayne a synopsis of everything else he'd done as well before they finished the call.

That night, Bruce studied what Wayne had sent him. There was a chart showing the distribution of genomic breeding values for his bulls. In addition, there were genomic breeding values for about ten traits listed for each of the bulls. The variation looked startling to Bruce. There was too much that looked below average. He'd have to wait to discuss it with Wayne.

Wayne rang at six-thirty on Tuesday morning. 'How's your head?' he asked.

'Muddled,' Bruce replied.

'Let's see if we can fix it,' Wayne suggested. Wayne waited while Bruce sat himself in front of his computer and opened the Excel file with the results. 'We'll look first at the sheet marked 'Graph'. Bruce clicked on the sheet where a colourful graph was displayed. 'That graph is your Herd Profile. The first observation I'd make for you, Bruce, is that even though it doesn't look brilliant, it's actually quite representative of herds in northern Australia. That means, judging from your bull herd, your cattle are average. That's fine. It simply reflects the bulls you've been buying. So, it will come as no surprise to you to learn that many of the studs are average to a bit above average too, because they haven't previously had access to this technology. The downside is, no matter how hard you've tried, you've just stayed with the pack. It's the old problem of bought bulls, not your female herd, driving your genetics. It's been impossible for you to get ahead of the studs while-ever you buy their bulls, unless you also use this technology, or you have your own stud and are better at bull breeding than the rest.'

'That's good news, Wayne. I was worried when I saw this that I had a problem that no-one else had. I feel a whole lot better,' Bruce said.

Wayne continued. 'You'll see a bar for each trait. Let's look at one bar, the one on the left for weight. That's weight at about eighteen months, so it's a measure of combined yearling growth and growth up to weaning. The red section of the bar shows what proportion of your bulls are in the bottom twenty percent for north Australian beef cattle. Yours looks about eighteen percent. At the top end, the blue shows what proportion of your herd is in the top twenty percent for the north Australian herd. You have about twenty-five percent there. The green shows what's above average, the yellow shows what's average and the orange is what proportion are below average. Overall, you are a bit above average.'

'Righto, I understand that now. Thanks, Wayne,' Bruce responded.

'Now look across at all the other bars on the graph,' Wayne directed. 'The more it's biased towards blue, the better your herd genetics are for that trait and the more biased towards red, the poorer your genetics are.'

'Mmmmm. I can see we're a bit up and down, Wayne,' Bruce said.

'Yes, I agree,' Wayne replied. 'If you refer to your breeding objectives, you'll know the most important is P4M. You are heavily biased to red, which is not good. But your herd genetics is average for ability to reach puberty early, which is fine. You're below par on hip height, but you're biased towards blue on the adaptation traits and temperament. My basic reading of this is, you need to put as much pressure on good P4M genetics as you can, but also try to avoid getting into the red for any traits.'

'I agree with that Wayne. It's a lot clearer to me now. That's a ripper graph,' Bruce suggested. 'How would you recommend I draft out the bulls I'm going to keep?'

You have thirty-two bulls that passed a breeding soundness evaluation, Bruce, and you can afford to cull twelve. You'll see in the right-hand column of the spreadsheet with the genomics breeding values, there is a list of all the traits with a number between one and one hundred beside each.'

'I've got it, Wayne,' Bruce acknowledged.

Wayne continued. 'What you do is type over each number with a threshold number for your bulls. For example, if you put twenty for each trait except P4M where you put forty, that means no selected bull will be in the bottom twenty percent for any trait, and all will be average to high for P4M, that is, in the top sixty percent of north Australian cattle. The number of your bulls that meet all these thresholds is shown at the top of the column.'

Bruce entered the values Wayne had suggested. 'When I do that, Wayne, I get twelve. Does that mean I have to drop my thresholds to push the total to twenty?'

'Exactly, Bruce,' Wayne replied. 'Maybe first put everything at one except P4M and leave it at forty. The answer you get then will tell you if you have any opportunity to select for other traits or not.'

Bruce did this. 'It now says nineteen, Wayne,' Bruce said. 'Bugger. I'm going to have to drop my P4M threshold to thirty at least.'

'You've got it, Bruce. You can probably manage it from here. Remember I told you that you'll want to cull a lot more than you can, Bruce. Sorry mate,' Wayne said. 'But the good news is that it might be tough initially, but if you keep working on it, after a few years, it'll become much easier.

'The other strategy you can test is to keep ramping up your thresholds to find your top one or two bulls,' Wayne added. 'You might find a diamond among them that could compare with Jasper.'

'I already have Droughtmaster breeding values for Jasper,' Bruce said. 'Do you think I should get him assessed using these multi-breed genomic breeding values?'

'I would recommend it, Bruce,' Wayne replied. 'You never know, one of your current bulls may be comparable, but from what you've told me, possibly not. Let's have a chat in a month or two to consolidate but ring me sooner if you need someone to talk through anything you're doing,' Wayne suggested.

'That sounds brilliant, Wayne,' Bruce replied.

Bruce had a few jobs to do before he could work on the bull selection. After lunch, he spent two hours working on it and finally settled on his top twenty bulls. He'd confirm that by yarding and drafting the bulls he and Col would make sure there was no bull obviously in either the culls or bulls he was keeping when it should be in the opposite group.

Chapter Thirteen

It was a busy time of the year at Bovale. The cattle and the business became highly-demanding until the season broke, and in an average year, that was Christmas day. Bruce enjoyed the three months of hard slog, despite the mounting heat exacerbated by the monotony of the dry season. It was late September and supplementation of all cattle was in full swing with the first cows expected to calve within weeks.

It was late on Monday morning when a semi-trailer drove into the station compound. Bruce greeted the truck driver. 'Gday, mate. We'll unload and get you going in no time.' Bruce had been advised the shipment was coming. He had the tractor ready with the forks fitted and set to work unloading the ten pallets of a specially-formulated supplement from Home Hill.

When he finished, the truck driver commented, 'I haven't delivered this type of mix before. Sorry to be nosy, but I'm just interested. What are you feeding this to, Bruce?'

'No problem, mate. It's for the heifers about to commence calving,' Bruce replied. 'We'll probably start feeding this tomorrow. We're aiming to get about one kilogram daily into each heifer. It gives them an energy boost, a bit like simulating green pick from an early storm. It's also got a yeast-extract product included that has been shown to significantly boost all responses to the supplements. We're aiming at two benefits. The first is it keeps their ovaries in good order. The eggs for the next pregnancy are being cooked up in late pregnancy and we don't want that set back. It's called spike feeding. It can boost pregnancy rates during lactation by up to twenty percent, which is a huge bonus.

'The second benefit is it helps the heifer switch from pregnancy mode to lactation mode on the day of calving. We've been losing too many newborn calves because many new mothers are not ready to start full milking on the day of calving, much like what happens in many women after they have a baby. Recent research shows that if we boost the quality of feed in the weeks before calving, we can reduce this problem and boost calf survival rates.'

'Gee, that's interesting,' the driver replied. 'Where do you learn all that stuff?'

'Well, I pay an advisor,' Bruce replied. 'I know not everyone does. I'm probably a reasonable cowboy. But there's lots I don't know. I'm finding out that if you pay the right people for professional support, it's amazing how much extra net benefit there can be for the business.'

'That's excellent,' the driver said. 'It's bloody good to see young people making good things happen.'

The next day, a full semi-trailer load with twenty-two tonnes of a phosphorus lick arrived from Townsville. The shipment included ten tonnes of the dry season to wet season transition supplement for the pregnant cows that would soon be calving and lactating. The potential provided by implementing the new supplementation regimes was an exciting prospect for Bruce.

Bruce rang Jane on Tuesday night. 'How's The Villa ladies going?' he asked.

'Great, Bruce,' she replied. 'It's a crazy house though. We're all getting ready for the ball. It's so much fun.'

'Yes, Therese and her mum are spending night and day on it, too. But, you'll know, I'm a bloke and we just don't go to the same heights as you ladies,' Bruce admitted.

'I know. We'll forgive you as long as you turn up looking a million dollars,' Jane said. 'Have you got your suit yet, Bruce?'

'Well, not yet, but I'm planning on coming into town on Thursday afternoon to fit myself out,' Bruce replied.

'Has Therese given you instructions?' Jane asked.

How come they know this stuff, Bruce wondered to himself. 'She has, Jane. I'll do my best,' Bruce replied.

'We can't risk anything, Bruce. You blokes are hopeless. You wouldn't know green from pink. I'm going to ring Therese and find out what she wants and I'm coming shopping with you,' Jane declared.

'I think I've been given an offer I can't refuse, Jane. Thanks,' Bruce said. 'But that's not why I rang.' Though it was. I tell a lie, he said to himself. 'If you see that Mick bloke around town, can you tell him, if it suits him, I'll choke down at his place on Thursday night? And I rang you because if there's an opportunity to play gangs on Thursday night, you'll know.'

'You bet,' said Jane. 'I reckon we could have Friday night on Thursday night. I'm sure the girls and Mick and Craig will be up for it. Unless you hear from me, she's on.'

'Thanks, Jane. Can we meet at four o'clock at Ranch Pants on Thursday afternoon?' Bruce asked.

'Done deal. See you then,' Jane said as they finished their call.

Never far from Bruce's mind was his debt. He did most of his selling once a year, though his account never stopped bleeding. Over a year, his costs averaged two and a half thousand dollars a day, every day, three hundred and sixty-five days a year. The extra debt burden had increased the risk associated with the business. But Bruce had confidence this was now considerably reduced due to the changes they were making on advice taken from Wayne. Apart from keeping a lid on costs, Bruce's focus was on live weight production and maximising sale values. For many years, the Bovale herd had been producing an average of a bit over eight hundred kilograms per day on an annual basis. This would hopefully increase to one thousand kilograms per day with the new system, an exciting prospect, especially if the prices kept improving, as they had steadily been doing all year, and stayed high.

The herd kept growing, and sales were needed. Bruce, like Merve before him, targeted selling in October. The prices were typically about ten cents per kilogram of live weight higher in October and November because it was late in the dry season and supply of high-quality cattle to the markets was always starting to dwindle. Not everyone could keep their cattle on as late in the year as Bruce could. He could do it because of the brilliant pasture management Merve had done over many years. Plentiful high-quality grass, combined with a large body of Seca stylo legume providing true protein, further underpinned by astute urea-based supplementation, ensured his cattle continued to achieve small weight gains and held good body condition well into the dry season.

Bruce had booked the slaughter of three hundred cows and twenty-five bulls at the Townsville abattoir. He would be trucking them in two weeks, on a Wednesday, for slaughter the next day. He was selling more cows than usual as part of the program to reduce stock numbers and prevent overgrazing when the phosphorus supplementation effect kicked in.

Bruce and Col were in the shed getting supplement loaded for feeding out on Wednesday morning. 'What's the plan for the steer sales this year, Bruce?' Col asked.

'I've been looking at the markets, Col, and I calculated our best option is to truck them to the Roma sale,' Bruce replied. 'I've booked in all four hundred steers and those two hundred heifers we've drafted off for the Tuesday sale in two weeks. We'll muster them on the Saturday. I've booked twenty-two decks to leave here early Sunday.' A truck usually pulled three trailers, each having two decks. Each deck was usually loaded with about ten tonnes of cattle.

'That will be an impressive sight, Bruce, four triples lined up ready to go to Roma. I'll get out the new drone we just got and get some photos and maybe a video. Lachlan will love that,' Col said.

'That's a champion idea, Col. I reckon you're right. She'll be impressive,' Bruce agreed.

'What's the trucking plans for the meatworks cattle?' Col asked.

'I've booked seventeen decks for the Wednesday, the day after the Roma sale,' Bruce replied.

'Changing the subject, have you and Simone got everything sorted for the ball yet?' Bruce asked.

'Funny you should ask. We're going in on Saturday to get frocked up. Simone has all sorts of plans. She's getting very excited, mate,' Col said.

'Col, she and your children do a lot for the station that I feel I don't always pay for, so I'd like to help,' Bruce said. 'When I'm in town on Thursday, I'm going to place a two-thousand-dollar credit at Ranch Pants for you guys. That will help you both a lot, I know. She'll be able to get the dress she really wants, Col, and the handbag, and the shoes, and the whatever else; you know what I mean.'

'Two thousand?' Col queried. 'That's very generous of you, Bruce, but it sounds way too much.'

'It is for blokes, Col. But when the sheilas are going to the ball, they want to be mistaken for a princess. And they want their prince to match their style. You'll need it, mate, trust me,' Bruce said.

Bruce was having lunch later that day when Simone came across to the homestead. 'Come in, Simone,' Bruce said. 'What's up? Everything okay?'

'Bruce, Col just told me about the deposit at Ranch Pants,' Simone replied. She had a tear in her eye. She was very happy. She went forward and gave Bruce a bear hug. 'Thanks, Bruce. Not every boss in Australia does what you do.'

'My absolute pleasure, Simone. Not everyone in Australia is lucky enough to have a Col and Simone working with them. That is special,' Bruce responded.

At Ranch Pants on Thursday afternoon, Jane assumed control. Bruce just did what he was told and paid for it when it was finished.

He hardly said a word as the sales lady and Jane almost treated him like a mannequin. He was given no say in whether he liked what they were fitting him with, only whether it felt comfortable or not. Bruce was quite pleased, because even though he always liked to be neat, he really didn't have much idea about what a prince would wear. If he did what he was told, he'd find out. Forty minutes after the quest began, he knew. Not only that, he knew it would match whatever Therese was wearing. Bruce had no idea. He was very thankful for secret women's business. It achieved beautiful magic.

As they left, Bruce asked Jane, 'Can you meet me at the florist now, Jane?'

'Can do,' she replied.

When they arrived, Bruce said to the florist, 'I want to order corsages for six ladies for the Cattleman's Ball, please. What do they call the equivalent for blokes?' he asked.

'Boutonnieres,' she said.

'Six of them too, please,' Bruce said.

He turned to Jane. 'Can you work out what we all need please, Jane? You know what the ladies are wearing and what will suit everyone. Is that okay?'

'Is that okay?' Jane replied rhetorically. 'That's fantastic. Thanks, Bruce. I'd love to.' Bruce watched as the ladies sorted the details. And then he paid. He was absolutely loving the experience. Balls are great things, he thought.

'Can you make sure everyone knows this is happening, please, Jane?' Bruce asked as they were leaving.

'Leave it with me,' Jane responded. Bruce had no doubt at all that Jane would manage the situation as she always did, with aplomb.

The gang all met at the pub at five-thirty. Even Eileen had finished at the surgery for the day, an unusual achievement. Veterinary clients and their animals are a demanding mob, and many feel they have the God-given right to descend on the surgery when it suits them best and not the poor old vets, who really like their job, but also really want to have a life. Eileen was treated like a queen. She was told to sit and relax. Bruce shouted drinks for everyone to start the night. After one drink, they all ordered a feed; Bruce paid for Eileen's.

After they finished their feed and their second drink, it was on to The Villa, where Brenda and Jane had prepared what they were calling smoko. 'It's not smoko,' Craig exclaimed. 'This is dessert. And she's a ripper by the look of it.'

'We've changed the rules, Craig,' Brenda told him, smirking. 'In The Villa, we don't have dessert because it causes good people to gain weight. So, we have smoko instead.'

'I'll let you get away with this one, Brenda,' Craig responded. 'You own me, I know. So, I'll accept whatever rules work for you.' He paused. 'As long they work for me,' he declared, returning her mischievous smirk.

'I reckon my dress will still fit if I eat all this,' Mick said.

'I'm not going to the ball with a bloke in a dress, I can assure you,' Jane sternly reacted, with a huge smile.

'Ah well, I'll just cuddle up with Bruce then,' Mick said, feigning complete naivety.

'Not a chance, Mick,' Jane said. 'Therese will have you branded, castrated and in the steer paddock straight up if you try that.'

The spirit of the upcoming ball had infected them all. 'Everyone all sorted for the ball?' Bruce asked.

'You can bet on that,' declared Jane. Bruce had been wondering who Eileen might have been going with, and hoped there was no way she was opting out. Jane's response to his question suggested she had a partner. Bruce was happy.

Oh Hell was as much fun as always. Eileen was last past the finishing post. 'Tell us something we don't know, Eileen,' Mick queried.

'Not your business, Mick,' Jane told him. The ladies all had big smiles and were saying nothing. The men kept their counsel. Whatever was afoot, it was obviously good. Bruce again marvelled at secret women's business.

Over coffee, after cards, the gang agreed the ladies would get dressed at The Villa, and that included Therese, Simone and Frances. The blokes would get dolled up at Mick's den and then they'd come to The Villa and collect the ladies. The blokes had not actually made any suggestions, nor had they verbally agreed. But they were good blokes and because it was the ball, they were all on their best behaviour, taking all suggestions as orders, and good ones at that. Their passive response was taken by the ladies as full agreement.

'I've organised my mum to be at Mick's place when you blokes get dressed. You'll need her to make sure you've all got your crowns on straight,' Jane told them. She was leaving nothing to chance.

'And Bruce, can you please tell Simone that my mum will look after Lachlan and Carina?' Jane asked. 'Carina can be here while we get ready, and Col can bring Lachlan over when you all come. Mum will come over at the same time and she'll stay here with them.'

'Thanks, Jane,' Bruce said.

On Friday morning, Bruce headed back to Bovale where he and Col pushed all the sale steers and heifers into Upriver paddock, in the north-west corner of the station, to make it easier for the trucking muster. They first mustered Hollywood paddock and walked them past the yards and through Bull paddock to the water in Upriver paddock. Early that morning, Col had slowly worked all the cattle in Duck paddock, in between Airstrip and Upriver paddocks, into Upriver paddock. The cattle were well-behaved as they had been well-trained as weaners, so it was a relatively easy job.

Every day was a long hot day at Bovale at this time of the year. So far, there were no signs of any storms. It did not appear the wet season was going to start early. Col and Bruce had worked out a good routine to get all the supplements out, check all the waters and keep an eye on the cattle. It could not consume all their time as they had plenty else to do. They had worked out their logistics details to truck all the cattle. Because they were mustering and trucking the cattle for the Roma sale on a weekend, that enabled all the Wattle family to be involved. Lachlan was beside himself with excitement. His recent accident, from which he had fully recovered, was a forgotten memory. Every day after school, he checked something for his father, whether it was cattle or licks. His most important task was keeping an eye on Jasper and his harem. Lachlan reported the bull was doing just fine.

It was the weekend before the ball. Lachlan was out of bed in the dark. Even though they were not mustering till later that day, he was impatient. Bruce timed it so they all met at the front grid of Bovale, which was in the north-east corner of the paddock. Simone was in the Kubota with Carina. The two men and Lachlan were on two-wheel motorbikes. Bruce had picked this time because all the cattle would most likely be at the waters, taking all the stress out of locating the cattle and bringing them together. Simone and Lachlan worked along the northern side of the paddock to the water near the centre of the paddock. They found a few grazing, but most of the two hundred and fifty cattle they ended up with at the water had already been camped there, ruminating after their morning graze and a drink. Once they had the mob settled there, Simone and Lachlan walked them three kilometres across to the south-east corner of the paddock. Bruce and Col worked the rest of the paddock to the east and west of the line Simone and Lachlan were on. Col brought another two hundred and fifty from the south-west water across to join the hundred or so that Bruce had in the south-east corner. A good muster is an uneventful one and this muster was uneventful.

Col and his mob were the last to arrive. Once the cattle were settled with the group Bruce had brought in, Simone radioed Bruce, 'Is it okay to film you guys bringing in that mob?' Simone had their drone in the Kubota.

'That's fine, Simone,' Bruce radioed back. 'Just keep behind Col and me and the mob in case it spooks them. And have Lachlan on alert when you send it up in case the mob you have gets upset.'

'Did you hear all that, Lachlan?' Simone asked.

'Yes, Mum,' he responded. Lachlan was sharp. He may have only been eight years of age, but bush children with his experience were as capable as many adults in situations like this.

'When I'm operating the drone, Lachlan, I won't be able to drive the Kubota, so you'll be on your own for a bit if the cattle spook. Is that okay, Lachlan?' Simone asked.

'Yes, Mum,' Lachlan radioed back, full of confidence.

The drone was compact. Simone unfolded it and clipped her mobile phone into it. And switched it all on. 'Starting up, boys,' she radioed.

The small drone buzzed and quickly rose as Simone steered it directly to the north, away from the cattle. The cattle reacted immediately. Many of those that had been lying down, stood up. They were alert to the strange object. But they did not try to take off.

'Looks like they're okay, Mum,' Lachlan radioed.

'Thanks, Lachlan,' Simone replied. From the drone images, she could see the strung-out approaching mob coming from the west. She started the camera video and skirted wide and to the north, circling in behind Col who was at the rear. Bruce was on the wing. It was an excellent shot of driving cattle. The distant yards were visible, almost in a direct line ahead as the camera filmed a bit to the south of east. Simone brought the drone down right in behind Col who waved. He turned and smiled like a tourist. The cattle ahead of him were also turning their heads, seeking to see what was buzzing in behind them.

'I'm bringing it back now,' Simone said. 'Thanks everyone.' Very quickly she brought the drone back the way she had taken it out.

'That toy might be real handy,' Bruce radioed. 'Do you reckon you could pick up cattle with that, like out of a chopper?'

'Easy, Bruce,' Simone replied. 'I'll contract my services at four hundred dollars an hour. Is that a good price?'

'Sounds perfect, Simone.' Bruce agreed.

The six hundred cattle now had to be pushed towards the yards across the southern side of Bull Paddock. Bruce drove up beside Simone. 'Can you please scout ahead with that toy and tell us where the bulls are, Simone?' he asked.

'No problem,' she replied. As she sent the drone up, Col went through the gate. His task now was keeping the bull herd well away from this mob as it was full of potential girlfriends. The bulls would have caused chaos if they were allowed anywhere near them.

There are about a dozen bulls around the water in front of us,' Simone said. 'I'll scout further down for you, Col.'

'Thanks, Simone,' Col replied. 'I'll start those guys off to the north. I'll come back if you find any ahead of you.'

It was about three kilometres across Bull paddock, well within the drone's range. As Simone scouted, Bruce came in to look over her shoulder. They didn't see another bull. 'Looks clear ahead, Col,' Bruce said. 'The rest must be up at the north-east water, out of our way. Once we get going, and you've got those bulls uninterested and out the road, can you get ahead of us and work up towards that north-east water?' Bruce asked. 'We'll start these cattle off now.'

Simone and Carina were on the tail of the mob as they slowly pushed them along. Once they were steadily moving, Simone stopped and put Carina in the driver's seat. Carina was almost in a standing position, keeping the accelerator down and steering at the same time, but it's amazing what determination can achieve. This allowed Simone to send the drone up again to get a video of them and the cattle as they went, and to scout ahead again to make sure it was clear. Lachlan was in the lead of the mob. 'Lachlan, Mum here. I'm sending the drone up and checking ahead. You won't be able to hear it, but just in case the cattle get a fright, you'll know why,' she radioed.

'Thanks, Mum,' Lachlan replied.

The rest of the muster was completely undramatic as they slowly pushed the cattle into the yards. After they allowed the cattle to rest for an hour, they drafted them into six groups of small, medium and large steers and heifers. All the cattle were then left to rest in the yards till the next morning. Four semi-trailers, up to fifty metres in length, arrived just after first light on Sunday morning. Three trucks had three trailers and one had two trailers. The leading truck was parked up beside the loading ramp with the gates set to take cattle. Before they started, Simone sent the drone up again to get some impressive aerial photos and a video of the yard full of cattle waiting to be loaded onto the lined-up trucks. The loading itself was a steady process. Col and Lachlan worked the cattle forward in the yards, as Bruce drafted groups of twelve to sixteen at a time, depending on weight, to load half of each deck at a time. Simone kept each small group going up the ramp into the truck, where the truck driver took control and penned them. Carina played with her dolls in the stock-free area in the centre of the yards. Loading all occurred through the front lower deck of each truck. The trailers were configured so a walkway with side panels could be lowered in between decks to allow cattle to walk from the front of the front trailer right to the rear of the last trailer. Between decks they waited while ramps were raised and lowered between decks in the truck and gates were re-set. The whole process went like clockwork. The Wattle family and Bruce stood together to watch the line of loaded trucks slowly pull away from the yards and head off to Roma, a drive of nine hundred kilometres. As the trucks drove off, Lachlan turned to Bruce. 'A job well done, Bruce. Thanks for letting me help.'

'Thank you for your help, Lachlan. You're a mighty young man. We're all proud of you,' Bruce replied. Bruce walked over to the Kubota and reached in to pick out a small parcel he had there that he had purchased the previous Thursday afternoon. 'Lachlan,' he said, 'I really appreciate what you do for me. The law does not allow me to pay you, but here's something that may help.'

Lachlan opened the parcel. 'Thank you, Bruce,' he exclaimed with the biggest grin he'd ever had. 'Dad, Mum, this is the best watch I've even seen. Wow.' A small man was very happy.

The muster on Tuesday was more challenging. There were four hundred cows to recover from Kenworth paddock, the place where Lachlan had his accident. The paddock was seven kilometres long, and over five kilometres wide on the eastern boundary, narrowing to only a one-kilometre-wide west boundary. Bruce had booked a chopper to bring the cattle in the eastern half of the paddock into the waters. Ian Spencer, the chopper pilot, started working the paddock at nine o'clock which meant most cattle were already on the waters, saving a lot of time and expense for Bruce. Bruce had been able to hire Scott Olden from next door again to help for a half a day. The on-ground team waited until Ian had the eastern half of the paddock clean before they started the mobs off towards the yards. As they did this, the chopper refuelled and then checked all was under control in the paddock, before checking out. As Bruce and Scott pushed mobs along the southern and northern boundaries, Col worked between them, ensuring all cattle in the western half joined the muster. It was nine kilometres from where they started the mobs off to the yards, which took a couple of hours. They left the cattle to rest, while they had lunch.

After lunch, Bruce and Col mustered Bull paddock. The bulls were remarkably well-behaved. As they neared the yards, the bulls detected it was full of female cattle, most of which were non-pregnant and many of which would have been in oestrus, very happy for a tryst with any old bull. It was bull heaven. The men had virtually no work to do to get the bulls into the yards. In the yards, they immediately drafted the bulls into those destined for the meatworks, into five smaller groups, and those to stay at Bovale. They spent half an hour scrutinising all the bulls and agreed no errors had been made in the draft before they took the keeper bulls back to their paddock. Ordinarily, this was a one-man job, but the bulls really didn't want to leave all their girlfriends in the yards.

When they got back to the homestead, Bruce had a message to ring the livestock selling agent in Roma. Bruce hurried over to his office to return the call. 'I have the results from the sale, Bruce,' the agent told him.

'Let me have it,' replied Bruce. He was trying to play down any optimism he could have had because he didn't want to be disappointed.

'It was an excellent sale, Bruce,' the agent told him. 'Your cattle presented well in good lines and they attracted strong interest on a rising market. The steers averaged four dollars twenty-five cents a kilogram at three hundred and fifty-one kilograms, the yearling heifers attracted three dollars eighty-five at three hundred and thirty kilograms, and the older heifers made three dollars fifty-seven at four hundred and nineteen kilograms. All up, that's eight hundred and seventy-two thousand, five hundred and ninety dollars less commission.'

Bruce let out a big sigh as he had found himself holding his breath. 'Wow,' he said. That's well beyond what I'd dreamt I could get. I'm ecstatic. Thanks.' They continued the discussion for a short while before the agent had to leave and call other clients.

Trucking of the cows and bulls the next day went well. They loaded soon after first light again, which enabled the whole Wattle family to help. It was time for Simone, Lachlan and Carina to head back and get ready for school when they finished.

On Friday morning, Bruce received an email from the meatworks with his kill sheet, a summary of the statistics of the cattle at slaughter and the prices he received. In a buoyant market, he was once again very happy with the result. It was a double bonus that he was reducing the herd size. The bulls' average carcass weight was three hundred and ninety kilograms paying six dollars thirty-four cents a kilogram; the cows made five dollars seventy-eight cents with an average carcass weight of two hundred and fifty-four point four kilograms. He was receiving a payment of four hundred and forty thousand, nine hundred and forty-two dollars.

It was the middle of the day, but he had to ring his dad. 'Dad, we've just completed our sales. Fantastic result.' Bruce explained the details to Merve. 'I've netted over three hundred thousand dollars more than I had budgeted on.'

'Bruce, I'm really happy for you. You've been very lucky to hit gold in your first year. Savour the experience. It won't always be like this,' Merve replied. It was sobering.

'Dad, the funny thing is that I'm not at all unhappy about all the angst I had when I was doing the budget. I've been thinking the best way to move now is to increase my resilience, on top of the other changes we're making. To me, I'm feeling it's weird I don't want to race into town and buy a truck like everyone else seems to do. Am I thinking straight?' Bruce asked.

'You're absolutely spot-on, Bruce,' Merve agreed. 'The advice I'd give you now though is, get a good lump into super while you can. That's what your mother and I did. It was the best investment we ever made because when it came to succession, we could achieve it painlessly. You can always extend your overdraft in tough years. But you can't always fill the super coffers like you can at present.'

'Great advice, Dad. Thanks,' Bruce responded.

Chapter Fourteen

The euphoria of the sales morphed into the euphoria of the ball. Before then, there were cattle to be fed. Bruce was more than happy doing the basic routine work. He derived daily exhilaration out of seeing the results of their endeavours. He was particularly pleased at present to have most of his pregnant cows on a high-phosphorus transition lick and his pregnant heifers on their spike feeding supplement. It was not possible for him to measure any response yet, but all the work they had done confirmed for him that what he was doing at Bovale now would increase both his profitability and resilience. Every day he thanked the stars that his father had made this possible through creating a fantastic pasture base that he was continuing; without that, he would be twenty years behind where he currently was.

On Saturday morning, Bruce cleaned his Land Cruiser. After lunch, he cleaned and preened his carcass. He was nearly ready for the ball. On the way into town, he kept thinking he may have forgotten something, but he eventually concluded he was overthinking the situation. His anticipation of the event was over-powering his rationality. He tried to relax himself and let the whole show take its own course. It couldn't go wrong with all the meticulous planning that had been done. Once he arrived at Mick's place, he couldn't relax. His mates were there, and they were amped up. It took all their willpower, and then some, to not have a few beers to settle their jingling nerves. Beers would not really help them, and they didn't want their partners to suffer the pong of beer breath before they even started. Mick had a few bottles of sparkling water.

They pulled out the cards and were having a great game till Jane's mother arrived. 'Righto you guys,' she declared, 'time to get frocked up.' This sparked them into action. When they were dressed, she produced their boutonnieres and pinned them on, satisfied with her charges. 'If I was thirty years younger, you blokes would be in trouble. All three of you are absolutely digestible,' she exclaimed. 'Before we go, can I get a photo, please?' It wasn't a request. It was an order. The boys were very happy to comply.

It was six-thirty, the appointed hour, when the men arrived at The Villa. Col and Lachlan arrived at the same time. Col didn't get two metres from his car before Jane's mum had him cornered, pinning on his boutonniere and ensuring he was as well preened as Bruce, Mick and Craig. Two other young blokes arrived at the same time. Bruce already knew one of them. They sauntered up to introduce themselves, but before they could do that, Jane's mum had done for them what she had for Col. Bruce was thinking, I now know why Jane is a brilliant organiser.

The first bloke introduced himself. 'G'day guys. I'm Tom Smythe, Eileen's partner.' Everyone shook hands and introduced themselves. 'Hello Bruce. Fancy meeting you here.'

Finally, the other bloke could introduce himself. 'G'day fellas. I'm Simon Casey, Frances's partner.'

Carina had been watching from the doorway of The Villa. She skipped down and hugged her dad. 'You look great, Dad,' she said. 'You should see all the ladies. They are beautiful.'

It was a casual but nervous walk for the men into The Villa where all the ladies were ready, waiting in the lounge room. 'Wow,' Bruce said, almost breathlessly, when he caught sight of Therese. She was stunning in a light blue jersey gown set off by gold and pearl jewellery. Bruce didn't even notice anyone else, not even his sister. He went forward and they lightly embraced, taking care not to undo any of her preparations. 'You are absolutely beautiful tonight,' he said. 'Your perfume is amazing too. Can't believe I'm so lucky to be your partner.'

'Thanks, Bruce. I'm absolutely sure I have the best-looking bloke in Australia in my arms just now,' Therese responded. They just looked at each other for a moment before they regained their senses sufficiently to realise they weren't the only people in the room.

Jane was once again master of ceremonies. 'Photo time,' she declared. Jane had a friend there with a camera who was not attending the ball. The ladies had prepared well for the photos. Each couple was positioned for a few glamour shots before the whole group of twelve was shot. It was ten minutes before the photographer was happy. As she had been clicking away, there were multiple mobile phones doing backup work over her shoulder.

It was ball time. Jane and her mother organised this with ceremony. They ushered everyone to their vehicles. Mick waited patiently till his beautifully-gowned partner ushered herself to his ute. The ball was being held at the cattle sale yards. Within ten minutes they had reached the yards, shown their tickets and been directed to parking. The organisers had cordoned off a large area between the selling arena and the canteen. Most of it was open air, so it was high risk to hold it in this spot at a time of the year when they could have been savaged by a tropical storm. However, they were lucky. There were no signs of storms. It was a typical, perfectly-dry, still and comfortable evening in Charters Towers. Rather than have a tent, the organisers had leased a large flat wooden surface that was the dance floor in the centre. There was a band set-up under the awning of the canteen. Tables were set up in adjacent nooks and crannies. A beautiful atmosphere had been created with hay bales, large potted plants, old utes and rural bric-a-brac from olden times highlighted with coloured and discrete lighting.

The group found their reserved table and immediately set about quenching their thirst, commandeering the services of a mobile drinks' waiter. Soft background music was playing as everyone went walk-about, catching up with everyone they knew in the growing crowd. Entrees were available from roaming waiters. Everyone knew everyone it seemed to Therese as Bruce introduced her to so many people within the first half hour, she simply decided she couldn't possibly remember all the names. It was a heady night, for sure, as all the young people from the bush were in town for a good time. The first beers here were not the first beers for many young blokes tonight and they were obviously warming to something as wild as riding a bull, if only they could drink and stay sober. The ladies were focussed on the glamour. The mingling was as much about catching up with each other as it was about seeing and congratulating each other on how beautifully dressed everyone was.

After the quick rounds, Bruce decided he and Therese should zero in on his sister and Eileen and their partners, to welcome them and share who they were. Frances was raging, so they found Eileen and Tom first. 'Sorry to be rude for not catching up earlier but had to say howdy to a few of my mates,' Bruce said to them. 'I'm sure Eileen has told you all about us, Tom. She is a great lady.'

'She is,' replied Tom. 'We met at a recent vet conference in Townsville. She was talking about cattle vet work in the region. As you know, I'm a ruminant nutritionist based in Townsville and was discussing nutrition with the vets. We just saw each other and clicked. Just like Eileen says you pair have. It's just fantastic,' he said as he and Eileen side-hugged and smiled at each other. After they chatted a bit, Bruce and Therese excused themselves and sought out Frances and Simon.

'Which rock have you been hiding this bloke under?' Bruce asked Frances when they finally cornered her. She had been catching up with the myriads of people she knew from her Charters Towers childhood.

'Funny you should ask that, brother. He's a geologist with a construction mob in Townsville. We've been hanging out for a bit,' Frances replied, snuggling into Simon. Bruce was very pleased for his sister. They would have to leave getting to know each other till another time as everyone in the mingling crowd was still clamouring to say howdy to those they hadn't seen in a while, sometimes years. Bruce and Frances were swept up in it.

As far as the gang knew, there were no formal sessions during the evening. It was simply about meeting, eating, dancing, grooving and anything else that felt good. At seven-thirty the music was gradually turned down and off. To everyone's pleasant surprise, a string quartet replaced the noise machine. The quartet had been contracted to produce tunes that would induce traditional dancing through to waltzing. It was beautiful music, and in a twinkle a majority of the crowd was dancing. Not one of the Bovale table's twelve had sat down yet. After half an hour of that, the quartet pulled up for a bit so the main course could be served at the tables. 'I was wondering whether we'd ever get to sit,' Brenda said. The evening mood was great. It had been a genius move to start the evening the way it had. A combination of classical music, a great ambience and a few beers had taken the let's-go-crazy edge out of the night, which was maturing into a memorable evening.

After another session from the string quartet accompanying dancing, a couple took the microphone and introduced themselves as the emcees, wishing everyone a great evening. Using a tag team approach, the pair then proceeded to inform the crowd there was a formal activity for the evening, designed to raise funds for the Royal Flying Doctors' Service, a very worthy cause for the bush folk. There was going to be a race. But it was no ordinary race. Only ladies could race. The participants first had to be selected. Nominations were called, with the instruction being one lady from each table. Immediately Jane announced, 'We nominate Therese.' This immediately elicited a resounding seconding by everyone at the table. Therese protested in vain. 'Therese,' Jane calmly informed her, 'you are one of our wonderful nurses who deal with the emergencies the RFDS delivers. You're it. Done deal.'

'I really don't want to race,' Therese said, horrified at the thought of having to dash around the saleyards in high heels, wearing her beautiful gown.

'Let's see,' Frances said. 'We understand. If it gets tricky, we'll call Mick, Michelle, and race him.'

'Fan bloody tastic idea,' Craig agreed, heartily endorsing Frances's suggestion. 'Here's to Michelle,' he said, raising his beer and toasting Mick's potential success.

'Righto,' the announcer declared, 'can we have all nominated fillies up here, please.' Therese, along with twenty-seven other reluctant ladies, all fashionably and elegantly attired, nervously met near the announcer. 'Now the fun begins,' the lady emcee said. 'We will auction each lady. The top bid for each will be a donation from the table with the winning bid. The ladies with the top eight bids will race. But they won't run. They will model their beautiful outfits. The race will be won by whoever attracts the biggest crowd roar. Your roars will be immediately after the race caller mentions the filly. The winning model will win for the table who bid for her, a two-thousand-dollar voucher from the Pioneer Hotel here in Charters Towers, the proud sponsor of tonight's race.' A hearty roar went up from the crowd, who were all right behind the concept. It was essentially a fashion parade with a beautiful twist, and many winners.

'I don't think they'll take you, Mick, even if there's a scratching,' Bruce said, which created quite a bit of mirth at the table.

Four local experienced auctioneers who each sold hundreds and thousands of cattle weekly, magically appeared and the auctions began. In very quick time, the first lady went for three thousand two hundred dollars, reflecting a buoyant cattle industry. As this happened, Jane went over to the bloke emcee and had a quiet word on the side with him. Jane knew everyone and no-one thought too much about it. When it became Therese's turn to be auctioned as she modelled, the bloke emcee announced, 'Ladies and gentlemen, we have a very special filly now. Recently the RFDS evacuated a seriously-injured boy from a local station, Bovale. You all know Bruce Arnold and you probably know what happened. Therese Pavarotti is a highly-trained emergency care nurse who was part of the team who welded young Lachlan back together and now have him back like a bought one. Lachlan's parents, Col and Simone Wattle, are here tonight and I'm sure they'd love to see this filly win.'

This fired off the auctioneer. 'Righto ladies and gentlemen, can I get two thousand dollars for Therese?' Mick's hand went high, firing off a bidding war. Bruce sat back, enjoying it immensely. He knew he'd pay whatever Mick bid, and Mick knew he would. Therese's absolute beauty and grace and her now-public background ensured she was going to race. 'Ladies and Gentlemen, at eight thousand four hundred dollars. Going once. Going twice. All done, out she goes. To the Bovale table. Thank you, bidders.' The auctioneer declared as he signed off for the next auction.

Bruce turned to Mick. 'Thanks mate, I'm stoked.' Mick gave him the thumbs up. Bruce then turned to Col and Simone who were both tearful. 'My shout,' he said, gently. It was the call of a legend. Everyone at the table was dealing with leaky lacrimal ducts, even Craig.

Therese was a race starter. The lady emcee lined up the eight ladies with the highest bids, instructing them to pretend they were on a cat-walk, slowly moving in a small circle in single file. She then introduced a local legendary race caller, eliciting a huge roar of approval from the crowd. Therese was feeling helplessly uncomfortable, but it seemed there was little she could do to escape the situation. Bruce looked like he was a cat that had just swallowed a mouse. Everyone else on the table was already shouting encouragement. She was racing, a first for her.

'And they're off,' the caller announced. Very quickly the crowd realised which lady he was calling as he went. 'Medical Emergency is making a move on the pack,' he said, referring to Therese, eliciting a massive roar from the Bovale table. The race had been going for a minute, with roars building for the favourites, when Mick introduced himself. He walked out on the dance floor in front of the catwalking ladies and started riding an imaginary racehorse, crouched, urging, hands pumping with the stride of his invisible horse, coupled with a massive roar any lion would have been proud of, each time Medical Emergency was mentioned. He had the crowd behind him and after another two minutes, when Mick was flagging but still roaring mightily, the race was called. Medical Emergency had blitzed the field by three lengths according to the caller.

Bruce walked over to Therese and took her hand. 'Thank you,' he said to her. 'If I didn't know before why Simone calls you the princess of Bovale, I sure do now,' he added, showing his immense pride in what she had just done. They had a hug which drew another huge roar. 'You might just be a bit famous after tonight,' Bruce whispered to her.

The end of the race signalled dessert, which was being served at the tables. This was done with amazing speed, as was demolition of the desserts, cueing the string quartet back to action. Just as Bruce and Therese were about to hit the dance floor, they were approached by a young lady. 'Hello, Therese,' she said and proceeded to introduce herself as a representative from the Royal Flying Doctors' Service. 'I took a few photos of you during the race. Do you mind if we put them on our social media site with a bit of a story? Our main message will be the funds raised that exceeded two hundred thousand dollars, which is amazing.'

'Can I see what you'll be putting up, please?' Therese asked. The lady complied.

'Those are stunning photos, Therese,' Bruce commented. Therese simply nodded in resigned agreement, though like all ladies, probably thought they didn't show her as they could have. The lady collected a few details Therese was happy to share for the worthy cause.

'Can you please introduce me to the parents of Lachlan?' the lady then asked. They had to retrieve Col and Simone from the dance floor, where they headed themselves while Simone and Col posed for a photo and shared details on the Lachlan story, including a recent photo of Lachlan mustering.

The Bovale team were all dancing. After another hour, the quartet were thanked for their amazing contribution to the evening. The emcees then introduced a well-known local band, who turned up the volume and the vigour of the music with some rock. It was a couple of hours later when a few slow dances were introduced. Bruce and Therese were certainly enjoying the experience. It was then that Bruce noticed that all five other couples from the Bovale table were doing more than just dancing.

The Villa ladies had told everyone that breakfast was at their place on Sunday morning. Though it was hard for everyone to extract themselves from their bunks after such a legendary night, they were glad to all get together and talk about what a brilliant evening it had been. Jane's mum arrived early to cater. She was reading all she could between the lines, and finally realised that six very personal relationships had either started or been cemented further. She was a very proud mum to make the breakfasts of such a wonderful group of young people.

'Hey, check this out,' Brenda exclaimed, coming to life. She had been sprawled on the couch, her legs resting on Craig's knees who sat at one end of the couch while both conducted their obligatory morning scrolls through social media. Brenda sprang to her feet, glued to her mobile phone. As she scrolled, everyone was peering over her shoulder, taking note of what she had found, then seeking it themselves if they had a phone at hand. 'You are a megastar, Therese. Simone, Col and Lachlan are right up there with you.'

'What does it say?' Carina asked eagerly.

Simone found the post on her phone. Lachlan and Col came in to look over her shoulders. 'It says, 'Princess Therese Pavarotti stimulates massive RFDS donation'. There are some lovely photos of Therese, of us and Lachlan and of lots of other people at the ball. Can you see under the picture of Lachlan, there are some words?' Carina nodded numbly in her awe. 'They're saying that Therese helped fix Lachlan.'

'This is embarrassing,' Therese said as she scrolled the post as well. Her new friends were not only checking out the post, they were also posting it to everyone they thought would like to see it.

Carina and Lachlan were in awe of Bruce, Therese, and all of their friends. They were most pleased to discover their princess and prince had been the stars. Carina approached Therese. 'Therese, were you a real princess last night?' she asked, trying to make sense of what she was hearing and seeing.

Craig overhead it. 'No, Carina, she wasn't. Mick was.' Carina turned to Craig with a large frown, absolutely confused.

'Craig, you are terrible,' Brenda scolded. 'Carina, she was. She still is.' Therese humbly took Carina in her arms and gave her a hug. Carina had seen Therese dressed for the ball last night. She had no doubt she was being hugged by a princess, every little girl's dream.

The goodbyes to the Townsville contingent were a very emotional experience after a long breakfast. Therese was on a late shift. She was not one to feign sickness as many workers did in situations like this. She knew she'd see Bruce and the gang soon enough. Bruce had never felt so gutted when she left. Even the thought of heading back to his beloved Bovale could not resolve his emptiness.

When Therese arrived at work that afternoon, it seemed the whole hospital was aware of her weekend. She was about to start changeovers with nurses from the previous shift when the shift manager approached her. 'Therese, I'm sorry, but we have a local television crew here asking to do a story about you at work. I've cleared it with management because it's good publicity for the RFDS and the hospital. If you don't mind, we've set up some patients who are willing to be in the background. Is that okay?' she asked. Therese was numbed, but she agreed. She settled her nerves and dealt with the filming and interview as best she could.

After the ordeal, Therese thought she'd better alert her family and friends. She sent a simple text with no explanation, 'Channel four news tonight.' They'll work out to watch it, she knew. She then immersed herself in emergency medical care till her shift finished. It was just before midnight when Therese turned on her phone to find her message box staggering under its burden. As Bruce had predicted, the social media story had gone viral and the television news story was brilliant. This is all because a crab bit Bruce's toe, she mused. Her romance and memories of the ball evoked a huge smile. The smile almost fell away as she thought about the public profile she had attracted from the ball. I'm glad I did that, she thought, but I don't want that too often, even if it does help the RFDS coffers.

Bovale was very demanding at this time of the year. However, Bruce ensured Col had a couple of days' break every week. Bruce didn't mind seven days a week, especially as Therese was now coming to Bovale for at least one whole day in between every second one of her shift breaks, which was about once a fortnight. Bruce arranged with her that she'd take the days off in Brandon every four weeks. That gave him a chance to have a break for a couple of days during which he'd see his family in Townsville, go fishing with Lenny if the weather and tides were right and spend time with Therese. On the way home he tried to stay in town for the night and catch up with the gang. It was a great routine.

A week after the ball, which was now becoming everyone's reference point for time, Bruce received a phone call from Wendy Olden next door. After catching up on each other's social news, including a synopsis on the ball of course, Wendy said, 'Bruce, there are a few places around here keen to form a business discussion group and we're wondering if you'd be keen to join?'

'Tell me more, Wendy. What's the objective?' Bruce asked.

'The basic objective is to accurately describe our businesses so that we may define what our specific problems and opportunities are,' Wendy replied. This sounded to Bruce like it strongly complimented what he was aiming to achieve with Wayne.

'That sounds interesting,' Bruce commented. 'How would we actually do this, Wendy?' Bruce asked.

'We have a lady from the agriculture department who will help us, Bruce,' Wendy explained. 'The interesting part is there's money available for us to select one of the group to be trained as a facilitator and then be paid a retainer, equivalent to about three-month's wages a year, to help each of us assemble and analyse the data we collect.'

'Now that is a good concept,' Bruce suggested. 'Can we involve others like Col and Simone from our business?'

'We sure can, Bruce. It's entirely up to each individual business who they involve, but there will be a confidentiality requirement for everyone involved,' Wendy explained. 'There's one other important aspect, Bruce. Every business had to contribute two thousand dollars each year to the group, which will be used for combined group activities, such as training or contracting professional services.'

'Count us in, Wendy,' Bruce said. 'I have no problem with the annual payment. When's the first get-together?'

'We're thinking mid-November here,' Wendy replied. The next day, Bruce explained the opportunity to Col and Simone. Both were very keen to participate.

Almost three weeks after the ball, Bruce contracted Eileen to come to Bovale and assess Jasper. After school on Wednesday afternoon, about two weeks after the calving season had started, Col and Lachlan biked out to Airstrip paddock, drafted Jasper out, and walked him to the yards. Jasper was in fine fettle. But he was unimpressed. He wanted to be back with his harem. 'It's okay, Jasper,' Lachlan told him as they walked along, blocking every move Jasper made to duck back to the paddock. 'We're taking you back in eight weeks, if you can wait that long.'

Eileen arrived on Thursday morning about seven-thirty, enabling all the Wattle family to be there when she conducted the breeding soundness evaluation of Jasper. 'Can you walk him around the yard, and I'll observe him?' she asked Lachlan.

'Sure can,' Lachlan replied. He had a bright pink plastic tube about twenty-five millimetres in diameter and a metre and a half long. Lachlan used this to gently tap Jasper on the butt and wave near his head, guiding him along in a steady walk around the yard.

'Thanks, Lachlan. Can you bring him up the race now, please?' Eileen asked after she had completed her observations. She turned to Bruce, 'That's a very impressive bull, Bruce. I can't say I've seen many bulls as physically sound and as athletic as he is. Congratulations. Hopefully he'll match that with high-quality semen.'

Col and Lachlan brought Jasper up into the veterinary chute. Eileen kicked the veterinary gate closed behind the big red bull. She grabbed Jasper's tail. 'Can you hang onto this please, Bruce?' she asked. Bruce took the tail, holding it just above the brush, preventing Jasper from flicking Eileen in the face. She reached down from behind, between his back legs, and gently grabbed the neck of Jasper's scrotum with her left hand. With both hands, she palpated his testes. Jasper stood with no reaction. Eileen reached into her back pocket and extracted a circular tape.

'What's that?' Lachlan asked.

'It's a Barth tape,' Eileen replied. 'We use it to measure how big his scrotum is.' Eileen encircled the widest part of the scrotum with the tape and drew it firmly up until a green button appeared out the end of the keeper, indicating the tension on the tape was perfect. 'Thirty-seven point five centimetres, pretty good,' Eileen said, as she pocketed the tape and backed out of the chute. After the previous bull assessments with Wayne, Eileen did not have to show Col how to insert the electroejaculation rectal probe. Very quickly, Eileen collected six millilitres of creamy semen via a collection funnel into a test tube. She used a pipette, to take a small drop and placed it on a microscope slide. 'Wow. This is amazing,' she said.

'Can we have a look?' Simone asked.

'By all means,' Eileen replied. She backed away as each of them, including Carina and Lachlan, viewed the swirling masses of sperm through the low-power objective lenses of the microscope, each of them suitably impressed with how active the semen was. 'Now I'm going to look at the individual sperm,' Eileen said. She then took another drop of semen from the test tube and placed it into a small tube of clear liquid that she capped and gently rotated to mix.

'Why are you doing that?' Lachlan asked.

'I'm diluting the semen, Lachlan,' Eileen explained. 'There could be as many as one billion sperm in the collection tube. Looking at individual sperm is very difficult when there's so many. So, I mix it with some special salty water and that spreads them out enough for me to see them. I'll take a small drop of this now, put it on the microscope slide and place a thin square piece of glass over the drop to spread it evenly.' Eileen did that and studied the diluted sample. 'Have a look at these guys now. They look excellent. I estimate about eighty-five percent motile, which is close to as good as it gets.' Each of them peered down the microscope to see hundreds of sperm vigorously swimming in all directions. Each sperm looked like an oval with a long tail. Eileen then took a drop of semen from the collection tube and added it to another bottle of clear liquid, capped it, and rotated it to achieve full mixing.

'Why are you doing it twice?' Lachlan asked.

'There is a different liquid in this bottle, Lachlan,' Eileen explained. It kills the sperm and then keeps them perfectly in shape. I'll send this to a lab in Goondiwindi where they'll check if there are any abnormal sperm.' Lachlan gave her his best blank look because he really didn't comprehend what was being explained to him.

Carina helped solve his confusion. 'What's the sperm do?' she asked.

Eileen did not reply immediately. She hoped Simone would answer. But then she realised Simone might have trouble creating a suitable explanation for a six-year-old and an eight-year-old. 'Well, the bull mounts the cow and puts some sperm under her tail. When this happens, the cow has a very tiny egg there that's so small you can't see it. When the sperm and the egg come together, they create a baby calf. The cow grows the calf in her belly for nine and a half months and then she calves. Now you know where calves come from. The reason we check the sperm is, sometimes it has a problem and can't make calves, so we have to replace the bull with one that makes good sperm. Does that make sense?' Eileen could see that both Carina and Lachlan now had a sufficiently-rudimentary understanding to satisfy their immediate curiosity as both nodded, looking up at her with understanding looks.

'You're a genius, Eileen,' Bruce said, smiling broadly at her explanation. After they finished, Col put Jasper into Cull Paddock, with several steers that had not been sold because they were too small, where they could keep a close eye on him, and he was unlikely to get into trouble.

A week later, Eileen rang Bruce. 'Results are back on Jasper's sperm morphology,' she said. 'He's very good. Eighty-nine percent, ready for mating.'

'Phew, ' Col responded. 'I've been sweating a bit on that result. I know bulls can have semen that looks good crush-side but in reality, can be rubbish, so that result is a ripper. Thanks.'

The following Monday, at about two o'clock, they headed next door to the Olden's where the business discussion group was holding its inaugural meeting. Wendy and the agriculture department extension officer, an enthusiastic young lady who everyone knew well, had trouble mustering the crowd together while they were topping themselves up with tea and cakes and catching up on everyone's gossip. The recent ball was the hottest topic. That was until they were eventually called to order. The extension officer explained the potential process, which was for each business to collect strategic data on their pastures, their herd and their costs. This would be analysed to describe production and performance of their pastures, their cattle and their overall business. These measures would be compared to achievable levels, thus initiating targeted and efficient business development. Everyone present was excited by the potential offered by the process. The unmentioned secondary social benefits were a highly-attractive bonus; everyone loved an excuse to get together as most of the time they worked in isolation.

Bruce asked, 'Can we give our group a name?'

'Absolutely, Bruce,' Wendy replied. 'I've been thinking about it and my suggestion is the Cockatoo River Beef Group.'

'What about Cockatoo River Advancing Beef Group,' Bruce suggested.

Not everyone initially twigged to Bruce's intention until Scott asked, 'Will that create a risk we'll be getting bitten, Bruce?' Bruce had been feigning seriousness. Scott's question, which was more a comment, caused his façade to break down to a broad grin. Scott suddenly had inspiration. 'Ah, I know what's going on here. He wants Therese to come out and treat his toe again.' Despite this causing much mirth in the camp, everyone agreed that Bruce's recommendation was a good one and the CRAB group was duly adopted.

'We need a facilitator,' Scott added. 'If Bruce is happy with it, I'd like to nominate Simone.'

'I like that,' Bruce responded. 'If Simone is happy, I'll second it.' Simone was very pleased, though she was not sure about the details. After the extension officer had explained the data needed to conduct analyses of the cattle production and performance, the group decided on where and when the next meeting would be and the agenda. Bruce, Col and Simone then met with the extension officer, separate from the group. 'Explain to us what this entails for Simone, please,' Bruce asked. She explained that Simone would be provided with some online and face-to-face facilitator training with all expenses paid. She would then be contracted to assist each group member collect data, with some expenses provided.

'I am keen,' Simone concluded.

Bruce had been keen to add more females to Jasper's harem to take maximum advantage of his mating potential. Later that week they scheduled a muster of the previously-unmated yearling heifers. There were two-hundred and twenty of them after the culls had gone to

Roma. They had the heifers in the yards by ten o'clock. After smoko, they went through the heifers. Col brought two to three at a time into the pound, a small drafting yard about eight metres in diameter with six gates. Bruce was in the pound. Col made his observations from the drafting yard as they agreed on whether each heifer should go to Jasper or not. Their decisions were using the same criteria based on the breeding objectives Bruce had worked out. By the end of the draft, they had sixty-two eligible heifers that both men were very pleased with. Col returned the main mob to their paddock while Bruce mustered Jasper's fifty pregnant heifers which were added to the sixty-two yearling heifers in the yards. Col then mustered the bulls in Bull paddock and pushed them into Airstrip, while Bruce took the expanded harem to Bull paddock, which was going to be Jasper's mating paddock. Jasper would not complain about having one hundred and twelve girlfriends, which was no challenge at all for a bull like him to impregnate as they each came on heat, even if twenty came on in one day.

A few weeks later in early December, it was Bruce's birthday. Therese was coming up for two days. She wouldn't get to Bovale till dinner time as she had to finish an early shift first. The Wattle family invited Bruce for breakfast. They put a candle in a fried egg, a very novel birthday cake. Carina said to Bruce as he went to blow out the candle, 'Make a wish,' which brought an even bigger smile to his face. 'Mum made you a cake too, Bruce. And we have a present for you,' Carina added. Simone produced the cake in a sealed container for Bruce while Lachlan gave Bruce the gift.

'What is it?' Bruce asked, receiving what was obviously a bottle of plonk.

'It's champagne for you and Therese to drink,' Carina informed him, absolutely thrilled with herself.

'Thank you,' Bruce said. He gave Carina and Simone a hug and firmly shook the hands of Col and Lachlan. 'Therese and I are lucky to have such a nice family living here.'

Bruce had a stuffed topside with spuds and pumpkin nearing the completion of roasting when Therese finally drove up to the homestead. As she stopped, Therese reached down into the well of the passenger seat to retrieve her gift. Bruce opened the car door, and she presented him with a small red kelpie puppy that was excitedly wriggling in her arms.

'Wow,' Bruce exclaimed. 'That's perfect.' They warmly embraced, with the poor pup desperately trying to attract attention to himself. They both reverted their attention to the pup that Bruce put down. 'What's his name?' he asked.

'I've been thinking, Caesar. As a Roman emperor, that will match Brutus. And also,' she said as she produced a wicked smile, 'it suggests what you can do to me.'

Bruce's forehead creased for a moment till he realised she was suggesting, seize her. 'Oh, I think I can do that,' he said.

The weekend was too short for both of them, even when they spent most of it working together. When Caesar met the Wattle children, he found two very willing playmates, relieving Bruce of having to keep him caged while they were out in the paddock.

Chapter Fifteen

The new year started well. Christmas had been memorable. Caesar was growing fast. Bruce loved his company. Whenever Bruce took him near cattle, his natural herding instincts kicked in, but he had to be kept away from the cattle for now in fear of him being kicked, which would have been devastating.

In mid-January on a Friday afternoon, his mum rang. 'I had a test for the cancer the other day, Bruce, and at this stage it looks clear.'

'That is so good to hear, Mum,' Bruce responded. It had been three months since Doris had finished six, two-week cycles of chemotherapy, which had been a taxing experience for her and for Merve. 'Your father and I are planning to come up at the end of next week to celebrate if that's okay with you,' she said.

'That would be terrific, Mum,' Bruce told her. 'I'd love to promise you green grass and pouring rain to go with your visit, but so far, we're still waiting for that.' The wet season was late. It was very concerning. Fortunately, Bruce had plenty of pasture and his cattle were strong, but the cows with small calves were losing weight rapidly as the energy-sapping process of making milk appeared to almost melt their body tissues, it was happening so fast. There had been a few storms, but they were isolated and had not delivered enough rain to achieve significant resurgence of green grasses and legumes. Bruce needed fifty millimetres or more across the station as soon as possible, but he just had to wait till the rain gods were ready to deliver.

The prevailing weather conditions did not affect the start of mating. It was as close to the fifteenth of January each year as they could achieve. The timing was dictated by the optimum calving period, starting nine and a half months after the start of mating. Mating itself was of no specific risk to the cattle. They could not predict the weather a year ahead, so they kept with the same start of mating date each year. On Saturday, Lachlan and Col mustered the bulls which were drafted into their allocated groups for mating. Lachlan was allowed to take Jasper by himself to Bull paddock. This was associated with virtually no risk at all because Jasper knew where he wanted to go and it matched where Lachlan was taking him. All Lachlan had to do was open the gates and shut them behind Jasper. Irrespective of this, Lachlan felt proud he had been allowed to do this alone. As soon as he had Jasper into Airstrip, he radioed in. 'Jasper's back with his girlfriends,' he said.

'Thanks, Lachlan,' Bruce radioed back. 'We'll meet you back at the yards.' When Col and Bruce arrived back from walking out a bull group each, Lachlan was waiting. 'Can you help Dad take the bulls to Kosciusczko, please, Lachlan?' Bruce asked him.

'Can you help me please, Dad?' Lachlan immediately said with a cheeky grin to his father who was clearly pleased to hear his son's display his confidence.

'Sure, I can do that,' Col replied.

Every day was getting more unbearable, exacerbated by a heat wave that lasted ten days. This typically occurred about every ten years. The birds were much less vocal and less active than they usually were. Bruce found a few dead magpies, victims of the extreme weather. Every day, the maximum reached the mid-forties mid-morning and hovered there till just before sundown. The cattle were lethargic and certainly could not be moved. Bruce noticed a few weak newborn calves that obviously were not getting sufficient to drink. Whenever he found one that needed help to survive, he captured it, easy to do when the calf was weak. He tied the calf up and placed it the back of the Kubota, taking it back to the small yards near the homestead where they had set up poddy feeding. Bruce setup tarpaulin shades for the calves. He had purchased a calf feeder, which was an elevated, small, elongated tank into which he placed milk twice daily. The tank had artificial teats attached along each side. The calves quickly learned that when the tank was filled, it was feed time, they clamoured for a teat, and as quickly as they could, sucked the tank dry. The milk was made by mixing powdered milk with clean water. This was standard practice on dairy farms across the world. The powdered milk was exactly what the calves needed for at least a few weeks, after which they were slowly transferred onto a pelted diet. Whenever else they needed a drink, Bruce had a small, shaded trough of water in the yards they could drink from. Carina and Lachlan loved poddy feeding. Carina spent a lot of time with the poddies, talking to them and cuddling them. It was school holidays, so she had plenty of opportunity. She gave every new poddy a name. Carina would take Caesar to the poddy yard as often as she could. While she played at being their mother, Caesar played predator-prey games, which he enjoyed immensely. The calves ignored him mostly.

Not all the poddies were destined to live. One of the first calves poddied had severe diarrhoea. Bruce judged he was unlikely to survive another day. 'What's wrong with him, Bruce?' Carina asked.

'He never got the first milk from his mum, Carina, so he has a very weak body and can't fight germs,' Bruce told her. 'Unfortunately, he has a really bad tummy ache now. He's in agony, I'm fairly sure, and he's not going to live. I'm sorry, but I need to put him down.' Carina had seen quite a few animals put down. Each time, either her dad or Bruce had shot them. No-one liked doing it.

'Does it hurt them when you shoot them, Bruce?' she asked.

'No, Carina,' he replied. 'They don't even know anything happens. It happens in an instant. They just go to sleep and never wake up.'

Simone missed five days of the heat wave. She was away for four days in the air-conditioning, travelling to Brisbane, and participating in facilitator training. Bruce caught up with her, bright-eyed and bushy-tailed on Thursday morning. 'How was it, Simone?' he asked.

'It was excellent,' Simone replied. 'I met eight other facilitators for groups across northern Australia. They were all terrific people and we clicked really well. The trainers, who came over from Western Australia, were also excellent. I learned heaps.'

'What was the highlight?' Bruce asked.

'Not being here getting fried alive, I think,' Simone responded, laughing. 'It's not too funny being back. I'm really looking forward to our next group meeting in April.'

'Me too, Simone,' Bruce said. 'I'm looking forward to getting more savvy on doing these cattle monitoring measurements, which will help our program with Wayne.'

Merve and Doris arrived on Friday night. It was eight-thirty. They stepped out of their air-conditioned vehicle into what felt like a blast furnace. 'Bruce, how can you stand this heat?' Doris asked him. Even though it was so late, it was still thirty-eight degrees.

'We just have to, Mum,' Bruce replied. 'It's okay for us. I just feel sorry for all the animals and plants.'

Therese had arrived two hours earlier. 'We have the air conditioners on and hope we don't get a power failure,' she added.

It was a languid weekend. Doris was wondering why they had come out. On the other hand, Merve was loving it. As depressing as the heat was, he enjoyed toddling off by himself around Bovale, checking waters and feeding lick, which was about all they could do at present. The pleasure of each other's company countered any negative impacts the heat could have had on Bruce and Therese as they did the same as Merve, but together in the trusty Kubota with Caesar riding shotgun. At Bruce's insistence, despite the dire situation at Bovale, Col had taken his family to the coast for a few days where the ocean kept the ambient temperatures a bit lower, though that was countered by stifling humidity.

Mid-week, the regional thermometers had a reprieve. January was almost done. As the brutal dry heat tapered off, the humidity built. The city folk were complaining bitterly about the discomfort. But

Bruce was loving it. His cattle were more comfortable. Better still, each day the afternoon cloud masses grew; it was the final stages of the build up to a break in the wet season.

On Sunday, Bruce woke to a clear sky and still day. The forecast was a high chance of a storm. Bruce had previously experienced these days that started off with no indication of what was to come and by nightfall, all hell had broken loose. Rather than do his water run as planned, which was optional today anyway, he decided to spend the day ensuring the Bovale homestead and surrounds were as secure as possible if a storm eventuated. If it didn't hit today, it was going to come any day soon. One of the first tasks was to pull the homestead water supply pump out of the river and secure it on high ground.

At about one o'clock in the afternoon, Bruce noticed a few small cells building to the west. She's on, he said to himself. He redoubled his efforts to have Bovale battened down. Col had made the same observation and joined Bruce. They also ensured the generator was fuelled and ready to go. As sure as night follows day, they'd have no power tonight if they had a major storm. The men also prepared the vehicles for fence repairs. Because they maintained fence lines so diligently at Bovale, the chances of falling timber breaking fences were not high. However, almost nothing could prevent the enormous power of flood waters, smashing any fence across a creek.

The clouds built at an incredible pace. By three o'clock, there were several towering tropical storm cells to the west of Bovale. Every time Bruce looked, he noted totally different cloud formations. The atmospheric conditions were highly volatile. Bruce had the feeling of electricity in the air. He didn't know whether such a thing was real; it may have just been a psychological effect created by the tension leading up to a dramatic event.

Earlier in the day, Bruce had created a secure area in an old saddle shed beside the yard, where the poddies could be temporarily housed for the night. He also took down their temporary shelters as the tarpaulins would be shredded if the storm was violent. With help from Lachlan and Carina, Bruce fed the poddies early and herded them into the shed enclosure as he knew it would be difficult to do so later. It wasn't going to be much fun for the poddies, but Bruce had done his best to make them safe and comfortable.

Just after four o'clock, Bruce and Col were in the shed when they heard the first rumble of distant thunder. The clouds were billowing and very dark, almost with a greenish tinge. A gusty easterly wind was building as the colossal updraughts in the approaching storm sucked in ground-level air, mainly from its front. The shading by the clouds and the high humidity of the gusting breezes created the same effect as an evaporative air conditioner; it was cool and very refreshing. It was so dark outside, it almost felt like it was seven o'clock. 'I don't think there's anything more we should or could do, Col,' Bruce said. 'Let's get safe before this thing hurts anyone.'

'Simone has prepared an early dinner and we're all about to have showers so if the power goes, we won't get caught short,' Col told Bruce. 'Simone has made spaghetti. She has a bowl full for you as well, Bruce. If you come past the house, pick it up, and that'll save you fumbling around in the dark later trying to make a feed.'

'Thanks, Col,' Bruce replied. 'That wife of yours is a champion.'

Bruce made sure Caesar was locked in his weather-proof cage and bolted inside the homestead. Just as Bruce shut the door behind him, there was a massive lightning strike, lighting up the dark afternoon. Almost simultaneously, there was a deafening crack. The lightning had struck frighteningly close. The power was gone. He had been about to ring Therese and his parents, but that was not going to be possible until they could get the generator going. There was nothing Bruce could or should do, so he sat down to the bowl of spaghetti and tried to enjoy the storm, knowing it could bring the rain he desperately needed, but he also knew it was going to cause some destruction.

The first drops of rain were intermittent and sounded like gravel hitting the iron roof of the homestead. Bruce looked hard through the front windows to the front lawn. He was sure he could see small lumps of glistening ice. Hail, he thought. Hail! He had never heard of or seen hail this far north, but seeing is believing. No wonder the first drops sounded like gravel. Very soon after, there was a massive gust of wind, coinciding with a sharp burst of very heavy rain. Momentarily the rain stopped. A massive, close lightning strike accompanied by more deafening thunder heralded continuous rainfall. The rain continually and violently changed from very heavy to heavy and back again, in concert with winds gusting to what may have been in excess of one hundred kilometres per hour to almost still. Lightning and thunder become incessant.

The storm must have been very wide because it raged for ages, never letting up in its ferocity. Finally, two hours later, it abated. The clouds almost limped away. The wind dropped. The sun came out. It was beautifully cool for a short while. But that didn't last long as the heat re-escalated, exacerbating the humidity. The storm was moving in a roughly easterly direction, which meant that as the rain stopped at the homestead, almost the whole of Bovale was still being pelted.

Bruce walked outside to survey a drenched landscape. He let Caesar out to be with him. Caesar was not moving far from Bruce. He'd obviously been spooked by the storm. 'It's okay, mate. All finished now,' Bruce soothingly said to him. Already Bruce could see flooding in the river. Birds were out. The thunder rolling from the east was punctured by bird songs with the background of the turbulent flood waters. Bruce saw Col heading to the shed to start the generator. Bruce headed to the rain gauge that was tied on the front fence. The wind had blown the top off, but would not have affected the collection, only subsequent evaporation. Bruce was not surprised when he measured out one hundred and eighty-three millimetres, seven and a half inches in the old money. Rainfall of that intensity only ever occurred every few decades at Bovale and Bruce had certainly not experienced anything like it.

With power now available, Bruce checked the radar, which showed the storm was almost two hundred kilometres wide and about to hit Townsville, with Brandon also in its path. Bruce rang his father. 'She's a big one, Dad. Hope you're battened down,' he told Merve.

'I think we're right, thanks, Bruce,' Merve replied. 'We secured the business this afternoon and everything's fine here. How'd you go? Did you get it?'

'Did we get it?' Bruce answered rhetorically. 'We just had a ripper.' He described the experience to his father. 'It's a bit late to check anything now, but we were well prepared, so hopefully we won't have too much damage repair in front of us.' After speaking to Merve, Bruce rang Therese, Frances and Lenny. It was comforting to know his and Therese's families were safe.

Bruce and Col spent the next few days in a slog. Fence lines across most creeks needed repair. All the licks they had out were spoiled and had to be tipped out and topped up with wet season lick. The cattle had been lethargic before the storm. Even though it takes many days for green shoot to come through, the cattle were walking long distances, seemingly much brighter, seeking what feed they could. This only exacerbated their weight loss in the short term, but once the green feed came, they would gain up to two kilograms a day for up to two weeks and then settle to one kilogram gained daily. Weight change would then gradually decrease as the tropical pastures matured.

They could not leave Bovale because of localised flooding. Cockatoo River raged for two days before it settled down to a steady low flow. That did not bother the Wattle family or Bruce. They were prepared for events like this, and they had neither planned to, nor needed to, go anywhere. Life was quickly back to normal with restored optimism.

After the storm, Bovale very quickly turned green. The days were clear. There were no signs of any impending storms or monsoonal rain. Long-term forecasts were not promising any useful rain. Bruce was worried. February rainfall makes or breaks the year in a cattle business in this part of the world. If it rains, no matter how dry it was before, the grass will grow like fury. If it doesn't rain, irrespective of what happened in the months before, hot dry February weather cooks whatever is standing to a crisp. Later rainfall was never as effective in generating pasture, except in years where it rained regularly. The dry tropics is a challenging environment for man and beast. Merve would regularly comment, 'There's a reason why almost no-one lives west of the Mossman to Charters Towers line and north of the Charters Towers to Camooweal line, an area approaching half a million square kilometres; Queensland's Gulf country and Peninsula have a brutal, harsh climate.'

The grass stayed green for weeks. The cattle consumed the phosphorus-based lick Bruce and Col were now feeding. Cattle growth rates were off the charts. But the days stayed hot and dry. Maximum temperature rarely varied from thirty-five to thirty-six degrees. It never dropped below thirty degrees till ten o'clock each night. Twice, Bovale received a patchy storm generating a total of thirty millimetres of rain that evaporated almost as quickly as it had fallen. By the end of February, it was clear, the wet season had failed. Bruce had pasture, but he also had a lot of cattle. Too many, if the available feed was going to last till the next wet season. He had to reduce his herd size. Quickly.

Bruce told Col he had made the decision to sell. Col had just returned from a water and lick run on a clear dry day. It was lunch time. Bruce was in the shed, having also just returned from a water and lick run. 'What are you going to sell?' Col asked Bruce.

'It has to be what has the lowest production potential, has high risk of incurring management costs, will attract the best prices right now, and or will be the easiest to replace if we need to buy back the equivalent in the future,' Bruce replied. 'It can't be bulls because we have already minimised our bull herd. It can't be yearling steers now. They are our major income later in the year, and we need that income next financial year; it's bad enough we have to sell more this financial year. We've already cut our heifers back to minimum numbers and they will be the lowest risk to induce costs. So, it has to be cows. Cows reach their maximum live weight production and efficiency at six years of age, so it has to be at least non-pregnant cows aged over six years.'

'We'd have four hundred to four-fifty of those, wouldn't we?' asked Col.

'Yes,' Bruce replied. 'I'm thinking the best and simplest strategy may be to brand as soon as we can, and when we have the cattle in, get Eileen here. All mature cows that are non-pregnant have to go. We'll reassess in another month. We'll just wean the calves of the first-lactation cows.'

'What about the market though, Bruce?' Col queried. 'It's coming back quickly from what I've heard. Will that hold you back from selling?'

'Yes, unfortunately, the market has plummeted. It usually is on the slide at this time of the year, but because of the failed wet season everywhere, it's on a massive slide. It's already down by nearly two dollars a kilogram at the meatworks,' Bruce commented. 'However, we cannot make something out of nothing. It's as crazy as wearing a coat in this weather as it is to keep cattle that will have nothing to eat. We just have to suck it up and sell. I'm very disappointed, but that's how it is.'

'I suppose the one good thing going for you is you have big cows and in fair condition,' Col remarked. 'I bet there's plenty of places around that don't have the options you have because they're consistently overgrazing their country. They smile in the years it rains, but what a disaster when it doesn't.'

'Pasture is everything, Col,' Bruce agreed. 'If there's one brilliant thing Dad taught me, it was to build the business on good pastures. I have seen no evidence to refute that. I could open the country we burnt last year or the country we want to spell this year, but that will just undo in one year what it's taken thirty years to create. We just can't do it, Col.'

'If you target non-pregnant cows for selling, you'll be selecting the poorer-conditioned ones, which will cause you to get a real caning in the market,' Col noted.

'That's true, Col,' Bruce agreed. 'But we can either sell them as is, or we can put them through a feedlot. I'll have to do my sums on what will work best.'

That night, Bruce worked out, based on the prevailing body condition of the cows which was moderate, that the best option for the cows was to consign direct to slaughter. The pressure was on. After he made the decision on slaughter, he spent the next few hours working on logistics. Bruce had to process four paddocks and brand a total of about eight hundred calves. The added complication to normal management was that he had to wean all the calves from the cull cows. If he was culling forty percent of the older cows, he had to find a solution to which calf belonged to the cull cows. In the end, he reasoned the simplest solution was to wean everything. Bruce came to the realisation that, because of the cattle nutrition failing much earlier in the year than usual, it was a smart move to wean all calves, even though some were as young as two months of age. This would preserve the condition on the cows and delay the costly exercise of having to feed energy-dense supplements to cows later in the year if the dry conditions persisted. As well, weaning the calves early would reduce mortality risk in the cows; mortalities were very expensive, costing the business about one thousand dollars per cow lost at current values. However, the downside was that it required him to supplement the weaners for much longer with higher-value supplements. Bruce arced up his spreadsheeting skills and did some calculations from which he concluded the cheapest option under the circumstances was to wean all calves in mid-March.

That was easier said than done. At relatively short notice, he had to plan and organise the slaughter date, helicopter for musters, extra men for mustering and branding, drafting, pregnancy diagnoses, weaning, holding paddocks, returning cows to paddocks, trucks, rations for small weaners, weaner training and branding. He spent another hour on logistics to ultimately get the cull cows on a truck in three weeks, having done all the mustering and pregnancy diagnoses. It would be possible if he could recruit his father, Eileen and Therese for Friday to Sunday at the end of the following week and then both days on the following weekend. He'd still be shy of help on the Monday when they trucked the cattle and on the following day. He decided he'd ask Mick or Craig if they were available. By this stage, it was too late to ring anyone.

Bruce was on the phone early the next morning. His first call was to his father at five-thirty as he knew Merve would be up. 'G'day, Dad.'

They had a quick general chat before Merve asked, 'What's up, Bruce? You don't usually ring this early?'

'Fancy a day or two on the tools out here, Dad?' Bruce asked him.

'Wild horses wouldn't keep me away, son,' Merve replied. 'I reckon your mother would be up for it too. She's good now and raring to get out to Bovale. What's the plan?' Bruce explained what he'd like. 'I reckon I could do that, Bruce. I'll put Farmin Stuff on automatic pilot for a few days and head out. The staff I have now are getting real handy and they can manage without me for a couple of days. And besides, I need some days off,' Merve responded.

'Everything depends on the meatworks, Dad,' Bruce said. 'I'll ring you back later if we can go as planned.'

Bruce then called the meatworks buyer. He was lucky. He could fit two hundred and fifty in for slaughter on Tuesday in three weeks' time. The buyer could not offer Bruce a price until the week before slaughter. Bruce had to accept that; he did not have a better alternative. Bruce then rang the chopper pilot, Ian Spencer, to organise the helicopter for the five musters he had planned. Ian could fit him in. I'm landing on my feet here, Bruce thought. It wasn't every day you could get the dates you wanted from multiple businesses at once.

Before ringing Merve back, Bruce rang both Therese and Eileen. Eileen booked him in. She loved going to Bovale. 'Would it work if the gang turned up, Bruce? I don't know what everyone's up to, but I'll ask,' she said.

'That would be terrific, Eileen. I need to ring Mick and Craig anyway, as I need one of them, if possible, for a couple of days outside a weekend. If you ask Jane and Brenda, that'd be great. And if Tom wants to come, please bring him. I'd love to get to know him better.'

Eileen was ecstatic. 'Thanks, Bruce. I'll ask him. I don't think we'll be able to keep him away.'

'If you're here, I don't doubt that for a moment, Eileen,' Bruce commented.

Therese was also keen to come. She should be able to swap shifts with someone else.

The primary unsecured missing component of the plan now was the trucks. Bruce rang a few operators and secured twelve decks. The only thing that looked like it could thwart the plan was big rain. That would not be a bad problem, Bruce thought. Not only would he get the extra grass he needed to hold the cattle, but also the cattle prices would be likely to sneak north again.

Bruce's next call was to Mick. 'Mate, is there any chance at all you could help me out?' Bruce asked. Mick was keen to do the Monday and Tuesday branding. 'Let Craig know what's on too please, Mick. Eileen was thinking about herding the gang out for the experience, so don't be surprised if Jane asks you to come out for a weekend or two.'

'Those ladies will be as keen as mustard. I reckon you'll have us, mate. I'm on a high already.' Mick told Bruce.

Bruce rang Merve back and confirmed the dates. He suggested to Merve his mother might find herself being chief caterer. He knew Doris would thrive on this, having a job to keep her busy. He then picked up the UHF. 'Col, are you there?'

'Here, Bruce. In the shed, loading some lick,' Col radioed back.

'I'm coming over to cross check some plans with you, if that's okay?' Bruce asked. Bruce thought he had a sound plan, but he needed to be sure. Col would quickly pick any holes in it for him. Bruce had a white board in the shed where him and Col listed jobs to do. He made some space on the board and mapped out the plan. The main challenge Col could see was dealing with the wayward fence-crawling behaviour of newly-weaned cows. Together, they worked out how they would do it.

Therese had a late shift on the Thursday before the muster. She had six hours' sleep before she headed out to Bovale. Merve and Doris had gone out Thursday night after Merve finished work. By the time Therese arrived, Bruce, Col and Merve already had the cattle in hand and the chopper had left to do another muster. As Therese came through the front gate of the homestead, Caesar was waiting. 'My, you are growing so fast,' she said to Caesar as he lapped up her cuddles and play. Therese left him, standing, watching in disappointment, as she went inside the homestead to greet Doris. She could hear the men making decisions on the UHF as they brought the mob out of the paddock, heading to the yards. She radioed Bruce. 'Bruce, Therese here. When will you get to the yards?'

'It's about four kilometres, so give us an hour and a half. The calves make it a bit slow,' he replied. 'We'll be back at the house in about two hours. Tell Mum we'll have lunch then. Eileen should be there by then too.' As the men arrived back when Bruce had suggested they would, Eileen drove in on cue. Therese was very pleased to see that Tom had come as well. She didn't know whether Bruce had organised a party or two or work, as she knew the rest of the gang was going to arrive that night, but then decided it was probably both.

After lunch, they descended on the yards. When they got out of their vehicles, they were met with the continual bawling of cows and calves. The yard held hundreds of red cattle, some of them light red, some of them dark red, and every shade in between. They were fairly settled, but some dust rose as a few within the mob milled slowly. Everything Therese was seeing, hearing and smelling, were all new. 'Do they always make that much racket?' she asked.

'Yep. That's not too bad,' Bruce replied. 'Wait till we start moving them and separating the calves from the cows, then they'll take it up a notch. And they'll keep going twenty-four hours a day for about three days, now we're weaning the calves.'

Bruce had some electronic gear and was busy organising the show, so Therese stuck with Eileen to start with. She had Caesar on a lead. Caesar was in heaven. Whatever was new to Therese was even newer to Caesar. He'd move a few paces, stop, cock his head and look. They went through several heavy steel gates that opened and shut with spring loaded catches. 'That's nifty,' Therese remarked. Eileen did not have much gear to carry. She had a small battery-powered ultrasound unit with a built-in screen and a two-metre lead and probe, plus a couple of buckets Therese carried for her holding two boxes of gloves, a four-litre pump pack of obstetrical lubricant, a large shoulder guard and a scrubbing brush. 'Is that all you need?' Therese asked her.

'Yes. These are cows, Therese,' Eileen explained. 'No consultation, no general checks, just a very quick rectal palpation, and they're done. You'll see.' Eileen secured Caesar to the base of a tree in the stock-free area adjacent to the veterinary chute. That was safest for everyone, especially Caesar.

The mixed mob of cows, calves and a few bulls were all in one large receiving yard. The ladies watched as Bruce, Col, Tom and Merve walked into the yard after opening some gates to a consecutive series of smaller yards that Eileen told her were called forcing yards. Therese thought they'd simply get behind them and chase. But they didn't. The men all walked wide around the mob to the left of the direction they wanted to push the cattle. Merve kept walking to the far corner of the yard, where he started pushing the cattle in the corner into the mob and towards where they wanted the cattle to go. Col went back with Merve and then moved back on the left of the cattle that Merve was pushing. Bruce was near the front of the mob pushing into it and peeling off a group that he started herding towards the gate. He didn't go too far, before he peeled back and took another group, making sure no cattle moved out behind him. Tom worked in between Col and Bruce. Therese could see the men were working as a team, keeping the mob against the yard fence on the mob's right-hand side, whilst they kept pushing the left-hand side, adjacent to them, forward towards the front of the mob. As they did this, some of the cattle at the front of the mob started to walk freely into the series of smaller yards. When the men had about half of the mob into the yards, Bruce called out, 'That's it,' and the three men quickly moved around the left of the mob, towards the gate, pinching the mob in two. They herded those in front of them through the gate and shut it; the cattle behind them stopped and started moving back to where they'd come from.

'Wow. Now that's what I call teamwork,' Therese exclaimed. 'They hardly seemed to communicate, and they had those cattle completely under control.'

'They're experienced stockman, Therese,' Eileen responded. 'I agree, it's beautiful to watch when you see people handle cattle like those blokes do. You wait till you see Lachlan tomorrow. He'll be in there too, working the cattle like a pro.'

The men had shut themselves into the first forcing yard. They then moved forward on the left of the cattle and split what they had herded into consecutive yards, without overcrowding them. Bruce came back to the ladies. 'Therese, if you don't mind, can you work with Col, please? He'll tell you what he wants you to do,' Bruce said to her. 'I'll work up here with Eileen catching the cows and drafting them. Tom, can you work the race, please?'

Col was in the pound, a circular yard about eight metres in diameter that was fed from the last small forcing yard. There were about twenty cows and calves in the forcing yard. The pound was a central thoroughfare in the yards. It had several other gates about three metres wide leading to other yards. It also had a gate that led into a race, which was a narrow laneway, just wide enough for one cow to walk comfortably through, leading to the veterinary chute where Eileen would be doing the pregnancy diagnoses. Between the stock-free area and the pound was a very narrow space between two posts that a person could squeeze through, but no cattle; it was a manway. Therese squeezed through into the pound. Col handed her the ubiquitous cattle herder. It was a bright pink hard-plastic pipe about twenty-five millimetres in diameter and about one and a half metres long. 'You'll need this, Therese,' he said. 'I'll work in the forcing yard with the gate open to the pound. I'll yell out what's coming. It'll be calves, cows or bulls. If it's cows, open the gate to the race. Just practise that to make sure you're comfortable with it.' Therese pulled the gate latch handle that unlatched the gate automatically as the handle turned. To close it, she held the gate, not the latch, and simply pushed the gate which latched automatically. 'When you do that, Therese, open the gate about halfway and stand out from the end so the gate cannot hit you if an animal knocks it on the way past,' Col explained as he demonstrated what he wanted her to do. 'Use the herder like an extension of your arm. You can reach behind the cattle and guide them forward. It'll be a bit scary to start with, but we'll go steady and you'll be right. We can't go any faster than Eileen can assess them anyway which is about one hundred an hour.'

'One hundred per hour?' Therese asked incredulously. 'I'm glad I'm not a cow. How can she possibly do that?'

'We'll be going very slow, Therese, so when the race is full, you can go forward and watch her. She'll explain,' Col replied. 'When I'm bringing up, if I yell 'calves', open that gate inwards, and send them out there. Bulls go in that yard,' Col said, pointing to where he wanted the cattle to be drafted.

'We're ready, Col,' Bruce shouted from the chute. He had to shout to be heard over the bellowing of the cattle. Therese could see Eileen standing at the back of the chute with an arm-length glove on her right arm, typical latex surgical gloves on both hands, and a large, bright yellow flexible plastic guard covering her right side from her neck to her waist. Bruce was standing at the front of the chute ready to operate the head bail.

'Are you ready, Therese?' Col asked.

'I hope so,' Therese replied.

Col opened the gate into the forcing yard. Almost immediately he yelled, 'Cows.'

Therese could see he had separated two cows at the front of the yard. They willingly moved into the pound. Therese opened the gate as she'd been instructed. The cows knew the routine well because they walked straight into the race without any encouragement. Just as Therese was about to close the gate, Col yelled, 'More cows.' She looked back and saw that Col had another three cows coming. Therese held the gate open and those three followed the first two.

The opening of the race was about three metres in front of the gate Therese had drafted the cows into. There was a vee from the gate to the race. At the front of the vee and at the back end of the race was a gate that slid across from the left side of the race. Tom slid the gate in behind the cows. 'When Tom opens the slide, you let me know you need more cows,' Col said to Therese. 'Is that okay?' he asked.

'I should be right with that,' Therese replied.

'I'll be right here for a bit. Just go up and see what they're doing at the chute,' Col said to Therese.

She squeezed through the manway. Caesar saw Therese coming and thought he was in for a pat, but when she went towards Bruce, he stopped wagging his tail, and cocked his head, staring at her. Therese stood back a bit to watch. Eileen let one cow in at a time through a slide gate like the one at the back of the race. The chute was in two sections. The front section was about two metres long. The rear section was about three-quarters of a metre long. There were two half gates, called vet gates, one above the other, as wide as the chute was, hinged on a side opening at the back of the chute. Eileen had the top one open and it stayed open with the ultrasound machine hanging on the inside where she could view the screen. She set the bottom vet gate set so it could allow a cow to pass as she opened the sliding gate from the race to let the cow in. As she closed the race gate, she kicked the vet gate, which automatically latched it in behind the cow, making it safe for her to stand immediately behind the cow. Eileen had the obstetrical lubricant sitting on an empty two-hundred-litre drum beside the chute. She pumped a small amount onto the back of her right hand. She lifted the ultrasound probe from the bucket of water beside the chute and palmed the probe. Eileen then stepped in behind the cow, grasping its tail as she did so. She wiped the lube on the backside of the cow and then entered the rectum up to her elbow, holding the probe in her hand. The cow didn't seem to mind. Eileen was only in the cow for about ten seconds when she withdrew and called some information to Bruce that Therese didn't understand. In response to the data, Bruce immediately tapped the information into what looked like a computer set on a frame beside the chute and attached to cables from under the chute. He then set gates in front of the chute and released the cow, as Eileen admitted another cow, repeating the cycle.

Bruce used opening and shutting of the front gate of the chute, the head bail, to lure each cow forward that Eileen admitted. As soon as one cow was set, Therese went forward to Bruce. 'Hope you don't mind me asking, Bruce, but what is the information Eileen is calling, and what are you typing into that device?' she asked.

'Well, the first thing that happens is that when the cow comes into the chute, that device hanging on the other side of the chute reads the small button tag in the cow's right ear. Can you see that?' he asked.

'Yes,' Therese replied.

'You can see on the monitor of this data recorder that this cow has a sixteen-digit number. We know she's the only cow in the world with that number. We have previously matched it to an age and sex. All the data we record is entered against her unique identification number. The first number Eileen calls is the body condition score of the cow between one and five, one being poor, three being moderate and five being fat,' Bruce explained. Therese was nodding. 'Then she calls the number of months pregnant, and then whether the cow is lactating or not. If the cow's lactating, Eileen calls 'wet', and she'll call 'dry' when she's not lactating. While that's all happening, the system automatically weighs the cow as the whole chute is set on load cells you can see under the front and back. I then draft all the non-pregnant cows one way and pregnant cows into another yard.'

Eileen called, 'Three, two, wet.'

Bruce typed the data into the data recorder, drafted the cow out of the chute and lured another cow forward to be restrained for assessment. 'Did you get that last cow when Elieen called body condition score three, two months pregnant, and lactating?' Bruce asked Therese.

'Yes, I understand now,' Therese replied. As Bruce went back to concentrating on his job, Therese asked Eileen, 'Can I watch your ultrasound screen, please, Eileen?'

'No problem, Therese,' she replied as she locked in another cow and proceeded to conduct the palpation and talk at the same time. 'These cows can only be up to two months pregnant, so I scan forward from the cervix over the uterus and check each side to see if there's any pregnancy. This cow is non-pregnant. Two, zero, wet,' she called to Bruce. Therese waited for the next cow. As soon as Eileen entered the cow, Therese could see the pregnancy. It didn't look any different to a human pregnancy on ultrasound. Eileen called to Bruce, 'Three, two, wet,' as she removed the probe and started looking for the next cow.

Therese went back to help Col. 'That's amazing how fast they do that, Col,' she said. She watched Tom as he worked the cattle on the race. He mostly kept about four metres from the race. If he wanted a cow to move, he approached from in front of and directly towards her head at about forty-five degrees, which seemed to cause the cow to move forward. As this occurred, Tom would immediately step directly back to the four-metre line. She must ask him about that later, she thought. Everyone kept plugging away at their jobs. Every time Col emptied the small forcing yard, he went to the yard behind and collected some more cattle. When all the forcing yards were empty, everyone stopped while the men went back and yarded the balance of the mob into the forcing yards. Within three hours, the job was finished.

Bruce had radioed his mother and Simone, giving them an estimated time when they'd finish. It was just after three o'clock and the last of the cows was being drafted off, when the homestead crew appeared with a cup of tea and some cake. The team wolfed it and then started drafting the calves through the chute into those less than one hundred kilograms, those bigger than one hundred and twenty-five kilograms and intermediate-weight calves. Col explained that the calves needed different rations during the weaning process and when they went out to their paddocks. The smallest would only get pellets in the yards. The biggest would get hay and some protein meal. The intermediate calves would get hay and pellets. Simone could see what Eileen was talking about when Lachlan entered the yard. He was like an over-eager pup, but well-trained.

When they finished weaner drafting, the calves were fed, and the cows were held in the receiving yard. They'd be let out the next morning. The team went back to the homestead where everyone congregated on the front lawn of the homestead for some deliciously cold beers and a snack that Doris had prepared. 'I'm amazed by everything I saw today, Bruce,' Therese said. 'I suppose me seeing what you do is like you seeing what we do farming sugar cane.'

'It's all fairly routine for us, Therese,' Bruce responded. 'Give it time, and you'll master it. You did a great job today. Thanks. Did you feel comfortable?'

'Not at first,' Therese said. 'But Col was great the way he taught me. By the end of the day, I was feeling much more comfortable.'

Dinner was a great party, after the rest of the gang arrived. Doris was in supreme catering mode. Bruce called the night early as they had a big day ahead of them, mustering Kosciuszko paddock. Therese was going on the muster in the Kubota buggy with Simone.

First bells were at four o'clock. They left the homestead at five o'clock. By the time they were in position in the paddock, Ian arrived in his chopper. He skirted along the southern edge of the paddock, taking instructions from Bruce based on what cattle he found where. Simone and Therese waited at Jindabyne dam where there was a water trough and blocked up cattle into a mob as they came ambling and trotting down Wild Horse Creek. There was not much to do initially, but as the muster progressed, more and more cattle came into their water. The sound of the chopper was clear as it moved across the paddock scouting for cattle, moving them on, and ensuring they all kept going in the right direction. Therese had not expected the rush she would get, witnessing the low-hovering chopper weaving behind the last mob into them. She had her mobile out, taking photos and videos as Simone masterfully positioned them to control the cattle.

Bruce radioed. 'Simone and Therese, can you move that mob off please, down the western side of Wild Horse Creek? I'll be there in five minutes to help you. Col and Lachlan, can you please move your cattle off and we'll meet on the northern fence line where we usually do? Tom, can you please work your mob down the western fence and join us in the corner?' Bruce received assent from everyone as the cattle were all started off. The chopper disappeared back to the homestead to fuel up.

'I thought it was going to be faster than this, Simone,' Therese remarked as they pushed the mob along. Their pace was slow as they kept circling behind the mob that was ambling along. Bruce did the same as Simone and Therese, but he was moving fast, checking well out from the mob to the east and west for other cattle to bring in. Ian returned and cross-checked behind the mobs and ensured everyone was under control before he signed off and disappeared.

Once they had the mob together, it totalled about five hundred cows with about four hundred calves. It was a sight to behold for Therese as they pushed them slowly to the yards. The final push as they yarded the mob created a bit of excitement as a few bigger calves decided they'd like to take off at high speed, straight back to where they came from. Therese marvelled at the skills of Col, Bruce and Tom as they rounded up these wayward individuals and brought them back into the mob as gently as they could.

By Sunday night after three big days, Therese was knackered, as was just about everyone else. After dinner, all the visitors left. It was just Bruce and Therese at the homestead, and it was very quiet. A good night to go to bed early. Therese was rejuvenated the next day. Bruce and Col had to leave early to attend to the yarded cattle and keep their water and lick runs going for cattle that had not been mustered. After giving the homestead a clean-up, Therese left for Townsville. The previous three days had been a very enlightening experience for her. She now had some idea how hard these cattlemen worked and how skilled they were. It was very different to farming.

Chapter Sixteen

The whole gang and Merve and Doris arrived back at Bovale for two full days the next weekend. Frances and Simon were lured out too, not wanting to miss the family action. On Saturday, they mustered the first-lactation cows, including Jasper's harem separately, to wean their calves. A few of these cows were not lactating. Bruce drafted them off to join the culls, which were being mustered the next day.

Saturday was not a big day with so many people helping. This ensured that both Friday night and Saturday nights were gala events hosted by Doris, Jane and Brenda who were having a field day. After a very ordinary twelve months, Doris was pumped to be back in full health and to be working with such wonderful young people in her favourite corner of heaven.

Branding, which is what the collective surgeries conducted on calves is called in northern Australia, started at daybreak on Sunday morning before the culls were mustered back out of Kenworth paddock. Despite all her medical experience, like every experience on this muster, branding was an eye-opener for Therese. She'd only ever seen a few consecutive surgeries. When she learned they were doing three hundred, she initially thought that was impossible. They did the surgeries in blocks of one hundred.

Today they were doing the biggest calves that had been weaned. The calves were initially put in the main race where a repeat injection gun was used to give each an injection of a meloxicam, a pain killer that had effect for three days. The group was then brought in single file through the smaller branding race, sized for calves. The end of the race opened to a cradle in which the calf was restrained and laid over on its right side. Two notches were cut out of the left ear, and it was fire branded on the left rump. The firebrand was in two parts; the station's symbol brand of M+D was branded above a 'one'. 'I understand where M+D comes from, but what does the one mean?' Therese asked.

'It means they were born in the twenty, twenty-one financial year and will be weaned in two thousand and twenty-one,' Eileen explained. 'Just about everyone in the north Australian industry uses the same system, which means we can instantly age almost any animal in northern Australia.'

All male calves were surgically castrated. Bruce did this at an incredible pace. Several had small horn buds that were scooped out to prevent further growth. Both the castration and disbudding wounds were medicated using a repeat-dosing gun that squeezed a local anaesthetic, antiseptic and haemostatic gel directly into the wounds. Eileen had gloves on, and she then placed a gauze surgical swab on disbudding wounds and held them there for at least twenty seconds, till the animal was released, to help reduce bleeding. The whole process from one calf to the next took less than sixty seconds. Therese was impressed.

The branded calves had been through training over the past week, which had dramatically reduced their fearfulness of man, of being handled, and of the yards. As soon as the surgery was completed for each calf, it was released to walk freely out of the yards into a small paddock where the group would recuperate for several days before Bruce and Col walked them to a weaner paddock.

After the surgery was completed for the day, the team had a late smoko and then mustered the cull cows from Kenworth paddock. On Monday morning, two triple-trailer trucks arrived. The cull cows were loaded by Bruce, Col and Mick before they turned their attention to another group of weaners that they branded. Branding, weaner training and taking cows back to their allotted paddock continued till Saturday.

On Friday, Bruce received an email from the meatworks with advice on the slaughter of the cull cows. He received an average of four dollars, twenty-five cents a kilogram of carcass weight, one dollar, sixty-four cents less than what he had received the previous year for cull cows. The meatworks had transferred two hundred and forty-three thousand, three hundred and thirty dollars into his account, which was ninety-three and a half thousand dollars less than he would have received on the previous year's market. It was a lot of money, but beef businesses are always exposed to unavoidable market fluctuations. Last year he was ahead; this year he was behind. Over time, whether he tried or not, he would simply receive average prices.

Bruce had been relieved there was no rain during the weaning and branding period, or they would have had to defer the branding.

When processing cattle at this time of the year would usually have been difficult because of wet conditions, they had a dream run with the now-completed muster. Bruce was lucky on that score. However, March remained dry. It was such a contrast to the previous year when everything had fallen in the business's favour. It was early April. Col and Bruce were helping each other load up for a lick and water run.

'Are we selling more cattle if this keeps up?' Col asked.

'By my reckoning, we have to Col,' Bruce replied. 'I can't see it raining any day soon. We simply have to plan for no useful rain till Christmas. She's an ugly thought,' Bruce added as he screwed up his face in disgust with the weather.

'What are you aiming to take out next?' Col asked.

'As much as I hate to do it, Col, it has to be non-pregnant first-lactation cows and the usual non-pregnant two-year-old heifers,' Bruce answered. 'There will be more this year than previously because of the rubbish weather, but we can only afford to keep what's going to produce the most amount of live weight in the next few years.'

Days later, the weather forecasters indicated a weather change may deliver rain. The Arnold and Wattle families remained pessimistic. It had been very dry for so long, other than the big storm at the end of January, that they refused to believe it would rain until it rained. A few days later Simone commented, 'They keep predicting rain, Bruce. My experience is when their forecast stays the same or even gets better for a week or more, they have it right.'

'We'll see, ' Bruce said with a smile. 'I want to believe you, but my business instincts are not to plan for it.'

Simone's assessment had been correct. A week later they received fifty-five millimetres of soaking rain at the homestead. It appeared the whole station had that amount or more. Everyone was ebullient. Bruce did not change his selling plans. The rain was certainly going to give them more feed and allow him to defer sales till the next financial year, but the rain had not broken the dry spell. It was still dry, even if it was temporarily wet.

The optimism that invaded the psyche of everyone in the region who had received the rain helped Bruce cement the decision he had made a long time ago but had been waiting for the right time to declare. He needed a ring first. Bruce had surreptitiously worked out the size and the style that was likely to suit. He had based his conclusions on his observations of Therese's jewellery. He had started investigating options online and found a Melbourne business that he rang. This advanced to zoom meetings, at which the specifications were agreed. Bruce contracted the finished item to be delivered in an innocuous oversized insured package by courier to Charters Towers. Delivery to a remote area was not possible, except in the post, and Bruce did not trust the postal system with such a precious item.

Bruce rang Mick, 'Mate, she's on.'

'What are you talking about, Bruce?' Mick asked. Bruce had Mick declare complete and absolute secrecy, first. He then asked Mick if the package could be delivered to his place and then kept secure until Bruce could retrieve it.

'Done deal,' Mick said. 'This is sensational. When's it all happening, Bruce?'

'You'll find out, Mick. All you have to do is see nothing, hear nothing, feel nothing and say nothing, especially at The Villa,' Bruce replied. 'When I'm in town getting that package, even when it's just us two, I want you to maintain complete ignorance. Those sheilas have special sensors, mate. You'll be right, I know, otherwise I wouldn't have asked you. It's great to have such a good mate who I can absolutely trust.'

***

A week later, Simone facilitated the second get-together of the CRAB group. At the first meeting, the group had decided to reconvene at Koolburra Station. The homestead was set in beautiful expansive lawns interspersed with shade trees watered from a large creek below the house. The creek naturally flowed almost continually, fed by aquifers and springs upstream. The impressive homestead was low set with a six-metre-wide veranda encircling it. It was a beautiful day with a bit of cloud. The very recent rain had covered the countryside with green grass and had boosted morale considerably. 'It's almost too good a day to be working,' Bruce commented.

Simone organised it for a Sunday so it could be a family affair. Every family brought food for themselves and everyone else, the usual generosity of good friends and neighbours who don't get a chance to see each other often enough. It didn't matter they'd take half of it home because it saved making dinner, a tiresome chore after a day out. The children and mothers enjoyed these days immensely. The children ran non-stop, playing games with friends they rarely saw. When Simone didn't have the team in hand, the mothers discussed all their family news and achievements, learning heaps that always delivered a few pearls of wisdom such as a new recipe. At the same time, the blokes liked it too, but in their casual way, stood around with beers in hand, solving world or regional issues using their in-built wisdom, or so they thought, rarely discussing the details of their own businesses except in generalities; the weird part was they usually went home thinking they'd been a lot of help to everyone.

After the small crowd had a hearty morning smoko, the children were banished to one side of the homestead. A few people volunteered for child minding duties. Simone opened the meeting on the homestead veranda on the opposite side to where the children were cavorting madly. The Koolburra owners had set chairs around several small tables so everyone was comfortable. 'Good morning, everyone. Today we have three main agenda items,' Simone told them. 'The first is training in how to monitor cattle herd performance and production effectively and efficiently. The agriculture department people here will do that. The second is a general discussion about the management, performance and production of our pastures, our herds and our businesses as a way to identify what we need to know more about. Finally, we'll decide where our next meeting is and what the agenda will be.'

After the training on herd monitoring and during lunch, Wendy Olden was having a cup of tea with Simone. 'That was excellent, Simone. Thanks for chairing that session. Scott and I came here thinking we'd learn some sophisticated system invented by a five-wheel chair rider from the air conditioning in Sydney. But it was simple and practical,' Wendy commented.

'I agree,' Simone said. 'At Bovale, we've already started working on this after Bruce contracted Wayne Greenhough to help improve the business. We had never counted how many in each age group of each sex before, but now we have NLIS tags in every animal, it's very easy. I am really looking forward to the analysis next year.'

'You're a year ahead of us already, Simone,' Wendy said. 'I know I'm keen to see what comes out of your analysis and where it leads you. I'd presume everyone else is just as keen.'

'We already had some of the data, which gave us a fair indication, Wendy,' Simone said. 'That's how Wayne worked out we were not supplementing with phosphorus correctly. Col said to me that Bruce might increase production by ten percent or more and profits by even more if we get it right. Col's never experienced the use of science in a business before, and he's learning a lot because Bruce shares all the business details with him and involves him in the decision-making.'

'Interesting comment that, Simone,' Wendy responded. 'When I think about it, most of us are completely protective of our business details and very few, other than us and the accountant, have any idea what's going on. What I think that's doing is blocking our ability to see where our problems and opportunities are and keeps us in the past and in the dark.'

'You're exactly right, Wendy,' Simone told her. 'That's one of my great learnings from the facilitator training. Improvement for most people requires us to amp up our communication. Some can get there without it but the rest of us need to analyse our own businesses better and see what analyses of other businesses show before we can effectively improve. Most of us can't do that in isolation. Without it, we're like subsistence farmers doing a small number of things well but unknowingly making a right royal stuff-up of many aspects.'

'Has the training been time-consuming, Simone?' Wendy asked.

'No,' Simone replied. 'The first stage was brilliant. I had a couple of days with a group all learning the same thing. And we've been doing further training through the internet at night. It's been perfect, especially because it's so interesting and will help us at Bovale and everyone in our group.'

The session after lunch was Simone's first big test of her new-found skills. What Bruce had learned from his father and the agriculture department about pastures and his recent experiences with Wayne Greenhough were very helpful in initiating discussion points. At the end of the session, Scott summed it up, 'It's been a very informative couple of hours, but I feel we're the blind leading the blind with some of what we've discussed. It's been good to draw on our collective wisdom and experience and the knowledge of agriculture department people here, but I suggest we temper future discussion when we find ourselves asking questions we're guessing the answers to. We can always get specialist help.'

'Well said,' Bruce agreed. 'The facets it appears most are struggling with are the science behind pastures and the mysteries of business analyses. I understand from speaking with Simone that we have the opportunity to get specialist training in both those areas, so let's target one at our next meeting,' he suggested. The group agreed with Bruce and asked Simone to organise a date for pasture monitoring training when a trainer could be accessed. That would be the main agenda item at the next meeting. The next meeting was likely to be at Bovale; it was agreed the site be selected based on what the trainer wanted and when the training could be done. Bruce agreed that when the meeting was next held at Bovale, he'd share details on his plans developed with Wayne's support.

Therese's birthday was fortuitously on a Friday in the middle of May. Bruce began organising a 'birthday party' for her at Bovale. The weather was likely to be excellent at that time of the year, important, as it made sleeping in swags a good option for a crowd. Bovale was likely to look good as well. He had already checked Thereses's roster and knew she had Thursday and Friday off. He asked her if she could wrangle the Saturday off and maybe the Sunday as well, so they could have a birthday bash at Bovale.

Not surprisingly, Bruce agreed she could ask her friends; the more the merrier Bruce had responded. He rang Lenny to make sure him and Maria would be there. He simply told them he had wanted them to come up for a long time and this was the best excuse he could think of to lure everyone up for a few days of fun, especially as he'd have Merve and Doris up and Merve was keen to give him a look over the station. Bruce also invited the whole gang plus Frances and Simon.

With at least twenty-four people to cater for, Bruce asked Wendy Olden from next door, would she mind bringing Scott and another couple over to do the catering. Wendy and Scott were familiar with Bovale and it would allow Doris and Therese to fully enjoy the birthday party, which it was, without having to worry about keeping everyone's glucose and alcohol levels topped up. They contracted to camp the night and cater for breakfast as well. Wendy was very happy. She got to attend a party she might not have ordinarily been invited to.

Usually, Bruce and Col would be busy at this time with stock work, but they had broken the back of that with the March muster. They would resume stock work in June. That gave Bruce time to fit in all the preparations he had to complete in between routine station work. I'm sure glad I'm not preparing for a wedding on Bovale, Bruce thought, as the pressure mounted to get every detail right.

It was Thursday. Therese was driving out to Bovale after finishing an early shift. Bruce caught up with Col in the shed before they both took off to do their agreed jobs for the day. 'Col, I need you to give me a hand with something, please,' Bruce said.

'No problem, Bruce,' Col replied. 'What can I do?' Bruce preceded his request with a request for absolute confidentiality, as he had with Mick. Bruce then explained what he wanted Col to do so he could deliver her 'birthday present' in a special place.

Therese, Lenny, Maria, Merve and Doris all arrived at Bovale on Thursday night. The Wattle family were over for the evening. Merve and Doris had previously met Lenny and Maria on one occasion in Townsville. But the Wattle family had not met them. Everyone had a great evening.

With both his and Therese's family in the homestead, Bruce was wearing better clothes than he usually did on a Friday at Bovale. Therese was wearing a very attractive frock. It was her birthday, and she was getting the royal treatment. Therese was all smiles as she had received some wonderful birthday gifts, including an exquisite pearl necklace from Bruce. The six of them were enjoying a very social morning after an extended breakfast, when Col came on the UHF. 'Are you there, Bruce?'

Bruce picked up the handset in the homestead. 'I'm here, Col. What's up?'

'Bruce, I'm out at Jindabyne dam. There are some cattle in the dam enclosure that need to be herded out. It looks like they've broken the fence up from the campsite and that'll need fixing too. I'm flat strap. Any chance you could come out and do that, please mate? Sorry to interrupt the party there.'

Bruce glanced across at Therese. He gave her the 'I don't know about this' look. Therese said, 'Bruce, it's okay. I'll come with you.'

Amazing, Bruce thought. She's straight on the hook; fishing was never this easy.

'Can do, Col,' Bruce radioed back. 'We'll be out there shortly. Anything else need doing while we're there?'

'No, Bruce. Everything else looks fine. Thanks,' Col replied.

'Let's have a cup of tea before you go,' Doris said.

'Let's,' Bruce agreed. He was very anxious and desperately trying to present his usual calm façade. Breathe steady, he told himself. It's just a question. Nothing bad can happen, so why are you trembling, he mused. The sooner I get in that Kubota, the better, he was thinking. He must have been doing okay with his façade because no-one commented on his shaky disposition. If they had, his story was going to be that having Lenny and Maria here was a big occasion.

'While you pair are fixing that problem, Bruce, I'll take Lenny for a scout around the ranch,' Merve suggested.

'That'd be brilliant. Thanks, Dad. Are you okay with that Lenny?' Bruce asked.

'Sounds sensational to me,' Lenny agreed.

'And we might go for a girl's drive,' Doris added. 'I'm sure Maria wants to see a bit of Bovale. And I want to see it as well.'

'Am I okay in the Kubota in this dress, Bruce?' Therese asked.

'It's perfect,' Bruce replied.

'Can we take Caesar?' Therese asked.

'Maybe not today,' Bruce replied. 'He's been out with me a fair bit lately and if he comes again, we might be overdoing it for a young pup.'

Bruce had carefully made sure the Kubota was as clean as a whistle, fuelled up and ready for the job. He had even put some fencing gear in the back to make it look right. Nothing could go wrong today. He drove at a very sedate pace just to be certain.

Half an hour later, as they approached Jindabyne dam, Therese remarked, 'This is my favourite spot on Bovale. I love it. It's where we first held hands, Bruce. Do you remember that?'

'Do one-legged ducks swim in circles?' Bruce replied. 'I've been on cloud nine ever since. I'm finding it hard to crawl off.' Therese gave him a beautiful smile and a side hug as he drove.

'I can't see the cattle,' Therese remarked as she surveyed the surrounds of the dam.

'They'll be there somewhere. Let's go to the picnic site, which gives us a good vantage point,' Bruce said, as calmly as he could. He pulled up at the gate that Therese opened for him. 'Leave it open so we can bring the cattle out this way, please,' Bruce asked.

At the picnic site, they climbed out of the Kubota. Bruce went around and took Therese's hand and escorted her towards a beautifully couched area beside the water's edge where the ground was firm. He had been out a few days earlier to select the spot, so it wasn't random. They were both panning the vista, Therese looking for cattle, Bruce feigning to do so. As they reached Bruce's target spot, he stopped. Therese turned and looked at him as he went down on one knee at the same time as he drew the small velvet box from his pocket using his free hand. He released Therese's hand and opened the box in front of her looking down. He looked up and said, 'Will you marry me?'

In front of Therese was the man of her dreams. She was in her dream spot on a property she had been dreaming about living on with Bruce. And she saw a magnificent, beautifully-faceted, large solitaire diamond mounted on a beautiful gold ring sitting in a small blue velvet box in

Bruce's palm. Her hands flew to her face. Her eyes instantly welled with tears. 'Yes. Yes,' she replied. Bruce was shaking. He was tearing up as well. He took the ring out of the box. Therese held out her left hand and he placed the ring on her third finger. Therese lifted her hand and stared at the ring as Bruce stood and they warmly embraced. 'It's absolutely beautiful, Bruce.'

Therese started weeping uncontrollably. 'I'm so happy, Bruce,' she managed to get out as they held each other gently.

'I'm now firmly wedged on cloud nine, Therese,' he responded. 'I can't imagine anything better than having you as my wife.' They stayed where they were for a while.

Therese stopped weeping. She looked up at Bruce. 'There are no stray cows and there isn't any broken fence, is there?' she asked.

'Not today.' Bruce replied, with the biggest smile he'd ever had. Therese plucked the water bottle out of the Kubota and she freshened her face. She wanted a couple of photos, including some selfies, to help remember the occasion.

They took their time getting home. No-one was at the homestead when they arrived as Doris and Maria were still out playing tourist on Bovale. They decided to just chill out for once in their lives and wait.

An hour later, the matriarchs waltzed into the homestead in high spirits. 'Bovale is beautiful,' Maria declared to Bruce and Therese.

Therese was standing facing her mother as she said this. Therese said nothing. She simply raised her hand to display the ring. Pandemonium, awash with tears of joy. Maria's response was underpinned by the wonderful Italian genes she carried for dramatic expression. When the dust settled, Therese said, 'Can we please have it so Bruce and I meet everyone who comes in and we'll do the same as we did for you? I don't want anything on social media till tomorrow.'

As the birthday party guests trickled in between lunch and dinner, all received the A grade surprise. Mick and Col were the only ones not bowled over by the revelation as they joined the party. Jane and Simone had both looked at their partners, initially shocked the blokes were not as happy as they both were, till both realised the lads had been in on the act. The night was every bit as memorable as Therese's first night at Bovale, when Mick had sold Craig. When that event was retold by Jane, Tom asked, 'Have you paid up yet, Brenda?'

'Not yet, Tom,' she replied. 'I haven't actually had the article delivered yet.'

'I reckon you might catch Therese's bouquet at the wedding, Brenda,' Mick suggested, which caused Craig intense momentary embarrassment.

Just like his mate Bruce had done, he was saying nothing. But he also wasn't missing any opportunity to get a notch in his belt. 'I'm just worried she'll be knocked out the way by Jane, lunging for it,' he added, looking down, trying to withhold his mirth.

Most of the guests left on Saturday after lunch. Bruce and Therese's parents stayed till Sunday afternoon. For Sunday lunch, Therese suggested they have a picnic lunch at Jindabyne dam. She wanted to make sure her parents didn't miss seeing one of her favourite places in the world. That night, it was just Therese, Bruce and Mick in the homestead. Mick was staying for two days to help with trucking, branding and getting cows just weaned back to their paddocks.

'I can't say I'm lonely, now all the crowd has gone,' Therese commented. They all went to bed early as Therese had an early shift tomorrow and she had to leave Bovale by four o'clock, leaving Bruce with a massive hole in his heart.

***

After the betrothment and the month of preparations that had gone into it, Bruce had to rapidly readjust to the realities of running his business. The primary incentive was that, since the early April rain, no more rain had been received. The rain gods hadn't become benevolent in response to the good things happening at Bovale. From this time onwards, any amount of rainfall would not achieve any grass growth until September, as once the first cool weather arrived, in late May or early June, it was too cold for tropical grasses to grow. Bruce knuckled down and began reviewing his available pasture and his cattle management to deal with the situation, based on no rain till mid-January. It was a daunting prospect after what they'd experienced, but his business nous indicated he was taking the best approach.

On Tuesday night, Doris rang Bruce. 'Hello, Bruce. Thanks so much for an incredible weekend. Your father and I are still on a high,' she said.

'I'm stoked too, Mum,' Bruce responded. 'It was the best weekend of my life.'

'Bruce, I have to tell you something you won't like. I'm sorry to take the shine off you and Therese. I had a routine test last week, and we got the result today. The cancer is back.'

Bruce was stunned. It was the last news he expected. 'Mum, I'm so sorry to hear that. Are you okay?' he asked.

'As you know from the weekend, I feel terrific. The test shows it's there so it must be quite small at this stage. That's good because it gives us a good chance of taking it out,' Doris replied.

'What treatment are you having, Mum?' Bruce asked.

'The same as last time, Bruce,' Doris told him. 'I start almost immediately, which gives us a lot of comfort.'

'I'll let Therese know. She will be upset. Mum,' Bruce said. 'But the upside is you now have two daughters in Townsville.'

'I do, Bruce,' Doris responded. 'We love Therese. We are so lucky. You have made a great choice.'

Therese had immediately set about wedding plans when she got back to Townsville. Her and Bruce had decided they wanted a rural setting for the marriage if possible. They wanted to get married before Christmas if a suitable reception venue was available, one that offered protection from peak summer conditions, preferably air conditioned. Anywhere between Home Hill and Townsville was suitable. Therese and Maria were a formidable pair, seeking the options, assessing features and suitability, and checking availability. It took them two weeks.

Therese rang Bruce. 'We're getting married on Wednesday, the first of December,' she told Bruce.

'That sounds great,' he responded. 'That'll be more than a month after Mum finishes her last cycle of chemotherapy, so she will be in excellent health again. Perfect. Tell me more.'

'It'll be a bit upriver from Ayr,' Therese replied. 'There's an old bush church there that a young couple have bought and set up as a wedding venue. They have put an extension on the church so it can accommodate at least one hundred people. They can do both the ceremony and the reception. It is beautiful inside and air conditioned.

And it has tropical gardens outside where everyone can also mingle. It's out of town, which means we can make any racket we like. It's a dream venue, Bruce. We had to pick mid-week because it is so popular, it's booked every weekend for the next year. Mum and I are really happy with it.'

'I haven't even seen it, but the way you describe it makes it sound like you could not have done better. Thanks, Therese.' Bruce said.

'When you're next down we can work out who we'd like to invite,' Therese suggested.

Bruce decided it was a good move to have a low profile in the wedding preparations. He had absolute faith in Therese and Maria. He adored beauty and what artists could create, but he had no creative bones at all. He was a pragmatist. He would offer opinion when asked, but otherwise would retain his counsel. He'd stick with developing his relationship with Therese, getting Bovale through this shocking dry spell, catching up with his family and Therese's whenever possible, and fishing when he had the chance.

Bruce now had a solid plan for the next six months and beyond. He had rung Wayne Greenhough and discussed it with him; Wayne had endorsed it. One of the first tasks they had was pregnancy diagnoses of the heifers. Jasper's harem and the first-lactation cows had been spared the axe at the muster back in March. They had been mustered to wean the calves, but no foetal ageing had been conducted as all Jasper's females were to be kept unless they were not found to be pregnant in June and the usual plan was that no first-lactation cows were culled unless they lost their calf, irrespective of pregnancy. On the first Tuesday in June, Col and Bruce mustered the remaining maiden two-year-old heifers from Clover paddock on the northern side of Bovale and Jasper's mating group from Bull paddock. They had mustered the already-weaned, first-lactation cows out of Stocking paddock the day before. Half of Jasper's females were maiden two-year-olds; the other half were a year older and had weaned a calf in March. The Wattle family was very keen to see the outcome, so they scheduled the pregnancy diagnoses to start after school that day. Eileen arrived without an ultrasound machine. She wouldn't need that today. Her trusty arm could do the job without any help from a very expensive toy.

'Can I enter the data please, Bruce?' Lachlan asked. For once, he was keen to be at the chute to witness the result rather than in the back yard herding cattle forward and drafting with his dad.

'I think you can Lachlan. I'll supervise and you can do it,' Bruce agreed.

The first of Jasper's two-year-old heifers came into the chute. She was a magnificent Droughtmaster, beautifully quiet, polled and well-grown. Eileen inserted her arm. 'Four, zero,' she said.

'What does that mean Bruce? What do I do?' Lachlan asked.

It means the heifer has a body condition score of four and she is not pregnant. When Eileen says zero, that means zero months pregnant. Can you see where to enter that?' Bruce asked. Lachlan was adapting to the system very quickly.

'That's ominous,' Bruce said to Eileen. 'I hope we don't see much more of that today.'

'It's a pity, Bruce. She looks good, but obviously isn't. It's just un-lucky that the first one up is the random non-pregnant heifer,' Eileen suggested. As they proceeded, it was evident that Jasper had done a good job. Eileen had been correct. Within his two-year-old heifers, only two were non-pregnant, one being the first heifer they assessed. In the other two-year-old heifers, there were only fifteen not pregnant. However, only half the three-year-olds were pregnant.

'I'm quite pleased with that result on the whole,' Bruce commented. 'Four decks of culls for now is what we needed.' Bruce returned pregnant three-year-olds to Stocking paddock and kept the other pregnant cattle in the yards overnight and gave them hay. He had two groups of pregnant heifers. One, numbering about seventy-five, were the bull-breeding harem. The others were all remaining two-year-olds on Bovale, numbering about one hundred and forty. Bruce decided he'd redraft each group. Any female in the harem showing evidence of not meeting his breeding objectives would switch mobs. The reverse was planned for the very best of the second group. This would leave the harem with about one hundred females, easy work for Jasper next year. The drafting was done early the next morning and the cattle walked back to their paddocks. Bruce finalised a sale of the non-pregnant cattle within a week, and they were gone in the first week of July, taking more pressure off the Bovale pastures.

Simone had been working on the next meeting for the CRAB group. She scheduled it for a full weekend in mid-July. The pasture monitoring trainer required two days. Usually, they did the training in a town, where people could get motel accommodation, but the group was versatile and preferred to camp at Bovale, especially so they could socialise as wildly as they liked without disturbing the city folk. Bruce was keen for it to be at Bovale as well because if they used his pastures, it might save him some legwork in getting an up-to-date calculation of his pasture reserves and review his stocking decisions. The only downside was it would be the middle of winter. They'd need a few campfires at night and that had to be managed very carefully to avoid sparking bush fires under the prevailing high-risk conditions.

As the CRAB group training weekend approached, Bruce was discussing preparations with Simone, 'We could do this one of two ways: one is to spend a fortune in time preparing for the herd to descend on us; or, we could do virtually no preparation and let it happen. Everyone coming can look after themselves if we provide the facilities. I'm inclined to have minimal preparation. Therese is coming and I want her to enjoy the weekend and not find herself being a slave. Do you agree?'

'You're right, Bruce,' she replied. 'That will keep it simple and create less work for everyone, especially Therese. I like it.' When the time came, it worked a treat. Bruce was spot on. The men were interested in beers and steaks, only. They loved simple. The children just wanted a sandwich or a biscuit when they were hungry and to be let run wild, preferably in the river. The added bonus of the river was it was full of water if they needed a drink, and bush kids were not shy in dipping their lips in a waterhole. The ladies prepared what suited their families and all were very well-organised. The evenings allowed everyone to let their hair down and socialise.

Best of all for Bruce, Therese was able to meet and socialise with the locals. On Saturday afternoon, the group was on the front veranda, with each station involved working on pasture data for their own place, downloaded from the internet. Therese was with Bruce and Simone, looking over Col's shoulder as he worked through the calculations for stocking rate using satellite data.

'I am so glad you invited me to be here this weekend,' Therese commented when they pulled up for a bit. 'Meeting all the neighbours and learning a little about what you do is very helpful. I have been fretting a bit about living here one day soon and being a fish out of water. This is like getting my gills wet. Thanks.'

On Saturday night, Scott commented to Bruce, 'This is fantastic, mate. Everyone on your front lawn with those drum heaters to keep us warm on a beautiful night is magic. I wouldn't be dead for quids.'

'Yes, I am really enjoying it too,' Bruce agreed. 'I'm glad we set up the TV inside for the children too. It's an easy way to manage them, putting a children's movie on. It stops them in their tracks and keeps them quiet while we get outside and play up like second-hand lawn mowers.'

When the two days were over, Wendy and Simone were once again ruminating on the two days. 'Gee that went well, Simone,' Wendy said. 'You are to be congratulated for your excellent management of the situation.'

'Thanks,' Simone replied. 'I enjoyed it too. I now understand what I've been watching Bruce do over the past year or two.'

'What I loved about doing it here, Simone, was that Bruce has done it all before, so it went like clockwork,' Wendy commented. 'We were all able to go through the full process of paddock pasture assessment and use the satellite imagery methods to not only calculate what was in your paddocks, but also how to safely stock them for the rest of the year. I know that helped Bruce review his stocking management, but it was a perfect way to learn. Scott and I will be getting into this as quickly as we can while it's fresh in our minds. Once we do it the first time, it will be a lot easier in the future.'

***

At the end of August, Bruce decided he had to sell his steers. He had sold all the female cattle he wanted to. There were three hundred and ninety steers to go. They were not as well-grown as they usually were, about thirty kilograms lighter, making them a less attractive market option. However, he had no choice, unless the market and weather gods intervened, and that didn't look likely. The next morning, Bruce discussed his thinking with Col. 'I've decided we have to bring forward the steer sales, Col. We can't afford to have them chewing any more grass. The paddocks have taken all they can cope with safely,' Bruce said.

'Where are you selling, Bruce? Same as last year?' Col asked.

'Yes,' Bruce replied. 'The Roma market was going down, but it's come up a bit in response to the reasonable winter they've had in southern Australia. It's good that someone's having a good year,' he added, wryly.

The muster and trucking were simple logistics. They mustered the following weekend so the whole Wattle family could be involved. Lachlan was now nine and becoming more useful every day. Carina was starting to shift a little bit of her focus to what was happening on Bovale and away from her dolls. The muster was a family affair for the Wattle's. Life can be a drudgery on a cattle station if you let that happen, but Bruce wasn't like that. He invited the gang for the weekend. It was a good opportunity to have a party on the homestead front lawn on Saturday night, when they couldn't see the tired, brown landscape. Mick commented during the night, 'Those steers won't beat us tomorrow. We'll have them outnumbered.' The muster felt like that to Bruce. It was good fun. Injecting a social atmosphere lifted the spirits of everyone on Bovale and the visitors loved it.

Bruce had booked twelve decks to ship the steers to Roma. The two triple-trailer trucks arrived at Bovale at five o'clock on Sunday afternoon. The steers had been drafted after lunch into three size categories to enhance market values. Everyone stayed to help with or watch the steers being loaded. The steers had a long overnight trip ahead of them, before having a rest leading up to Tuesday's sale.

At four o'clock on Tuesday afternoon, the selling agent rang. 'The market was firm today, Bruce. Your steers looked great compared to a lot of what's been coming down from the north. So, even though they were a bit light, the backgrounders were keen to take them.'

'That's good to hear,' Bruce replied. 'We need all the good news we can get.' Bruce knew the news would not be brilliant. The steers sold for an average of three dollars a kilogram, seventy-five cents lower than the previous year. Bovale's account was going to swell by a bit under four hundred and forty thousand dollars, less selling commission. This was about ninety-four thousand dollars less than he would have re-ceived the previous year. It was a hard pill to swallow, but Bruce knew the cattle business had tough years and good years. He'd had one of each so far and was hoping the balance would swing more to good in the future.

September was done. Still no rain. October was the same, only the days were quite hot. All of Bruce's preparations were paying dividends, but the cattle, the people, the wildlife, and the trees and grass would have kissed the gods' feet if they'd just delivered an early break to the wet season. There were no signs it was coming.

One early-October afternoon, when Col and Bruce were in the shed, getting ready for water and lick runs, Col looked at the sky. 'Crikey, batten the hatches. The wet is coming,' he exclaimed, smiling at his own joke.

'How do you know that?' Bruce asked.

'There's a cloud on the horizon. See that, about due east,' Col said, pointing to a very small piece of fluffy cloud that had cropped up.

'I think you need a break Col,' Bruce responded. 'How about I fill your dual-cab with diesel and book you a family room for three nights in Cairns and you take Simone and the children up there for the weekend? It's always green and it rains so much the locals whinge about it.'

Col didn't know what to say for a minute. He was hot, sweaty and dirty. The thought of relaxing in a wet green place sounded even better than cold beer. 'I'd like that, Bruce, as long as you're not joking.'

'I'm not joking, Col,' Bruce said. 'This weather is slowly sending us all troppo. I'm getting down to the irrigated country once a month when I visit Therese and her folks, but you're not getting a real break from this oppression. How about if you get Simone to work out where you'd like to go, and when she's done that, she can come over to the homestead and I'll book and pay for it?'

At about seven-thirty that night, Simone was on the UHF. 'Bruce, are you there?

'I'm here, Simone,' Bruce replied.

'Okay if I come over now?' Simone asked.

'Come on down,' Bruce declared. He was elated Simone was coming over to book the weekend. They had decided to head to Cairns on the coming weekend. They needed a break from a parched brown landscape. Bruce made sure they left immediately after school on Friday and didn't come home till early Monday. School commitments were the problem, but leaving very early on Monday from Cairns was not a problem when it gave them another whole day to relax. They also avoided the early-morning city traffic, getting out of the city in the predawn hours.

One day on the reef and another day in the jungle in the mountains behind Cairns refreshed the whole family's perspective. They arrived home with only fifteen minutes to spare before school started. Bruce knew they were coming and greeted them as they parked their car. Carina was the first out. 'Bruce, it was amazing. We saw a huge shark,' she said.

'I hope he wasn't eating anyone,' Bruce commented.

'No, silly,' Carina replied. 'He was in the water near the boat. Lachlan was going to jump in, but I told him not to.' Lachlan was standing beside her laughing his liver out. He'd obviously also been transformed back into a normal human after the wet and green weekend.

Simone and Col were also rejuvenated. They both got out of the car with huge grins. 'Man, that was a good couple of days,' Col said as he stretched his limbs.

'Thanks for the weekend, Bruce,' Simone said. 'I think you know how good it was for us. We didn't know how good green therapy is till now.'

'My pleasure,' Bruce responded. He was pumped as he watched the family hurry to get back into Bovale mode, buoyed by what they had just experienced.

Chapter Seventeen

The dry season may have been wringing the life out of everyone and everything in the north Australian beef business, but it couldn't depress Bruce. Not a chance. He was getting married to the number one sheila in the country. It was seven weeks away. So far, he had not been asked to help with wedding preparations, but Therese had made him a to-do list. It was quite simple: rings, best man, speeches, suits. Therese knew Bruce was under the pump with Bovale, which is why she had left him with little to do. She was a city girl and only worked forty hours a week. Bruce, like most station people, had never worked a week as short as that. It didn't bother Bruce at all. Rather, he thrived on it. He had no idea how anyone could enjoy working for someone else for just seven to eight hours a day, but then, he'd never done it, and he knew he shouldn't judge because of that.

It was a Wednesday afternoon in mid-October, another hot, dry, cloudless day that sucked the juices out of anything it could. Lachlan was still running on all cylinders though. He'd hopped on his motorbike, soon after he'd finished school and topped up his ravenous hunger with two scones and a sandwich. 'Where do you put all that food?' Simone asked him.

'I'm hungry, Mum,' he replied. It's what happens when you're nine years old in perpetual motion, except when the schoolteacher straightjackets you for five hours a day. Lachlan's dream was to be just like his dad one day. No school. Working outside all day, every day, with cattle. How could it be better than that? Col had asked him to check on Jasper's harem in Bull paddock. Jasper was nearby in Airstrip paddock with all the other bulls and nothing to do except eat, fight and wait till Bruce let him back to do his favourite job in January. It didn't seem that Lachlan had gone long when his excited voice came over the UHF. 'Dad, Bruce, one of Jasper's heifers has had a calf.'

Bruce was in the Kubota, working on the southern side of the station. 'Is it a bloke calf or a sheila calf?' Bruce radioed.

'It's a bloke,' Lachlan almost shouted, he was so excited.

'That's brilliant. The more bull calves, the better in Jasper's mob. Does he look good?' Bruce asked.

'He's a little ripper, Bruce,' Lachlan told him. 'I'll go home and ask Mum if I can get a lend of her phone and come back and take a photo and a video if you want.'

'That's good Lachlan, 'Bruce said. 'But please be careful. Sometimes a cow with a newborn calf can get very angry if you get close, even if she usually doesn't mind you being there.'

'I will, Bruce,' Lachlan responded. Bruce knew Simone would lend him the phone, and to avoid any stress to the cows, he'd just take a look at whatever Lachlan was able to photograph. The cattle were quite accustomed to Lachlan slowly biking through them and checking them, virtually ignoring him. Bruce sometimes gave them supplement, and he was certainly not treated as any threat by the cattle, but they would not be accustomed to him doing what Lachlan was doing. Cattle were very astute observers and would immediately detect a different person riding around them, irrespective of what bike they were riding. In addition, if Bruce arrived, they would immediately run towards the lick troughs, expecting their lolly; any cows that had just calved, charging off after Bruce, would create a risk for newborn calves.

There were no calves in that paddock for another week, when Lachlan again radioed in that he'd found a second new calf. This time it was a heifer. The next day, he was checking the group again when he radioed, 'Bruce, Lachlan here, can you hear me?'

'I can hear you, Lachlan,' Bruce replied. Bruce was fixing a leaking pipeline he'd found in Emu paddock. 'Everything okay?'

'I'm good, Bruce. But the heifer that was born yesterday looks weak to me,' Lachlan radioed.

'Thanks, Lachlan, Bruce replied. 'Col, can you hear me?'

'Col here, Bruce.'

'Col, when you can spare a minute, can you please check that calf with Lachlan. See if you reckon she's delivering milk. Just because she's bagged up, doesn't mean she's milking. If you suspect she's not, catch the calf and give it a drink.'

'Will do, Bruce. What suggestions do you have for giving it a drink?' Col asked.

'Try and pour at least two litres of water into it,' Bruce told him. 'Better if you can get five litres down. A soft drink bottle would be good if you can find one.'

An hour later, Col radioed Bruce. 'We're going out to catch that calf and give it a drink, Bruce.'

'Thanks, Col,' Bruce replied.

Bruce was waiting in the shed when Col and Lachlan returned. 'How did it go?' he asked them.

'I reckon you're right, that it wasn't getting a drink, Bruce,' Col replied. 'I couldn't pick from the cow what was happening but because she looked very tight in the udder, I thought it was likely she wasn't milking. So, we caught the calf. It was easy to get the water in because the calf was very thirsty. I can't remember Wayne's explanation of why this happens. Can you remind me, please, Bruce?'

'From what Wayne told us, the problem is the same as what happens in women,' Bruce explained. 'Sometimes the mother's hormones have not switched from pregnancy mode to milking mode at birth. When this happens, the body panics and takes about three days to sort out the problem. In the meantime, junior goes without. That's why we build up the gravel around troughs before calving, so these milk-deprived calves can get a drink till their mothers start milking properly. If you give the calf a drink like you did today, it will spark up almost immediately, and if you get enough water into it, the calf will be right till when the cow can look after it.'

'That's exactly what happened, Bruce,' Col responded. 'When we let the calf go, she was almost normal immediately. It was like magic.'

'It's good alright, but it's not the total solution for the calf, apparently,' Bruce added. 'Wayne said most of these calves don't get their mother's first milk within twenty-four hours of birth, which means that, until they slowly build up their own immune system, they are very susceptible to generally-innocuous bugs that can give them severe diarrhoea or pneumonia and kill them. Remember those poddies from last year?'

'That makes sense, Bruce,' Col replied.

Bruce continued. 'That special supplement we've been feeding to those young late-pregnant females is designed specifically to reduce the chances of the problem, but obviously it doesn't work all the time. I estimated we've been losing up to twenty percent of our calves from that problem in the first-calvers and hopefully we'll now get it back to under ten percent, which is the achievable level in this tough country, even in a mongrel year like this.'

'But those heifers were in good body condition, Bruce. Isn't that all that is needed?' Col asked.

'Good body condition helps, Col,' Bruce explained. 'But what makes all the difference is the quality of their diet in the last couple of weeks of pregnancy, whether they're fat or skinny themselves, as well as whether they're holding or losing weight. That's why we give them extra protein and energy in their supplement, compared to the older cows. It's not much, but it makes a big difference.'

Calving started in earnest in the first week of November. Because of the breed and the diets the cattle had throughout pregnancy, assisted calving was rarely required, so daily inspection of the calving cows was not required. It would have been an impossible task anyway, with the cows spread over about sixty square kilometres of open forest. This was true for all groups except Jasper's harem. Lachlan's intense interest in the bull-breeding enterprise at Bovale ensured he was keeping a very close eye on them. This was one less job for Bruce and Col and it also gave them a continuous update.

Three weeks into November, Bruce asked Lachlan, 'How many calves now?'

'Thirty-three, Bruce,' Lachlan replied. 'There's eighteen bulls and fifteen heifers so far. One heifer calf died too, but you know about that.' Lachlan had regularly borrowed a phone to get photos that he eagerly shared with everyone.

'Do they all look healthy?' Bruce asked.

'They do, Bruce,' Lachlan replied. 'They look really good. But their mums are tired.'

That night, Bruce had a call from Dennis Seccombe, the bloke who'd sold him Jasper. After the usual informal chat, catching up with each other's family and social life, Dennis asked him, 'How are the calves looking out of that bull I sold you?'

'Brilliant, Dennis. We couldn't be happier,' Bruce replied. Bruce was intrigued by the call and the question, and a red flag went up for him. 'Is there some potential problem?'

'Most likely not,' Dennis replied. 'I'm just checking. One other bull I sold has sired some odd calves and we're looking into it. I'd appreciate it if you treat this as confidential information. I'm just trying to resolve the situation. It's good to hear you have no problem, but I'll let you know what's happening once the vets have worked it out.'

When Bruce got off the phone, he was worried. But then he realised that worrying would achieve nothing. He couldn't undo what was done if there was anything wrong with Jasper. The immediacy of his wedding made sure it wasn't in the front of his mind for too long.

Bruce was in no position to be having a traditional buck's party. Mick, his best man, organised dinner at the pub and cards at The Villa on the Saturday night before the wedding. The whole gang was there, unfortunately without Therese, but Frances and Simon came up. Bruce was expected to be absolutely motherless last at Oh Hell, but he wasn't. Craig took the wooden spoon, prompting Mick to again warn him about Brenda catching the bride's bouquet. Brenda smiled. The group was in high spirits as Bruce left to go back to Bovale. He couldn't spare even a night away as he was away for over a week after the wedding.

On Sunday night, Bruce read the weather forecast. Storms were predicted in the following days. This gave him a huge lift. If Bovale could just jag a wayward storm, that would take a lot of pressure off, especially for Col and Simone who would be here alone for over a week in the middle of calving, with lick feeding going at full pace. Fortunately, the water system remained intact with only the odd minor leak. Bruce was heading to Townsville on Tuesday morning for final wedding preparations. Therese and her family and friends had all preparations running smoothly.

On Monday morning, Col remarked to Bruce, 'This weather looks ominous Bruce. Do you think you should head off now in case we do get a storm like we had in January?'

'I can't see that happening, Col,' Bruce replied.

'I hope you're right, Bruce,' Col responded. The sky was clear. There was hardly any breeze. Col said he felt electricity in the air. 'For what it's worth, Bruce, if I was you, I'd be packing my bags and getting out now. If you get stuck here, the sky will fall in. And that's minor compared to what the women in your life will do to you if you don't turn up on Wednesday afternoon.'

'I'll take my chances, Col. Thanks for the concern, but I just can't see anything that catastrophic happening,' Bruce replied. At lunch time when they met up again, Col asked Bruce again if he should head to Townsville that afternoon rather than in the morning. There was a bit of fluffy cloud around, but it did not look threatening enough to Bruce for him to be bolting out of Bovale.

Bruce was focussed on getting his lick run done and dusted and was not paying much attention to the weather. At about four o'clock, he stopped for a drink and casually glanced to the west, probably subconsciously primed by the sudden darkening of the day. He was shocked. A huge bank of cloud had grown out of seemingly nothing in no time. He needed to act, and quickly. 'Col, are you there?' he radioed.

'Yes boss,' Col said, returning his call. He's never called me 'boss' before, thought Bruce. I've stuffed up, and he's a bit miffed that I didn't take his advice for sure. Damn.

'Col, it might be too late to get out now. From the look of this sky, I should have taken your advice. Sorry. I should be back at the homestead within twenty minutes.' Bruce pushed the Kubota as hard as it would go all the way back to the homestead. By the time he got there, the storm was almost upon them. The day had darkened as the huge bank of cloud shielded the sun. To the east, the sky was still clear, but it would not stay that way for long. Caesar jumped out of the Kubota, his tail down between his legs and sticking close to Bruce. The pair of them raced to the homestead. Bruce secured Caesar. He raced around the homestead, shutting windows and doors. He then picked up the UHF. 'Are you guys all safe, Col?' he radioed.

'We are, Bruce. Are you?' Col asked.

'I am, Col,' Bruce replied.

'I've set up the generator ready to fire when this is over in case you were wondering about that, Bruce,' Col said.

'Thanks, Col. I feel like a right royal idiot. If this storm sends the situation pear-shaped, I have no idea how I'm going to explain this to the bride when she rings tonight.'

Just as he finished, the afternoon suddenly went from dark to intensely bright as a bolt of lightning struck very close by, accompanied by the deafening roar of thunder. The radio went dead. The mains power supply was gone. About twenty seconds later, the first few huge drops of rain splattered down on the homestead, driven by a strong gust of wind. The wind died and the drops stopped momentarily before another lightning strike heralded the front of the torrential, gusting rain.

It was a beautiful sound, one of the best, after having been so dry on Bovale for so long. Bruce was torn between not being already in Townsville and the pure pleasure of being safely cocooned in the storm. He knew for certain where he should have been. He knew Therese would have been monitoring the radar and would have seen Bovale being hit. She would be pleased the station was finally receiving rain, but also very concerned. Bruce wasn't that concerned. Solutions were available. He'd assess the situation after the storm. Until then, there was no value in acting on pre-emptive assessment of what he might need to deal with.

The storm raged for half an hour. It was well below the ferocity and scale of what had occurred in January, but it still delivered excellent rainfall. As the storm passed, Bruce released Caesar who was now much happier. While Caesar explored the consequences of the storm in the homestead enclosure, Bruce checked the rain gauge. He emptied fifty-nine millimetres. That was enough to create good grass regrowth. Fortunately, it was just enough to cause a few creeks to flow for a couple of hours, but not enough to cut any roads.

Col came over to see Bruce after having cranked over the generator. 'You're off the hook, Bruce. We can all go to the wedding now,' Col said, grinning from ear to ear. Both the men were very happy.

Simone was not far behind with Lachlan and Carina. They were also in high spirits. Caesar was overjoyed to have Carina and Lachlan to play with. There would be plenty of that over the next couple of weeks in Bruce's absence. 'We were really worried about you, Bruce,' Simone told him. 'How would you have gotten out if the storm had been like the one in January?'

'I probably would have chartered a light aircraft, Simone. The only risk was if one wasn't available, but I thought I could plead a fairly good case in an emergency,' Bruce replied, smiling.

Bruce's phone rang. 'Therese,' he said to Col and Simone, who both realised they'd have no chance of an audience with Bruce for half an hour. They collected the children and toddled off home.

***

The wedding was everything it could have been, and more, as far as Bruce and Therese were concerned. They had made the ultra-smart move of having Jane as the emcee. She was brilliant, ensuring all attention was on the radiant and beautiful bride and her handsome groom. A feature of the evening was a string quartet, quietly playing beautiful music as required, and amping up for waltzing when the opportunity arose. Maria and Doris both felt like it was a scene from Utopia. The speeches were done, everyone had been fed, and the cake had been cut and munched on.

Jane announced, 'Ladies, Therese is now going to throw the bouquet.'

Bruce walked over to Jane. 'Can I have the mic please?' he asked her.

'I've just sacked the emcee,' Bruce announced. 'Just for a bit. Jane is going to join the ladies.'

Jane mouthed, 'Thank you,' to Bruce and gleefully joined the group positioning to pounce on the bouquet when it came hurtling over Therese's right shoulder.

Therese was standing on the elevated area at the back of the former church and where the string quartet was sitting. All the guests were keen to see who was going to be the lucky lady. The volume of the discussion increased as wild, unsubstantiated and hilarious speculation was rife. The group of young ladies, all keen to catch the bouquet were obviously restless, and desperately trying to maintain some composure in the middle of what could easily have become a rugby scrum. It was going to be like an Aussie Rules throw-in or a rugby line-out with a penalty for lifting. Bruce announced, 'Everyone ready?' The catchers had their arms extended, willing the bouquet their way. Therese was smiling radiantly. She looked at the ladies and scrunched up her nose and squinted, showing she didn't want to disappoint anyone. Therese turned and tossed the bouquet high and what she hoped was into the midst of the waiting ladies. She immediately turned, following the flight of her bouquet, to see who would catch it.

It was a neat throw. Immediately, all the catchers crushed into what was going to be the landing zone. A couple of ladies almost tripped but no-one went down. As the bouquet was about to hit, there were about a dozen hands extended with a chance, pushing on each other, vying for the flowers. The bouquet hit and immediately disappeared into the throng as the winner snatched it firmly. She then thrust it upwards to claim her victory. 'Eileen has the bouquet,' Bruce declared, delighting everyone. Therese was very pleased and clapped.

Mick sidled up to Craig and out of the corner of his mouth said to his mate, 'Don't worry, Craig. You can still pop the question when they don't have a handful of flowers.'

'Are you telling me that, or are you talking to yourself, again, Mick?' Craig replied, grinning broadly as they both started laughing uproariously.

Jane saw them and came over. 'What's happened?' she asked.

Craig tried to get himself back together and portray a serious mode. 'Mick just asked me to marry him,' he replied to Jane. 'I told him he was too ugly.'

Mick couldn't stop laughing. He added, 'But you didn't add the part about still wanting to give me a kiss,' he said, tears of laughter blurring his vision.

'The grog's got to you both,' Jane told them. She shook her head and walked away.

Bruce and Therese disappeared for a week onto a Great Barrier Reef island resort. Both were very active people. Despite them enjoying each other's company immensely, neither could emulate the life of a sloth for any more than a week. They returned to Townsville initially because Therese's work colleagues had organised a send-off for her. It was a very emotional event. Bruce had not previously had the chance to meet most of these people. It was no surprise to him when he found that Therese was held in incredibly high regard. He had briefly seen her in a professional capacity the first time he saw her, and even then, it just wasn't her stunning beauty that caught his eye; she had an aura of competence and leadership, that was confirmed in the many congratulatory speeches made.

In his young life, Bruce had some major achievements already behind him, but nothing compared to bringing home his new bride. He was at home. Caesar had another companion. And Therese had fulfilled a dream. It was a major transition for Therese. She had to move from a professional medical environment to a cattle station environment. It was a massive change, and it took her some time to adjust. The support of Bruce, Simone and her mother were instrumental. With the break in the wet season behind them, it allowed Bruce more time with Therese, and whenever she could, she accompanied Bruce and Caesar around the station.

Christmas celebrations, which had all the families together, also eased the transition for Therese. It was mid-January after dinner one night when she said to Bruce, 'When I thought about home today, I thought about here, not Brandon and not Townsville. I'm happy.'

A week later, on Friday night, which was nearly a week after the bulls had been mustered, drafted, and taken out to their paddocks for mating, Dennis Seccombe rang again. 'Bruce, we've made a fair bit of progress on the problem I was discussing with you back in December. A genetic disease has been diagnosed. The name is a proper mouthful. It's called *epitheliogenesis imperfecta*; apparently, it's usually abbreviated as EI.'

'That does not sound good, Dennis. Can you explain what it means, please?' Bruce asked.

'It's a bit of a story, Bruce, so please bear with me,' Dennis replied. 'Unfortunately, it has some ordinary consequences for me, and I ask you treat this as completely confidential.'

'I will, Dennis. Sorry to hear you're having a rough trot with it,' Bruce replied.

Dennis continued. 'The disease is caused by a simple gene mutation. If an animal has one copy, it's a carrier. If it gets two copies, it's affected and will die soon after birth. The calves are born with the skin completely missing on their lower limbs, around the mouth and back end. One in four calves is affected if both their parents are carriers. If one parent is a carrier, half the calves will be carriers and the rest normal.'

'I understand so far, Dennis,' Bruce said.

'In a way we've been lucky,' Dennis said. 'As part of generating breeding values from our herd, we get DNA samples from everything, and we know full pedigrees. We traced back the problem bull I sold, and it's revealed that in its lineage there is Sahiwal.'

'Is that a breed, Dennis?' Bruce asked.

'Yes,' Dennis replied. 'A group of scientists, in all their wisdom, probably the cane toad team, brought ten of them into Australia from Pakistan over fifty years ago. They are a red *Bos indicus* breed, a bit like a red Brahman. The main differences are they are at least ten percent smaller, though have higher milking capacity. The Queensland government tried to make a milking breed out of crossing them with Friesians, but that failed because of their poor temperaments. Those kept for beef were also duds, not only because of their poor growth, but also, they had a very high incidence of calf mortality that appears related to their poor behaviour and their very poor udders. Anyhow, one of the imports carried the EI gene, which was its death knell as a significant breed.'

'I can see where this is going, Dennis. Ouch,' Bruce said.

'Yes. Ouch,' Dennis said, wryly. 'The stud that infused this breed now has a high prevalence of carriers. They're in real trouble as they've essentially had half their stud herd devalued overnight to meatworks values. I can't divulge who they are. However, quite a few years ago now, I skilfully bought one of their cows, didn't I. Thankfully it was a cow and not a bull. So, this cow had a calf, which was also a heifer and a carrier, that in turn bore a bull after we artificially mated it using a few semen straws from that same stud. Obviously, the straws came from a bull that was a carrier.'

'Wow,' Bruce exclaimed. 'You've brought it in, but it sounds like you've been incredibly fortunate to do it in a way with minimal impact on you.'

'That's correct, Bruce,' Dennis replied. 'We've identified what we believe are a handful of potential carriers and they're all out of the stud now. We've gotten out of it fairly lightly. But the poor bugger who got the bull we sold, he'd also been buying bulls from the source stud of the EI. He had been merrily creating heaps of carriers and just had to buy another bull and mate him to expose it. In a way, it's fortunate it's our bull and not just another one of the source stud bulls, because that's enabled us to clean our herd up with almost no damage.'

'So, you will have the problem of replacing that bull, Dennis?' Bruce queried.

'Yes, spot on,' Dennis said. 'But it's not so straightforward. As part of the investigation, everything was re-checked, including the bull we sold. We made another discovery that will have some impact on you,

Bruce. We've found that when those bulls went to Charters Towers as a truck load, a couple of them lost their tags, causing a mix-up. The carrier bull was the bull you bought. You ended up with another bull. They looked very similar, which is why the accidental switch was not noticed.'

'What?' Bruce exclaimed. 'What a nuisance.'

'It doesn't appear to be anyone's fault other than the bulls themselves. You know how they like to fight all the time,' Dennis said.

'So, Jasper's not Jasper, but hopefully we'll get a new Jasper?' Bruce queried, quite sullen at the thought of losing the bull. 'From what you've said, this mishap is also fortunate for us because it has kept the gene out of my herd. Is that correct?' Bruce asked.

'You're correct, Bruce,' Dennis replied. 'Unless you've picked it up elsewhere, you should be clear. However, the bloke who bought the bull you ended up with wants him back to replace the dud you were supposed to get. And he wants that bull as soon as possible so he can get calves out of him this year. He's holding off the mating of his group till he can get him. Legally, he owns the bull. We stuffed up. Sorry.'

'That's okay, Dennis. I sincerely appreciate you being completely honest with me. It's brilliant.' Bruce thought for a minute. 'I'll be okay if I can get a bull from you immediately. My situation is that I'm really lean for a whole lot of excellent reasons. Jasper has a hundred females in his mating group. I can't have them without a bull, and I don't have spares. If you have a few to pick from available right now, with acceptable breeding values and they've passed a breeding soundness evaluation, can we come down and pick one?'

'We anticipated this, Bruce. Yes, come as soon as you're ready,' Dennis replied.

'Are you able to email me right now what you have on those bulls, please, Dennis?' Bruce asked. 'That way I can do a bit of homework before we arrive, and I'll waste less of your time.'

'Can do,' Dennis replied.

When Bruce finished the call with Dennis, he turned to Therese. 'Want to go for a drive in the country?' he asked her.

'Where to?' she asked.

'Blackwater, to select a bull,' Bruce replied. He told Therese the story. They agreed to go the next day. Bruce picked up the UHF handset. 'Col, are you there?'

'Yes, Bruce. What's wrong?' Col asked.

'Col, seems we have a bit of a bull glitch. I'll explain the details later, but the bottom line is there was an accidental bull switch with Jasper. We have to send him where he's supposed to go as soon as possible. Therese and I are heading to Blackwater tomorrow to select a replacement. We'll see you when you get back. I'll let you know when I want Jasper shipped out. Sorry about this.'

'That's not good news, Bruce,' Col said. 'I'll wait till I hear from you before I do anything. In the meantime, we'll cheer Jasper on to get as much out of him as we can before he goes.'

It was an eight-hour drive to Blackwater from Bovale. Bruce had gone to bed late after poring over the data Dennis had sent him. Even so, he and Therese still left early. On the way down, Bruce dialled Mick. After they had the usual chat, Bruce asked him, 'Mick, I'm looking to buy a bull from Blackwater today to replace Jasper who we have to let go almost immediately. I'll explain another day. When would you be right to collect him for us?'

'I could do it Tuesday, Bruce,' Mick replied. 'I don't mind the long drive. I won't get back to Bovale till maybe nine o'clock. Is it okay if I camp there the night?'

'You are always welcome Mick. Pick up Jane on the way through Charters Towers and we'll host the pair of you. Does that sound like a deal?' Bruce asked.

'Jane will be thrilled, Bruce. Thanks. I'll hear from you,' Mick responded.

They were in Blackwater by two o'clock. Dennis and Greta met them warmly. 'Therese, it is so lovely to meet you. Tell me all about the wedding,' Greta said as the ladies, instantly friends, disappeared to build a cup of tea for all four of them.

After smoko, the four of them went to the yards where Dennis had three bulls. Bruce had all the paperwork on hand, but he really didn't need it. He had decided the previous night and confirmed it in further discussion with Therese on the way down, that only one of the bulls met his breeding objectives. Bruce desperately hoped the bull would meet his expectations. He did. Within ten minutes, a deal had been done. Bruce rang Mick immediately to confirm the trucking. He also rang Col and asked him to get Jasper in on Tuesday. Dennis rang Jasper's correct owner, who was happy for Mick to take Jasper to his new owner on Wednesday morning.

'Where are you staying tonight?' Greta asked Therese.

'We were thinking of heading over to the coast and getting a motel somewhere,' Therese replied.

'Would you like to stay here the night?' Greta asked.

It was agreed they would. The Seccombe and Arnold families became even more firm friends that night. On Sunday, Bruce and

Therese headed to Brandon. Maria and Lenny were overjoyed. After spending a night in Townsville with an equally-pleased Doris, Merve, Frances and Simon, Therese and Bruce headed back to Bovale on Tuesday to get ready for Mick and Jane's arrival with the new bull.

Mick and Jane arrived at five o'clock on Tuesday afternoon. Mick had an opportunity to go most of the way on Monday afternoon and was able to pick the bull up a lot earlier. Jane jumped out of the truck, Bruce jumped in, and he and Mick headed to the yards to unload the new bull. Lachlan and Col were ahead of them on their bikes. Bruce let the bull out into the yards, where he could have a drink.

'He looks great, Bruce,' Lachlan commented. 'But I don't think he likes Jasper.' The two bulls were facing off to each other with necks flexed and eyes bulging. Fortunately, there was a fence between them.

'Thanks, Lachlan,' Bruce said. He's every bit as good as Jasper, just a different bull. Give him half an hour to get his feet and you can both walk him out to the harem in Bull Paddock. The next morning, Mick and Bruce loaded Jasper. Carina came down with them to the yards. 'Goodbye Jasper,' she said, waving her little hand as Jasper calmly walked onto the truck.

'What are we going to call the new bull, Carina?' Bruce asked.

'Does he look like Jasper, Bruce?' she asked.

'He sure does,' Bruce told her.

Carina was stumped for a little bit. Her little mind was racing. She looked around at nowhere in particular, and then she looked back to Bruce. 'I want to call him Topside.'

'Topside. That's a great name. Why did you pick that?' Bruce asked.

'Because he's a lovely big red chunk. And I like topside. It's yummy,' she told him.

'Topside, it is,' Bruce agreed.

***

Simone was organising the Cockatoo River Advancing Beef group for another meeting. She had been in constant contact with all group members, travelling to each property when she could to assist in organising and or collecting cattle and pasture data after the previous meetings. The enthusiasm for the process was building as all members anticipated starting to get an objective understanding of how their business operated and was performing. After consulting with all members, the consensus was to have some training on business management. A packaged course was available. It was akin to mustering cats, but eventually Simone was able to get all group members to agree on three days the course would take. It seemed a lot, but formal business skills were one of the most obvious skills all of them lacked, and these skills were core to good decision making.

All the group wanted to have a weekend on genetics as well, but it was decided they'd defer that till after they'd done the business skills development. The course would be in late February in the air conditioning in Charters Towers. The Monday to Wednesday dates were selected because the children doing distance education, including Lachlan and Carina, were already attending a camp in Charters Towers where they would be with all their friends they rarely saw.

***

It was Monday night in mid-February. Bruce and Therese had just had a sensational weekend in Brandon and Townsville. They had just finished dinner and before doing the dishes, they were sitting in the lounge, talking and occasionally checking the television news that was on. Bruce was having a beer. Therese was having an alcohol-free wine. Bruce asked her, 'How come you decided to drink that, and not have a beer with me?' Therese had bought a few bottles at a bottle shop on their way home.

'Well, that's a good question, Bruce,' she said. She snuggled up to Bruce. There's been a few changes, and when I was in Townsville, I bought a test kit that I tried out today. Twice.' She looked at Bruce with a beautiful smile. 'I'm pregnant.'

Bruce was stunned. He grinned broadly. 'That is fantastic!' He put down his beer and hugged his wife. 'Wow,' he said as he looked again at his radiant wife. 'How come I am so lucky?' Therese was clearly adjusting to the knowledge. It was a big step for Bruce, but massive for her. She didn't respond to Bruce's comment other than to embrace him warmly. 'How far? Do you know?' Bruce asked.

'My calculations suggest six weeks and if I'm correct, I'll be due to have the baby at the beginning of October,' she replied. It was very sobering for them both. 'I haven't done anything yet, but on our next trip to the coast, I'll get an appointment to confirm. We can tell the world around about the first week of April if everything stays on course. There's always the chance it's a false alarm, and that's why we just have to keep it a secret for now.'

***

Once again, Simone excelled. The CRAB group's business training course was a fabulous success. Everyone said they'd learned things they'd never heard of but were very useful. They saw how it integrated with what they'd learned and were now implementing on herd and pasture monitoring. Simone was being given the credit, which she tried to deny, but had to concede eventually that she did a lot of work, culminating in the successful meetings they had.

A month later, at the beginning of April, Bruce and Col were discussing plans for the station on the Friday afternoon. They were sitting on the front veranda of the homestead. Caesar was laying under Bruce's feet, content. Simone and the children were coming over shortly to join the Arnold family for dinner. It was drizzling rain and both men kept commenting on how beautiful the rain was. Unlike the previous year, average rainfall had been received in February and the pastures had responded with tonnes of high-quality feed to put Bovale in good stead for the rest of the year.

When they'd worked out their plan, Col said, 'Bruce, last week, I got an interesting phone call.' Bruce's mind immediately went wild. Oh no, I might lose this bloke, he was thinking. Stay calm, boy; it might be nothing. Listen. Col continued. 'A place north of Cloncurry offered me a job. They made it sound very good. And they offered to employ Simone as well. Her reputation is going viral, because of the excellent work she's been doing with the CRAB group.'

'What did you decide, Col,' Bruce asked, dreading the answer, but he had to know.

'Simone and I gave it some serious consideration because it looked like a very good job, and our combined income would have been much better than here. But, Bruce, we're staying if you'll have us.'

'That's excellent, Col,' Bruce responded, suddenly able to breathe again. 'Thanks. I can't imagine having better people to work with than you and Simone and your children.'

'That's why we're staying, Bruce,' Col told him. 'We opted to stay where we know the situation is excellent and is only getting better. You and Therese are terrific to work with. The place is great for Lachlan and Carina. This latest gig that Simone has taken on, cemented our decision. It is what she needed and what she likes. Unless she is ul-tra-lucky, she's not going to score this opportunity anywhere else.'

While they were having dessert later, Bruce commented to Simone, 'Col told me about the offer you had. Thanks for wanting to stay here. I'm chuffed and I'm sure Therese is as well.' Simone gave Therese a brief synopsis of what had occurred, and Therese agreed with Bruce.

After they finished talking about the job offer, Therese said, 'We have some news too.' She paused as Bruce and she smiled at each other. I have been on the phone to both Doris and Mum today, and also Frances. It's time to tell you guys that we're pregnant.'

Simone was ecstatic. Col shook Bruce's hand, 'Congratulations!' he said.

'First of October,' Therese said, anticipating the obvious question.

Without thinking, Col said, 'You've synchronised with the cattle breeding.' Bruce and Therese thought it was hilarious, but Simone gave Col a glaring scowl. 'Sorry,' Col said.

'Don't be sorry, Col. It's true,' Bruce said. 'And it's all good news. It's what Bovale is all about, breeding.'

Carina just caught the gist of the conversation. 'Are you having a baby, Therese?' she asked.

'I am,' Therese replied.

'What's its name going to be?' Carina asked.

'You name the bulls and Bruce names the babies,' Col responded, which caused a lot of mirth. 'Sorry Carina, but we have to wait till the baby's born before we'll know its name.'

'Just keep it under your hat for a few days until I can tell everyone, please?' Therese asked. We're going to ring all the gang later. They will be happy. I'm waiting for what Mick has to say. He is a dear friend, and his banter is always entertaining.'

Chapter Eighteen

The branding had been done and dusted for the year. The calves were back on their mothers in their final growth spurts before weaning, which was planned for the first week of June. Supplementation and water checks never stopped on Bovale. Therese was becoming an accomplished station hand. She could fix a water leak, build or fix a fence, muster cattle and brand, skills she never dreamed she'd have two years earlier. Bruce and Col found her an amazing asset when it came to vehicle maintenance or any engineering, which was her background. The men were learning too. Therese was enjoying station life with Bruce immensely. So far, the pregnancy had not caused her to miss a beat when it came to station life. She planned to let her body tell her when it was time to slow down and by how much. Until then, she was another part of the work team. This made it easier on both Col and Bruce. Simone was very thankful because it gave Col more time with their family.

Bruce and Therese were having smoko one morning in the latter half of May. They had met at Jindabyne dam, always their favourite spot. The dam was handy this day as they were working independently in its vicinity. Caesar was laid out like a lizard, soaking up the warm sun after a morning with a slight chill in the air; winter, well, the dry tropical north Queensland version, was not far away. 'That dog has switched his allegiance since you've been living here,' Bruce said. 'He would never leave my side before.'

'He's great, Bruce,' Therese commented. 'He gives me a feeling of security. One thing I still find a bit daunting is when I stop for a drink, for example. The vehicle motor's off. I'm not making any noise from my work. It's still. There are only bush sounds. I'm miles from anywhere and anyone. Just me. But it's not just me. I have Caesar. I don't know what I'd do without him.'

'I'm so glad, Therese,' Bruce said. 'He's a beautiful dog. He's paying you back for bringing him to Bovale. He must have known you'd eventually be camping here.' Caesar lifted his head and flicked his eyes from Bruce to Therese. 'I think he knows we're talking about him,' Bruce said. For now, life was idyllic for Bruce and Therese as it ever was for Caesar. However, both knew having a child would change that and they looked forward to it.

Early on Monday morning, they drove to Townsville. Therese was having a mid-term ultrasound examination of the baby. They had timed their drive so they could go straight to the radiography clinic to have the ultrasound, which was an uneventful process for them both. After that, they went around to Bruce's parents place for lunch. Merve came home for lunch to see them; Frances and Simon did the same as it wasn't often enough they were able to see each other. At two o'clock, they arrived at the specialist's rooms to get a report. They were ushered in. The doctor greeted them warmly and sat them together on a bench couch. They had the usual quick hello chat followed by a rapid general health question and answer check. All sounded excellent.

The doctor then assumed a serious look. 'I'm sorry, Therese and Bruce, but we've found a problem.' Bruce and Therese both went cold with fear and grabbed each other's hands, glancing at each other. Therese's bottom lip was trembling, and she had tears welling up. Bruce also had some tears. It was an awful moment. The doctor continued. 'The first thing you need to know is that the baby is fine and in excellent health.'

Therese immediately turned to Bruce. They smiled at each other through their tears, before returning their attention to the doctor. 'Let me show you what we found.' The doctor swivelled her large computer monitor so the three of them could see it clearly. The doctor had a mouse controlling a recording of the ultrasound. The machine had pointers, markers and measurers she could use to highlight the image. She manipulated the video till it got to a certain point and then froze the image, before making a few marks on it. Bruce had no idea what he was looking at, though he could clearly see his baby. Therese's medical background helped her a lot more, but she was insufficiently familiar with obstetrics and gynaecology to discern exactly what the doctor was highlighting.

The doctor turned to them. 'We are looking at what is called placenta previa. It occurs in about one in two hundred pregnancies. It is totally manageable, but it can be a jolly nuisance. What happens in a completely normal pregnancy is the placenta attaches to the inside of the uterus on the upper area and sides. In placenta previa, the placenta is also attached to the lower part of the uterus and can cover the cervix.' The doctor swivelled on her chair, back to look at the screen, outlining what she had just told them.

'I can see it now,' Therese said in a soft quivering voice. She was terrified. 'So, everything may still proceed fairly normally?' she asked.

Bruce was numb. He understood what was being said and also appreciated what the ultrasound images showed.

'Yes, it can,' the doctor replied. 'In some cases, it resolves itself and the pregnancy and birth proceeds in a completely normal fashion. But we cannot assume that will happen. In very simple and crude terms, we need to plan for the worst and hope for the best. I'll explain what that means.'

Bruce felt Therese's hand constricting his as her fear mounted. He shifted her grip to his other hand and put his arm firmly around her in a warm side embrace.

'The primary consequence of this condition is it makes you highly susceptible to bleeding. If you start bleeding from now on, it's an emergency,' the doctor explained. 'I'm sorry that's not such good news. The prevention is quite simply to cut out exercise, especially lifting and get off your feet as much as possible.'

Therese looked at Bruce and then snuggled her head into his shoulder. This was almost like a death sentence for someone with her lifestyle. Therese was so numb she couldn't get a word out. Bruce was much the same. Both simply nodded as the doctor went on to explain more about what was ahead of them and how they should manage it.

Bruce and Therese had been looking forward to an overnight stay in Brandon. It was now doubly important. Mothers are invaluable when their daughter is in distress. When they arrived in Brandon, Lenny and

Maria were on top of the world. They loved these visits. Maria detected a problem the instant she saw Therese. She was all tears as Therese explained the situation over a cup of tea. Lenny was numb, looking alternately at Bruce and his daughter, his only child. Previously, Lenny had been full of cheek, he was so happy. He joked to Bruce they were breeding a cane farmer, not a grazier. This child would come back and take over the Brandon farm, according to Lenny. The wind had gone completely out of Lenny's sails. His dreams had no clear ending.

Bruce was trying to think ahead through the blur of what he'd learned that day. It wasn't easy when fear grabs you by the heart, he found, as his mind kept wandering to awful potential outcomes. He tried to be positive. 'Maria and Lenny,' he said, 'I haven't discussed this with Therese yet, but what I'm totally fearful of is her having an emergency at Bovale. The quickest we could get her into a hospital would be more than an hour. That may be too much. I'm thinking that Therese might be much safer here if you would like that. What do you reckon, Therese?'

She nodded numbly, looking at her mother who replied, 'Bruce, we'd do anything for Therese, you know that. It's lovely that you want her here with us.'

Bruce continued. 'I will enjoy it as much as a smack in the ear with a burning log, but Therese's and the baby's health and safety come first, not the pleasure of us having each other at Bovale. My suggestion is Therese comes here in four weeks' time and stays till not long before the baby is due to be born, and then I come down and we shift to Townsville to be as close to the hospital as possible.' Therese, Maria and Lenny all nodded.

'Three months here is a long time Bruce,' Lenny said. 'Your suggestion is great, but are you okay with Therese being away for that long?'

'I have to be, Lenny,' Bruce replied. 'It's gut wrenching, but I just have to be.'

***

Life changed dramatically back at Bovale. Therese felt like she'd been put in irons and thrown into solitary confinement when Bruce was not in the homestead. Physically, she felt great, no different to normal. It was only the ticking bomb inside her that kept her disciplined into no physical activity. It almost felt unreal that she had a problem, but she'd better believe it she told herself. Caesar was totally confused. He wanted to be with Therese and was stumped when she did not continue what had become her normal station life. When Bruce called him to jump onto the back of his Land Cruiser when he went to work, Caesar would stop and look desperately into the homestead, wanting Therese to come out and take him in the Kubota. But she wouldn't. After a minute, he'd look backwards and forwards to where Bruce was and where Therese was in the homestead before he'd reluctantly canter off and join Bruce.

The week after Therese's diagnosis, Bruce and Col started the weaning muster. Unlike the previous year's condensed process, this year they could stagger the musters of each paddock and slowly work their way through the herd. When they needed a hand, Scott would come over, and in return, they helped Scott when he needed an extra hand or two. Bruce planned for Eileen to do pregnancy diagnoses on each mob of cows as they came through. The much better seasonal conditions, coupled with obvious dramatic effects on cow growth and body condition resulting from the improved supplementation program, bode well for high pregnancy rates. Bruce was planning to cull any non-pregnant female, which meant that most lactating cows had to conceive within four months of calving. The scientists called this P4M; it was top of Bruce's priorities when selecting bulls using their breeding values. With Simone's help, he'd set his data collection up so they could quickly analyse last years' production and the performance of the herd, once the muster was complete. Everyone was looking forward to seeing the results of the changes that had been made.

***

It was nine o'clock on Tuesday morning. School had just started at the Wattle's house. Therese had been lying down with a novel, feeling completely healthy and completely useless. It was depressing. She felt something odd and looked down. Bright red blood. Oh no, she thought. She had her mobile phone with her. She laid back down immediately and dialled the emergency number.

'Emergency. Who do you want to speak to please, police, ambulance or fire brigade?' the lady at the other end asked.

'Royal Flying Doctors, please,' Therese said, stumbling over the words. She was crying. 'I require an emergency evacuation.'

'Hold the line please,' the efficient operator replied.

Another lady answered the phone almost immediately. Therese knew her script. She told them very quickly what the problem was,

401

what she needed, where the station was, what the UHF channel was, and she gave them the airstrip coordinates that were stored on her phone. 'Do you want me to stay on the line with you, Therese?' the operator asked.

'No, thank you,' Therese replied. 'I have to organise help here. Thank you.' She stopped the call and rang Simone who answered immediately. 'Simone, please get Bruce for me. It's an emergency. I have a bleed. I'm lying down in the homestead. I've already called the RFDS. Thanks.' She hung up. She knew Simone would act like lightning. She wasn't wasting words and she was determined to relax and let everyone look after her. Her medical experience told her that trying to help herself could be lethal.

Bruce and Col were mustering. The chopper had just checked out and they had the cows and calves under control, slowly moving towards the yards. 'Bruce, are you there?' came over the UHF from Simone.

'I'm here, Simone. Is everything okay?'

'No. Emergency. Therese has a bleed. The RFDS is on its way.' Simone was equally as brief as Therese had been. She had told Bruce everything he needed to know for now. He would know exactly what to do. And now she needed to rush to Therese.

Bruce looked over to where Col was, who was looking back. Bruce pushed the button on his handset. 'Let's go,' he said, quietly and firmly. The men abandoned the cattle and raced off at high speed on their two-wheel motorbikes, straight for the homestead. Bruce was crying, his tears wetting the inner padding of his helmet. 'Please let her be okay,' he pleaded, probably to some deaf God somewhere.

Bruce charged at the shed like Evel Knievel, ploughing up the gravel as he slewed to a stop in front of the Land Cruiser. Caesar was in the homestead yard watching him approach with great curiosity. The dog knew something serious was afoot but didn't know exactly what. Caesar had been at home today for a change, so Therese could have some company when she was completely bored. Bruce ran into the homestead. 'How is she?' he asked Simone, who was sitting at her head. Therese looked like she was sleeping.

'She's getting dopey, Bruce. I'm worried.' Simone was crying. Bruce gently kissed Therese.

Bruce had not planned on how to get Therese from the house to the plane, but he had to rig something up that was safe and quick. As he charged back to the shed, his mind was racing. A mattress on the tray back would work. He furiously went to work, cleaning all the gear off the tray back. He then pushed the button on his UHF. 'Col, I know you're heading to the airstrip. Thanks. When you're done there, can you scoot back here please?'

'Will do,' Col replied.

Col had gone directly to the airstrip to ensure no stray animals were on it and everything was in order for the plane to land. He also set the gates open so when Therese came through, there would be no need for stopping. When Col had set the gates, he stopped and pushed the handset button of his UHF. 'Lachlan, can you hear me?'

'Yes, Dad,' Lachlan replied.

'Can you look after your sister, please. We're helping Therese,' Col told him.

'We're okay, Dad,' Lachlan radioed back.

'I'm on my way, Bruce,' Col radioed.

At the shed, Col found Bruce nailing a piece of ply to two lengths of wood. 'Rigging up a stretcher, Col. We'll take this into the house and drop a mattress on it. When Therese is ready to move, we'll get her on it, and we'll carry her and put her on the tray of the ute.' No more words were needed. The men read each other's minds as they finished the wooden base, put it on the tray back and drove the ute into the homestead yard, reversing up to the front steps, ready to receive Therese. They took an end each of the stretcher and carried it into the lounge where Simone was sitting beside Therese, holding her hand.

Bruce took one look. Therese looked content as she slept. Simone looked up, crying. She didn't know what to do. Bruce said, 'Col, mattress in there,' as he pointed to a room. Col dashed in, collected the mattress, and set up the stretcher adjacent to the couch. Bruce went to the kitchen sink and filled a glass of water. He gently replaced Simone. He kissed Therese. He was crying. He then tried to dribble some water into her mouth. His logic was she was losing blood. At least he could try and replace some of the fluid.

As he did this, a UHF call came through. 'This is the RFDS. Bovale, can you hear me?'

Col picked up the handset. 'We're in the homestead now. Airstrip clear and ready. How far out are you?' Col asked.

'Eight minutes,' the pilot replied.

'We'll have Therese there when you arrive. She is weak.'

'Roger. Thanks,' the pilot replied.

Bruce, Simone and Col then manoeuvred Therese onto the makeshift stretcher. She was limp. There was a lot of blood. But they could not afford to take heed of that. There was nothing they could do on that front. Simone grabbed Therese's large hat as the men carried her out and placed her on the back of the ute. Col then drove. Bruce and Simone were on either side of Therese, shading her and making sure she was as comfortable as possible.

As they drove into the airstrip enclosure, the twin-engine King Air B350 touched down. Bruce was weeping uncontrollably, which was causing Simone to do the same. The plane had come to a full stop and switched off as the ute pulled up beside it. Very quickly the doors of the plane opened, and the medical team emerged. They were like ants into sugar. They hardly said a word. They knew their drills. They knew what they had to do. Bruce and Simone retreated as the medical team took control. In no time Therese was in the plane, the doors were shut, and the plane took off. Bruce, Simone and Col stood there watching it go. All crying. All numb. It was extremely painful for them all. Simone turned and hugged Bruce. Col was on his other side and joined the hug.

Col drove back to the homestead. Bruce opted to sit on the back. Caesar was nonplussed. He couldn't work out what was going on. He stood and watched as the three went into the homestead. Simone immediately set to work, cleaning up. Bruce found his mobile phone and started making calls. He rang Maria first. The worst part was, he had no idea what the prognosis was. He just had to hope those useless Gods, who couldn't even make it rain when it was needed, would at least sort this situation out and deliver his beautiful wife and unborn baby back to him alive and healthy.

After the dreadful job of informing his and Therese's families what was happening, Bruce packed a bag. He then packed a couple of suit-cases for Therese. He knew she would not be back till after the baby was born. That was very depressing. If he forgot something, he'd get it next trip. He tried to stay positive. He had great faith in the RFDS. He also knew the Townsville University Hospital emergency department would know they were about to receive one of their own. She could not be in better hands.

After a quick shower, Bruce was ready to leave. Col had fuelled Bruce's vehicle for him. 'Bovale's all yours for a couple of days,' Bruce told him. 'I'll ring when I know what's happening. Thank you both for everything. I hate to think what would have happened if I didn't have you two here.' Bruce shook Col's hand firmly, nodding at this wonderful man. He gave Simone a bear hug. They were all crying again. 'It'll be okay. You'll see,' Bruce said. He jumped into his ute and drove off.

For much of the drive, there was no mobile phone coverage. All he could do for now was to safely get to the hospital. He arrived at one o'clock. When he walked in and asked to be directed to where Therese was, the staff were ready for him. Therese was a celebrity in this place after the Cattlemen's Ball publicity. It seemed the whole hospital knew what had happened.

As Bruce was being escorted through the corridors, a doctor approached him, 'I'm Doctor Bryce,' he said, introducing himself. They shook hands. 'Let's walk together, and I'll update you. Therese is okay.' Bruce stopped and lapsed into almost convulsive weeping. The nurse who had been escorting him embraced him for his comfort. Bruce was going nowhere till he regained his composure. He didn't care about moving just now. He had heard some magical words spoken.

'Eventually, through the blur of tears, he turned to the doctor, 'She's okay?' he asked, seeking to hear it again, in case he'd mis-heard.

'She's okay,' the doctor gently replied as he nodded.

'And the baby?' Bruce asked.

'It's fine too,' the doctor confirmed.

'Sorry,' Bruce said.

He untangled himself from the nurse, embarrassed he'd needed her support. The nurse went over to a nearby nurse's station and picked up a box of tissues and brought it back for Bruce. 'Thanks,' he said. After he'd composed himself, he asked, 'Can I just quickly sneak into a bathroom somewhere and clean myself up, please? I don't want to look like a sorry mess when I see Therese.' The nurse ushered him to a bathroom, while her and the doctor waited. They then resumed the walk to see Therese, with the doctor filling Bruce in on the details of what had happened. When they arrived at her bay in the intensive care unit, they stopped. Bruce thanked the doctor and nurse who excused themselves.

He walked into the bay. Therese was laying there, looking comfortable, but with a wan smile. 'G'day handsome,' she said.

Bruce went forward and they kissed. An embrace was not possible as she was hooked up with a mob of strings to all sorts of medical gear. The only bit that Bruce recognised was a bag of blood being slowly dripped into her. 'You gave us a big scare,' Bruce said. 'You were lying there peacefully like nothing was happening and we were all a blithering mess. It is so nice to have you back to normal.'

'Thank you, Bruce,' Therese said. 'The doctors tell me that you, Simone and Col were absolutely amazing. If you hadn't been, my mum would have been very sad.'

'Your mum and everyone else in the world,' Bruce responded, warming up to a big smile. He was still in shock; his emotions were shot, something he'd never experienced. 'The baby's fine too, I'm told.

I'm so happy,' Bruce said. 'Let's not do this again,' he suggested, which made Therese smile. He kissed her again.

'It's not going to be a fun three months in front of me, Bruce,' Therese said. 'But I'll do anything to have our baby, so it's okay. Mum will be happy too.'

Bruce stayed for a while and then left to allow Therese to get more rest and the medical attention she needed. She wasn't in ICU for laughs. As he walked out of the hospital, he rang Maria and gave her the amazing news. He sent a text to Simone. And then he messaged his mum to tell her he'd be at her place shortly. He added that Therese was fine. He'd give the details when he got there.

Doris offered Maria a bed for as long as Therese was in hospital, which she gratefully accepted. Maria did not want to be too far from her daughter, right now, and for the rest of the pregnancy. Maria arrived that afternoon. Doris and her were a great comfort for each other. Bruce took both ladies to briefly visit Therese late in the afternoon.

The next day, Therese was sufficiently stable for further assessment by her obstetrician who ordered some ultrasound. She visited Therese at her hospital bed and examined her. She told Therese, the baby was in excellent health. Bruce was in attendance. When the doctor went to leave, she beckoned Bruce to follow her. In the corridor, she turned to Bruce. 'I didn't want to upset Therese at all while she's in the state she is. However, I need to at least tell you that, even though the baby is fine, it's currently in the breech position. That may resolve, but given she has placenta previa, it is not likely it will. Overall, it's not a big issue for now, which is why I didn't want to inadvertently create any unnecessary worry for Therese. Whether the baby turns or not, she is still destined to have a caesar.'

'We already have one of those,' Bruce told the doctor, straight-faced.

The doctor looked at Bruce in puzzlement. 'How's that?' she asked.

'That's the name of Therese's dog,' Bruce said. 'Sorry, sick joke. I need humour right now. I apologise for my silly joke.' The doctor was laughing. She was happy that Bruce was happy. His joke was a good one and she told him. 'Thanks for looking after Therese so well,' Bruce said to her as she left.

Later that day, Therese was transferred to a general ward where she could receive the many visitors she had. She liked the visitors as there was nothing else to do in the hospital most of the time other than read a novel or watch the box. Therese expected to be in the hospital for five days in total. Bruce was not going to stay in Townsville that long and Therese knew it. She sensed he was like a dog on a chain, straining to get off and work. Two days after the drama, she said to him, 'Bruce, I think you should go home. I love you being here, but if it's boring for me, it's dreadfully boring for you. You'll be happy and I'll be happy if you get back to your first love and finish that muster.' Bruce was not going to deny her logic. She was going to be in the very capable hands of their unborn child's grandmothers. He agreed it was better to be useful. He rang Col and was back at Bovale that night.

It appeared the whole countryside was aware of what happened at Bovale. Bruce had many well-wishing text messages. The grapevine was fueled to some degree by Simone who was working with a lot of local businesses, who in turn had lots of contacts. Anything of significance that happened to a popular couple like Bruce and Therese, especially after the Cattlemen's Ball, was bound for the high-speed gossip channels. Bruce didn't mind. Most of these people were his friends and their hearts were definitely in the right place. What it meant was that, when he and Col went to fire up the muster again, everyone he asked for help bent over backwards to do so. Bruce was humbled. When he rang Therese each night, he was almost crying, telling her about what nice things people had said to him about the pair of them and how generous everyone was. Merve had always said to Bruce, 'If you want respect, give it.' Bruce had always been respectful wherever he went, whatever he did and with whomever he did it with. It was paying big dividends when it mattered most.

The muster went even better than Bruce hoped. The deferment had caused much of the muster to coincide with the mid-year school holidays. Simone and Lachlan were in seventh heaven. They were able to participate all day, every day. Simone had scheduled the next CRAB meeting for mid-July. The focus was going to be genetics. It would be at Bovale, one year after the previous CRAB group meeting there. The reason for Bovale being the venue was two-fold. Bruce, Col and Simone would be able to present results from the pastures and herd monitoring. The second was that Bruce's passion for cattle breeding had created some great outcomes. There was plenty to discuss and see on this topic at Bovale. Bruce's only regret was Therese could not join them. She was safely leading a so-far-uneventful slothful existence in Brandon, where he visited as often as he could.

Bruce and Simone set aside a whole day to work on the cattle data after the muster. Col continued to feed lick and check waters and cattle. Lachlan went with Col. Carina spent the day in the homestead, playing with her dolls and being the resident tea lady when Simone decided she should be. The numbers were very good. Wayne's forecasts were largely realised. The complex system change Bruce had planned and implemented was working. Live weight production was up twenty percent on the long-term average with no change in pasture utilisation. That meant efficiency had also been dramatically increased. Overall business costs were not increased much, despite the extra supplements, which meant the cost of production per kilogram of live weight was down by about twenty percent from where it had been to a bit over two dollars and ten cents. Bruce said to Simone, 'I have the artistic skill of a chook. It'll be a lot better if you prepare the presentations for the CRAB group meeting. Col and I will do what we're told.'

'I'm happy with that,' Simone replied. She wasn't just happy. She was absolutely delighted.

Chapter Nineteen

The CRAB meeting at Bovale a couple of weekends later was a sensational success. Simone had invited Chantelle Menzies, a geneticist from Longreach who had presented at the Koolburra field day two years earlier, to participate. The entire meeting was informal. Simone masterly applied her newly-acquired facilitation skills, orchestrating informative discussion for two straight days, whether it was on the homestead veranda, or in the paddock evaluating pastures or breeding cattle.

The evenings were once again as brilliant as ever. The crowd stayed Sunday night, even though they didn't need to. They wanted to. A CRAB group meeting at Bovale was one helluva social event and more than one person suggested that Bruce cement the mid-July meeting in place for years to come. Wendy knew the importance of Bruce's group of friends and had invited them and Bruce's family to join them on Sunday evening. The CRAB group meeting wound up at about three o'clock in the afternoon. Not long after that the gang arrived to join the festivities. It was a fantastic surprise for Bruce when Frances and Simon also turned up, not far behind. Even better was when Merve and Doris rolled in a short while later. Bruce was all smiles. So far, he had rung Therese four times already today. She was excited for Bruce, and stoically told him to have a few beers for her and the baby.

After dinner on Sunday night, Wendy called the group to order. Bruce looked over and saw she was standing with a stranger. Worse still, there was what looked like a photographer with them who started to video Wendy and the crowd. In all that had been going on, he had completely missed two new arrivals. Damn, he thought. At least Wendy was looking after them. He was embarrassed, but now was not the time to fix his lapse. He'd do it after Wendy finished saying whatever she was going to say.

'Sorry to interrupt the banter, but we have to add a little bit of formality to the weekend,' she announced. Everyone was attentive. 'I know I speak for everyone when I offer a sincere thanks to Bruce, Simone, Col, Lachlan and Carina for hosting us to this incredible weekend where we have learned so much that we can take home and put into practice in our own businesses. Simone, without you, the CRAB group wouldn't be a patch on what it is. Thank you.'

There was cheering and clapping as Simone stood with a smile, looking around the crowd with unspoken thanks.

Wendy continued. 'We all know the princess of Bovale would have made the weekend even more special, and we ask you Bruce, to thank Therese for supporting you all here at Bovale.' The crowd clapped furiously. Bruce stood and nodded his thanks.

Wendy went on as the crowd again became completely silent. 'Bruce, we have to make a change. Sorry Merve and Doris. We are going to elevate Therese to queen status. That's because, Bruce, you are the new king.' A huge cheer went up.

They silenced as Wendy raised her hand and went on. 'What you have achieved here in just a couple of years, much of it under trying circumstances, and your leadership with our group and elsewhere, is exceptional. The details of your business analysis that yourself, Simone and Col shared with our group earlier today, totally confirms this.' Wendy paused for the applause. 'I don't think you have any idea just how amazing it was for the community and for those of who were there, to experience what Therese and yourself did at the Cattlemen's Ball.'

There were more cheers and clapping.

'Because of all this and more, unbeknown to you, the CRAB group nominated you for an award as Australia's best farmer. This award is hosted by the federal government's agriculture department who is keen to improve the business skills in the farming sector. We are honoured tonight to have the federal minister for agriculture, the Honourable Mister Darcy Benson here this evening to tell us about that award. Please welcome him.'

There was very polite applause.

Bruce now knew who the stranger was. He was getting jittery about where this was leading. He decided to dial Therese so she could listen too, as best she could via the phone. He whispered into the phone when she answered, 'Speeches here tonight. I have to stay quiet,' he said. 'I'll try and pick up for you what's being said.' Bruce held his phone so Therese might be able to hear. Simone was standing next to him and heard the exchange. She looked at Bruce, took the phone from him, walked over to the minister, and held it close to him.

'Thank you for the welcome,' the minister began. 'I'm sorry we've snuck in on you, Bruce. It was not an accident. The reason I came was that the committee made its decision recently. We also decided that gala events for awards is often mostly for the benefit of the politicians. My first announcement is that we wanted to change that and transfer most of the potential expenditure on a gala event to award recipients. We're fat enough with big-enough egos already.' This comment elicited a few laughs which quickly built to cheers and clapping. 'We also decided to deliver awards to the recipients on a staged basis within their peer groups. Tonight, I am very pleased to announce the last of this year's awards, the big one. The winner is Bruce Arnold.'

The crowd was on its feet, screaming, wolf whistling, cheering, and clapping.

Simone talked to Therese on Bruce's phone. 'Did you hear that?'

'I did, Simone. I am so happy for Bruce and all of you.'

The crowd was finally settling. The minister waited till they were ready for more. The photographer had found Bruce and the Wattle family and was taking them in on a regular basis.

'Wendy has told you the basics of why Bruce received this award ahead of all farmers in Australia, young and old. He is an inspiration. He has superb technical skills augmented by a flair for business, which is all brought together by his outstanding leadership. I am reliably informed that his wife is no lesser person.' There were more cheers and clapping before the minister could continue. 'It has been said, if good things are happening in a business, you'll find a good person at the top; the corollary is also true, always. Wendy and her team of conspirators have told me that if I'd met Simone and Col, I'd be as impressed as if I'd met Bruce. I'm not surprised at all.' There was more cheering.

The minister continued. 'The award Bruce has won, will total one hundred thousand dollars.' There were 'wows' softly being spoken throughout the crowd. 'It includes a cash component of half that amount. The rest is to be used on study travel for the business's benefit, wherever and whoever being decided by the recipient. Thank you.' There was very loud clapping for Bruce.

Wendy took the microphone she had been using back from the minister and asked Bruce to come forward and accept the award. Bruce shook the Minister's hand and thanked him. Wendy passed the microphone to Bruce, 'If you want to say something ...' she said.

Bruce turned to face his family and friends, minus Therese, though he knew she could hear. He was pumping out a few tears, and he let them dry up as he composed himself. 'Thank you, everyone. Therese and I will treasure this award and use it wisely. My fervent wish is that Simone and Col use a significant proportion of the study travel funds. They deserve it. Bovale could not be what it is without them. Thank you.'

Bruce was exhausted when he finally got to bed that night. He didn't know where his life was headed, but it was comforting to know that he and Therese had mobs of such good friends.

Bruce headed to Brandon on Monday after the clean-up and the crowd dispersed. He was taking Therese to Townsville on Tuesday for her regular check. The local news bulletins had ensured everyone in the region knew about Bruce's award. The Pavarotti family were very impressed. The young Mrs Arnold embraced her husband in congratulations as best she could without popping a rivet in her fragile uterus.

Doris met them for a relaxing cup of tea next to the radiographer's building after her ultrasound and before her specialist appointment. There was too much risk for Therese to stop at the Arnold's as well as meeting her medical attendants and much safer to travel directly back to Brandon after visiting the specialist. The specialist confirmed that all was sailing along as best as could be expected. The baby remained safely in the breech position, and the placenta previa had not resolved. Therese was booked in for a caesarean section in late September, about ten days before the baby's due date.

Two weeks later, Bruce had a phone call from Merve who wanted to chat about how everything was going at Bovale. He was very proud of his son, who was increasingly needing less of his advice. Merve could sense that Bruce was increasingly excited about the imminent start to the calving season, especially in Topsides's harem where they would see the foundation of future Bovale cattle generations being born. This surpassed any anticipation of the sales of surplus female cattle and steers which would provide the income for the entire year's operations. At the end of the conversation, Merve said, 'I'll pass you over to your mother. She has some news.' Bruce steeled himself. He'd heard that line before and it had not heralded revelations he was ever pleased to know.

'Bruce, I had another test last week and we got the result today,' Doris told him. 'I'm completely free of cancer.'

'Yahoo!' Bruce screamed down the phone. 'Whoops. Sorry, Mum. I probably just broke your ear with that. I'm stoked to hear that.'

'Thank you, Bruce. Your father and I are also very pleased.' The mother-son chat after that was like singing for Bruce, he was so happy.

***

It seemed like almost no time, and Bruce was back in Brandon, collecting Therese for the big day. Maria was following them to Townsville and would stay with Doris and Merve until Therese was discharged and they took the baby back to Bovale. Maria was going out to Bovale as well because she knew Therese would need all the help she could get. Bruce could not take leave like a typical worker.

Therese was having the baby in a private hospital where her specialist usually operated. When she arrived, it was almost a relief for her not to be treated like a celebrity, as she had recently experienced in the public hospital. Bruce would not let her walk to admissions. He disappeared into the hospital and was followed out almost immediately by a team with a mobile hospital bed. Her admission was low-key. All the staff, orderlies through to senior doctors, were very respectful, friendly, and highly professional, providing a sense of security for both Therese and Bruce. Their room could easily be mistaken for a good-quality motel room, other than for the typical hospital fittings added. They had a double bed, a single bed and a crib for the baby.

Preparations for surgical procedures were not new for Therese, only that she was the patient for a change. It was done quickly. Two orderlies arrived at her room. 'Ready to have your baby?' one beamed.

'I am. Thank you,' she replied as they helped her onto the bed on which she would have the surgery. Off she was wheeled.

A nurse said to Bruce, 'Let's get you prepped as well.' She had him change into surgical scrubs, along with a mask. 'You'll pass as a doctor she said,' checking him to make sure he was geared up correctly.

She threw her stethoscope around his neck and said, 'A quick photo for your wife before we head in.' Bruce was laughing. What service, he exclaimed to himself. The nurse retrieved her stethoscope and led Bruce to where Therese was being prepared. He was given a chair beside Therese's head.

The anaesthetist introduced herself and her assistants. The specialist introduced her staff. Nods were the order of the day as handshakes were not good practice in a surgery. Bruce was highly impressed with these people and how they performed. Therese was rolled on her side and an epidural anaesthetic was administered via a needle inserted into her back. This would numb everything below the chest for Therese. Nothing was being given via the drip inserted into Therese's arm to ensure the baby did not also get a dose of sleeping juice. A large green surgical sheet was then raised as a screen above Therese's chest. Neither Bruce nor Therese could see past the screen.

Ten minutes after the epidural injection, the specialist asked, 'Can you feel this?'

'I can feel you're poking around, but there is no pain,' Therese replied.

'Are you ready, Therese?' she asked.

'Yes,' Therese said. She held Bruce's hand in trepidation. After all she had been through, this was not the time for anything to go wrong. The anaesthetist discretely nodded to the specialist and the team went into surgical action. The whole time, one of the anaesthetist's assistants was taking photos and videos of Therese and Bruce.

Almost a minute after the team started, Therese felt weight suddenly being lifted from her abdomen. Immediately after, she heard a small cry. Bruce and her looked at each other. As they did this, the specialist lifted the baby above the screen so they could see it. 'It's a healthy boy,' the specialist said.

They had already known this and had a name, Hamish. Hamish looked adorable. His body was wet. His small hands were bunched up. His relatively long legs were moving with the still-functional umbilical cord spiralling down between them. Hamish had thin black hair and brown eyes. The photographer was catching all of this. Both Therese and Bruce were in awe. Very quickly, Hamish was transferred to a nurse who wrapped him in a towel and brought him around the screen to rest on Therese's chest. She cradled him and looked into his beautiful face, barely fifty millimetres from hers. Bruce kissed his wife's forehead. He was back on cloud nine, his usual position when he was with Therese.

A short while later, after Therese had been reconstructed and brought back to their room with Hamish, Bruce dialled Maria and put the phone on speaker. He knew both Doris and Lenny were with Maria at Doris and Merve's place and waiting for the call. Maria didn't even say hello.

'Have you had the baby?' she asked, the excitement in her voice lifting its pitch to a thrill.

Therese smiled. 'Hamish was born half an hour ago,' she replied. Maria, Doris and Lenny were over the moon. Therese shared all the important details before they finished the call.

Bruce then rang his father. 'Your first grandson, Hamish, was born forty-five minutes ago, Dad,' he proudly announced.

'Congratulations on your successful breeding,' Merve replied.

He knew his son well.

About the Author

Geoffry Fordyce hails from north Australia's beef cattle and sugar cane country. After completing a veterinary science degree, augmented with post-graduate study, research of beef cattle systems, especially of reproducing cattle in the tropical world, has been his life's work. Geoffry most recently worked for the University of Queensland and collaborated with beef business operators and other scientists across northern Australia, Indonesia and Timor-Leste, ultimately developing new business practices that can improve the profitability of beef systems, while also having significant welfare benefits for the animals, the environment and the people.

His endeavours resulted in him being awarded the inaugural medal for Excellence in Research by the North Australian Beef Research Council in 2006.

In 2021, Geoffry was bestowed with a prestigious Honorary Doctor of Science degree by James Cook University in recognition of his contributions to the international cattle industry and rural communities. Geoffry has hundreds of scientific publications, highlighted by almost 80 papers in international peer-review science journals (eg, doi.org/10.1071/AN20342) and a few books.

'Breeding' is Geoffry's first expedition into fiction writing. Geoffry lives outside Charters Towers with his wife, Linda, continuing his work through his small business, GALF Cattle.

www.ingramcontent.com/pod-product-compliance
Lightning Source LLC
Chambersburg PA
CBHW070345170726
48291CB00001B/185